D0366686

Dear Readers,

You're never too old to learn—I found this out the hard way. In *Heaven Knows,* I wrote my first letter to readers saying how sad it was to finish the Mackinnon books. I learned to never say never!

Over six hundred letters arrived telling me the Mackinnon saga was NOT over. It was this overwhelming interest in the Mackinnons that inspired Fletcher's story, *When Love Comes Along.* Now before you go and grab your pen and start another letter, let me say that I have just finished writing Margery's story. *If You Love Me* will be released by Warner Books in the fall of 1996.

Please know that I always love hearing from my readers, both the old faithfuls who have been with me from the start and the new arrivals. It is knowing how eagerly you await my next novel that keeps me going, your encouragement to "write just a little faster" that keeps me sitting up late at night, when anyone with half a brain would have gone to bed. You are my inspiration and my guiding light.

With much appreciation,

Elaine Coffman

Look for these other titles in the Mackinnon series
of historical romanes by Elaine Coffman:

ANGEL IN MARBLE
FOR ALL THE RIGHT REASONS
SOMEWHERE ALONG THE WAY
SO THIS IS LOVE
HEAVEN KNOWS

And watch for *IF YOU LOVE ME*, a Mackinnon
historical romance coming from Warner Books
in the Fall of 1996.

ELAINE COFFMAN

WHEN LOVE COMES ALONG

WARNER
VISION

A Time Warner Company

WARNER BOOKS EDITION

Copyright © 1995 by Elaine Coffman
All rights reserved.

Cover design by Diane Luger
Cover illustration by James Griffin
Hand lettering by Carl Dellacroce

Warner Vision is a trademark of Warner Books, Inc.

Warner Books, Inc.
1271 Avenue of the Americas
New York, NY 10020

Ⓦ A Time Warner Company

Printed in the United States of America

First Printing: November, 1995

10 9 8 7 6 5 4 3 2 1

WHEN LOVE COMES ALONG

Alasdair Ramsay, Eighth Duke

Douglas	Alexander

Beneath that was written: Which of these Douglas Ramsay's

Douglas Ramsay, m. Bride
|
Ian

Next came the following headings:

Bruce Ramsay's line
|
Ian Ramsay, m. Moina
|
Angus Ramsay, m. Bethia
|
Dugan Ramsay, m. Elspeth
|
Bruce Ramsay, m. Maggie
|
Fletcher Ramsay

of Glengarry, m. Maude

Beitris	Tibbie

was Alasdair Ramsay's true son and which was the imposter?

or   Douglas Ramsay, m. Jean

Ian

Adair Ramsay's line

|

Ian Ramsay, m. Isobel

|

Robert Ramsay, m. Anna

|

David Ramsay, m. Robina

|

Adair Ramsay, m. Brina

|

No male heir

Prologue

The time was late. The house was still. The dream came to him again, for the first time in ten years.

Fletcher Ramsay slept fitfully, consumed by a drowsy numbness, troubled by haunting dreams. A sudden gust of wind blew into the room, wailing like a woman's sorrow and sending a shower of imaginary leaves skittering across the floor.

Out of the darkness and into his room a silent guest had come, lingering in the hovering shades of night.

His eyes opened. Was he awake, or asleep? He couldn't see a thing, and yet he saw himself standing in an unknown place, upon a dark, unfamiliar summit, looking down at a wild and churning sea. And all about him, the world lay infinitely still.

It was night, nothing more than a shadow of darkness upon

a treeless moor, yet the crags were white as milk and the moon pale as cream. Overhead, the stars hung thick in a black velvet night.

The wind carried the smell of a pungent sea and the haunting lilt of bagpipes. He saw his homeland, a place of bleak heath and shaggy wood, of high corries and stormy seas, and against a gleam of fading light, he saw the ghostly spires of a castle rising in silhouette, infinitely gray, infinitely silent, and calling out to him.

Lightning ripped the sky. A brilliant, blinding light appeared before him, and something seemed to suspend time.

From the intense brightness a man came forth, dressed in white and hovering just above the ground. His being shone, and his countenance was one of immeasurable beauty.

Wait, Fletcher. The time is soon. . . .

The wind died down, and the eerie moans of a voice hung in the air, as dry and flintlike as the ancient syllables of a Gaelic chant, before fading away. The vision dimmed, becoming no more than a pale vapor, growing obscure, then disappearing completely. But like a faded flower whose fragrance lingers, the memory stayed. Fletcher closed his eyes. The speaking silence of the dream had passed, and at last his body slept.

But his mind could find no rest. His soul was awakened. His spirit was ready.

It was now twenty-one years since the murder of his father, Bruce Ramsay, the Duke of Glengarry. The year was 1878 and Fletcher Ramsay was twenty-eight.

The time had come.

Chapter One

Northern California, June 1878

Fletcher stood on the cliffs where the great, swelling waves of the Pacific crashed against the rocks below, churning the water and turning it to foam. He was restless and on edge. He had been that way for three months now, ever since the dream had come to him. He knew why he was restless and he knew what the dream meant. He did not know what he was going to do about it.

He had always known that there would come a time when he would go back, a time when he would avenge his father's death and set everything right. Recompense and restitution. They were two words he learned to live with, two words that shaped his life.

His father had been murdered, his birthright had been stolen from him. The time had come to take it back. He knew that, and yet the vision confused him.

Wait, Fletcher. The time is soon. . . .

"I thought I would find you here."

Fletcher turned around and saw his mother, Maggie Mackinnon, walking toward him, the wind whipping her hair and skirts about her. As she drew even with him, she paused, looking out far over the water.

He saw the way she stared as if in a trance and knew that she did not really see this place, but another. "This place has always reminded you of Scotland, hasn't it?"

"Aye. I ken that is because they are both places born of the violence of the earth." Maggie did not say more, but he knew her well enough to know that something grave distressed her.

"What troubles you, Mother? What are you thinking?"

She turned toward him, a bittersweet look upon her face as she lifted her hand and touched his cheek. "I was remembering."

He gave her a smile. All that he was or ever hoped to be, he owed to his mother. "And what were you remembering?"

She sighed. "A lot of things, things I ken you will find silly . . . forgotten evenings when you used to walk with me here when you were just a wee lad, your hand warm in mine, your pockets crammed with rocks and string, and a snail shell or two." She looked down and drew her shawl more tightly around her shoulders, and he knew that she was fighting back the urge to cry.

"It's too cold for you out here, Mother. Let me take you back to the house."

"No. I want to walk out here, Fletcher, along the cliffs with you."

"Why?"

"It seems appropriate somehow."

"Appropriate?"

"Aye. Like you said, this place has always reminded me of Scotland."

"And that makes it appropriate?"

She nodded.

"For what?"

"For what I have to tell you." He could almost hear the

heartache he saw in her eyes. She smoothed the collar of his jacket. "How like your father you are: tall, with a slimness that is just now beginning to fill out. You have his smile, his wit, his intelligence, his gentleness—" she smiled sadly— "and that same stubborn streak."

He had seen her in these moods before and understood how hard it sometimes was for her to see her children grow up. "I know you'll be telling me next how my eyes are the same dark blue as my father's."

"Aye, but they have none of Bruce Ramsay's teasing lightness, for you were ever a serious lad, Fletcher."

He was concerned now, for instead of her mood lightening, she seemed to grow more melancholy. "You aren't ill, are you, Mother?"

"No, it's nothing like that."

"Are you certain?"

"Aye."

"Then what is it?"

She put her hand up, pushing his hair back from his eyes as she had done so many times before. "Even the texture of your hair is the same."

He nodded. "But lighter brown."

"Aye, but not too much lighter."

He smiled at her motherly ways. Taking her hand in his, he turned it to kiss the palm, hoping to cast her somber thoughts away. "Always the mother," he said, reaching out to draw her shawl up over her shoulders. He paused to stroke the soft wool, as he rubbed the fringe between his fingers. He gave her a winsome smile. "I used to wonder why it was that your clothes always felt different from anyone else's in my hands."

Tears welled in her eyes. "Oh, Fletcher, how can I bear to let you go?"

"Go?" He looked down into her face, his eyes searching hers as if he could see the sadness there. "Mother, what's wrong?"

"Let's walk to the end of the trail," she said, and took Fletcher's arm as she started up the well-worn path.

"You are greatly troubled," he said.

"I received a letter from Scotland today." She glanced at him. "It was from my sister, Doroty. My brother, Ian, is dead."

Fletcher drew up short. "Ian? My uncle Ian is dead?"

"Aye," Maggie said, "Ian Alexander Sinclair, the twelfth Earl of Caithness, is dead, and you, my son, are now thirteenth. *Thirteen*. Not exactly a good omen."

But Fletcher wasn't interested in omens right now. "What do you mean I am the thirteenth?"

"You are now the Earl of Caithness, Fletcher.

"But how? I'm not a Sinclair, Mother. I'm a Ramsay."

"Aye, you are a Ramsay through and through, and proud as a peacock about it, too. I ken hearing all of this seems strange to you since you never knew my brother."

"No, I never knew much about him."

"He was a widower. He had no children. My two older brothers have been dead a long time. There are none of us Sinclairs left now, save myself and my sister, Doroty."

"So the title passed to me?"

"You are the closest male heir."

Fletcher was dumbfounded. "I had no idea. You never mentioned the possibility."

"I never gave it much thought. Ian was not that old. I always thought he might one day remarry and have children. He did write that he was quite interested in a young widow."

"I . . . I don't know what to say."

Maggie smiled. "It is a rare thing indeed to see you flustered and uncertain."

"It is a rare thing for me to hear I've just inherited a title."

"I know the news is staggering to you," she said. "Hout! It is staggering to me as well."

"Was there anything else in the letter?"

"You mean as to what happens now?"

"Yes. I . . ." He paused, turning to look at her, taking her hands in his. "I have to go, Mother. It's what I've always wanted. To return to Scotland. You know that I must go, don't you?"

"Aye, although those are the words I have dreaded hearing for a good part of my life. My heart is crying out with unbearable grief, now. I would have kept you young, Fletcher, and playing about my skirts if I could. . . ."

"I know. But you've always known I wouldn't stay here in California. It was never right for me. Never."

"Oh, Fletcher, how can I bear this?"

He heard the pain in her voice and knew how difficult this was for her. She was not the kind of woman to control her children or interfere in their lives. It was only her love for him—and her fear—that forced her to try now.

"I have to go."

"Aye, I've always known you would, just as I've always known I would do everything I could to stop you. I fear for your life, Fletcher, every bit as much as I did the day I left Scotland. Adair Ramsay may be an old man now, but he is still formidable. Once he finds out you are in Scotland, he will stop at nothing."

"Don't worry. I can take care of myself."

"Aye," she said, wiping at her eyes. "That's what your father said the day before they found his body on the cliffs." Maggie's lip trembled as she studied her son's face. "Is there nothing I can say, nothing I can do that will keep you here?"

"No," he said. "Nothing."

"Well then, there is no more to be said. You will return to Scotland, and my heart is breaking. I fear I may never see you again, Fletcher. You, my firstborn." Her voice broke.

"I would never allow anything to happen to sadden you. You know that. Give me your blessing, Mother."

"I have experienced much pain in my life, but none that has cut so deeply as this. I want to give you my blessing, Fletcher, but I canna. How can I bless something that will tear out my heart?"

He nodded. He understood that. After all, she was only being the woman he had always loved and admired. It was her love for him that stirred this protectiveness within her. She had lived with her fears, her feelings of dread, since his father's death.

In some ways it seemed like such a long time ago, but in reality it had only been some twenty years ago that a man by the name of Adair Ramsay had come into their lives and destroyed them—a greedy little man who had tried to usurp the title, Duke of Glengarry, from Fletcher's father, Bruce.

Protecting his title had cost Bruce Ramsay his life, and for what? A few months after Bruce's death, Adair Ramsay had laid claim to the title again, and this time the courts in Edinburgh had awarded it to him. No one had been able to prove that Adair had taken Bruce Ramsay's life. But that mattered little to Fletcher.

In his heart, he knew it was so.

His mother knew too, for she had told him often enough that as long as he lived, he was a threat to what Adair Ramsay had taken.

Maggie put her hand on his arm. He turned toward her and saw that she was crying.

How small she looked. How broken. It cut into the heart of him that he was the one to do this to her. "Please don't cry, Mother."

"I canna help it. I canna let you go, Fletcher. I did not invest so much of my life in you to have you throw it away. Adair is a very dangerous man. If you go back, your life will be in grave, grave danger. Not even the passing of twenty years has been able to erase the memory of those horrible words he spoke to me that day so long ago, the day I left Glengarry Castle for good."

"What words? You never told me."

"I had hoped to persuade you without having to tell you." She paused. "I will go to my grave remembering the way he said, 'I would warn you, madam, to rid yourself of any fancy notions of regaining the dukedom or Glengarry Castle.' I told him the warning was pointless, that my husband was already dead, that the title could not pass to me."

"What did he say to that?"

"He said, 'I speak of your son.' When I accused him of threatening me, he said, 'I am merely giving you advice, madam. Leave things as they are. If you set about stirring up a hornet's nest, it might be you that gets stung. You may have nothing to lose, but your son has.'"

Fletcher scoffed. "How could I lose something a second time? He already had my title."

"He said he wasn't speaking of a title. And then he said, 'Start digging around in all these ashes again, and I will see that you regret it. There is no place you can go, no place you can hide that I won't find you. The lad takes after his father. I would hate to see him follow in his footsteps.'"

Fletcher felt a cold shudder pass over him. He put his arms around her, and holding his mother close, he listened to the heartbreaking sound of her crying. "I could never bear to hear you cry," he said, "and to think that I am the cause of it."

"It isn't that you are the cause, it's . . ."

"I know," he said, handing her his handkerchief. "I know why you left Scotland, why you found a place to hide halfway around the world. You left everything you held dear in order to marry Adrian Mackinnon and bring my sisters and me to California. You feared for my life and you took great sacrifice and risk to protect me."

"Aye, and it's fear for your life that makes me want to keep you here now."

Fletcher put his arm over her shoulders as they strolled a bit further.

"How many times have we walked along these cliffs, talking?" she said softly. "And how many of those times have I worried that you would one day grow up and leave?"

He looked at her.

"Aye, I've known since you were a lad and close to your mother's hip, but knowing doesna make it easy. Is there nothing I can do, Fletcher, no reason I can give to turn you from this?"

"No. You can't turn me away from my destiny."

Maggie sighed in defeat. "That is the same thing Adrian said. *Destiny*. How I hate that word. I want to scream and stomp my foot every time I hear it, for I'd like nothing better than to crush all it means beneath my heel."

"Tell me you understand."

She looked up and he knew that she could see the hope in his eyes. He did not want to leave her like this, without her blessing. He knew the understanding was there, for she was discerning enough to know that no man ever escaped his destiny. Nor could he fault her for being mother enough to want to try.

"Well then, if you must go, I can only pray that something will change your thirst for vengeance. You canna live by the sword, Fletcher."

Fletcher's face hardened. He rammed his hands deep into his pockets and looked out over the water. "Nothing can stop me."

"You never know, Fletcher, what will happen."

"I know nothing will sway me from two goals in life. I will get my title back and I will destroy Adair Ramsay. I never told anyone this, but I had a dream a long time ago, a dream that confirmed what I always knew."

Wiping the tears from her face with the back of her hand, Maggie looked at him and waited.

"The dream came to me ten years ago, when I had just turned eighteen, but even then I was already obsessed with going back to take back what was rightfully mine. Adair Ramsay took more than just the title Duke of Glengarry from me. He took my father's life. It was only that dream that kept me from going back before now."

"A dream kept you from returning? I dinna understand."

"I dreamed of a place very much like this one, a towering summit where the waves crashed against the rocks below. A man that was all goodness and light appeared and I could see that his face was one of celestial beauty. He called my name, then put his hand on my shoulder and quoted from Ecclesiastes:

" *'There is a time to be born, and a time to die; a time to plant, and a time to pluck up that which is planted; A time to kill, and a time to heal; a time to break down, and a time to build up; A time to weep, and a time to laugh; a time to mourn, and a time to dance . . . '*

"And then he said, 'Wait, Fletcher. Wait for your time. Wait until the time is right.'"

"Perhaps that was an omen, then," Maggie said. "Why did you never tell me?"

"I didn't want you to worry any more than necessary."

Maggie sniffed. "I ken I have made up for it in these past two hours."

He smiled at her. " I know. You're like a mother chicken, one with twenty chicks who counts only nineteen, then frets for that one lost one, as if nineteen wasn't enough."

"It seems like just yesterday that you were a young boy, Fletcher. There were so many things I wanted to teach you, but there never seemed enough time, and now it is too late."

"Your heart was always my schoolroom, Mother. You have taught me much more than you will ever know."

"I have always thanked God for your loving ways, Fletcher. But tell me more of this dream of yours."

"I knew the dream meant that I would one day go back, but that I should wait for a sign, or for some inner assurance that the time to avenge father's death had come. I understood it, but understanding did not make the waiting easy. I was eighteen, young and eager to prove myself."

"Aye, you were ever a restless one," she said, and he could tell by the way she looked that her heart was filled with memories.

"I had the same dream again."

"You mean recently?"

He nodded. "Three months ago." The words had no more than left his mouth when something startling occurred to him. Turning he placed his hands on Maggie's arms. "Mother, when did my uncle die? Do you have the exact date?"

"Aye," she said. "April twenty-eighth."

Fletcher's heart began to hammer. The blood ran thick and cold in his veins. His palms were damp. He knew his life was no longer his, but part of a bigger and greater plan. "It was on the night of April twenty-eighth that I had the dream again. I was eight when my father died; eighteen when I had the dream the first time; twenty-eight when it came the second time; and the year is 1878."

"It is a coincidence."

"It is more than a coincidence. Is an omen," he said, "and you are Scot enough to know it. In my first dream, I was told to wait until the time was right."

"And the second time?"

"I was told to wait, that the time was soon. Don't you understand now? The vision came again on the same day my uncle died. I was supposed to wait until I had a reason to go back, a reason other than to avenge my father's death. Now I know that I was supposed to wait until I was the Earl of Caithness."

"Aye," Maggie said, "you are the earl and nothing can change that."

He shook his head. "I still can't believe it. Don't you understand what this means, Mother? After all this time, I am finally going home . . . home to Scotland."

"Aye, I suppose I've always known the life Adrian carved from the forests was not for you. Your half-brothers love the life of a timber baron, but it has never suited you as well. But dinna forget you go as the Earl of Caithness, Fletcher, not the Duke of Glengarry. Caithness Castle will be your home, not Glengarry."

He patted her hand. "All in due time, Mother. All in due time."

Chapter Two

Scotland, August 1878

Cathleen Lindsay reached the fork in the road and saw red hair. She smiled, knowing it had to be Maude Campbell coming toward her, ambling along like a dog who has buried a bone and cannot quite remember where.

Cathleen paused, watching Maude for a moment. *"A man that hath friends must show himself friendly,"* she reminded herself. *Proverbs.* And with that she waved and called out, "Hello, Maude! Are you on your way to Drummond's field?"

Maude looked up in the dazed way she had when she had been daydreaming and was caught off guard. "Aye," she called back. "Is that where you are going?"

Cathleen gazed at Maude's round, red face and smiled. "Aye. Shall we walk on together, then?"

Maude nodded and put more spirit into her step. Soon she caught up to where Cathleen waited. "I'm glad to see you,

Cathleen. I tried to catch you after church yesterday. I wanted to thank you for the christening dress you made for Mary. It was such a lovely little dress . . . and all that smocking and embroidery. Why, it looked as if it was sewn by fairies, or angels, at least."

Cathleen looked amused, then she laughed. "No angel, I fear, but it was a task which brought me much pleasure," she said, then fell into step with Maude. "I must say I thought little Mary looked verra bonny, although the dress had little to do with it. My grandfather said he had never baptized a prettier baby."

Maude seemed to swell with pride at hearing such a compliment on her baby sister. "I ken David MacDonald says that about every baby he sprinkles . . . as long as they dinna sprinkle him first."

Cathleen laughed, then opened her mouth to speak, but the sound of a horse galloping up the road behind them drew her attention. Stepping into the ditch alongside the road, she and Maude turned to watch Adair Ramsay, the Duke of Glengarry, thundering toward them on a great black horse.

They watched him gallop past, throwing up a cloud of choking dust, without so much as a look in their direction.

"Hout! There goes the devil on horseback!" Maude said. Then, as if suddenly aware that she had been a bit carried away by her feelings, she blushed uncomfortably, and the tone of her voice was less passionate as she said, "I wonder where he is going in such a hurry?"

"*He that doeth evil hateth the light,*" Cathleen said.

"Is that from the Bible?"

Cathleen nodded. "John."

Maude shrugged. "Scripture or not, it's the truth. His kind only come out at night. I ken everyone knows he is an evil one, all right, although no one ever seems to witness any wrongdoing."

"I ken if they did, they wouldna live long enough to tell about it. My grandfather says, 'They that deal wi' the de'il get a dear pennyworth.'"

"I hear he has taken over the Widow McCutchin's farm, and poor William is hardly cold in his grave."

"Her farm? But how could he get it? I know Margaret McCutchin wouldna sell her farm."

"She didna sell it. It seems the duke produced some signed papers that said William deeded the farm to him upon his death. I have a feeling that if William signed those papers, he did so with the duke's dirk at his throat."

"Poor Margaret," Cathleen said. "Do you ken where she has gone?"

"Aye. She is living with her daughter, Elspeth."

"With Elspeth? But her husband hasna been right in his head since he fell in that well last summer and spent three days there. He canna provide for his family as it is. How will he provide for one more mouth to feed?"

"I dinna ken how they will get by. Everyone is talking about it."

A gloomy silence fell over them, as if each was cudgeling her brain in search of a source for funds. "Weel," Cathleen said after a bit, "talk willna fill their bellies. I shall speak to my grandfather. Perhaps we can take donations at church on Sunday. In the meantime, I will take some of the vegetables I have preserved from the garden over to them this evening." She paused for only a second. "And the leg of mutton Rob Stuart brought over yesterday."

"Your leg o' mutton? You canna."

"It is far too much for grandfather and me. We couldn't eat it in a month of Sundays."

"You canna give away the mutton."

"Dinna fret," Cathleen said with a laugh. "There is always a good way of looking at things."

"I dinna ken there is a good way of looking at starving to death."

"Have you not thought that if I give the mutton away, I willna have to cook it?"

Maude did not look convinced. "I dinna understand your being so happy about having nothing left to eat."

"*'God loveth a cheerful giver,'*" she said. When she saw her friend's puzzled expression, she added, "Corinthians."

Maude shook her head. "Weel, if you are bent upon starving, you might as well have company. I will give you the two loaves of bread I baked this morning," she said in a burst of benevolence. Then, giving Cathleen a sideways glance, she added, "But I willna laugh about it."

Cathleen smiled. "Ah, Maude, cheerfulness is as natural to you as the color on your cheek."

Maude smiled back at Cathleen and they walked on up the road. Soon they reached Drummond's field, where the workers had been haying for most of the morning, and it wasn't long until Cathleen lost herself in the task she had set for herself. After all, today was Tuesday, and Tuesday was her day to "do unto others."

It was a hot summer day, the kind of weather that was perfect for haying. As she always did whenever the village folk were gathered for work, Cathleen made her way among the hot, thirsty laborers, giving them a drink of the cool water she had just drawn from a nearby well. She stood in the midst of the hay field, pouring the last of the water from her jug into Mariah Duncan's dented tin cup. She listened patiently to Mariah, who thought Cathleen knew everything, simply because her grandfather was a minister.

"Fionn Alexander has asked me to marry him," Mariah said, her gazed fixed on a point behind Cathleen. "Do you think I should marry him?"

Cathleen turned, following the direction of Mariah's gaze, and saw Fionn working with a pitchfork, the muscles in his back flexing from the effort. "Fionn is a hard worker," she said. "I ken he will be a good provider."

"Aye," Mariah said, gazing at Fionn thoughtfully and putting a dent in her chin with her forefinger. "Do you think I should marry him?"

Cathleen looked at Mariah, seeing the anxiety and hope struggling in her expressive eyes. "I don't think it's my opinion that is important here. If you love him, Mariah, then marriage seems to be the natural progression of things, does it not?"

"I suppose," Mariah said, sounding as if her thoughts were drifting off in another direction entirely. "Were you ever in love?"

Cathleen felt her heart lurch. She willed her voice not to betray the anxiety she felt. "No."

"I ken this will sound silly to you, but what do you think about marriage?"

"I think it is a blessed and holy union sanctified by God."

Mariah seemed surprised. "Then why have you never married?"

"Only for myself," Cathleen said. "Now, why don't you stop worrying?"

"I ken worry comes to me as naturally as breathing. My ma says if I wasna worrying about marriage, I would be worrying about something else. Deep down in the innermost part of your heart, should I marry Fionn?"

Cathleen looked at Fionn. She looked at Mariah. Seeing the hungry look in Mariah's eyes, the way her gaze seemed to devour Fionn, she fought to overcome the unholy desire to laugh. "Aye. *'It is better to marry than to burn,'*" she said. "Corinthians."

Fletcher had originally planned to go straight to Caithness once he reached Edinburgh, but the moment his foot touched upon Scottish soil, he knew that was not to be.

Something called out to him—to seek the place of his birth, the place he had seen in his dream, the place where the crags were as white as milk and the wind carried the smell of a pungent sea. He sought instead black heath and shaggy wood, high corries and stormy seas, and the ghostly spires of a castle that rose, infinitely gray, infinitely silent, calling out to him.

Glengarry Castle.

Although he knew that something greater than himself drew him there, he knew also that he was not meant to stay. At least, not yet.

He purchased a sturdy horse and rode over the often treacherous terrain, aware of nothing save his great desire to see his home again. He stopped to sleep only when necessary, then was off again, drawn by a great and mighty force sweeping him toward his destiny.

It was early morning when he reached the base of a road and looked up to see his first glimpse of Glengarry Castle in twenty years. He had been only eight when he had last seen it, and he had a memory of the chilly haunted glory that he felt when he gazed at it now.

The castle sat on a promontory that seemed to separate the village that lay down the mountain to one side and the fringe of forest that lay on the other. And above it all rose the tall towers and turrets of the castle.

The sight of it gave him a thrill of awe and caution. He felt as if he were unprotected, naked. There was something inviting and familiar here, but there was also something treacherous; something dark and dangerous that warned him away.

He understood, then, just why he had come here first. He had to know what he was fighting for, important to know what he was up against.

After staring at it for quite a long time, he turned his horse away and set his sights on Caithness and the properties that were already his, content for now with the title, Earl of Caithness. He felt calm, assured, for he knew in his heart that the time would come when he would be the Duke of Glengarry as well.

He had waited a long time for this. He could be patient for a little longer.

Having ridden a mile from Glengarry and the rugged coast, he passed a field where a few of the village folk were working. He might have taken no notice of this pastoral scene at all, had it not been for a head had reflected in the sunshine every rosy hue of wine-dark hair.

Distracted by this, Fletcher reigned in his horse and watched a woman who stood out from the rest. He was not a man given to heart palpitations over every woman he saw, yet he sensed she was unusual.

He was not certain why he felt this way, but he intended to find out.

Watching her, his first impression was that he was delirious, or that he was fantasizing, for there was something almost ethereal about her. Her every motion was deft, yet fluid; purposeful, yet full of grace. Each line of her body seemed to move and bend like the reeds that danced in the wind at the edge of the loch.

Her dress was faded and well worn, and even from this distance he could tell that her face glowed with beauty and rustic health. Even then, he might have ridden on past her had not something about the bucolic scene called out to him, beckoning him closer.

He felt himself drawn to her, not simply by his attraction to her but by some stronger force. She must have felt no such thing, for she took no notice of him. She was busy drawing water from a well. It was a hot summer day and she had been raking a field sweet with hay.

He urged his horse forward, riding toward her, the aroma of peat and hay mixed with perspiration and the warmth of the workers. He paused at the well just a short distance from her, and when she turned to look at him, he immediately noticed her beautiful eyes. They were large, innocent and violet, and they sparkled with happiness, as if she was enjoying the hard work and relentless heat. He was struck by the way she looked at him with obvious discomfort.

Her dress was blue, in a simple style, with a white fichu, crossed in front, as was the fashion of many Highland women. Behind the fichu, he noticed, she was filled out nicely. He could not help thinking that beneath that fichu her life throbbed quick and warm.

She had lovely skin, the color and texture of heavy cream. Like a painting of the Madonna, her face seemed radiant, as if something delightful and wonderful dwelled within her, the result of which shone through her. He was overcome with the impulse to grab her and throw her across the saddle in front of him and to ride off with her to some secret place, where she would belong to him and to him alone.

But the words he wanted to say were too thick and foreign to leave his mouth. He wanted to surround her, to hold her so close that they became one thought, one body.

Was he out of his mind?

Do something. Say something. Anything besides sitting here on your horse grinning like a fool.

"Hello," he said, instantly aware that she rendered him speechless.

He noticed then the way she was looking at him, as if she

couldn't decide if she should scream or take off running. He saw fear in her eyes, and that leveled him. He had never frightened a woman in his life.

"I didn't mean to frighten you. I am new here and unfamiliar with your ways. Have I acted improperly? Is there some irate father hiding in the hay field ready to shoot out my eyes?"

She stared at him, not saying a word—not that he could blame her, for the way he had been behaving, she probably thought she had come across a lunatic.

He smiled at her and held up both hands in a display of innocence. "I meant no disrespect. My name is Fletcher Ramsay. I'm on my way from Glengarry. I saw you drawing water and thought I'd stop by. It's a hot day."

She gave him a shy smile. "Would you like a drink? The water is verra cold for such a warm day."

Even her voice sounded like none he had heard before. She was an angel, an apparition, and he found himself wondering if this was real. He glanced back at the workers to see if they were taking any notice, wanting some confirmation that this was happening, but they simply went on about their work. He couldn't seem to wipe that silly grin off his face.

He prayed that she liked grinning fools. "Indeed, I would love a drink," he said at last.

Without a word, she turned, giving him her profile—which, like the rest of her, was just about perfect—before dropping the bucket into the well again. She handled that bucket like some women handle a baby. He closed his eyes, imagining her hands on his naked body. He opened his eyes.

He was an idiot. Pure and simple.

A moment later, she drew the bucket up and set it on the edge of the well. The sun seemed to pull a burst of color from her rich mahogany hair as she leaned over to fill a tin cup.

A breeze wafted across the field, rippling the shafts of hay and causing the loose tendrils of hair to dance about her face. Turning back to him, she handed him the cup.

He reached for it, and their hands touched briefly before she drew hers away, blushed, and looked down at her bare feet and worn, faded gown.

"You are very shy," he said.

She lowered her eyes. "I dinna encounter many foreigners."

Foreigner? He could not help smiling. "I am not foreign. I was raised in America, but I was born not far from here."

She said nothing, so he drank the water and handed her the cup. "Thank you. The water was, as you said, very cold."

"Would you like more?"

He wondered what she would say if he told her he could sit here drinking water from her cup until he'd had enough to float a battleship. "No."

The wind ruffling the hay field became stronger. The sun went behind a cloud and stayed there. He glanced up. "Those are mighty inhospitable-looking clouds."

"Rain," she said, glancing up, then looking at him through long-lashed eyes for just a moment. "But I ken it will go as quickly as it comes."

"Do you live around here?"

"Aye."

"And you work these fields every day?"

"No, I come here . . . sometimes."

"To work?"

"To bring the workers food, or to draw them a drink of water."

He raised his brows. "How fortunate for me, then, that I happened by on a day you were here, drawing water."

Her violet eyes questioned him, as if she did not understand what he was saying. *God, are there really people this innocent?* She looked down at her feet again, and he could not help noticing that her cheeks had colored. So she was a shy lass, and not very talkative—something that would have sent him on his way, had she not been so fair.

But she was fair.

And he was intrigued with her, this shy lass with skin as pure and undefiled as he knew she was.

"What is your name?"

"Cathleen," she said softly. "Mary Cathleen Lindsay."

He forced the conversation a bit longer, making an even

bigger fool of himself than he had done before, until she picked up her jug of water.

Out of sheer boredom, more than likely.

"I must go now," she said. "The workers grow thirsty."

Not moving, he sat there for a moment, just looking at her, something about the scene familiar to him. "The woman at the well," he said, wondering why he thought of that biblical reference, since his thoughts were far from pure just now.

"Aye, *'Everyone who drinks of this water shall thirst again,'* " she said. "John." She turned away then and walked off, balancing the jug on her shoulder.

He watched her go, then started to turn and ride away when he noticed a white cloth lying next to the bucket. He urged his horse closer and, leaning down, picked it up.

It was a woman's kerchief, the kind the women in the field wore in their hair. He rubbed it with his thumb. The fabric was coarse and not expensive, but it was delicately made and edged with intricate embroidery.

Somehow he knew it belonged to her, that those hands that drew the water had crafted it, that it was she who had toiled for hours over this coarse piece of cloth to lovingly embroider it and turn it into a work of art.

He looked toward her, wondering if she was as inexplicably drawn to him as he was to her.

If she turns around. If she looks back at me. She is!

She turned her head, nothing more than a quick glance, but it was enough.

Ahhhh, sweetheart, do you know what you've done?

He smiled at her and lifted the kerchief like a salute, then brought it to his nose. He inhaled her fragrance, which smelled of summer rain and fresh-cut hay, a scent as fresh and natural as he found her to be. With a light kiss, he tucked it into his pocket.

She turned around suddenly and ran across the field, not stopping until she disappeared behind a group of thirsty workers.

Without another look, he turned his horse and rode back the way he had come. He wished he had asked more about where she lived. He reminded himself that in any case, such a beauty would not be hard to find again. And then he thought that perhaps it was a good thing he had met her, for now he had two reasons to come back. One for business and one for pleasure.

He couldn't have asked for more.

As she walked home, Cathleen Lindsay tried to think about what she would serve for dinner, but all she could think about was her encounter with the man at the well.

The American with the strange ways and the odd speech.

Images of his deep blue eyes and smiling mouth, his teasing words, kept haunting her, and she was reminded of the nights she would lie in bed, hugging herself and weeping, overcome with loneliness, wanting so desperately to be loved, knowing she never would be.

She chastised herself for allowing herself even to think about a loving relationship. Such notions were not for her, nor would they ever be. A long time ago she had made her peace with her lot in life. She was satisfied with her existence; she had cultivated sadness as a product of her suffering, and she had become used to its occurrence and predictability. She was the product of her past, resolute and obstinate. She wanted this man out of her thoughts, and she willed it to be so.

In an effort to distract herself, she reached up to take her kerchief from her head in order to wipe the perspiration from her face. Suddenly she remembered leaving it at the well. She not only remembered where that kerchief was now, but the way he had looked when he brought it to his lips.

She decided he was a bit eccentric, and yet he had seemed quite congenial for a stranger. He was very bold, and talkative. She knew that his world and hers were quite separate from each other, for there was nothing poor about him. His manner was refined and quite elegant. He was dressed as a gentleman, with his polished boots and perfectly tied cravat, and the horse he rode was blooded, the saddle expensive.

She was unaccustomed to such as he. There was no reason for her to be thinking about him. No reason at all. But she was.

She found that baffling.

She told herself that this was simply because he was the first American she had ever met—and she did consider him an American, in spite of his telling her he was Scots born. His accent was as American as his straightforward manner.

She decided she liked Americans.

Perhaps this was because he had kind eyes. Or because he smiled a great deal. Or because she found him pleasing to look at. And then it just might be all three.

There was much character in his face, and much understanding in his eyes—so much understanding, in fact, that she sensed he knew exactly what she was thinking. This was the only thing she found disconcerting about him. It left her at a loss to think that someone could read her thoughts—little that it mattered, since she would never see him again anyway.

"Good afternoon to you, Cathleen."

Startled, she looked up to see Henry Darnley riding toward her. She stopped, holding her hand up to shade the late afternoon sun from her eyes. "Good afternoon, Mr. Darnley. How is that leg of yours doing?"

Henry looked down at his leg, where his black bull had gored it less than a fortnight ago. "It is still sore, but I'm walking on it now, God be praised."

"Aye," she said, "'in everything give thanks.' First Thessalonians. You had a verra close call, I remember."

"Too close. If you had not happened by when you did, I might well have bled to death."

"I ken it was a blessing that I chose to go home early that day."

"A blessing indeed. You are a saint in my book, Cathleen. I ken why everyone calls you an angel of mercy."

She felt her face grow warm, and she dropped her hand and looked up the road. "Weel, I ken I had best be getting myself home. I wouldna want to give my grandfather cause to worry."

"Nor would I wish to be the cause of it," he said. "Give my best to David."

"I will," Cathleen said.

"Good day to you, then."

"Good day, Mr. Darnley," she replied, waiting until Henry

had passed before starting up the road again. She had not gone very far when her thoughts returned to the man at the well.

Cathleen was surprised to be thinking about him. It wasn't her wont to allow her thoughts to dwell upon men. And yet for the past half hour she had done just that.

Try as she would, she could not understand it.

She forced the image of the smiling American away, putting her mind, for the second or third time, to what she would prepare for her grandfather and herself for dinner.

Tatties, turnips, and oatmeal, more than likely, for that was their usual fare.

But in between tatties, turnips, and oatmeal came the memory of his features, full of expression; of an elegant stretch of mouth and eyes that held a thousand secrets. His eyes were the darkest hue of blue, a step away from black, but in the sunlight they were like deep pools that absorbed the light, appearing much lighter than they really were. Those eyes held a gaze that had reached out to her, touching her gently, moving over her body briefly, leaving her breathless, but never with the feeling that he was looking through layers of clothes to see what lay beneath.

How fortunate for me, then, that I happened by on a day that you were here, drawing water . . .

His words stayed with her. His voice had a slow, almost lazy ease and tone to it. How strange she felt. How odd. She glanced around her, seeing the same trees, the same burn tumbling down the fellside on its way to the dell below. Nothing about her world had changed. And yet, everything within her seemed different.

Why did she feel light-headed and weak when she thought about him? Why did she feel as if he had reached inside of her and touched something that so desperately needed to be touched? She reminded herself again that she had no right to be thinking like this.

She began gathering wildflowers, telling herself that these were probably the last she would see this season.

Some time later, she reached the cottage she shared on the small farm with her grandfather. She peered over the bounty of flowers in her arms to see Pedair Wass in their front yard. He was delivering a load of peat he had cut in the bog.

"I can cut a thousand peats in a hour and keep on going," Pedair was telling her grandfather.

"Aye," David said. "You are a dab hand with a tuskar. Will you be coming in to have some tea and scones?"

"I am as empty as a widow's purse, but the missus will be waiting dinner and I've three more deliveries to make before I go home. Tell Cathleen we are beholden to her for her help with the cooking while young Jamie was so ill."

"You can tell her yourself," David said, nodding in Cathleen's direction, "for here she comes now . . . at least I ken it is her, for I see a bouquet of flowers coming this way with her same color of hair."

Cathleen laughed at her grandfather's attempt at humor. "Tell Mrs. Wass I was glad to help," Cathleen said, lowering the flowers to peer over the top. "Master Jamie is getting on well, then?"

"Aye. As fit as a fiddle, he is," Pedair said, glancing at Cathleen. He put a thick peat on top of the others, as if that little something extra was for Jamie. "Weel now, I guess that about does it."

David counted out his coin, handing it to Pedair.

Pedair didn't count it but simply shoved it into his pocket, tipping his cap to them as he spoke. "Good day to you then."

"Goodbye, Pedair," Cathleen and her grandfather said in unison.

They watched Pedair leave before turning toward the house. "You need a haircut, Grandpa," Cathleen said, giving the longish gray hair at his nape a yank. "I'll give you one before dinner."

David drew up his shoulders. "I ken it would wait another week or two."

She laughed. "You always say that."

"Aye, and sometimes it works."

"Next week, then," she said, taking his arm as they walked toward the thick-walled cottage, pausing for a moment to let three fat ducks waddle by.

"Those ducks seem to have recovered," David said.

"Aye, they are good as new."

"Dinna you ken it is time to return them to Mary Mac-Gregor?"

"I have returned them to her three times, Grandpa. They keep coming back here."

"They are not your ducks, Cathleen."

"Aye, but the ducks dinna seem to ken that."

"You will have to tell Mary they are here."

"I stopped at her house on the way to the hay field this morning."

"Will she be coming after them, then?"

"Aye. She said she would come tomorrow."

David watched the ducks waddle down to the loch.

"Dinna fret, Grandpa. She will come after them, I promise."

Cathleen and her grandfather watched the ducks swim until they disappeared in the reeds that edged the loch.

"I hope they dinna come back again," David said. "I dinna ken you need three ducks."

"I dinna need those three," Cathleen said. "What would I do with them? I couldna eat them after nursing them back to health."

David flicked away a bee that had landed on his sleeve. "No, I suppose not."

Cathleen looked at her grandfather. She knew he was thinking about the three kittens she had pulled from the river, and the fawn whose mother she had found shot on the moor.

He did not mention the kittens or the fawn, however, and neither did Cathleen.

Once they were in the house, Cathleen left her grandfather in the parlor and went to the kitchen, her favorite room. She took her apron from the hook near the door and, tying it, went to wash her hands.

The room was small but pleasant. Overhead, where rough-hewn beams were exposed, Cathleen dried flowers and herbs. Strings of onions hung on the whitewashed walls below. A stone fireplace took up one corner. Near the fireplace stood her butter churn, the peat box, and two large kettles, one stacked inside the other.

The hutch that held her mother's dishes covered the opposite wall. In the center was a stout-legged table with three chairs, the fourth having been broken some five years before. An old spinning wheel occupied the same corner it had been in for a hundred years.

Cathleen did not know how to spin, but she liked the spinning wheel, knowing it had been used by generations of women in her family before her.

Filling a pot with water, she peeled a few potatoes and turnips, then put them on to boil. Soon a cloud of steam rose from the iron pot, and she went through the motions of preparing dinner the same way she had done all her life.

Some things never change, she thought, only to find herself wondering why she had the strangest feeling that something had.

Chapter Three

Fletcher Ramsay was left standing in front of Caithness Castle in a downpour for a full ten minutes before it was announced that Lady Doroty Lamont would see him.

Shown inside by a large, stout woman in gray linen and a white apron, who introduced herself as Mrs. MacCauley, he asked if he might have something to dry himself off a bit.

The woman looked him over good and proper, her shrewd little eyes narrowing. "Stand in front of the fire, laddie, and dry yerself."

Fletcher glanced toward the fire, but he did not move. "I would prefer not to stand dripping on the carpets the first time I meet my aunt," he said.

"Och! Yer aunt, you say? Now, why didna you tell me that in the first place?"

"My good woman, you didn't give me time to say much more than hello."

"Lose an hour in the morning and spend the rest of the day looking for it," she said. "I dinna have time to waste."

Fletcher blinked and stared at Mrs. MacCauley. His mother had warned him about the Scots and their abrupt, often dour ways. Apparently she had forgotten to mention their knack for shrewd evaluation.

"Weel now, if you'll be excusing me, laddie, I'll be fetchin' yer aunt . . . *if* Lady Lamont be yer aunt, that is."

"She *is* my aunt," he said with firm conviction.

"Time tries all things," she said and quit the room.

After she left, Fletcher began to study his surroundings. It was a large room, rich with paintings and tapestries hung over old stone walls. On one side stood an Elizabethan table with drawing leaves and carved bulbous supports, flanked by a pair of walnut armchairs with four finely carved cabriole legs. Opposite it stood a massive pedestal and urn, carved and inlaid with neoclassical decoration. He moved closer to the warmly glowing fire, feeling quite welcome here, in spite of the chill of the rain outside and the wintry reception he'd received from Mrs. MacCauley.

He gazed at several of the paintings, figuring that those were the faces of his ancestors staring back at him. He looked down at the worn stone floor and the old Persian carpets and found himself thinking that these were probably the same carpets his mother had played on as a young girl.

In one corner of the room was a piano, and he recalled his mother telling him about how she had learned to play. He crossed the room to stand before it.

This has to be her Cristofori.

"It was a lovely Cristofori, made in 1720," Fletcher remembered her saying. "I began to play the piano when I was four. Your grandfather, the earl, was an accomplished pianist. He taught me to play himself."

Fletcher touched the keys and felt his mother's strength reaching out to him. He was about to plunk a key or two when heard a noise and turned around.

A woman, whom he assumed to be his aunt, Doroty Lamont, swept into the room and stopped abruptly. "Sweet merciful heavens!" She looked as if she had seen a ghost.

Apparently regaining control of herself, she stepped farther into the room. "I am Lady Doroty Lamont. Who the devil are you?"

"I am your nephew, Fletcher Ramsay," he said, thinking it hadn't been such a good idea to surprise her.

"*Fletcher*? Fletcher Ramsay?"

Judging from the look on her face, he thought his words had shocked her, so he asked, "You were not expecting me?"

Her hand came up to her throat. "Bless me! Of course I was expecting my sister's son, the heir of Caithness Castle. I was not expecting him to look so much like his father." She rubbed her arms as if she were feeling chills. "Makes a body shudder, it does. I feel like I'm looking upon the face of the dead, and I canna help wondering if I am seeing things, or if it really is the Duke of Glengarry come back to life."

Fletcher could not help his smile any more than he could help his thoughts, for he knew that right now she was thinking that Bruce Ramsay's son smiled exactly the same way his father had. It was a comparison he had heard from his mother often enough.

"Maybe it's a little of both," he said. "I will be the Duke of Glengarry . . . and before too much longer." He could tell by the way she smiled at him that she did not miss the strength in his voice or the conviction with which he spoke.

"Aye, your mother wrote me about the task you have set for yourself," she said. "It wilna be easy, lad. It cost your father his life."

"I will be more careful."

Doroty Lamont studied him and he wondered what she was thinking. "Come," she said, "let us sit here by the fire."

Fletcher took the chair she indicated. "You think I am wrong to want my father's title—to go after what is rightfully mine?"

"For now, I withhold my opinion. If you have inherited as much of your father's Highlander blood as his looks, then I could hardly blame you. The Scots way is one of extremes. Compromise is a foreign word to us. Ever the romantics, we always have a cause. Consequently, it has become a way of life for us to live on the knife's edge."

"I will remember that."

"I would not be completely honest if I didna tell you I feel a twinge of pity for you, lad."

"Why is that?"

"Your Highlander blood can just as easily work against you. You will have to be cautious if you are to succeed."

"I can be careful."

"I can see that you have much of your father in you, and that may be more hindrance than help. A Highlander was never a man to take the easier way. We set impossible tasks for ourselves."

He chuckled. "My mother has often said the same thing."

"And did you understand what Maggie was telling you?"

"Sometimes," he said, grinning.

"It has never been a Highlander's way to harbor malice, Fletcher, and it is difficult for him to take his revenge cold. We are quick to anger and just as quick in the cooling of it."

"Then we have found one area in which I do not take after my father, for I have harbored malice toward Adair Ramsay for a very long time," he said. "It hasn't cooled in twenty years."

"Heed my words, Fletcher. Your father made a deadly mistake. It was in his blood and it may be in yours."

"What mistake was that?"

"He was too swift to forgive and just as fatally forgot. In spite of your mother's admonitions, Bruce did not think Adair Ramsay capable of treachery. It was the opening Adair needed. We are a strong people and history has shown we are without equal in the attack, but our defense has too often been weak. From what I know of Adair Ramsay, he will not be a man to take the threat of losing the title he usurped lying down. He will come at you, and come with everything he has," she said. "I canna help wondering if you will be strong enough and canny enough to stand up to that."

"I am prepared for that," he said. "And as for whether I will be canny enough and strong enough, I must say I've inherited those qualities from my mother."

She nodded. "Aye, Maggie was always gifted with both. I pray you have learned from her. From what she wrote about her husband, I find myself thinking you have acquired some of Adrian Mackinnon's sound judgment as well."

Fletcher smiled at that. He paused for a moment. "Forgive me, Aunt. In my eagerness to discuss the loss of my father's title, I did not mean to imply that I take the title I inherited from Uncle Ian lightly. With your help, I will learn what is required of me here, even before I begin my quest to regain Glengarry and my title."

"You have a bit of the tactician in you, Fletcher. It is something I am happy to see. *That* is something you inherited from your mother. Maggie always had a way about her." She paused. "Weel now, enough of that. I didna mean to talk your ears off. You have traveled far and will be here for the rest of your life. I ken we can continue this talk at another time."

Doroty rang for Mrs. MacCauley, then instructed her to have Fletcher's room made ready. "Are you weary, Fletcher? Would you like to rest a bit?"

"No. I'd like to spend more time talking to you, if you don't mind. There is much I need to learn."

"Aye," Doroty said, "there is, at that. Come with me then."

Leading him from the room, he followed her down a long, narrow passageway, unlit except by a pair of sconces, before going into a large study, its walls crammed with books and documents.

"Have a seat there before the fire. Your clothes are still damp."

She watched Fletcher as he settled into a leather chair, commenting to him that it had been used by four generations of the earls of Caithness. She offered him whisky, which he declined, then green China tea, which he accepted.

As she poured, they exchanged pleasantries—questions about his mother, his sisters, Ainsley and Barrie, and the rest of the Mackinnon family; his trip here; his life in California.

Then they began to speak of the title Earl of Caithness, which he had inherited from Doroty's brother, Ian. After much conversation, Fletcher changed the subject. "What do you know about my father's death and the loss of his title?"

She put her teacup on the table beside her and thought for a moment. At last she said, "I fear you will be disappointed, for I canna tell you more than you already know. I ken your mother has told you everything."

"My mother talks when the subject interests her. This one did not. I understood that she feared any discussion would only strengthen my resolve to return. I would like to hear your recollections."

Doroty nodded. "Then I suppose it best to start at the beginning," she said. "Your father was about your age—twenty-seven, I think—when Adair Ramsay first showed up on the doorstep of Glengarry. He brought with him some papers that he said proved his lineage back to Alasdair Ramsay, the eighth Duke of Glengarry."

"And Alasdair's son was Douglas, and Douglas was my great-great-great-grandfather."

"Aye, but have you been told that Adair Ramsay had a great-great grandfather by the same name, and his Douglas was also the son of an Alasdair Ramsay?"

"Yes, Mother said there were two Douglas Ramsays, with Father's named Alasdair. She also said *mine* was the duke."

"That was the way of it, but it seems that Adair had proof of his lineage, whereas your father did not. The first time this was challenged in court, it was thrown out, simply because your father's title had been handed down to him, so they took it to be right. Your father, after all, was alive, and quite well liked."

"And after he was murdered . . ."

She frowned. "That was never proven."

"But Mother said . . ."

"I know what Maggie believed, so I can well imagine what she said, and in my heart I feel she is right. Your father was an expert horseman and he knew the area around Glengarry like the back of his hand. It is hard to believe he would have ridden his horse over the cliffs, even harder to believe that the horse would have gone . . ."

"Unless he was forced."

"Exactly." Doroty leaned back, placing her hands on the arms of her chair. "Shortly after your father's death, Adair brought his suit again, and this time the courts accepted his proof as valid."

"And they stripped the title from me and gave it to Adair."

"Aye, that was the way of it."

"But why? That is what I don't understand. What was his proof? Mother mentioned that it had something to do with a marriage that never took place."

"Aye," she said, and then went on to explain, in detail, what had happened and how his father, the Duke of Glengarry, lost his title. Having no documented proof to counter Adair Ramsey's attack, Fletcher's father could do little to preserve his inheritance. As Dorothy sketched a family tree for Fletcher she explained who was related to whom.

"Study this and we will talk about it later," she said, handing the diagram to him.

Fletcher took the paper, folded it, and placed it in his pocket. "Thank you, Aunt. This"—he patted his pocket—"makes it much simpler to understand."

"It may sound simple, but the proving of it will be something else entirely."

"Perhaps," he said, "but I *will* prove it."

It must have been the way he said it that made Doroty look up. "What makes you so certain you can prove something your father could not?"

"Because my father will be guiding my steps. I cannot fail." He gave her a direct look. "Do I shock you? Do you think me daft?"

"No," she said, suddenly understanding. "We Scots were ever a superstitious people. You've had a vision, then?"

"Yes," he said, and told her about the two dreams.

"And so you had to wait ten years after the first dream before you had the second."

"Yes, and I had a hard time of it. I was never known for my patience."

Doroty laughed, as if she had no trouble believing that. "Aye, patience is a good nag, but she'll bolt."

Fletcher went on to tell her that he believed his acquiring the title of Earl of Caithness was a sign—a sign that it was time for him to come back.

"I am glad you mentioned Caithness. I thought you had forgotten it. Hout! You had *me* forgetting it."

"I'll give you no cause to worry on that score," he said. "I will do all I can to honor the title. What my mother lacked in telling me about my Ramsay ancestors, she more than made up for in speaking of my Sinclair ones."

Doroty nodded. "Ours is a rich history and a proud one."

"Yes, I know, and for that reason I came to love this place long before I saw it, and even now I feel a closeness to it, knowing it is where my mother was born, where she acquired all the qualities I so admire in her ... as well as a few I don't."

Doroty laughed at that. "Aye, your mother was ever a strong-willed lass, and my father spoiled her shamelessly. She was the baby, you see, and born quite some time after the rest of us. There are ... that is, there were five children in all, three boys—all dead now—and two girls. Did she tell you much about us?"

"Yes, she often said it was like having two mothers and four fathers."

"Aye, and Maggie had need of every one of them—a handful, she was."

Fletcher was amused at that. "She chose not to tell me about that either," he said.

"Well, remind me to speak at length about it sometime."

Fletcher nodded. "I will, and I will also do everything in my power to be an earl you will be proud of."

"Somehow I knew you would. Caithness is not a wealthy earldom, but it is rich in more important ways. The people here are good and will serve you properly if you do well by them."

"And I shall endeavor to do so, if you will agree to be my tutor. Mother said you knew more about Caithness than anyone."

"Aye, I've lived here long enough ... since the death of my husband, some forty years ago. My father was old and almost blind and I was his eyes and ears. Once Ian inherited the title, I continued to run things." As if she saw his surprise, she added, "Ian preferred the social life of the country earl, which he found in Edinburgh, to what he called the solitary confinement of these cold, stone walls."

Fletcher studied her for a moment. "So, in essence, you've been the Earl of Caithness for quite some time."

"Aye, and it pains me to think upon it. I could never understand why a woman couldna inherit a title. She can inherit the lairdship of a clan, but not a title. It doesna make any sense to me."

"Perhaps things will change."

"Not in my lifetime," she said, "or in yours either."

Mrs. MacCauley entered the room and stopped, looking from one to the other.

"Are you going to talk yer aunt to death?"

"We have reached a stopping point." Doroty came to her feet. "Well, I ken you could go on with this for another hour or two, but these old bones dinna have the stamina they once had. It is time for me to rest. I ken your journey was long and hard, in spite of your youth. A little rest willna be a bad idea for you as well."

"Of course," he said, rising to his feet. "I apologize for keeping you awake at such a late hour."

"I ken I enjoyed our talk more than an hour of sleep."

"I would like to talk again tomorrow . . . if it's all right with you."

"Ah, the young are ever restless," she said, smiling.

Chapter Four

Fletcher sat at one end of the massive dining table, his aunt, Doroty, at the other. If he had learned anything in the many weeks he had been at Caithness Castle, it was that she was both formidable and striking.

At sixty-eight, she was tall and as regal as Queen Victoria, with white hair and that aloof confidence that he had already learned to associate with Scots. Her clothes were always black or gray, or a combination of the two, and as elegant as they were out of style. She was opinionated, prejudiced, dour, and steeped in tradition and the past. Upon their first meeting, he had thought her quite inhospitable—after all, he had been left standing outside in the rain for a full ten minutes before being shown inside.

But now that he had gotten to know her, he saw her as the wisest, strongest, most loving woman in the world, and he adored her. There was much about her that reminded him of his mother, and, like his mother, she taught him much. It was his aunt who spent her days telling him the history of his mother's family; his aunt who advised him not to be so eager, but to proceed slowly and with great caution if he was determined to prove Adair Ramsay an impostor.

Fletcher learned much about his mother's family from Dorothy. But he also learned a great deal about it from Caithness Castle itself. Although he was living in the earl's chamber, he spent a great deal of time in his mother's old room, a room filled with things from her life with Bruce Ramsay, things she had brought with her from Glengarry Castle after his death. Everything in her room was just as she had left it, and every time Fletcher went there, he felt as if he were stepping back in time.

Sorting through her belongings, Fletcher could not help smiling. His mother was shrewd enough to know that she should not take the reminders of one marriage into another, yet she was woman enough to want to keep the mementos of a past love, and Scot enough not to throw anything away.

Of all Maggie's belongings, the one thing that interested him most was a large, humpbacked trunk. It was quite old, much older than most of the possessions it contained. Inside the trunk, Fletcher found some of his father's clothes and personal property, like his watch and his brush and comb, but deeper down, toward the bottom of the trunk, lay many documents and ledgers that belonged to Bruce Ramsay as well. And there, below the documents, Fletcher found a false bottom concealing a very old book. He realized at once that it was a Bible, but it was written in French. The moment he touched it, his hands began to tremble. About him, the room seemed to grow brighter, and he had the strangest feeling that someone else was with him. There was an inscription on the inside cover, but it too was in French, and the brown ink had faded. He was barely able to make out *Brigitte de Compiegne, Honfleur, France, 1740*.

There was something special about this Bible. He knew that instinctively, but he did not know exactly what made it so.

When he had replaced the Bible, restored all the contents, and closed the trunk, he wondered if he had just imagined the intense sensations that had coursed through him or if the belongings really could speak to him so powerfully.

A few days later, Fletcher went to Edinburgh to hire a solicitor, then spent the afternoon reading over the documents pertaining to the hearing between his father and Adair Ramsay, as well as those to the hearing after his father's death, when the courts had stripped him of his title and given it to Adair.

As he began to learn the ways of the Scots and the role of the Earl of Caithness, he understood what Doroty meant when she said to him one evening, "Power and respect will serve you well. You will need both to gain the trust of those you will rely on to help you. Regaining your title will be difficult, and I need not tell you, Fletcher, that it is not an easy path you have chosen for yourself. Adair Ramsay is a very powerful man."

"I am not afraid of Adair Ramsay," Fletcher said, taking a bite of salmon.

Doroty put down her wineglass. "That is foolishness talking. The greater the power, the more dangerous the man. You would do well to remember that."

He did remember it, but it did not stop him from the task he had set for himself.

"I dinna think you have heard a word I've said," Aunt Doroty said, waving the butler away when he offered her more wine.

At the sound of Doroty's voice, Fletcher said, "What? Oh ... I'm sorry, Aunt. My thoughts have wandered."

"In the direction of Glengarry Castle, I'll wager."

"I've decided it's time to pay a visit to Glengarry."

"You willna find any proof there, but I ken you are itching to go. I've known for days that I will be continuing in my role as the *Earless* of Caithness a bit longer."

Fletcher grinned. "Is that Ear-less or Earl-ess?"

"It's Earl-ess, but sometimes I would prefer the former, especially after listening to all the bickering that comes when it's time to collect the rents. When do you plan to leave, lad?"

"By the end of the week."

"I dinna need to warn you to be careful. The village of Glengarry is small, and it has been Adair Ramsay's home for twenty years. He will have plenty of ears about."

"I know."

"Where will you stay?"

"I will find something when I get there. Don't worry about me."

"Humph! I will worry regardless."

Fletcher finished his wine. "I know you will. You are much like my mother in that regard."

"It was ever a woman's way," she said, "to worry about her menfolk, but I ken you heard enough of that before you left California. What are your plans?"

He shook his head. "I don't know. I only know that it's time for me to go there, that there is something . . . someone in Glengarry that holds a key to all of this."

"Trust no one, Fletcher," Doroty warned. "Except . . ."

"Except whom?"

"I was thinking you might pay a visit to that nice parson, the one who married your mother and father. MacDonald, his name was. David MacDonald. Of course, he would be getting on up in years by now, but still, he might be of some help. He baptized you . . . and your two sisters too, if I remember right."

"My mother told me about him, and, like you, she advised me to seek his counsel. She has corresponded with him over these past years."

"I ken you plan to heed her advice?"

He smiled. "Of course. I am ever the dutiful son, am I not?"

"Aye, when it pleases you."

"Rest easy, Aunt. I plan to make it a point to call on him," Fletcher said. "It couldn't hurt to have a man of God on my side."

"You had best be praying you have God himself on your side," she said.

"I have always prayed for that."

Two days later, Fletcher received his first invitation as the new Earl of Caithness.

He had just come in from riding a gelding he had purchased at a fair the week before, when Mrs. MacCauley handed him a cream-colored envelope.

His brows narrowed as he turned the envelope over, studying it. "Who is this from?"

"You might find the answer to your question if you would open it," Mrs. MacCauley said.

Giving Mrs. MacCauley a teasing look, Fletcher took the envelope to his study, where he opened it.

"Who is Annora Fraser?" he asked his aunt at dinner that night.

Doroty paused with a bite of mutton midway to her mouth. "Where did you hear of Annora?"

"I received an invitation from her today—for a ball she is giving."

"And you are thinking of accepting?"

"I don't know. What do you think?"

"No matter what I said, I ken you would go anyway," Doroty said, "as soon as you learned that Annora Fraser's home is quite close to Glengarry."

That definitely piqued Fletcher's interest, and he leaned back from the table, his meal forgotten. "Do tell me more."

"You will love this next part," Doroty said. "Annora is young, wealthy, and very beautiful. She is also a widow."

Fletcher grinned. "Are you proposing marriage?"

"It crosses the mind of every man who meets her."

"And her husband? What happened to him?"

"He died of old age." Doroty paused. "Annora married for money. She was a poor village girl, until she caught the eye of a wealthy landowner."

"Any children?"

"No. Simon Fraser died before his wife could bear him an heir."

"How unfortunate."

"For Simon, perhaps, but as for Annora, it makes her all the more appealing."

"Appealing enough to interest me. After what you've said, I would be a fool to refuse, even if her home wasn't close to Glengarry."

Fletcher was silent for a moment, reflecting.

"Something is troubling you."

"I was just wondering how she had heard of me."

"Annora did not get where she is by oversight. You can bet she knows all about you, just as surely as you can bet she will know even more after she meets you. She has more than being neighborly on her mind, I am certain. You must not forget that she is as cunning as she is beautiful."

"You make her sound like a witch."

"She isn't an evil woman, just determined enough to do whatever is necessary to accomplish what she desires." Doroty paused. "There must be some English blood in her somewhere."

Fletcher laughed, then pushed his chair back and rose to his feet. "I think you exaggerate, Aunt. I doubt that Annora Fraser will even notice I am there."

"Who is that?" Annora whispered, keeping her gaze fastened upon the back of the tall, brown-haired man across the room. She had spied him the moment he entered the room, wearing the kilt with the sporran hanging from his waist, the silver-handled dirk in his heavy knit sock, the tartan riding his broad shoulder, held in place with a laird's badge.

Her gaze dropped lower.

He had long, muscular legs and looked as if he would sit a horse well. She wondered if the same was true about women.

"That is the Earl of Caithness," the doorman replied.

"Well, well, well," Annora said, studying him with increased vigor, her face alight with curiosity. She had a vision of him with his thick brown hair rumpled from sleep, his voice low and throbbing with desire. He looked marvelous—and why not? He was tall, and fit, and wealthy, and available.

"The Earl of Caithness," she repeated, thinking she had been wise to invite the new earl to her home. "How fortunate it is that I'm a woman with an ear finely tuned for gossip. He looks even better than I was led to believe."

A second later, Annora turned away, adjusting the front of her tight-fitting princesse Basque, tugging the low-cut square neck of her dress so that it plunged just a little lower. Then she headed across the room, the long green faille train held in place by a spray of black poppies swishing seductively as she went.

* * *

He saw her coming and was more than interested. Hell, a man would have to be blind to admit otherwise.

He had noticed her the moment he entered the room, for she was all the beauty his aunt had said she was and then some. He had noticed her even before she turned around, for from the back, her figure was long, lean, and curvaceous, and beautifully seductive in yards of a perfectly fitted emerald-green gown. Never had he seen hair so blue-black or skin so fair and white, and, now that he thought about it, he had never feasted his gaze upon such a shapely derriere. He wondered what she would do if he tried to pick one of those black poppies.

When she turned around he could think of only one word to describe her bosom: Magnificent.

When she started across the room, he almost laughed outright, for she reminded him of a falcon swooping in for the kill. The urge to laugh vanished when he realized that he was the intended prey.

Feeling the need for fortification, he took a drink from a passing servant's tray and tossed it down quickly, then stood with a wide-legged stance and watched her. Although he knew she realized that he was watching, she did not react as most women would have done. She didn't blush, avert her eyes, or do any of the other silly things a woman might do when a man looked at her with thoughts he had no business thinking. He thought that her boldness was probably due to the fact that she was no simpering virgin, that she had been married. More than likely she hadn't been a virgin when she took her vows.

It was more than obvious that she was an experienced woman and that she wasn't too proud to reveal her interest in a man. These two things set to work on him immediately. Before the night was out, he would do more than look.

"Shame on you for being so late," she said, coming up to him. "I've been waiting for you all evening. I'm Annora Fraser, and you must be the Earl of Caithness. I would have recognized you anywhere."

"Why is that?"

"Because you are undeniably handsome, and because I was told you were American and it shows."

"Is it that obvious?"

She smiled, looping her arm through his. "Did I say it was obvious? It simply shows, that's all."

"In what way?" he asked, hoping she wasn't going to say it was because of the way he looked in a kilt. It hadn't been easy for him to put this rigging on tonight, and he had agreed only because he knew it was expected of him. Damn drafty, it was.

She shrugged, and he could not help noticing how the gesture increased her cleavage.

"You Americans have a certain air of defiance, a nonconformist demeanor about you that makes you stand out in a room," she said.

"Then it must be acquired, for I am a Scot through and through."

"Oh, I know who you are. I know all about you and why you've come to Scotland."

He stiffened and came to an abrupt stop.

"And why have I come?" he asked, his voice harsher than he'd intended.

She gave him a coy smile, pressing closer than was considered acceptable. "Why, to inherit your uncle's title, of course."

"Of course."

She tightened her grasp on his arm. "Now do come along. I've dozens and dozens of people to introduce you to."

"All males, I'll wager."

Annora gave him an appraising look, then threw back her head with a throaty laugh, the emeralds and diamonds riding the crests of her breasts glinting in his eyes. "We shall get on," she said. "I'm glad we understand each other."

"Do we?"

"Aye. Tell me, did you not know that you would bed me even before we spoke?" She led him through a set of double doors and onto a small, private balcony.

"I knew," he said. "Hell, the whole room knew."

She laughed at that, and he found himself liking that throaty pitch. The sound of it was as arousing as her forwardness. He had never met a woman like her.

"Then we shall be careful not to disappoint them. You will stay the night, won't you?"

Something within Fletcher prevented him from saying that he would, despite the interest his body was showing. "Perhaps," he said.

She smiled, coming up on her toes to kiss his mouth. Her lips were soft and warm, coaxing. He was tempted to open his mouth to her kiss, but something stopped him.

Annora drew back. "A man who plays hard to get?" she teased. "I am intrigued and find myself challenged. Come along then. It's time to make all the women in the room jealous."

At that, Fletcher threw back his head and laughed.

A few minutes later, he stood with Annora in a circle of people as she introduced him. There were probably twelve men clustered around them, all of them about his age or older.

"I would like to present Scotland's newest acquisition, straight off the boat from America. Gentlemen, this is the Earl of Caithness. Most of you knew his uncle, Ian, and the tragedy that took his life. And now the new earl is here, and it is up to us to make him feel welcome."

The men didn't exactly jump at the chance to welcome him. A couple of months ago, Fletcher might have been worried, but not now. In the short time he'd been in the country, he had learned that it was the Scots' way not to form instant opinions. Yet, a few of them did smile weakly, and one or two went so far as to act mildly polite.

"What part of America are you from?" asked a man who called himself Fergus McAlpin.

"California," Fletcher replied, noticing that the reply seemed to be acceptable.

"You are the late earl's nephew, so that must make you a Sinclair, but I wasna aware any of the Sinclairs went to America," Colin Ferguson remarked.

"My mother was a Sinclair. She married an American after my father died."

That comment sparked new interest, especially from a short,

stout man he remembered as Gavin MacPhail. "Your name wouldna be—"

"Ramsay. Fletcher Ramsay." He noticed how Gavin's eyes seemed to dart across the room, but when Fletcher looked in that direction he saw nothing out of the ordinary.

"Ramsay," Colin Ferguson said. "Your father was . . ."

"The Duke of Glengarry."

A hush fell around them.

Tension was evident now in every person present. Even Annora seemed to be at a loss for words. Fletcher thought it was simply because none of them wanted to become involved in an old feud, and he couldn't blame them.

As he expected, one by one the gentlemen made their excuses and turned away.

It was only after they had gone that he had time to think about their reactions upon learning who he was. A few minutes later, none of them stood out in his mind—except one man.

Gavin MacPhail.

After quickly glancing around the room, Fletcher saw Gavin just as he was disappearing through the doors that led outside, his head bent, as if deep in conversation with the man beside him, a man of small stature and gray hair.

Suddenly Fletcher felt as if a cold draft had swept into the room.

He watched until the two men were out of sight, wondering what it was about Gavin MacPhail that bothered him. The eyes, he thought. The shifty, not-to-be-trusted eyes. Yes, it was the eyes, he reminded himself, as Annora led him around the room like a prize stallion she had just won. The pale blue, ice-cold eyes.

"Who was that man?" Fletcher asked Annora.

"What man?" she asked, turning toward him, her hands on his arms.

"The one that just went outside with Gavin MacPhail."

The color faded from Annora's face. Her gaze flicked away, then quickly came back to him. She recovered herself well, he noted, as she said smoothly, "Why, I don't know. What did he look like?"

"Never mind," Fletcher said. "I'll find out later."

Later came half an hour afterward, when Annora excused herself, leaving Fletcher to talk to a small group of men and women.

Before long, the conversation died down, and one by one they began to drift away, all save an older woman who spoke quite fondly of Fletcher's aunt. It was at that point that he noticed the gray-haired man he had seen go outside with Gavin MacPhail; but MacPhail was nowhere in sight. The gray-haired man was talking to Annora. Once or twice they glanced his way.

Fletcher felt the same cold chill he had felt before. This time, when Fletcher asked who the man was, he got an answer.

The woman who spoke so fondly of his aunt looked across the room. "The man talking to Annora?"

Fletcher nodded.

"Why, that is Adair Ramsay, the Duke of Glengarry."

Chapter Five

The day after Annora Fraser's ball, Adair Ramsay sat behind his desk in the massive library of Glengarry Castle.

The library, although beautifully appointed with priceless antiques and rugs, had a heavy, gloomy appearance. Even the narrow windows behind the desk—set deep into the castle wall—seemed to exclude rather than to admit the sunlight.

Adair twirled a silver-handled letter opener in his hands. The oil lamp on his desk threw a deep golden glow across the room, casting his shadow upon the wall behind him. He was a small man, with dark penetrating eyes, stooped shoulders, thinning gray hair, and a thin, weasel-like face. His countenance was both shrewd and sinister. He was a man who graced those in disfavor with a full portion of his hatred.

Using the letter opener to clean his fingernails, he leaned back in his leather chair and waited.

A few minutes later, the door to the library opened and Gavin MacPhail entered, a man of middle years, with graying red hair and a stocky build that suggested his Gaelic heritage.

He made his way across the highly polished floors to one of two massive, carved chairs before the desk. In the Scottish tradition, the chairs' legs had been lathed to resemble sticks of barley sugar.

Looking like a man relieved to have his journey over with, he dropped into the chair. "I ken you want to know what I've found out," he said.

"Blithering fool! I haven't been waiting all this time to hear about your wife's health. Where is he? Have you learned why he's here?"

"He is on his way to Glengarry. Word has it he's come here to pay his respects to David MacDonald."

"His respects to the retired minister? Why would he do that?"

Gavin shrugged. "Nostalgia, from what I hear. It seems his mother has always spoken fondly of the good minister and wished him to pay her respects."

Adair scowled. "A good alibi. But not, I think, the real reason for his coming."

"Perhaps you are wrong. After all, it is my understanding that MacDonald did baptize the boy and his sisters, and he married his parents."

"He also performed Bruce Ramsay's funeral, and he was here at Glengarry the day Maggie Ramsay packed the last of her belongings and left for good. I would not be surprised if the minister has kept in touch with her all these years."

"The earl's going to visit MacDonald doesna prove anything."

"Why is he in Scotland?"

"I ken it is because he is the Earl of Caithness."

Adair rose to his feet and slammed his hands on the desk, the sharp point of the letter opener jabbing into the pad of his finger. "Idiot! That is not an important title, nor a wealthy one. Fletcher Ramsay's stepfather is a millionaire, and Fletcher was reared in America. That would make him more American than Scottish. Titles don't appeal to Americans. I dinna ken for one minute that it was that measly title that brought him scampering over here."

"What then?"

"Revenge. Justice. My destruction. Regaining his father's title." Adair regained his composure and lowered himself into his chair, where he sat for a moment staring at the scarlet drop of blood that welled on his finger. "He is the avenger of blood come to retaliate for the death of a kinsman."

"His father?"

"Aye, you fool, and what better way to avenge his untimely demise than by reclaiming his title?"

"I thought you said titles weren't important to Americans."

"*This* title would be important, you imbecile."

Gavin said nothing, but his discomfort was obvious. A moment later, he rose to his feet. "Whatever the reason, there is little we can do about it. He is here, and he is the Earl of Caithness, like it or no. We have no proof that he has come for any other reason. If that is all he's after, then all our worries will not come to a muckle. There is no point in muddying a river you dinna intend to cross."

"As long as he is content to be the Earl of Caithness—and that means keeping his nose out of Glengarry and my business—then I won't have to do anything about it. But if he becomes greedy, if he starts setting his sights on bigger fish—Glengarry castle, for one thing—then I will do something about it. I won't see everything I've worked for taken from me."

"What are you saying?"

"That it would be a pity for him to end up like his father."

"You mean, losing his title?"

"I mean, dead."

It is said that memory is the treasury of the mind, and perhaps it is, for Cathleen was in the kitchen sweeping the floor when she suddenly realized that she wasn't sweeping at all; she was standing in the middle of the kitchen floor, her hands folded over the top of the broom, her chin resting on her hands, her gaze fixed on the big rowan tree in the yard, her thoughts a million miles away . . . perhaps as far away as America. Well, not America, perhaps, but upon a certain American—the one she had met in Drummond's hay field when he had ridden up, out of the blue, and she had given him a drink of water.

Just like the woman at the well in the Bible.

She thought about that day, wondering why her mind had chosen to build a monument to that particular memory. Was it because a monument in her memory was all she would ever have?

She gave herself a mental shake, telling herself that the likes of him were not for her and that it did precious little good to covet something she could never have. A normal life, a husband, children ... these things would never be for her. Yet that strange-talking American had disturbed her thoughts and caused her to be just a little dissatisfied with her life.

Picking up the broom, she admonished herself as she began sweeping furiously. "*Fais toujours aucune chose de bien, que le diable ne te trouve oyseux* [Do always some good deed that the devil may not find you idle]," she said. "Saint Jerome, Epistles, 125."

She quoted Saint Jerome in French because she felt entitled at least to this little bit of extravagance in her life.

She swept the dust out the door, pausing in the doorway to gaze down the road toward the village of Glengarry. She was remembering the way *he* had ridden into the hay field that day, looking as bonny as a Highland regiment, then found herself imagining what it would be like to see him riding down the road and into her yard. What would it feel to have a man like him come courting?

"Aye," she said, "what would it be like to have *any* man come courting?" She shook the rug and placed it back on the stoop. "You know, the trouble with you, Cathleen, is that you want it all—even when you know you canna have it. '*Lay not up for yourselves treasures upon earth, where moth and rust doth corrupt, and where thieves break through and steal: But lay up for yourselves treasures in heaven, where neither moth nor rust doth corrupt, and where thieves do not break through nor steal: For where your treasure is, there will your heart be also,*'" she said. "Matthew."

"Did you say something, Cathleen?"

Cathleen turned around to see her grandfather, David, walk into the room. "I was just quoting Saint Jerome, Grandpa."

"Ahhh, *'I have revered always not crude verbosity, but holy simplicity.'*"

Cathleen blushed and looked down at her toes. "That isna the one I was quoting."

With that, David MacDonald threw back his head and laughed.

Chapter Six

The journey to Glengarry was not a difficult one, for Glengarry lay not more than half a day's ride from Annora Fraser's grand house.

For Fletcher, it was so pleasing to take such a journey, for it put him out of doors and in touch with a part of his heritage he had never known. Riding to the village of Glengarry, he crossed fragrant, heather-covered moors and passed dark, mysterious lochs where uneasy winds stirred pine trees that looked black against the gray sky, while ever in the distance rose the moorland ridges and tors, wreathed in mist and majestic silence.

He rode over rocks dappled with lichen, scattered between puffy tufts of heather, passing very few villages and not minding that in the least. Having spent most of his life in the timber forests of Northern California, he preferred the mirrored lochs and silent hills to the clamor of village life.

It was late afternoon when he reached Glengarry, a hamlet of cottages that he thought of as Presbyterian gray and white, nestled between Glengarry Castle and an excitable burn that tumbled over smooth, round rocks on its way to the loch below. A short distance away lay the sea, and the smell of it lingered in the air.

He pulled his horse to a stop.

The village was quiet as he looked across to the fragmented ruins of a cross at least two hundred years old. A few yards farther he saw a group of ornate gravestones resplendent with carvings of armed lairds and clan shields. Beyond, down the street, the steeple of a church rose above it all, while across from that a pub advertised fresh salmon and venison pie. And towering over it all was the place of his heritage, Glengarry Castle, riding the high ridges that separated the town from the pine forests.

Something about the place reached out to him. The spirit of the Highlands was an almost tangible thing. He'd been born here, and his father and a legion of other Ramsay ancestors were buried in that castle.

Yet he was a stranger here.

He made his way through the main street of town, thinking that Glengarry wasn't much bigger than its name. He rode toward the steeple until he drew even with St. Andrew's Presbyterian Church, where he stopped.

Going inside, he saw a man in somber clothing working near the pulpit. "Hello," he said.

Fletcher had never before encountered anyone who managed to exude annoyance at fifty yards.

"Pardon the intrusion," he added. "My name is Fletcher Ramsay. Do you work here?"

"I am the minister, Robert Cameron."

"I am looking for Reverend MacDonald."

"David MacDonald?"

Fletcher shook his head. "Yes, I believe he used to be the minister here."

"Aye, he was, but David MacDonald has retired. He doesna preach the gospel anymore."

"Do you know where I might find him? Does he live nearby?"

"Aye. He lives on a small farm at the edge of town. Lives there with his granddaughter."

"I would like to pay him a visit. How might I get there?"

"And what business would you be having with him?"

"He is a longtime family friend. He married my parents and baptized me and my sisters. He also buried my father. My mother asked me to stop by when I came here."

Apparently satisfied, Robert Cameron gave him directions to David MacDonald's farm.

After thanking Robert for his help, Fletcher left Glengarry, riding back the way he had come, following Reverend Cameron's directions.

A curlew gave a dismal warning that soon faded, leaving only chirping of meadow pipits and greenshanks. He continued on down the well-traveled road, riding across a bridge that spanned the river Garry, turning right at the waterfall. The road narrowed somewhat before it continued along a straight, tree-lined course, where it passed a small, partly hidden loch that he noticed only when distracted by the sudden flight of waterfowl.

Wild, grim, and black, the clouds began to swirl and churn overhead, bringing close the smell of heather and newly cut hay. He thought of the girl he had met that day in the field and wondered if she was out in this weather now, carrying water to those working in the fields and finding herself caught in this sudden downpour.

Wrapped in a whirl of wind and splattered with rain, he tried to turn his thoughts away from her, but it was no use. By the time the rain began to come down harder, he could not stop wondering if she, like him, was soaked to the skin.

He remembered how her white bodice filled out nicely. He imagined it wet and clinging to her skin. Realizing that he had better stop thinking about such things, he shifted his weight uncomfortably in the saddle, shifting his thoughts as well.

Passing a crumbling stone wall, black in the rain, he turned in at the gate, and, just as Robert Cameron had said, there stood a thatched cottage, its windows warm from the glow of a light inside.

He dismounted and a moment later knocked at the door.

Fletcher would never know who was more surprised: himself when the door opened and there stood the woman from the well, or the woman the moment she recognized him.

"Good morning—that is, good afternoon. Is your husband ... er—father ... Is anyone at home?"

She smiled. "Aye, I am."

He felt like an idiot.

He cleared his throat, forcing a gruffness into his tone. "I came to see David MacDonald. Is he in?"

She smiled. "Aye, my grandfather is here. Is he expecting you?"

"No."

She frowned and glanced behind her, and Fletcher saw that she was very protective of her grandfather.

Fletcher did not wait for her to turn down his request. "He was a friend of my mother and father. I have traveled a long way to see him—all the way from America. If you would tell him that Fletcher Ramsay is here, I am certain he would see me."

She stepped back from the door, opening it wider. "Come in, please."

He entered; removing his hat and apologizing for his wet clothing.

She took his hat. "It is of no consequence," she said. "Rain is something we've learned to live with. Wait here. I'll get something to dry you off a wee bit, then I'll tell grandfather you are here."

She left the room for only a moment, returning with a length of clean, dry cloth. While he dried himself, she left the room again.

A few minutes later, a man of small stature entered the room. His back was slightly stooped and his hair was quite gray, but his face was remarkably unlined. Fletcher noticed all these things, but it was David MacDonald's eyes that struck him most. Never had he seen eyes that reflected such peace. For a moment he was envious.

"Cathleen said your name was Fletcher Ramsay."

"Yes, my father was—"

"Bruce Ramsay," David said with a smile. He offered Fletcher his hand. "It is a real pleasure to see you again after all these years. You were no bigger than a bull calf the last time I saw you."

Fletcher smiled. "I feel I should warn you . . . you're shaking hands with a sinner."

Amusement danced in David's eyes. "Something I do quite regularly."

"My mother has told me much about you."

"All good, I hope."

"Of course. She said you were known for being the best minister in the Highlands."

"I fear I was known for being long on sermons and short on patience."

Fletcher laughed. "I see she was also right about something else."

"Oh? And what is that?"

"She said you were quite modest."

David looked as if he was lost in recollections, then he said, "Ahhh, Maggie . . . Some of the brightness was gone out of the Highlands after she left." He paused. "Forgive an old man's ruminations. Maggie is where she should be, and happy as a clam, I understand."

"Yes. Very happy."

"And now you are here and I canna believe you are Bruce and Maggie's son. Of course I would have known who you were even if you hadn't given your name. You are your father's double, but I ken this is not the first time you have heard that."

Before Fletcher could reply, David said, "Come sit down, lad, and tell me all about your mother. She doesna write as often now as she once did, and I find myself wondering from time to time just how Maggie is doing."

They started to walk into the other room when Cathleen reached for the wet towel Fletcher had used. Giving her a quick glance, David said, "Would you bring tea and some of your shortbread into the parlor, Cathleen?"

Cathleen did not answer, and when he looked at her, Fletcher saw that she was staring at him.

David MacDonald looked at his granddaughter. Then he looked at Fletcher.

Fletcher and Cathleen seemed locked in their gaze.

Somewhat bewildered, David said, "Do forgive me for not introducing you. This is my granddaughter, Mary Cathleen Lindsay."

She gave a quick nod, then darted through the door before Fletcher could say anything.

David, looking a bit puzzled, said, "You've met before?"

"Yes. I saw your granddaughter a few weeks ago. She was in a hay field drawing water from a well as I rode by."

"Barefoot and covered with dust, no doubt," David said, then glanced toward the door.

Fletcher could not help seeing the wealth of emotion in that look.

"Cathleen has ever been a helpful lass. When she isn't helping me, she is attending to others. Everyone in the village has come to depend upon her in one way or another. An angel of mercy, they call her." David paused, then drew his gaze from the door to look at Fletcher. "Well, enough of that. I ken you didna come all this way to hear me expound upon the virtues of my granddaughter. Beside, I am eager to hear of Maggie. Let's go to the parlor, shall we?"

Fletcher followed him into a small parlor and saw immediately that the reverend had been working on something, for papers were scattered across the library table and sheets of music lay stacked upon the piano bench.

David seated himself in a worn, comfortable-looking chair beside the fireplace and indicated for Fletcher to take the one across from him.

"Now then, tell me about Maggie and your sisters."

In the kitchen, Cathleen put on a pot of water to heat, then took down a small plate and the best teacups, placing several pieces of shortbread on the plate, then arranging everything on a tray that had belonged to the grandmother she never knew. While she waited for the water to boil, she listened to her grandfather talking with Fletcher Ramsay but catching only bits and pieces of their conversation.

When the tea was ready, she put the pot on the tray with the cups and shortbread and carried it into the parlor.

David glanced up as she entered. "Ah, things will seem ever so much better after a nice cup of hot tea and a bite of Cathleen's shortbread," he said to Fletcher, shoving papers aside and clearing a place for the tray on a low table next to a small chair, which Cathleen lowered herself into as gracefully as possible, considering that she was feeling a bit self-conscious because Fletcher Ramsay was watching her every move.

"How do you take your tea, Mr. Ramsay?" she asked, not looking at him.

"No cream, no sugar."

"Fletcher is the Earl of Caithness, Cathleen, so you must address him properly," David said.

Cathleen glanced quickly at Fletcher, then back down. She felt a burst of flame cross her cheeks and knew they would be red enough for the Earl of Caithness to notice, which only added to her discomfort.

Before she could ask his pardon, Fletcher said, "Please, just call me Fletcher."

Her eyes went quickly to her grandfather, then she nodded, but said nothing, giving her attention to pouring the tea, hating the way the cup rattled when she handed it to Fletcher.

As if trying to put her at ease, he smiled warmly and said, "Thank you, Cathleen."

She loved the sound of her name on his tongue, but she gave no hint as she nodded and cast a quick glance in her grandfather's direction, noticing the merry twinkle in his eyes as he looked speculatively from her to Fletcher and back to her.

Her grandfather was ever a perceptive man.

More from embarrassment than anything else, she rose and crossed the room, intending to return to the kitchen, but her grandfather stopped her, saying, "Please join us, Cathleen."

She took a seat at the piano bench, a place where she spent a good amount of time, and consequently felt more comfortable—comfort being something she had felt precious little of since Fletcher Ramsay's coming.

Once she was seated, her grandfather went on to tell her briefly about Fletcher and his family.

"I am sure the gaining of your uncle's title grieved your mother doubly," Cathleen said.

"How so?" asked Fletcher, giving her a curious look.

Cathleen felt a chill sweep over her and she drew her shawl up over her shoulders. "For the loss of a brother and a son," she said. "It is difficult to lose your children, even when they are grown, and Scotland and America are a long way apart."

"You have children, then?"

Cathleen's heart skittered, then seemed to plummet to her feet. Her face grew warm. "No, I have never married," she said softly.

She felt his gaze upon her and knew he stared at her over-long. At last he looked off, as if sensing that this was a painful subject for her. Cathleen rose quickly to her feet. "If you will excuse me, I've some things to attend to in the kitchen. I will join you when I finish."

David and Fletcher watched her go before resuming their conversation.

"You were saying you came to Scotland because of your uncle's death," David prompted.

"Partly, but I would have returned to Scotland even without my uncle's title. I have a title of my own ... the one that belonged to my father."

David cleared his throat. "You must be careful who you say things like that to around here," he said. "There are those who would not understand as I do. If you speak of it, it must be with caution, Fletcher. That is something your father should have done."

"I won't make the mistake of underestimating Adair, as my father did."

David nodded. "Bruce had a very clean heart and that made him a trusting man. You know, it has always interested me just how it was that Adair managed to take the title." He looked at Fletcher. "I ken you have been given all the information by your mother."

"Aye, I have been given a detailed account—but not by my mother."

David's brows went up in question.

"My mother always lived with the fear that I would come back to claim my title one day, and for that reason she was hesitant to speak of it."

"I can understand that. Maggie was upset with your coming back because she feared for your life. That is normal."

"Yes," Fletcher said, thinking about her. "I suppose that's because she is a woman."

"It is because she is a mother," David said. "But at least you were able to find someone to give you the details."

"It was my aunt, Doroty, who filled in the blank spaces I had about everything. She left no stone unturned."

"Neither did Adair, if I remember right."

"True. My aunt said he did quite a bit of work before he went to my father that first time."

"What exactly was his claim?"

"It seems that there is proof that the eighth Duke of Glengarry married a woman named Maude and that they had four children, one of whom was a son, Douglas, who was my great-great-great-grandfather—and the ninth Duke of Glengarry. Douglas supposedly had a wife named Bride, but, as Adair was able to prove in court, there is no record of this marriage of Douglas and Bride, nor is there a record of the birth of their son Ian, who was the tenth duke and my great-great-grandfather. Unfortunately, Adair had ancestors with the same names."

David leaned forward, and his voice reflected his interest. "And because there was no proof of your line and there was proof of his, they gave the title to Adair?"

"Yes because he had proof and my mother had none."

"I never really understood just how it happened, but even knowing now, it doesn't make sense."

"That is what I said the first time I heard it, but my aunt disagreed. After she explained, I understood. The courts had no choice. Although everyone was loyal to the memory of my father, they had to go with the proof. Adair, it seems, had undeniable proof of his ancestors. My father did not."

"But your father and his father before him were the dukes. So how did Adair's ancestor end up with the title?"

"It was Adair's contention that my ancestor Douglas took

the title of Duke of Glengarry when it rightfully belonged to his ancestor Douglas.''

''But how?''

Fletcher reached into his pocket and withdrew an oiled pouch. Opening it, he took out the family tree his aunt had designed for him. He handed it to David and watched his face as he studied it.

When David finished reading the diagram, Fletcher said, ''Now, as you can see, there was only one Alasdair Ramsay, the eighth Duke of Glengarry, but there were two Douglas Ramsays, and both of them had fathers named Alasdair and mothers named Maude, and both of these Douglas Ramsays had sons named Ian.''

David looked at the paper again. ''This is very coincidental, and that alone will make your search difficult.''

''Difficult, but not impossible,'' Fletcher said. ''I know what it is I need to search for, and I will find it.''

''You say that with much conviction. However, I must remind you that your father searched the whole of Scotland, Fletcher. There are no records.''

''There must be. If my ancestor was an impostor, they would never have allowed him to take the title.''

''How did Adair explain that away?'' asked David.

''It was Adair's contention that because this had all taken place during the time of Bonnie Prince Charlie, and that since his ancestor Douglas was killed in the battle of Culloden Moor, it would have been easy for my ancestor Douglas to lay claim to the title. He even went so far as to suggest that my Douglas had fought on the side of the English and that the title was awarded him because of this service.''

David nodded. ''Aye, those were times of great sadness and turmoil. Anything could have happened.'' He looked back at the paper in his hands. ''So the key to all of this lies in your proving that your great-great-great-grandfather, Douglas Ramsay, married a woman named Bride, and proving too that they had a son Ian.''

''Yes.''

David folded the paper and handed it back to Fletcher. ''Well, I am pleased to know how it all happened. I had often wondered, of course, but never wanted to trouble Maggie for the details."

"It is a sensitive subject with her even now."

"Well, I find myself terribly interested in this. I would like to help you in any way I can."

Fletcher started to speak just as Cathleen walked into the room.

Taking her chair, Cathleen could not help noticing the way her grandfather and Fletcher grew suddenly quiet. She felt something akin to fear grip her heart. Something about this did not feel right. She looked from Fletcher to David. "What has all of this got to do with you, Grandpa?"

David gave her a reassuring smile. "Nothing, my dear. Fletcher was just asking about some of the old church records—those pertaining to his ancestors and such."

"You mean his ancestors lived here? In Glengarry?"

"Aye," David said, looking like he was trying to keep something from her, which made her even more inquisitive.

Looking at Fletcher, Cathleen said, "And your mother and father—they lived here as well?"

"Yes."

"And your father's title and estates? They were here?"

Fletcher nodded.

Cathleen was about to ask more, when her grandfather sighed and said, "I might as well tell you, for you will ferret it out anyway. Fletcher's father was the Duke of Glengarry."

"Oh my," Cathleen said, sitting back on the bench, feeling she needed the support to keep from falling off. Again she looked from her grandfather to Fletcher. A vision of Adair Ramsay's face rose up before her and she shuddered. She did not like the present Duke of Glengarry. His cruelty to the poor was well known. "And you want my grandfather to risk his life helping you take your title back?"

Fletcher came to his feet.

She could see that he was a bit put off by her comment. *Well, let him be,* she thought. *He has no right to involve my grandfather.*

"I have not asked for help," Fletcher said. "I simply want some questions answered, nothing more."

Cathleen released a breath of relief. Her grandfather was old, and he was all she had.

"My granddaughter can be a bit overprotective at times," David said.

"And my grandfather has a tendency to be overindulgent," she said, wounded.

"Cathleen thinks I sometimes get carried away with tending my flock."

"You are retired, Grandpa, and your flock now belongs to Robert."

Fletcher laughed. "It's hard to teach an old horse how to pull a new plow."

There was no humor in Cathleen's voice. "That is not it at all. My grandfather involves himself in things he would do better to stay out of," she said with iron-hard determination. "He is no as young as he once was and sometimes he needs to be reminded of that."

Fletcher smiled, as if finding her mother-hen tendency amusing.

"Stop giving away all my shortcomings, Cathleen," David said. Then he turned to Fletcher and winked. "I will be happy to help in any way I can."

"I dare not ask," Fletcher said, "for fear of stirring up your granddaughter's wrath."

David laughed. "She has a loud bark, but rarely bites."

Seeing the determination in her grandfather's eyes, Cathleen sighed.

"The rain has let up. I'd best be going," Fletcher said at last, as if he could both sense the tension in the room and read her thoughts.

Whatever the reason, she was glad to see him on his way. Nothing had gone right since he had arrived. Never had her emotions been in such a jumble.

With a lively gait David walked Fletcher to the door, talking in that hospitable manner he had with all of God's creatures.

Silently, Cathleen followed.

"I would be happy to meet you at the church tomorrow,

to show you the old records," David was saying. "Where are you staying?"

"I haven't decided yet. I thought I would locate an inn. One nearby."

"Och, laddie, there is no inn here in Glengarry. The nearest one is more than ten miles away, but not to worry. We have a small crofter's hut here on our farm. Humble though it is, you are most welcome to it."

Cathleen cringed. The milk of human kindness went only so far.

"I wouldn't want to impose," Fletcher said, glancing at Cathleen.

Ignoring him, Cathleen gave her grandfather "the look"—the one that was supposed to silence him.

The one that he ignored.

"Nonsense," David said. "It would be no imposition. It has been vacant since the Clearances emptied the Highlands of crofters. We would welcome the company, wouldn't we, Cathleen?"

"Oh, aye," she said with little enthusiasm, trying not to appear horribly rude. Mildly rude was all right, but horribly rude would bring a chastening word from her grandfather, and more than likely a scripture or two, something about helping those in need, or entertaining angels unawares.

She narrowed her eyes and gave Fletcher a speculative look. If there was anything this man did not look like, it was an angel.

"I wouldn't want to be a bother," Fletcher said. "I will make a few inquiries in town."

"I have heard the widow Davidson has a room to let," Cathleen said quickly.

"I won't hear of your staying anywhere else," David insisted, ignoring her. "Why, just the other day I was discussing with Cathleen the possibility of renting the crofter's hut."

Cathleen wanted to gag her grandfather. He was involving himself in a matter that was none of his business, and she felt helpless to prevent it. Call it her woman's sensibility or simply an inclination, but this man was up to something dangerous, something her grandfather had no business involving himself in. She could not help being worried any more than she could help being so stubborn in her opposition. She just could not give in to this. She did not know why.

"Well," Fletcher said, unable to say more, for at that moment Cathleen interrupted.

"The hut is overly small and quite humble. I am certain you are accustomed to more," she said, hoping he wasn't as thick-witted as he appeared.

Fletcher gave her a pensive look, one that sent a shiver over her.

"You might be surprised," he replied. Then, looking at David, he went on, "I would be delighted to take your offer of the crofter's hut, but only if you would let me rent it from you."

David laughed. "Weel now, I wouldna be a true Scot if I didna like the clink of money, would I? Parsons were ever a poor lot."

She saw the look of understanding that passed between them. "Then I will stay there tonight," Fletcher said. He turned to Cathleen. "If that is all right with you."

She glanced at her grandfather, who gave her a perfectly innocent look. "Whatever my grandfather wishes," she said, thinking that she sounded a bit melodramatic.

A quick glance at Fletcher said he was thinking the same thing, for a wide grin stretched across his face.

"How long will you be staying?" David asked.

"I don't know. I feel certain the answer lies here in Glengarry, so I will stay as long as it takes, rather than go back and forth."

David agreed. "Aye, it is too long a ride from Caithness to make every day."

"Of course you will be going back . . . *frequently*, I would imagine," Cathleen said.

His eyes lit up with amusement. "Oh, I don't know how *frequently*, but I do plan to return there from time to time, to see how things are going. But Caithness is in very capable hands."

David laughed. "Aye, if your aunt, Doroty, is still tending things."

"She is," Fletcher said, "and she has taught me much."

"You have her blessing, then, to spend time here, looking for proof?"

"She said she would have done the same thing if she were in my place . . . only sooner."

David laughed and shook his head, a look of fond recollection upon his face. "I have a feeling she would have, too."

"I *know* she would have," Fletcher said. "She likes to complain that she is too old, that she is creaking with age, but she is too much like my mother to forsake something she believes in."

David's look turned serious. "What if you don't find what you seek?"

"I will look someplace else, and I will keep on looking until I find it. The proof is out there somewhere. I know it is."

"Aye, I ken it is as well," David said, "and I want to help you find it."

No! Not you, Grandpa. You canna involve yourself in this! At her grandfather's words, Cathleen's heart seemed to swell painfully. How well she remembered the time a young man named Ian Scott had involved himself in the Duke of Glengarry's affairs. Ian had a friend, Andrew Stewart. Andrew had a lovely sister, Fiona, who gave birth out of wedlock. Fiona would not divulge the name of her child's father, but it was rumored to be the Duke of Glengarry. Another rumor had it that the child had been fathered by the devil himself—not that there was much difference in the two, thought Cathleen.

No one was ever certain why Fiona did it, but when her baby was two weeks old, she jumped off a bridge and drowned herself, with her baby in her arms. Perhaps it was out of shame, because of the insatiable curiosity of the villagers and their constant speculations as to who the baby's father was.

After his sister's death, Andrew vowed to find out who had fathered Fiona's child. Because of his friendship, Ian involved himself in Andrew's search. Two days later, Ian and Andrew were found with their throats cut, lying in the road from

Glengarry Castle to the village. The day after his death, Ian's mother came to see David MacDonald, telling him that her son had told her the night before he died that he and Andrew had found proof that the Duke of Glengarry was the father of Fiona's child. Because she was afraid of what might happen to her, Ian's mother had never told anyone else what she knew.

And now her grandfather was involving himself in something that was sure to set the teeth of the Duke of Glengarry on edge.

Why couldn't he be content to finish out his years working on the Psalms? Why was he so insistent on involving himself in this? She could not understand it. She glared at Fletcher as if she knew the devil himself had sent him here to be purposefully disruptive.

Fletcher's words were for her grandfather, but his gaze was fastened upon Cathleen. "Thank you," he said, "but I wouldn't feel right involving you."

"Laddie, I involved myself in this years ago, before your father was killed. I will not forget the day your mother left Glengarry Castle. I swore then that if I could ever do anything to help, I would gladly do it. Perhaps this is my chance."

"You were a much younger man then, Grandpa," Cathleen said, curling her arm possessively through his.

"Aye," David said, "I was a young minister and there wasn't much excitement in my life. Now I am an old man and there still isn't."

"*Blessed are the meek,*" Cathleen said. "John."

David laughed. "Aye, but I ken I would welcome the feel of a bit of excitement before I go to meet my maker."

Cathleen could not believe her grandfather was speaking like this. "But what about the Psalms . . . our translations?"

David put his arm around her. "I willna forget the Psalms, my bonny Cathleen, but the days are long and the nights too, and I ken I have time enough for both. Now, if you will be a good lass and show our guest the way to the crofter's hut, I will finish the translations we started on this morning. Good day to you, Fletcher Ramsay. Come early for a bit o' porridge and a scone or two, and then I will go to St. Andrew's Church with you."

"Aye," Cathleen said, surrendering at last. "I will go as well." She caught Fletcher's curious stare. She was determined to not let her grandfather out of her sight.

Fletcher waited for Cathleen to gather a few things, then he followed her down the path from the cottage to the crofter's hut. He made a few attempts at conversation, but all fell as flat as his mother's pancakes.

"You don't like me, do you?"

"I dinna know you, so how could I dislike you?" she replied, marching ahead of him.

He caught up to her. "Are you always this put out with strangers, then?"

She stopped in the middle of the path, the basket on her arm swinging to and fro. "No."

"Then why me? Is it because I took your kerchief?"

"No, it isn't that. I have quite forgotten about that tattered kerchief. My grandfather is *old*."

He grinned. "You aren't blaming me for that, are you?"

"No," she said, with no humor.

"I haven't come to do him harm."

"Not intentionally, perhaps." She started walking again. "'*Out of thine own mouth I will judge thee,*'" she said. "Luke."

They reached the hut, and she opened the door, taking the lamp she carried and placing it on the table.

He followed her inside and gave the place a quick look around.

There wasn't much to it, just two rooms. The main room, which served as kitchen and parlor, was the larger of the two. The smaller was for sleeping and contained a small bed, a few hooks on the wall for clothes, and a chair and table by the bed.

While he looked at the bedroom, he heard her call out to him, "There is peat stacked outside by the door, if you wish a fire. I'll straighten up in here before I put the linens on your bed."

He went outside and carried in a load of peat. Not accustomed to peat fires, it took him a while to get it started, but he did manage to get a small blaze going. Then he looked around the room for signs of what she had done. He smiled. On the kitchen table she had placed a yellow cloth and a butter crock full of flowers. A loaf of bread and a cup, spoon, and bowl sat next to the flowers. Near the fireplace was a chair and an ottoman, and beside those a small table with a lamp, which she had lit.

He walked to the bedroom door and saw that she had spread another embroidered cloth on the table beside the bed, where a small lamp glowed. Beside it lay a Bible. He could not help smiling at that. Was it a hint, then? No doubt she had the appropriate verses underlined. She was an odd little creature, as strange as she was lovely.

His gaze moved to her as she leaned across the bed, smoothing the sheets in place. Once again he was mesmerized by her hands. She had a quiet, efficient way of working. She also had a way of slapping things around when she was angry. He watched her shake the coverlet harder than was necessary. When she punched the pillow, he wondered if she was thinking of him.

She had a tiny waist. He had better think of something else, he thought; then he remembered the flowers. He was touched by the fact that despite her obvious displeasure regarding his stay, she had taken the time to put flowers on the table.

"Thank you for the flowers."

She jumped, whirling so fast that she thumped against the table. The lamp teetered, and Fletcher made a dash for it, catching it just before it fell off the table. When he had steadied it, he looked up and saw her standing quite close, trapped, so to speak, between him, the wall, and the bed. He could see that this position made her mighty uncomfortable.

"Let me by," she said.

Finding that he liked her where she was, he said, "Why?"

"Because, if you don't, your other leg may be hurting."

He gave her an odd look. "But my leg isn't hurting."

She hauled off and kicked it. Hard. "It is now." She scampered around him.

He caught her by the wrist, turning her around to face him. Her body against his was warm and soft in all the right places. He might have taken advantage of that, but she was trembling, and her eyes were dark with fear. He wondered if she thought he was going to toss her onto the bed and have a go at her, and then he wondered why she would think that. "I'm not trying to frighten you."

"Then let me go."

"I just want to talk."

"I haven't time. My grandfather is waiting for his dinner."

He released her. She snatched up a stack of linens from the chair and held them in front of her, as a physical reminder of the barrier between them.

"You're angry," he said. "Why? Is it because of my staying here?"

She hugged the linens to her breast. "Aye," she said softly. "I know my grandfather. If you stay here, he'll want to be involved."

"And you are taking that out on me?"

"I heard the warning in his voice when you spoke of your father being the Duke of Glengarry. I have heard stories about the present duke. Whatever you do is your own affair, but my grandfather has no business in this. It could be dangerous. I don't want him hurt."

"Neither do I, but I would say that the decision to help me search the records is his, wouldn't you?"

She gave him her back and began shoving and punching the linens into the basket. "I did not expect you to understand."

"Perhaps if you explained, I might."

She slammed the basket down on the bed and whirled around. "I've already explained. He is old. He has done his job—he's given his life to the church—and he's earned the right to spend his remaining years working on his book."

"What book?"

She sighed. *"The Metrical Version of the Psalms."*

"Which is?"

She did not bother to hide her exasperation as she answered, "It is my grandfather's lifelong memories of German, French, and English versions of the Psalms that were set to music.

The words to many of them have never been written down. I play them on the piano and sing the words, and my grandfather writes them down, translating the French and German into English."

"I see. Would it help, then, if I told you that I did not visit here to come between you and your grandfather, or to slow down his work?"

"It is not your intentions but the result that counts."

"David has offered to show me the church record I seek. I will then work alone. You have nothing to worry about."

"Perhaps not, but I have a feeling you will come between us, nevertheless. Nothing is the same since you arrived."

He wondered what she meant by that, but he did not question her. "I assure you, that is not my intention."

"Then why did you come?"

"We went over all that before."

"I ken you said you wanted to regain your title, but I dinna ken why. You have a title now, and while an earl might not be as high on the peerage charts as a duke, it is a powerful and respected title, and more than enough to keep you busy. I have seen Caithness Castle, and in every sense it rivals Glengarry."

"I agree, but there is one thing you've overlooked."

"And what is that?

"Caithness has always belonged to the Sinclairs and Glengarry to the Ramsays. I am a Ramsay."

"You are *half* Ramsay. Your mother was a Sinclair."

"My name is Ramsay, my father was the duke, and his father before him. The Glengarry title is rightfully mine. Perhaps the problem is that you can't understand what it's like to grow up with part of your life missing."

"Oh, aye, I canna understand that, since you lost only a title and your father, while I lost both father and mother and my future as well."

He saw the way her expression froze when she uttered those last four words. He regretted his harshness with her. "What future are you talking about?" he asked softly.

Her face paled. "Nothing," she said, looking like she had said far too much already. "It isna important."

"And if I said it was important to me?"

Some of the fight seemed to go out of her. "I am sorry for my behavior. It isna like me to be so hard and uncompromising. I ken I am a bit too protective of my grandfather, like an old broody hen. It isna you and it isna me, or even my grandfather. It is the circumstances. I know the way Adair Ramsay's mind works. I have seen the results of his contempt in the village. If what you say is true, he willna take this lying down. A war between the two of you is understandable, but sometimes it is the innocent ones who pay the highest price. I don't want my grandfather hurt. He is all I have."

"You are right to feel that way, Cathleen. As I said before, I don't want him hurt either. I only want him to answer a few questions and to show me the church records. Nothing more. I promise." He held up his hand.

Again she ignored his attempt at levity, and Fletcher wondered if these Scots were always so dour.

"You dinna ken my grandfather," she said. "When he adopts a cause, there is no stopping him."

Fletcher smiled, wanting above all things to put her fears to rest. She seemed very small and very fragile to him, and that part of him that he called protectiveness was stirred. "Then I will see to it that my cause does not become his."

"That is the problem," she said softly. "I fear it already has."

He found himself lost in the depths of her violet eyes, not really listening to what she was saying. He wondered if she knew just how damnably close he was to dragging her into his arms and kissing her until she responded to him with something besides anger. He also wondered if she was as uncomfortable around other men as she was with him. Had she been jilted? Was there something painful in her past, something cruel or lewd a man had done to her? Or had she simply devoted so much of her life to her grandfather that no man had ever had the chance to get close to her?

He did not know the answer, but he vowed that before he left here, he would find out.

Chapter Seven

Early the next morning, they were at St. Andrew's Church, a place Fletcher found as old and drafty as a spinster's nightie.

Cathleen sat between him and her grandfather at the table as they looked diligently through a large, leather-bound volume of records for the parish. In it were recorded generations of the Ramsay family births, marriages, deaths, and baptisms, including those of Fletcher's parents, grandparents, and great-grandparents.

Fletcher scanned the pages with a keen and critical eye, but to no avail. When it came to his great-great-grandparents, Ian Ramsay and his wife, Moina, there was only the record of the marriage, the births and baptisms of their children, and their deaths.

There was no record of Ian's birth, nor was there any mention that he was the son of Douglas Ramsay and his wife, Bride, just as there was no record of the marriage of Bride and Douglas.

Fletcher could not hide his disappointment.

"I fear that proof is critical to your claim," David said, putting his hand on Fletcher's shoulder.

Fletcher's tone held a mixture of disappointment and frustration as he replied, "Without it, I have no claim. The proof should be here!" He slammed his fist down angrily upon the registry.

"But it isn't. You can't make proof where none exists, and you shouldn't take your disappointment out on a book," Cathleen said, moving the dusty volume out of Fletcher's reach. "Perhaps you should look elsewhere."

"The proof has to be in Glengarry somewhere," he said. "It's the logical place. This is where the Ramsays have lived for centuries." He turned to David. "Is there any way a marriage or birth could have been overlooked and not recorded?"

David shook his head. "If it took place here and was performed by a man of the cloth, then it would be here. And don't be forgetting this is the Duke of Glengarry we're talking about. A marriage or birth in his family would have been of the utmost importance."

"I just don't understand how this could have happened. Why isn't it here when it should be?" Fletcher reached for the book and pulled it toward him, ignoring Cathleen's scowl. He flipped through a few pages. "It doesn't look like there are any pages missing."

"No," David said, "these pages are all in tact, but there are pages missing in some of the minutes from the church meetings during the times in question. I've often wondered if they might have contained some reference to your Douglas and Bride or to the fact that Ian was their son."

"We'll never know," Fletcher said, frowning, puzzled by the lack of information on his ancestors. "If I am to have any hope of regaining my title, I need strong, legitimate documentation. The courts in Edinburgh will require hard proof that Douglas and Bride were legally married and that Ian was their legitimate issue."

David nodded in agreement. "Aye, they will need that. It was the same after your father died. Without that proof, Maggie had no case."

"Then how did Adair prove they weren't married?" Cathleen asked, sounding excited and quite interested despite her determination to stay out of it.

Fletcher gave her a surprised but agreeable look. She was such a small thing to command so much of his speculation, but she did. He had to admit that she baffled him. One minute she was tremendously fierce, protecting her grandfather like she was born to the task; the next she was joining in the search, as eager as a youth with his bow bent.

"Adair didn't prove they weren't married," he answered. "He didn't have to. His contention was that *his* ancestor Ian Ramsay, who married a woman named Isobel, was the Ian who should have inherited, and who was, according to him, the only rightful heir to the dukedom."

"He had proof of that?" she asked.

"He had proof that his Ian was the son of a Douglas Ramsay who had a wife named Jean, and that this Douglas Ramsay was the son of Alasdair Ramsay and his wife, Maude."

"I thought your ancestors were Alasdair and Maude Ramsay," she said.

"They were. According to my mother, my father believed there must have been two men named Douglas Ramsay who lived about the same time—one a Highlander and one a Lowlander, and both of them had a father named Alisdair."

Cathleen put her hand to her head. "Hout! This is getting too complicated. Two Douglas Ramsays? How will you be able to tell them apart?"

"There is only one way. By their wives. My ancestor was married to Bride, while Adair's was married to Jean."

"And your ancestor—the one married to Bride—is the one who was the Duke of Glengarry?"

"Yes," Fletcher said, "he was the eighth duke."

She shook her head. "This will be very difficult to prove, if for no other reason than that it is very complicated."

Fletcher agreed. "Things are further tangled by the fact that each of these men named Douglas had a son named Ian . . ."

"Two Douglases and two Ians," Cathleen said. "No wonder this is so confusing. And the only way you can tell them apart is by the names of the women they married." She paused. "But that still doesn't prove Adair's claim."

"True. Unfortunately, it does not prove mine, either. The courts ruled that since Adair had valid proof of all his marriages and births, his must be the true line."

"But how did your father become Duke of Glengarry if he was an impostor?" Cathleen asked.

"No one will ever know the answer to that, I fear. The barrister I hired to look over the hearing records said that all of this mix-up occurred about the time of Culloden. Adair supposedly had proof that his ancestor Douglas was killed at Culloden. He had some documents proving that there was another Douglas Ramsay living then, a man who was sympathetic to the Hanoverian cause against the Jacobites. It was Adair's contention that this Douglas Ramsay—who befriended the Duke of Cumberland—was my Douglas Ramsay, who married Bride. He further contended that out of gratitude, Cumberland gave the title Duke of Glengarry to my ancestor upon learning that Adair's ancestor Douglas Ramsay was dead. Since Adair had proof of all his births and marriages and my father did not, the courts were persuaded."

"And by that time your father was dead, you were just a boy of eight, and your mother feared for your safety, so she did nothing to challenge Adair's claim," Cathleen concluded.

"Aye, Maggie was afraid . . . so afraid that she married by proxy a man she had never met and sailed halfway around the world to start a new life, in order to protect her family," David added. "She was a very brave and courageous woman."

"She still is," Fletcher said. "I know that I was the reason my mother turned her back on everything she held dear. She was afraid for my safety, for she knew that as long as Adair Ramsay was alive, I was a threat to him. She was a young woman, only twenty-eight, when she left her father, sister, and brothers to go to America. She's never seen any of them again."

"But it worked out well and she is happy in America," David reminded him.

The gloomy expression on Fletcher's face was instantly replaced with one of fond recollection. "Very happy. She and

Adrian love each other very much and they are perfectly matched." He smiled. "Although it did take Adrian a while to realize that."

"What do you mean?" asked Cathleen.

Fletcher chuckled, looking down at her small, expectant face. "Well, it seems Adrian's brother, Ross, who happens to be the Duke of Dunford, was the one who did all the matchmaking, but he forgot to tell his brother one important fact about my mother."

Cathleen leaned forward, her elbows on the table, her chin resting in her hands, and Fletcher wanted to laugh at the sight. Last night she had been worried about her grandfather's involvement, yet now she seemed more intrigued with his family's history than David was.

"Well, tell us," Cathleen said, her impatience obvious in her voice. "What did his brother not mention?"

"That my mother was a widow with three children."

Cathleen sat up straight, her hands falling away. "You mean her husband thought he was marrying—"

"A woman who had never been married," Fletcher finished.

David raised his brows. "I never heard this story before."

"Small wonder," Fletcher replied, laughing. "It almost caused the end of their short marriage. Adrian had been *very* adamant about the kind of woman he wanted, and his requirements did not include a widow or children."

"Poor man. I can well imagine his shock when your mother arrived with three children in tow," Cathleen said.

Again Fletcher laughed. "Well, that isn't exactly the way it was."

"No, that is right," David said, looking at Cathleen. "I remember now. Maggie left her children behind. They sailed with their nanny some three or four months later."

"And her husband never knew about the children until the three of you showed up?" she asked.

"That was the way of it."

"I'm surprised he didn't send *all* of you back," she said.

"He wanted to, but my youngest sister, Ainsley, was deathly ill. By the time she was well, she had Adrian wrapped around her little finger."

Fletcher looked at Cathleen then and saw the strangest expression upon her features, one he could only describe as bittersweet understanding. "Aye," she said, "sometimes a child can soften the hardest heart and bring a barren life to full bloom."

"As you did mine," David said, putting his hand over hers and giving it a squeeze.

Cathleen scoffed. "You didn't have a hard heart, Grandpa. Just a broken one."

"Aye, and you mended it."

Cathleen smiled at her grandfather, then looked at Fletcher. "Beg your pardon," she said. "We seem to have gotten you a bit off your course."

"I don't mind."

"I do," Cathleen said. "Your mother has solved her problem. What I want to know is, how are we going to solve yours?"

Fletcher glanced at David, who also seemed surprised at the seriousness with which Cathleen now regarded Fletcher's task.

Tapping her finger against her cheek, Cathleen said, "So, until we find proof that your Ian was the son of Douglas and Bride, and proof that Douglas and Bride were married, you have little hope of regaining your title."

"What is this *we*?" Fletcher asked. "The burden of proof lies with me, not you."

Cathleen glanced down and began fidgeting with her hands in her lap. Her cheeks were flushed. "I meant you, of course," she said softly.

"I thought that's what you meant," Fletcher said.

"Weel, now what?" David asked.

"I keep looking. There must be other records of my family around here somewhere, records of land transactions, deeds, and such. I'd like to check a few graveyards for clues ... perhaps even families that intermarried with mine, just to see if any of them might have some record in an old family Bible, or a strongbox full of documents no one has looked through."

"Old documents? I hadna thought of that. There are plenty of those stored in the church attic," David said.

"What kind of documents?" asked Fletcher.

"Just a jumble of things. Some are illegible; some damaged, and some are there for no apparent reason. It would take quite a bit of time to go through them all. You would have to work slowly, for due to their age, the paper crumbles easily. A magnifying glass would have to be used on many of them."

"I've got the time," Fletcher said. "Would we have to go through the trunks in the attic, or would I be able to move them to another location?"

David thought about that for a moment. "Ordinarily, I'd say they would have to remain here, but if I were to explain to Robert that they would be coming to my house, and that I would be solely responsible for their safe return, then I think something might be arranged."

Fletcher frowned, remembering his words to Cathleen the night before about not intending to involve her grandfather. "I wouldn't want to impose. Perhaps it would be best if I worked on them at the crofter's hut."

"Nonsense. There isna room for the trunks, let alone enough space to spread the documents about. We'll bring them to my house. Cathleen will make room for them, won't you, lassie?"

Fletcher looked at her.

She compressed her mouth and said nothing.

Finally, Fletcher asked, "Would you mind having the trunks and documents scattered about your house?"

Cathleen did not answer Fletcher, but spoke to her grandfather. "Grandpa, what about the Psalms?"

David gave her an affectionate pat on the hand. "We've time and space for both, I ken."

Chapter Eight

The trunks came, all eight of them. They were quite large and filled up the parlor, which now seemed divided between the Psalms and what they had come to call "The Search."

The Psalms and The Search. These were the two things Fletcher had a feeling Cathleen was torn between. Because of her obvious displeasure in having him here, Fletcher had insisted that Cathleen and David go on with their lives and work just as they had before.

Cathleen had happily agreed that this was best, but David had not. It had left her a bit piqued that her grandfather preferred to work with Fletcher, and it was for that reason, Fletcher suspected, that she was determined not to join them.

In the past two days of sorting through the trunks, he had more than one opportunity to observe her working quietly across the room, occasionally picking out a tune, even singing at times, then meticulously writing down the notes and words, while he and her grandfather examined the old documents.

From time to time he would catch her stealing a look at

them, and whenever they came upon something of interest, she would stop work and stare off into space, pretending to be engrossed in thought, but it was more than obvious to Fletcher, and David too, that she was listening to every word they whispered.

He found it amusing that regardless of her efforts to appear otherwise, Cathleen was every bit as interested in his work as he was.

She was too stubborn for her own good, but that only made Fletcher see her as more vulnerable, for despite her determination, there were moments when she lapsed into a sadness that attracted him profoundly. Initially, her beauty had drawn him to her, but the secret life she kept hidden from him was what he now found most intriguing. He could not help but think it was another man who had caused her sadness, another man who had given her that unapproachable serenity that he longed to breach. It was not so much her tranquility that bothered him but the fact that he was not the one who had caused it.

A knock at the door turned out to be a neighbor who stopped by to visit with David. Walking outside with the neighbor, David left the door ajar, which was the perfect opportunity for Cathleen's three orphan kittens to creep inside.

Seeing them come into the room now, Fletcher watched them make their way to where Cathleen sat at the piano. One of the kittens, a yellow tabby, stopped under the piano, so fascinated with the swinging motion of Cathleen's foot that it took an occasional swat. The other two kittens hopped up on the piano bench, the orange and white one climbing into her lap, watching her hands move fluidly over the keys, unable to resist taking a swat as well. The gray tabby was more captivated with the idea of jumping on the keys. He pounced, and Cathleen ignored him for a minute, but when he began to make a nuisance of himself, she picked him up and gave him a good scolding, then reached down to gather up the other two.

Fletcher was fascinated, seeing her with her arms full of three squirming, mewling kittens. She had a great deal more patience with animals, he noted, than she did with him.

A warm sensation traveled through him as he watched the orange and white kitten climb up the bodice of her simple gray dress, following the curve of her breast, digging its claws into her collarbone—for which he received a firm scolding and prompt removal.

"Would you like me to put them out for you?"

"No, I can manage." She rose, carrying the three kittens from the room.

When she returned a moment later she did not even look in his direction.

She had shut him out, retreating into that unapproachable serenity again. He was determined to break in to it, so he tried distracting her with conversation. "What did you do? Drown them?"

She gave him a frank look. "No. I rescued them from that."

"An angel of mercy."

"It is a commission: *'Blessed are the merciful, for they shall obtain mercy.'* Matthew."

Amusement danced in his voice. "Haven't you heard, Mercy killed the cat?"

"What?"

"I heard a story once about a man who had a dog named Mercy. It seems that this dog killed a neighbor's cat, and when the woman came to complain, she rapped smartly upon the door, and when the man opened the door, she said, 'Mercy killed my cat.'"

For a moment, Cathleen simply stared at Fletcher, and he fully expected her to say something about his stupid attempt at levity, when suddenly she began to laugh—a full-bodied laugh that made her so weak she had to hold on to the piano for support.

David walked into the room at that moment, pausing to look from one to the other. "Seems you two are getting along fine without me."

Cathleen was using the sleeve of her dress to wipe the tears from her eyes. "Just don't listen when he tries to impress you with his wit," she said weakly.

David was smiling. "Why is that?"

"Because he hasn't any."

"Am I that bad?" Fletcher asked.

"Aye. You are awful."

After that, they settled back to work. An hour or so passed before Fletcher glanced up and caught her looking at him. He gave her his most inviting look. "You are welcome to join us," he said.

She jerked her head around quickly. Without a smile or a word to him, she gave the impression that she was enthralled with her work, but he knew that was not the way of it.

He exchanged amused glances with David and chuckled to himself, deciding he'd give her another day. *One day,* he thought, *and then she'll abandon the Psalms to work on The Search.*

It was a bet he made with himself, and if he was right, the reward would be . . .

He thought for a moment and decided that just to have her work with them would be reward enough. Then he found himself deep in thought about that. He was getting to know her a bit better, but he did not even begin to understand her, and he found that to be a great challenge.

Fletcher loved challenges.

He had learned much about both Cathleen and her grandfather in the few days he had been with them. For obvious reasons, it was mostly his observations about Cathleen that interested him. She was an early riser, a woman who did her farm chores quite routinely each morning. By the time she prepared the noon meal, she had milked the cow, gathered the eggs, fed the animals—both her own and the orphans she had inherited—and worked in her garden. In the afternoons she did her charity work, which he found was quite varied. In the evenings she sat with her grandfather, going over the notes he had taken on the Psalms, then picking out tunes on the piano and singing the verses to songs she had learned as a child, her voice high pitched and quite the loveliest thing he had ever heard. After an hour or so, David would leave her to work alone while he crossed the room to work with Fletcher.

Already, Fletcher had found many things about Cathleen

that reminded him of his mother, and it was at these times, when she sat before the piano, playing and singing, that he found himself missing his family the most, for it had been Maggie Mackinnon's way to play the piano and sing in the evening, with the children joining in when they were young.

Often, he would find himself watching her, learning her movements—the exact tilt of her head when she was thinking, the way she closed her eyes sometimes when she played, the way she looked at her grandfather when he didn't know she was looking. He wondered what it would be like to have her look at him with the same tender concern.

As always, he was amused at the way Cathleen tried to maintain her distance and disinterest while at the same time giving in to her natural feminine curiosity. It did not take him long to learn that she, like her grandfather, was more than interested in his work. He was now certain that her coolness toward him was not because she did not care for him but simply because she wanted to protect herself as well as her grandfather.

Defending those she loved was one of many things he admired about her, and one more thing that reminded him of his mother, for Maggie fiercely safeguarded those she loved.

"There isn't anything in this batch worth looking at," David said, moving a stack of papers to his left. "Have you found anything?"

Fletcher sighed and dropped his head, rubbing the tired muscles of his neck. "No. Nothing more than some minutes of the church session and a few references to the making of pewter communion tokens. The only wedding mentioned was for Ann Granger and Adam Fife. Nary a Ramsay in the bunch." He leaned back, placing his hands at the back of his waist and massaging there. He was unaccustomed to sitting for such long spells, and his back ached. At that moment, his gaze locked with Cathleen's. For a second they looked at each other, then she looked away.

As David had predicted, sorting through the documents in the trunks was slow, tedious work, and besides cramps in his neck and back, it was hard on Fletcher's eyes. More than once he had sighed and leaned back in his chair, twisting and stretching, his hands wearily rubbing the exhaustion from his eyes, only to open them and see Cathleen watching him. She would then use this as an opportunity to ask him a question.

Today he was surprised when the question turned out to be, "Do you want me to help?"

He forced himself not to smile. It had taken her only a few days. "I can always use another good pair of eyes," he said.

As if she had been waiting for the invitation, Cathleen stood, closed the cover over the keyboard, and crossed to the table where he and David worked.

"Would you like me to bring you some tea and shortbread first?" she asked.

"That would be a most welcome diversion," Fletcher replied.

"None for me," David said, rising. "I think it's time for me to retire. My heart wants to continue, but my poor old eyes have given out."

"Good night, Grandfather," Cathleen said, kissing his cheek. "Sleep well."

"Like a babe," David said, giving Fletcher a wink.

" *'The sleep of a laboring man is sweet,'* " she whispered softly. "Ecclesiastes."

Cathleen went into the kitchen, and by the time she came out with two cups of tea and a plate of shortbread, Fletcher was back at work.

She put the cups and plate down between them, then took her grandfather's seat next to Fletcher. "What would you like me to do?"

He carefully placed a stack of fragile papers in front of her. "Search through these. Look for anything that has the name Ramsay or Duke of Glengarry on it."

Cathleen nodded, then glanced at the clock. It was half past nine. As she began to read the first document, she understood why this was so hard on his eyes. The paper was water-marked and yellowed with age; the ink had faded to a light brown. In many cases the penmanship was overly ornate, making the words difficult to decipher.

She sipped at her tea as she worked, but she became so

engrossed in what she was doing that she did not look up until she finished the stack Fletcher had given her and her tea had grown cold.

She was about to reach for another pile of papers, when he covered her hand with his, his hand warm, his fingers intertwining with hers. She flinched, and her gaze lifted to meet his. She stared at him, mesmerized, until she realized what she was doing and had to look away.

"Cathleen . . ." he said, and she glanced back at him. He gave her one of his charming, lopsided smiles that had become so familiar to her. "Even you must rest sometime. It's after midnight. Already I fear you will hate me in the morning for keeping you up so late."

She looked down to where his large brown hand covered her small white one. She had never allowed a man to hold her hand before, and she was amazed that she could feel the effect of it throughout her body. She tried to pull her hand away, but he held it fast.

"Why have you never married?"

"No one ever asked me," she said, as she again tried to withdraw her hand.

But he continued to hold it firmly. "I find that hard to believe."

She jerked her hand, and still it did not come free. "Perhaps that is because you don't understand what it means to be kind and understanding. The men I know would never force themselves upon a woman."

"And you think I would?"

"You are forcing your attentions upon me now."

"Am I?"

"You are holding my hand . . . against my will."

"And no fine Scots gentleman would dare such a thing?" Her heart pounded. "No, he would not."

"Then I am surprised any of them marry," he said. "Often a woman doesn't know what she wants . . . until a man shows her." He released her hand.

"And you have a lot of knowledge about women, I would imagine."

"Enough," he said. "I did have a mother and two sisters."

As if he knew what she was thinking, he grinned. "Why, Miss Cathleen, you weren't referring to *amorous* knowledge, were you?"

Her mouth took on all the characteristics of a prune. "Of course not!" she snapped.

"That's what I thought. I can't imagine your thoughts ever straying to subjects such as reproduction or fornication."

"Isn't that amazing, for I don't picture yours straying to such thoughts either. No, I don't picture your thoughts straying at all. *Wallowing* would be a better word."

At that, he threw back his head and laughed heartily.

She was mortified over what she had said. If her grandfather knew . . . "Shhhhh," she said hotly. "You'll wake Grandfather."

"And we wouldn't want him to think you were enjoying yourself, would we?"

She came to her feet. "I think it's time for me to go to bed. Good night, Your Lordship."

" 'Fletcher,' " he corrected, rising. "I have asked you to call me Fletcher."

Before she could turn away, his hands closed over her arms, holding her immobile. His gaze traveled over her face as if he was searching for something. "Have you ever kissed a man?"

She laughed. "I just told you I haven't held hands with a man before, and now you ask if I've kissed one."

He cocked his head and looked at her as if trying to figure something out. "You don't hate men?"

"Of course not. I like them very much . . . as long as they behave themselves."

"And you aren't afraid of them?"

"Not unless there is a reason to be."

"And yet you won't let them close to you, will you, Cathleen?"

She stiffened. "I see no reason to."

"You have no desire to marry and have a family?"

Cathleen cringed. There would be no family for her. Not ever. "My grandfather is my family."

"That isn't what I mean, and you know it. David is old. What will you do when he is gone?"

"I will continue to live as I do now. I am happy with my life."

"Are you now?"

"Of course. I stay busy . . ."

"Ah yes, a life filled with stray and orphaned animals, as well as an abundance of good Christian charity for the needy. You seem to meet everyone's needs but your own. I wonder why that is."

"I am happy, so what concern is it of yours?"

"You could be happier," he said. "What has turned you against marriage?"

"I am not against marriage. It simply isn't for me."

"What happened to your parents?"

"My mother died."

"When?"

"When I was six."

"And your father?"

"He was killed in the Crimea."

Fletcher searched her face silently for a moment, then shook his head. "And what happened to you? Why are you so set against marriage?"

She tried to pull away but again he held her fast. Her gaze was drawn to his. He was smiling at her in a way she found threatening. "I don't think my views on marriage are any of your business. You are older than I am, and *you* aren't married."

She had no idea what he would do next, so she was surprised when he released her hand and drew the back of his fingers down the side of her face, making her shudder.

The warmth of his fingers seemed to sear her skin. Ripples of goosebumps spread over her, and she found it difficult to breathe. When she thought she might faint from lack of air, she inhaled, dragging in a lungful, not missing the amusement in his eyes.

"No, I'm not married, but unlike you, I have been kissed, and I hope to marry and have a family one day."

His words sent a chill down her spine. A painful memory surfaced in her mind, a reminder that let her see clearly just how wide the gulf was between them. They were opposites in every way. He was a brave and bold American, confident and sure of himself, a man who knew what he wanted and went after it. And he wanted everything life had to offer— wealth, a title, a wife, children. And what was she? A shy and timid Scot, a spinster with a painful past and no hope of ever having the things in life that Fletcher had a right to expect. She would eke out an existence on this humble farm, taking care of her grandfather in his old age, ministering to the needs of the village, finding what solace she could in the words, *It is more blessed to give than to receive.*

She took a step back. He was nothing but a spoiled and pampered upper-class American who was finding some sort of jaded pleasure in tormenting a shy and backward Scots spinster. Well, she would show him she had a little spunk. "There are a lot of things worse than not being married, but that is beside the point. I am trying to do my Christian duty to help you with your past, but I am not interested in the least in your future. I will thank you not to be interested in mine."

Instinct warned her to move farther away, but not in time to prevent him from taking her in his arms and drawing her close. Every part of her was perfectly aligned with him, and that realization brought her even more discomfort.

Everything within her seemed to stop, and even to look away from the fathomless blue depths of his eyes was impossible. Her breathing was rapid and shallow, until the flow of air stopped completely when his lips came against hers with firm, warm pressure. She could not have moved her head even if she had wanted to, for one hand held her around the waist and the other held the back of her head, where his fingers spread through her hair.

Her heart hammered in her throat. She felt light-headed. And everywhere he touched her, she felt the branding heat of his body burning against hers.

"There now," he whispered, "that isn't so bad, is it?"

She turned her head away, his face blurring. He caught her face with his hands and, turning it back to him, he kissed her. She returned his kiss willingly, so puzzled at her response that she felt angry.

She slapped him.

She heard her hand crack against his cheek and felt its stinging consequence. It wasn't something she had thought about or even decided to do. It had been simply a reaction, but even so, she was mortified. She had never struck anyone or anything in her life. That she was capable of doing so now shamed her.

But what embarrassed her more was the fact that she wanted to slap him again, that she wanted to take the palm of her hand and lay it against his face as hard as she could. As if sensing that, Fletcher caught her hand in his, holding it firmly enough to cause her pain. Then instantly he released her.

"I'm sorry. I didn't intend to do that. It's just that whenever I look at you, kissing you comes to mind."

She wiped his kiss from her mouth with the back of her hand. "You play with something holy as if it were a trinket sold by Gypsies at the fair."

Without another word, she turned and fled to her room, not bothering to see him out, or to lock the door, or to turn out the lamps, or to do any one of the dozen things she always did at night before going to bed. But then, why should she? Tonight was nothing like the countless other nights she had gone to bed.

Tonight she had been kissed.

In her room, she closed the door and decided to wait until she saw his light in the crofter's hut, then she would close up the house for the night. In the meantime, she would ready herself for bed.

She went to her bureau, and poured a pan of water to wash her face and hands. She looked at herself in the faded mirror in front of her. Of its own accord, her hand came up, her fingers curling under as she brushed them across her cheek in much the same manner as Fletcher had done.

The act was the same, but oh, the feeling was ever so much different.

It was late the next afternoon when Cathleen returned home to find Fletcher and her grandfather bent over the documents scattered across the table. As she entered the room, both men looked up.

David's eyes lit up. "You've been gone a long time, Cathleen. I was beginning to worry about you."

She sighed as she removed her bonnet. Her cheeks were flushed, her eyes bright and merry. Crossing the room, she gave her grandfather a kiss on the cheek.

She did not look at Fletcher.

"I rushed through my chores this morning," she said, "because I had so much to do today. Mrs. MacElroy is sick, so I cleaned her house and did some cooking—enough to last the rest of the week." She put the bonnet on a chair as she continued speaking. "After I left the MacElroys', I went to Widow Bennie's."

David's brows went up. "What ails Widow Bennie?"

"Rheumatism racks her joints. Dr. Scott has been giving her James's powder, which helps her legs, but seems to have no effect upon her hands." Cathleen shook her head. "Poor woman."

"And so you were her hands?"

"Aye. She was in too much pain to be making candles."

David frowned, looking at her hands. "What is that all over you?"

She held her hands out in front of her, staring at the deep blue stains. "Indigo," she said. Her gaze flicked over to Fletcher, then she looked away.

"Indigo?" David said. "Where did you get into that?"

She burst out laughing. It was the second time Fletcher had heard her laugh like that, and a shame it was, too, for her laughter rivaled her piano playing, so musical it was.

"I didna get into indigo. Myles Ballantyne did. He painted his little brother, Robbie, from head to foot. Dr. Scott was afraid it would do him bodily harm, so he asked me to help scrub the lad. Hout! Robbie was as squealy and pink as a suckling pig when we finished with him."

"And Myles?"

Her laughter was infectious and Fletcher could only join in. "His backside was pink as well. I ken he wilna be painting young Robbie with anything for a verra long time."

Fletcher watched her sink down into a chair, and upon closer examination he saw exhaustion in the grayness beneath her eyes. She pushed herself overmuch.

Apparently David thought the same. "It would do you well, lass, to rest a wee bit on the morrow. It willna do you or the village folk any good if you wear yourself to the bone. You canna be everything to everyone, Cathleen. I ken I have told you that before."

"Aye," she said, "you have, but I ken it went over my bonnet. I canna rest tomorrow, Grandfather, for I promised I would bring water to the workers haying in Ashton's fields." She came to her feet. "I'll see to dinner now."

"Why not give us a joint of cold mutton, and take yourself to bed early?"

"And miss all the things you and Fletcher talk about?" she said, and with a laugh that was not as light or as merry as her previous one, she left the room.

Fletcher watched her go. "She worries you."

"Aye. She works overmuch," David said. "It was true, what I said. She does try to be everything to everyone."

"Why is that?"

"I dinna ken. Perhaps she does it to feel needed, to fill the emptiness in her own life."

"And is it empty?"

David smiled sadly. "Is a wee old man like me enough to fill a young lassie's heart and life?"

"She seems happy enough, but I have wondered about her. Why doesn't she marry?"

The humor left David's face. "She willna."

"But why?"

David looked troubled. "I have my suspicions, but she doesn't like to talk about it, and I respect that. So it isn't for me to say."

"But you know the reason?"

David sighed, his gaze going to the door to the kitchen. "As I said, I have my suspicions, and then it may be more than mere suspicion. If I were completely truthful, I suppose I would have to say that I do know the reason. Let's just say there were things in her past—things to make her feel as she does." He looked at Fletcher. "It isn't because she has not had offers."

"Oh, I can believe that. She is fair of face and has a sweet nature about her. She would have attracted many a beau, I'll wager."

"Aye, she had more than her share."

"And she never cared for any of them?"

"She never allowed herself to care, not in that way. She is as loving as the day is long, but whenever things progressed beyond mere friendship, she took great care to stop it."

"And that never worried you?"

"Aye, it worried me, but there was precious little I could do about it. I would not force her to marry . . . ever."

"No, of course not. But it does seem odd. It's almost as if she were afraid."

"She *is* afraid."

"Doesn't that bother you?"

"Aye. It bothers me as a man, as her grandfather, who has known love, and it bothers me as a man of God, knowing as the scriptures say, *'There is no fear in love but perfect love casteth out fear'*."

David rose. "Weel now, I ken I had best be washing myself up a bit before dinner. There is much to be done yet, and a hungry stomach was never a good worker."

Fletcher watched him go, his mind upon the words David had quoted: *Perfect love casteth out fear.*

The phrase seemed to engrave itself upon his heart and echo through his mind. He could not help wondering which, in Cathleen's case, would prove the stronger: fear or love?

He was not so foolish as to think he might show her love or even perfect love, but perhaps in time he could teach her to trust. It would be a beginning.

Cathleen poked her head through the door at that moment. "Dinner is ready," she said, then disappeared behind it.

Fletcher stared at the door for a long time after she had gone, the words of Shakespeare coming softly to his mind:

> *What is your substance, whereof are you made,*
> *That millions of strange shadows on you tend?*

Chapter Nine

Her laughter drew him to her.

It was early the next morning, and Fletcher had just stepped outside the crofter's hut and heard the musical notes of her laughter drift toward him. Intrigued, he followed the sound until he came upon Cathleen.

He found her sitting on a tumble-down stone fence that edged a small field where a herd of fat sheep grazed. Above her were the gray branches of a dead tree, and her hands were folded in her lap as the three orphaned kittens tumbled about her. It was obvious that she was not aware of his presence.

A bird, perched in the tree, warbled and sung his heart out. She answered him with her own musical notes, replying as if she knew his song, his habits, his way.

Fletcher had never seen her look so lovely. Her long white neck and the flushed curves of her cheek were set off to perfection by the simple construction of her dress and the rich color of her hair.

In truth, her beauty seemed in perfect harmony with everything that surrounded her. Her profile was cameo perfect. Her hair was brushed back from the temples, but the curls about her face had been cunning enough to find their way back. The rest of the heavy, wavy mass was tied back with a yellow ribbon, and so lovely was the effect of it all that it mattered not that the ribbon was faded or its ends a bit frayed.

Beside her on the fence was a straw bonnet, which looked every bit as old and worn as the yellow satin ribbon, lovingly loaded with flowers and bits of trailing vine. Her yellow muslin dress was set off with a white fichu, untrimmed but for a stingy little ruffle.

Everywhere he looked, she was all yellow and white, and virginally plain. He could no more keep away from her than he could have cut off his right arm.

Quietly, he made his way toward her, walking softly so as not to disturb her.

Not far from the main flock of sheep, several lambs were cavorting, and Cathleen was watching them with avid interest. Each time they jumped and ran, their tails held straight, she laughed at their antics.

Amused, he stood there watching—not the antics of the lambs, but the unassuming innocence of her.

He stopped a few feet behind her and lost himself in study of the delicate curve of her ear, the dusky rose hue of her cheek . . . the soft nape of her neck. He was close enough now to bend down and kiss it where the fine determined curls ran truant from her hair ribbon.

In this setting she was not the shy parson's granddaughter who thought him disruptive and unkind. Here, among nature's bounty, she was a nymph, a sun sprite, who thought him disruptive and unkind.

The thought of that brought a smile to Fletcher's lips and grief to his heart, but the sight of her was the joy of his eye. He stepped closer, almost touching her now, looking down at the wealth of her hair—hair the color of dark red cherries and smelling of roses.

For a moment he felt he could not resist leaning farther down, allowing his lips to glide freely over the beauty of her face, to kiss her lips and whisper softly in her ear. But that, he knew, would send her running away from him.

He would have to settle for less. At least for now. But even so, while feeling the intensity of her, he could no more stop himself from sitting beside her than he could call off his search for proof of his ancestry.

He stepped over the fence where the stones had fallen away and moved closer to her. When he reached her side, she made no move to get up, but as a precaution he put his hand on her shoulder as he sat down beside her.

It was then that he noticed the fawn sleeping contentedly just a few feet away, for when he sat down, the fawn lifted its head, looking at him curiously with dark polished eyes, its large ears alert and standing up.

"Who is your friend?"

"Bathsheba."

"Another orphan?"

"Aye. The mother was shot."

"Well, let's see. That makes three kittens, three ducks, and a fawn."

"The ducks are gone. Mary MacGregor came after them."

"Anything else in your nursery?"

"Rabbits."

"Oh dear. How many?"

She rolled her eyes in an adorable way that crinkled her nose. "As of the last count there were five . . . and this one makes six," she said, holding up a smoky gray rabbit that began to kick furiously. She put the rabbit down in front of her and watched as it hopped a few feet away before turning to watch them, the sun shining behind its long ears and making them transparent.

"All I see is a pair of ears and two big feet."

She laughed. "Those are the important parts," she said. "But he does have an adorable twitching nose and wonderfully soft fur."

"Enough to line a pair of gloves, I'd say."

She whipped her head around to look at him. "I could never—"

He laughed and held up his arms in surrender. "I was only teasing." He looked at the rabbit. "On second thought, he isn't big enough for a pair of gloves."

She smiled.

"That would take at least *two* rabbits."

"Keep talking like that and they will leave."

"Maybe they should be leaving anyway. They look healthy enough to me. Are they ill?"

She laughed again. "No . . . at least not now, although they all had something wrong with them, at one time or the other."

"You mean the usual bunny maladies like overproduction?"

"No, they were ill, or orphaned. Some had broken bones."

"Which ones had the broken bones?"

"The black one. I also had a bird with a broken leg, and a squirrel, too."

"They are long gone, I gather?"

"Aye, most of them are, but sometimes I find some that don't want to leave, even when they've recovered."

"I can understand that," he said, giving her a soft look.

"Fie for shame!" she said, laughing.

"I love to hear you laugh."

She stopped and turned to give him a strange look. "Why?"

He shrugged. "Why do men enjoy the company of a beautiful woman? Why do you love your grandfather? Why do the capers of these lambs amuse you? Why do you feel sorry for wounded animals? How can you talk to the birds? It is something you feel, that's all."

She looked deeply into his face, as if searching for something. "That is a strange admission coming from a man."

"Why? You think a man cannot feel? That he cannot be moved, that he cannot be touched by the gentler things?"

She looked away. "Not many men are."

"I am not *many* men."

"Aye," she said, with an expression that showed her thoughts were miles and miles away. He found he did not mind that in the least, for it gave him time to study her more closely.

Sunlight worshipped her face, clarifying the amethyst color of her eyes. He wanted to lose himself in those purple pools. Was he going mad? He could never remember a woman having such an effect upon him. For a moment, he could not help wondering if she had any idea just how badly he wanted to take her to bed.

But he knew that she did not. It had become quite clear in the past few days that her only interest in him was inspired by her interest in his quest. His cause had become her cause, but by no means had his hunger become hers, or his desire, either.

Her gaze came back to him. There was something about the way she looked, or perhaps it was simply the nearness of her, or perhaps it was any of a hundred other reasons that made him reach out and take her in his arms.

She pulled back immediately.

He allowed her to go just so far before tightening his hold on her.

"Let me go, Fletcher."

"And if I can't?"

"Find some other method of amusing yourself. Don't use me this way."

He released her. "Is that what you thought? That I was using you?"

"Aye. If the feeling wasn't mutual, then you were demanding your feelings be given attention, and ignoring mine."

"The feeling was not mutual? You may push me away, but it isn't what you want."

"It *is* what I want. I feel nothing when you touch me. Nothing!"

His hands gripped her shoulders, close enough to her neck that when he lifted his thumb, it brushed the sensitive hairs at her nape.

She drew up her shoulders like a turtle drawing into its shell, and he couldn't help smiling. "You see? You do feel something."

"Aye. Irritation and revulsion."

"I think a good, upright Christian girl like you should know better than to tell falsehoods. You seem to believe things that are not true."

"They are true."

"Let's see," he said, turning her to face him. "Kiss me

and let's see if what you say is true. Kiss me, Cathleen, and we'll decide afterward if it is revulsion."

He saw the anger that flared deep in her eyes. He puzzled her, that much he knew, for it was as obvious to her as it was to him that he had laid bare her lame excuses.

He made no move to kiss her, and he saw the confusion on her face, confusion that gradually gave way to embarrassment. Tears formed and shimmered in her eyes, but she did not cry. "It isn't just you," she said at last.

"I know," he said softly. "Want to talk about it?"

"No."

"Are you afraid?"

"Aye. Afraid I might cry. Afraid I might end up feeling sorry for myself. Afraid I might make a fool of myself. I don't know you, Fletcher Ramsay ... not well enough to speak of such. Sharing that which is private is not my way."

"Perhaps you will feel differently before long." He kissed her then, drawing her firmly against him, allowing his tongue slowly to penetrate her mouth.

At last he broke the kiss, then chuckled. "At least you didn't slap me this time, Cathleen. I would say we have made a little progress here and that you now know a few things you did not know before."

She shoved against him, breaking his hold. "Aye, I know plenty. I know enough not to trust you again," she said, coming to her feet.

He reached for her hand, but she was quicker. "My grandfather always taught me that we cannot change our past, but we can learn from it."

"And have you learned something?"

"Aye, I have learned you are a man who likes to take hold of a woman."

"Not just any woman, Cathleen. Only you."

She looked away. "I cannot change what has happened, but I can prevent its happening again."

"You really want that?"

"Aye. It would be best for both of us if you would keep your mind on the reason you came here. I like you, Fletcher

Ramsay, more than I should, I ken, but willna tolerate your advances. To persist will only ruin our friendship."

She turned away, picked up her straw bonnet, and dumped the flowers on the ground. Without a word, she put the bonnet on her head, tying the strings as she started walking back to the house, cutting across the meadow, scattering sheep as she went. A moment later, the bonnet slid from her head and hung down her back.

For a moment he watched her go, her body a black silhouette against a backdrop of brilliant sun. He rose to his feet then and went after her. When he caught up to her, the two of them walked along in silence, until they came upon a ewe that had separated herself from the rest of the flock. Seeing that the ewe was down, Cathleen ran toward her.

Ever the helper, Fletcher thought, when suddenly she jerked to a stop. There was something quite strange about the way she stopped, the way she looked down, and he paused for a moment to watch her. Even from where he stood, he saw that her body was rigid and trembling.

"Cathleen," he said, and ran until he reached the place where she stood. The moment he reached her side, he started to put his arm around her, but she whipped around, pure terror in her eyes.

"Don't touch me!" she screamed, backing away. "Don't ever touch me again!"

Before he could decide what to do or ask what was wrong, she whirled around and ran back the way she had come, scattering the flock of sheep once more.

For a second, Fletcher stood there watching her, then he looked down at the ewe. He wondered what she had seen that terrorized her so.

There was nothing wrong with the ewe—aside from the fact that she was giving birth. From what he could tell, she was about halfway through the process. Seeing that things looked to be going along in a normal manner, he glanced in the direction Cathleen had taken, just as she climbed over the fence they had sat a few minutes before.

With one more glance at the ewe, he turned and went after Cathleen.

He might not have found her, had it not been for the dew that was still upon the meadow, which made it easy to see which direction she had taken, for her skirts had brushed the top of the grass, absorbing the moisture and leaving a dark trail for him to follow.

He walked the length of the field before he came upon her. She sat upon a jagged rock that hung over a small pool formed by a bubbling burn. She seemed forlorn and terribly lonely, more isolated than he knew he had ever felt in his entire life. As he went to her, his only thought was to comfort her. He dropped to his knees beside her.

"Go away," she sobbed. "G-go away and leave me alone."

"I can't. You know that." He spread his hand out across her back and began to rub, consoling her in the only way he knew, and feeling supremely clumsy and inept. However, this had worked with his mother and his sisters, so he thought Cathleen, being a woman, couldn't be much different. "What's wrong? What upset you so?"

She said nothing, but she did shake her head, as if even the act of speaking were too much for her. He sat upon the ground next to her, massaging her back in silence as she cried. He hoped this would show her that he wasn't a heartless, lecherous bastard, as she supposed.

After a while, her sobs became hiccups, and after a time, those too began to grow quiet. When she was calmer, he thought that perhaps she was too shy or embarrassed to look at him, and he toyed with the idea of leaving her here alone to salvage her scarred pride.

In the end, he decided he couldn't leave her, at least not until he found out what it was about her, what strange thing had occurred in her life that made her so afraid.

"Want to talk about it?"

"No."

"Want to talk about something else?"

"No."

"Want to talk about anything?"

"No. I . . . Why can't you leave me alone?"

"Cathleen," he said, taking her by the shoulders. "When are you going to realize that I only want to help you?"

"When are you going to realize I don't want your help?" she asked, turning her head away and looking off.

"What happened out there? What did you see that upset you?"

She picked a leaf that clung to her skirts and tossed it into the water. "I didn't see anything."

"You don't lie very well, I'll say that much for you." He smiled. "I would suppose that is because you haven't had much practice, but you saw something." He knew it was something about that ewe, and not the flock of sheep, that had upset her.

"Was it because you thought the ewe was sick? Did you think she was going to die?" he asked. Perhaps the thought of death reminded her of the deaths of her parents. Was that why she was so protective of her grandfather? Because she was terrified that he might die?

"The ewe wasna sick." She gave him an irritated look. "I know the difference between sick and . . . I am no idiot. I k-know what was happening."

He noticed the way her voice broke. Was her fear related to the fact that the ewe was giving birth?

"How did your mother die, Cathleen? Was it an accident? Illness?"

He knew how shaken she was now, for her breathing was rapid, and her eyes kept darting around, as if she was considering her chances of bolting from him.

"You wouldn't get very far," he said. "I am bigger than you and I can run faster."

"Aye, I ken you would run as fast as it took."

"I *ken* you are right. There will be no escaping now. If I have to toss you over my shoulder and carry you back to the house to confront your grandfather, I will. Or, we can stay out here in this field until the sun has roasted both our hides. What's it to be? Talk or bake?"

"Why does everything with you end up in talking?"

He grinned. "There are *other* alternatives. Would you like to try one?"

A flush spread across her cheeks. "Put that way, I prefer talking."

"I thought you'd see it that way."

"Are all Americans so prone to . . . to speech?"

"Probably. But we'll discuss that to your heart's content at another time. How did your mother die?"

She turned her head and stared out over the water, pushing her hair back from where it had fallen about her face. She did not answer him for a long time. At last, when she glanced back at him, she must have seen the resolve in his eyes, for she sighed and looked off again. "My mother . . . died in childbirth."

"I see," he said.

She scrambled to her feet. "No, you don't see!" she screamed, her hands curled into fists at her sides. "Who do you think you are, some magician who can cure my poor, sick mind? Well, if you want a challenge, I'll give you one. Aye, my mother died in childbirth when I was six, and my stepfather almost beat me to death because of it. And there is nothing . . . *nothing*, do you hear, that you can do about it. Now are you satisfied?"

He came to his feet beside her, noticing how her hands were now locked around her waist. She rocked back and forth, her eyes wild, as if she were not really standing here on this rock with him. Her eyes were fixed on the field beyond him, on some mysterious, dark point in her past, visible only to her.

No, she was not here. She was a child of six, reliving the horror that had left her shattered and so afraid.

"Come on," he said, "let's walk. Sometimes walking helps when you need to talk." He was careful not to touch her.

"I dinna need to talk and I dinna need to walk."

"Yes, you do," he said.

She did not say anything, nor did she look at him, but he had expected that. At least she did not run away from him.

"Our home in California was on the coast—a place very much like Scotland—where the trees grew right down to the cliffs that ran along the water's edge. My mother was a walker, and you could always see her in the evenings walking along the cliffs with a big yellow dog at her side. It's what she always did when she was upset or needed to think, and if there was a problem with one of us, she would take us down to the cliffs with her and make us walk.''

He shook his head, remembering. ''Walk and talk, we did, until we had talked out the things that bothered us.''

Silent, she simply stood there, staring off in the distance as she had done before, but his words seemed to have a calming effect upon her, so he went on talking.

He shoved his hands deep into his pockets and, standing beside her, stared out over the pool of water to the fields beyond. ''I could always tell what kind of mood my mother was in just by watching her walk. When she was happy, her walk was moderately fast, her steps light and lively. When she was upset about something, her steps were slower and more ponderous. I suppose my favorite was her angry walk, fast and furious it was, and she would be talking to herself, waving her arms this way and that. I was always curious to know just what sort of things she said to herself when she was out there walking off her anger.''

He started walking then, slowly, with his hands still in his pockets.

She started walking, not at his side, but trailing a bit behind.

''When she first came to California,'' Fletcher continued, ''my mother was the only one who walked along the cliffs regularly, but before long she had all of us out there stomping along the path, pounding out our anger, our frustrations. And a good cure it was, too.'' He paused and glanced back at her.

She stopped, giving him a skeptical look. ''You ken that *walking* will help? When nothing else has?''

''I know it will.'' He smiled at her, then turned and resumed his pace. ''Besides, what have you tried, besides keeping it bottled up inside you?''

She did not answer, but he was pleased when she fell in step beside him. ''I ken you miss your family verra much.''

''Yes, more than I would have thought possible.''

''You said you have two sisters?''

''Barrie and Ainsley. They are both married now and living near the Mackinnon side of the family in Texas.''

''No brothers?''

''I have three stepbrothers. They are a bit younger than I,

but we are very close. I was always the big brother and their idol. My mother said her first four gray hairs were for the four of us.''

She smiled shyly then. "Will you go back?"

"Not to live. This is my home now. It is where I want to be."

"I think it would be nice to have the choice . . . to be able to live anywhere you wanted."

"Where would you live, if you had the choice?"

She thought about that for a moment, then laughed. "Here, I suppose."

"Why did your father beat you?" he asked without looking at her.

"He was my stepfather. My father was killed in the Crimean War. My mother married again three years after my father's death."

"You didn't like him?"

"No, I didn't. He was always hitting my mother."

"Did he hit her the night she lost the baby?"

"Aye, several times. Then he left, and I knew he was going to get drunk."

"He drank a lot?"

"He never stopped drinking. He was drunk that night. He was always drunk."

"And while he was gone, your mother gave birth?"

"She was crying when he left, but soon she was crying harder and calling for me. When I went to her, she said the baby was coming, that she needed my help. I helped her to bed, but I didn't know what to do. There was so much blood. I tried to boil water like she said, but I couldna get the fire going. Then she kept saying the baby was coming, but it never did. There was nothing but blood and more blood. It was everywhere . . . soaking the bed, all over the floor, all over me. I didn't know what to do, so I sat on the bed beside her and held her hand. I didn't even know she was dead until my stepfather came home. When he saw her, he pulled off his belt and began whipping me. He kept on beating me, the buckle cutting into my skin. Pretty soon I couldn't tell if it was my blood or my mother's that soaked my clothes. I don't remember much after that. I remember crying and curling into a ball in the corner while he kept on hitting me. I don't remember when he stopped."

"And afterward, he just left?"

"Grandpa said one of the neighbors came by and found my mother dead and me unconscious in the corner. My father had passed out on the floor. By the time he was sober, Grandpa was there, and the village folk set upon my stepfather, chasing him away and telling him they would kill him if he ever set foot in the Highlands again."

"And you never heard from him again?"

"No."

"I'm sorry," he said.

She turned to look at him.

"Would you mind if I held you?" he asked.

"Why? Do you think it would make me feel better?"

"No, I think it would make me feel better."

They stood there in the middle of the field, looking at each other as if they were both trying to figure out what the other was thinking. She probably thought him an idiot, asking if he could hold her, when there were a dozen other things he could have said, all of them more poetic or romantic. But somehow he could not put what he was feeling into words right now. The need to put his arms around her and comfort her was strong. He sensed that the silent, caring touch of another human being would carry the healing power Cathleen needed then.

"I don't understand you," she said.

"What is there to understand? I want to share with you the warmth of my affection, to give food to that aching emptiness inside you. My heart is too swollen with feeling to explain, but sometimes we can tell more by a look, a touch, than we ever can with words."

"But why hold me?"

"Because you are no longer a child and I cannot take you in my lap to ease the torment you have suffered, nor can I bathe your wounds with lavender-water and kiss them away. What else is left?"

She had an almost winsome look about her as she asked, "Is that what your mother did?"

"Always...." He smiled at her. "At least until I was too big to hold on her lap and too manly to suffer the likes of lavender-water, but even then, she was always there with a loving caress and words of understanding and encouragement. It was a love that guided, yet encouraged me to grow away from her and become independent."

She looked terribly sad. "I have never met anyone like you. You have feelings and insight most men could never realize. How I envy you. You must have a wonderful mother."

"I do."

"Can we walk more? I would like to hear about her."

"She was the most important person in my life for a long, long time. Whenever one of us hurt, she was there. She loved us when we needed it, and pushed us away when it was necessary for us to stand alone. Her kitchen was a remarkable place and each illness had its own special foods. I did most of my studying at the big table in the kitchen while my mother baked. Even now, there are times when I am working with figures and I find myself remembering the smell of Linzer slices and hazelnut pastry, or the exact aroma of cinnamon stars. If it had not been for my mother's conviction and determination, I might have come to Scotland to kill Adair Ramsay, instead of take his title away."

"You hated him that much?"

"Oh yes. I still do. He took something from me that can never be replaced."

"Your father?"

"Yes."

"Well, at least you had your mother, and a loving stepfather ... something I never had."

"Do you remember your mother at all?"

"I try, but it seems the more I do, the more the memory of her eludes me. When I ask my grandfather about her, he tells me she was a loving, gentle person and that she loved me more than anything in the world, but it is difficult to pin a face on such a description. There are no pictures of her, only her name written in her Bible, and a small figure of her cut from black paper—a silhouette made when she was eight or ten. Often I would sit and stare at that silhouette, trying to breathe life into it, willing it to speak to me, to tell me things about herself. I remember trying to see if I had some resemblance to that small nose and round forehead. It's all so strange, really, for as the years have passed, I have grown up and become a woman, but my mother will always be a child."

He saw the path of tears down her face.

Her pain reached out and engulfed him. The admiration he felt overwhelmed his compassion. He was understanding her more now, and he came to a conclusion. She would never trust a man who felt sorry for her or who showed his pity. She would remain stubborn, aloof, and very private, neither relinquishing her privacy nor giving her trust without putting him to the test. And so he was considerate, understanding, and careful, determined not to humiliate her by his sympathy. She was like no one he had ever met. She was simply herself, a being who existed alone, abandoned, defeated, bruised, and shaken, but fortified by energy and incredible strength.

For a while, he forgot about Adair Ramsay and why he had come to Scotland. For a while, all he could think about was how much he wanted to touch her. But he dared not.

"It seems we both understand loss," he said, feeling that the words were a poor second to the comforting he wanted to give her.

Cathleen stopped suddenly and turned to him. "Will you hold me now?" she asked in a quiet little voice.

"Nothing would give me greater pleasure." Looking down at her, he opened his arms.

She stepped into them.

That night, in bed, Cathleen stared into the darkness, unable to sleep, thoughts of Fletcher Ramsay keeping her awake. His words haunted her. How could a man of eight and twenty years have so much feeling, so much understanding and compassion? There was a gentleness in him that seemed to reach out to her. She had never met anyone like him. Never.

Like her, he had suffered loss and tragedy, and yet how

different from her he was, being a man who confronted life; a strong and brave man who weathered whatever life offered him and met it face to face. While she was a woman who would avoid confrontation at all costs, a woman who chose to run, to hide from the things that could cause her pain, he met his fear, challenged it, and would not back down. She had let her fear take control of her life and could not imagine conquering it.

She rolled over, remembering the touch of his hand, the feel of his lips upon hers. Even more than the memory of desire was the memory of there being no fear. He had gained an access to her that no one else had, not even her grandfather, and yet she was not afraid of him.

Why?

She closed her eyes to say her prayers, and was reminded of a piece of scripture that spoke to her heart. " *'Fear not,'* " she whispered. "Genesis."

When her prayers were finished, she thought again of the man called Fletcher Ramsay. She had known him only a short while. It was much too soon to form any opinion. He might appear to be gentle and kind and understanding for now, but time would tell. She knew that the devil's principal method of attack was by temptation. Was that what Fletcher Ramsay was about?

Was she deceiving herself, then? Was he, like the devil, a creature of beguiling and deception? " *'Bread of deceit is sweet to a man; but afterwards his mouth shall be filled with gravel,'* " she whispered. "Proverbs."

But even as she said the words, her thoughts were elsewhere. *He is a good man*, she thought. *He is good to all things . . . just like water*.

And with the smoothness of water running over stones, Cathleen Lindsay drifted off to sleep.

Chapter Ten

B y the time Fletcher arrived at David's house the next morning, the old minister was sitting in the parlor, sorting through documents.

"You are working early."

"Thought I'd get an early start," David said, looking up. "Have you eaten?"

"No."

"Cathleen made breakfast before she left. There is still plenty in the kitchen, if you're hungry."

Fletcher grinned and rubbed his stomach. "I think I'll take you up on that."

He went into the cozy, warm kitchen, where the table was covered with a simple cloth, the customary pot of flowers in the center. A crockery bowl and a spoon had been set out for him. He looked around the room as if for the first time. Her presence hovered about him, almost a tangible thing, for she was here, in this room, even when she was not present.

This was Cathleen ... this kitchen that displayed such

loving care, this kitchen with its soft touches, this kitchen where everything had order and a purpose.

After eating the scones and porridge she had left for him, he returned to the parlor. "Where is Cathleen today?" he asked David.

"Tuesday is her day to minister to the poor," David said, without looking up from his work.

"She must have left early."

"Oh aye, she is always out early on Tuesdays. Excited as a hen walking on hot coals, she was. It does my heart good to see her so happy."

While he was glad to hear of her happy mood, Fletcher could not help wondering what day was Cathleen's day to minister to herself. The word *no* seemed unacceptable to her, for over and over he had seen and heard about how she gave effortlessly of her time and support to others, never thinking to save a little of it for herself.

Taking a seat across from David, Fletcher turned his attention to the document. Soon he was lost in his task, unaware that he had been working for three hours straight, until he heard David sigh wearily. Looking up, he asked, "Find anything?"

David shook his head. "Nothing with your family name on it."

Fletcher heard the weariness in David's voice and, upon closer inspection, saw the fatigue in his face, the faint circles under his eyes. He felt guilty for allowing his enthusiasm and his drive to spread to David. The minister wasn't a young man, and now that Fletcher looked, he saw many signs that David was pushing himself more than he should.

Knowing that the man would never admit to his own exhaustion, Fletcher feigned his by rising wearily to his feet and rubbing the back of his neck. "How about calling things to a halt for today?" he asked. "I don't seem able to concentrate. After five or six hours of this, I start feeling worn out and frustrated. Perhaps I'll go for a ride. I was raised to be a lumbering man, don't forget. I'm not accustomed to spending so much time indoors."

Going outside, Fletcher knew he had done the right thing

when David rose to his feet and said something about taking a little nap.

Going outside, Fletcher mounted his horse and took off down the lane at a fast clip. Before he knew it, he had ridden all the way to Glengarry.

While he was in town, he decided to post a letter he had written to his mother. Then, as he rode out, he noticed a crowd gathering for the Tuesday sheep auction. He decided to turn down a narrow lane, hoping to avoid the babble of men and sheep that enveloped the narrow streets around the pens. He had no idea where the lane would take him, but he would soon find out.

Before long he found himself in the poorer section of the village, a place where the houses were built one against the other and sewage ran in an open gutter in the middle of the street. Even the smell here was different from the rest of the village, as if it was a way to confirm the degradation and wretchedness of the poorer classes who lived here. Everywhere he looked he saw poverty, ignorance, and idleness.

He also saw Cathleen.

Just as he rode past a long row of ramshackle houses at the edge of town where a group of dirty children played shinty with sticks in the street, he saw her—or rather her wine-colored hair flashing brilliantly in the midday sun. She was surrounded by a group of ragamuffin children and did not see him.

Fletcher pulled his horse to a stop. It was his intention to watch for just a moment, but the instant his gaze rested upon her, awareness seemed to explode inside him in a rainbow of bright, intense colors. How odd that even in a crowd he could sense her presence; how odd to find her in this group of children as if time had handed him a miracle.

He was always learning something new about her and he realized that today was no different. It hadn't taken him long to learn that Cathleen did not lead an idle life. Now, it was apparent to him that these poor people knew her very well—knew her and loved her, for every person she passed nodded at her and said, "God bless you."

Even when surrounded by poverty, there was a heart-wrenching charm about the children scattered around her, and how lovely they were, how beautiful in their innocent frankness—ignorant, poverty-stricken children utterly unskilled in the art of hiding their feelings, which were as pure and beautiful as Cathleen appeared to him now.

He watched her lithe, graceful motions with a mixture of awe and delight. Her bonnet was thrown back, and the richness of the sun's bounty fell full upon her. How fair and sweet that face, and how vivid the color of her hair that curled as innocently as a child's about her forehead.

Never had he seen her face so radiant as when she stooped down, took the hem of her apron, and wiped the dirty smudges from the face of a little girl. The child then put her arms around Cathleen, who hugged her tightly. Fletcher felt a hard, jealous pang in the vicinity of his heart as he observed this.

Even from where he sat upon his horse, he could see that Cathleen was moved almost to the point of tears. How sad it was that a woman who obviously loved children as much as she did was destined to live the life of a spinster.

And yet, in spite of her own lackluster future, she inspired such hope in these people. How much right she did for these who had been done a great and inexplicable wrong. As he watched her gather the children about her beneath the lofty branches of a great, sweeping tree, he realized that the soul and nature of Cathleen was revealing itself to him in yet another way—through her interactions with others.

She seemed to him very alone, even while surrounded by children. Something fluttered in his chest, a tender regard for her, and it struck him that he was experiencing emotion on a level that he had never experienced before. He was aware of the sun's warmth upon his face, the flutter of leaves overhead, the gentle breathing of his horse, the grass that grew on the fellside—all things he had taken no notice of before. It was a strange, new awareness. One that he could not let go any more than he could let go of the feelings for her that grew inside him.

She was no more beautiful than a hundred women he had seen and had before, yet there was something about her that kept him entranced, kept him looking just a little harder and digging just a little deeper to find the treasure that he knew lay deep inside her.

Other women he had known possessed certain predictable traits that made him know their coyness, and their flirty ways could never be mistaken for sincerity. Cathleen had no time or use for other women's mental trappings. Life, for her, was not a game, something to take out and pleasure herself with like a frivolous party dress and then put away. The will to survive was strong within her. As was the will to protect.

Fletcher was reminded of a dove that flies off in the opposite direction from her nest, hoping to draw the intruder away. He had a suspicion that Cathleen was like that, doing her deeds of benevolence, her acts of kindness and Christian charity, in order to draw attention away from the loneliness and unfulfillment, from all the things that were lacking in her life.

He watched her movements as she told the children a story, her voice soft and comforting, her hands moving in a way that was both captivating and feminine. He realized then that she had looked up and seen him, and he was instantly aware of her discomfort, her insecurity. Cathleen could be friends with a man, but she was wary of anything beyond that.

Why was it so damned important to him to try to change that for her? He realized suddenly that he wanted her to look at him with an expression that was different from those she bestowed upon her neighbors and her animals, and even her grandfather for that matter. He wanted to see her eyes light up the moment he walked into the room. He wanted her to seek out his company. He wanted her to give him some small token of recognition, to show that his presence in her life meant something to her.

He saw her look away, returning her attention to the children, and he realized that he would never get those things from her. But then, it seemed not to matter. He could no more stop his fascination with her than he could stop his quest to restore his father's title. Spurring his horse, he rode toward her.

Cathleen had hoped that Fletcher would keep his distance. Now, as he approached, she knew that even this part of her existence, where she worked with the poor children of the village, was not to be hers alone. He would disrupt the story she had started telling the children.

Such were her thoughts, so she was completely dumbfounded when he rode on past her without so much as a wave and stopped where a group of older boys were playing shinty.

She could only watch as he dismounted and tied his horse, then walked toward the boys. After talking to them for a few minutes, he did the strangest thing. He began playing shinty with them, taking up the stick to strike the ball of hair, sending it rolling down the street.

Soon the younger children lost interest and she went on with her story. When she finished and the younger children scattered, she stayed where she was, content to watch Fletcher play.

When the game was over, he untied his horse and walked toward her, his clothes torn and soiled, his face dirty.

"I didn't know you played shinty," she said, smiling at the sight of him.

He laughed. "I didn't, but I sure do now."

"Aye," she said, "you were quite good, especially for your first time."

"Tomorrow I will be black and blue and sore all over. I have a feeling I will decide then that it was also my *last* time."

She laughed.

"Want me to give you a ride home?"

"I enjoy walking at this time of day."

"Mind if I walk with you?"

"No."

He tucked the reins to his horse in the back of his belt and fell in step along side her.

They walked along, talking about the children, the problems with the poor in the village, the weather, California. Then the talk dwindled and they walked on in silence.

Not far from her cottage, she broke the silence. "Are you hungry?"

"Starving. I'm hungry enough to eat a dried buffalo."

Cathleen stopped and gave him a curious stare. "A what?"

"A dried buffalo."

"What in heaven's name is a dried buffalo?"

"It's buffalo meat that has been dried."

She rolled her eyes. "All right. What is a *buffalo*?"

"It's a big animal with a hump—"

"Oh, like a camel."

"No, it's nothing like a camel. Its hump begins right behind its horns."

"Horns? Oh, it's more like a cow, then?"

"Well, not exactly. It is sort of like a cross between—that is, it resembles . . . It's more like a . . ."

"Yes?"

"What's for dinner?"

She laughed. "Perhaps you can draw me a picture sometime," she said, turning in at the gate and following the lane to the cottage.

Fletcher did not arrive back at David's house until after ten the next morning, and when he did, he met David coming out the front door.

"Go on inside," David said. "I'm on my way to town. Robert Cameron has sent word that he has some important church matters to discuss with me. I'll be staying for dinner."

Fletcher nodded. "I'll get started, then. Say hello to Robert."

"I will. Oh, before I forget—Cathleen is over at Mrs. Drummond's. Her husband was in an accident with a haying machine and Cathleen is helping the doctor set his leg."

"When will she be back?"

David shrugged. "Who knows? Cathleen will return when she is ready . . . or when she runs out of causes. And one more thing. Don't be surprised when you go into the kitchen, and be sure you leave the door closed."

At Fletcher's curious look, David added, "Old Mrs. Tawesson sent over a basket of goodies for Cathleen."

"Hmmmm. Maybe I'd better have a look, just in case I get hungry."

David laughed. "You willna get more than a mouthful of feathers."

"Feathers? As in birds?"

"Feathers as in owls. There are two baby ones in the basket. Seems they fell out of a nest and Mrs. Tawesson was afraid they would die."

"So she brought them to Cathleen."

"Aye, it is a common enough occurrence."

"And keeping the door closed? Is that because of the cats?"

"Aye."

"What do baby owls eat?"

David chuckled and shrugged his shoulders. "Cathleen will know."

Yes, Fletcher thought, *she will*.

Fletcher saw David off in his gig, then went inside to work. After two hours he found a faded piece of paper that had the name Douglas Ramsay written on it, but the rest of the page was water marked and illegible. It wasn't a bit of help to his cause, but simply finding one of his ancestor's names spurred him on.

His stomach growled. He realized how hungry he was, so he stopped working and made his way toward the kitchen, stumbling over the yellow tabby that was sleeping in the middle of the floor. The tabby let out a hissing squeal and shot beneath a nearby chair.

Shaking his head, Fletcher went into the kitchen. Once there, he spied the basket Mrs. Tawesson had left, sitting on the table. A white cloth covered the top. Lifting the cloth just enough to peer into the basket, he saw two little owlets blinking their eyes against the sudden glare of light, staring back at him in a drowsy sort of way.

Take away their head and there wasn't much to them, for they were mostly gray balls of fluff with big yellow eyes surrounded by a ruff that gave them a dish-shaped face. "Well, hello there," he said. "Fancy meeting you here. Are you fellows hungry?"

Buttery yellow eyes blinked at him, as they began to swivel their heads to look at him in a manner that made him think his clever attempt at conversation was not enough to forgive him for waking them. As if worried that he would not get the message, they began to chatter in a high-pitched way that sounded remarkably like a scolding.

He smiled and looked around the room. "We seem to be fresh out of mouse meat," he said, eyeing a pot left on the hob. Going to the pot, he lifted the lid and peered inside. "I don't suppose you like porridge, so it seems you will have to wait until your mother comes home."

That set them off into a fresh round of chattering, so he covered the basket again, then he realized he had left the door open when the orange and white kitten hopped into the chair beside him. Picking up the kitten, he carried it from the kitchen, then closed the door.

He passed over the porridge for a meal of cold potatoes and mutton. Once he finished, he peeked at the owls again and, finding them asleep, returned to his work.

But his task was not what his mind was interested in, and before long he found his thoughts drifting to Cathleen.

She was such a private person who ministered tirelessly to others. He felt anger at her mother and father for dying and leaving her to the cruelties of the world, and even a little anger at David, for being too old and out of touch to see what the kind of life she led was doing to her. God, she deserved so much more. Once, just once, he would like to see her put on a scarlet dress and let down all her glorious hair.

And then he remembered why he was here, why he had come. Attracted to her though he was, he could not, would not, allow anything to come between him and his work. Closing his eyes, he searched the deep reaches of his mind, calling up bits and pieces of memory, scenes of happier times, times he had shared with his father.

There were glimpses of a father's loving arms lifting him into the saddle of his first pony, of the silvery flash of a salmon jumping out of the water and the sound of splashing water when the fish proved to be more than Fletcher could handle and he fell into the river.

He could hear the faint echo of a gunshot—the one he had taken at his first grouse; the gentle instruction of his father teaching him to butcher a deer he had just shot. There were memories of Bruce Ramsay's broad shoulders and how the world seemed ever so much larger when he observed it from their lofty heights, and the pride in his father's eyes when Fletcher had gotten all of his Latin phrases right.

And he could remember gentler times, when the family gathered near the fire and his sisters clustered about his mother's feet as he climbed into his father's lap. Even now he could feel the comforting weight of his father's hand stroking his head, and falling asleep with the rough texture of his father's tweed jacket against his cheek, the scent of tobacco reminding him that his father would always be there for him. Always.

Only he hadn't been.

Bruce Ramsay had been ripped from Fletcher's life as savagely as a wolf tears out a deer's throat. Fletcher had been robbed of his father's presence, his love, his guidance, and *these* were the reasons why Fletcher wanted back his title.

Not for what he would gain, but for what he had lost.

He had never forgotten his vow to avenge his father's death. He had lived with it for a long time, and it was as much a part of him now as the blood that flowed in his veins. Nothing would come between him and his goal. Nothing.

Not even Cathleen.

It was much later that evening when Cathleen came home and found the house dark, save for a stingy wedge of light beneath the kitchen door.

Hanging her cape and bonnet on the peg by the door, she went to the kitchen door and opened it just a little. Inside, she saw Fletcher crouched near a chair, his hands in the basket that held the baby owls.

She stared in wonder at the gentleness in the way he cupped his hand to hold a tiny owl that seemed bent upon giving him a good fussing, and how his finger found the right place to stroke behind its head.

The owl grew suddenly quiet, and for a moment Cathleen was distracted by the memory of seeing Fletcher with the children in the village, and how they had left her to cluster about him for a moment, a crippled little boy with bent legs tugging on his coattails, and how Fletcher had lifted him onto the back of his horse and given the boy a ride. She smiled, remembering how afterward the clamoring children would not be quiet until he had promised to visit again and give each of them a ride. And then she remembered the sight of him playing shinty with the older boys.

She remembered the faces of even those boys, whom she had not been able to reach, as they looked up at Fletcher with expressions of both delight and awe—expressions quite similar to the way she looked at him now.

Children and owls loved him, it seemed.

The yellow tabby bounded across the floor, jumped into his lap, and came to a screeching halt when it saw the two owls. Arching its back high, the fur that ran along its backbone standing straight, the kitten hissed.

Cathleen put her hand over her mouth but apparently it wasn't enough to completely stifle her laugh, for Fletcher turned his head toward her.

"Hello," he said, giving her a welcoming smile. "I'm glad you're home. I could use a little help. I seem to have more than I can manage right now."

"Aye," she said, "so it seems." She went to him, leaning over the yellow tabby in his lap to peer at the owls in the basket. "Oh, how darling," she said, taking the tiny balls of down in her hands. The owlets began chattering again, voicing their displeasure in being separated from the warm spots they had occupied moments ago. "They are so small. They must be verra young."

"And very hungry, I think. I didn't know what to feed them, but they kept making such a ruckus, I couldn't work. The only way I could keep them quiet was to hold them."

"Where did you find them?"

"Here in the kitchen," he said. Then, seeing her surprised look, he laughed and went on to tell her how Mrs. Tawesson had left them with David.

"What will you feed them?"

She cradled the blinking babies against her. "Dried buffalo," she said, laughing.

"And if you can't find that?" he asked softly.

"Then I'll chop up some raw mutton." Giving him a shy

but friendly smile, she asked, "Would you rather hold or chop?"

He eyed the owls. "I'll hold. I've more experience at that." He sat down at the table.

"Here," she said, coming to stand beside him and handing him the owlets. Suddenly she realized how close his body was to hers, how warm his thigh was as it pressed against her leg. The shocking pleasure of it caused her breath to catch. Her gaze dropped unconsciously to his legs, and she found herself fascinated at the way his lean muscles seemed to tug at the fine fabric of his pants. She followed the tight line upward . . . until she realized what she was doing. Feeling the heat rushing to her face, she knew her cheeks flushed red.

She might have run from the room, had he not had the decency to ignore it by giving the owlets a questioning look and saying, "Uh, don't they need something—that is, do I need to put a cloth under them? . . . Aw, hell, you know what I mean."

Then she was laughing so hard that she forgot all about her embarrassment. "They dinna need to wear nappies, if that is what you are asking."

He eyed the baby owls again. "Couldn't we just drop them back in the basket?"

"No. I want them to get accustomed to being held."

"Shouldn't they get used to *you* holding them?"

She turned, a knife in her hand. "I don't think it will matter much to them who does the holding." Then, turning around, she cut a wedge of mutton from a joint. "A fine father you will make."

He knitted his brows together. "I don't plan to have baby owls."

"There isn't much difference. Babies or owls. They are both helpless." She gave the mutton another whack. "I must admit that I am rather surprised at you."

"Why is that?"

"I would have thought you the type to catch all sorts of animals when you were a boy."

"I did," he said, giving her a little grin, "when I was a

boy. Unlike you, I outgrew it . . . much to my mother's eternal gratification."

Her gaze flew to his and held there for a moment, suspended in the awareness, the tenderness, the inviting light she saw dancing in his eyes. Turning away, she began working, filling her mind with the rapid tempo of the knife chopping the meat.

When she finished a few minutes later, she carried a bowl of finely chopped meat to the table. "You hold and I'll feed," she said, taking the chair next to his and offering one of the owls a bit of meat on the handle of an old wooden spoon.

It did not take the owls long to figure out that although it was a mighty strange-looking contraption that came at them, there was something good to eat at the end of it. Soon, both owlets were gobbling down bits of mutton.

"They may be owls," Fletcher said, "but they eat like pigs."

"They were starving, poor babies." She finished feeding them, stuffing them until neither of the owls would eat any more, then she watched as Fletcher returned them to the basket. "I'll fix them a better place to stay tomorrow," she said. "But for now they will have to make do with the basket."

She drew the cloth over the top of the basket, feeling suddenly awkward when he reached out to take her hands in his. Beneath the sturdy strength of them she felt her own hands trembling, and as if he sensed her uneasiness, his gaze came to rest upon her face, searching her eyes as if looking for the reason.

"Do I frighten you?"

"No." She whispered the word and tried to tug her hands from his, unable to decide if it was the holding of her hands that made her so uneasy or the warmth of his leg pressed against the length of hers. "Please stop. I don't want this."

He released her, watching her as she crossed the room and busied herself with cleaning up the chopped mutton. She glanced at him once, and, seeing an odd expression on his face, she found herself wondering if it was because he was a man unaccustomed to being told no. But even as she thought it, she knew that had no bearing here. Somehow she knew that no matter how many women there had been before her, it did not alter or detract in any way from what had passed between them.

She turned away to wash her hands, then dried them. She heard him rise, heard the chair scrape. She closed her eyes, listening to his footfalls as he crossed the room. He was standing behind her now, close enough that she could smell him, close enough that their bodies touched, ever so lightly. She fought against the urge to lean back against him, to feel the warmth and strength of him, the security. She felt the caress of his hands as they cupped her shoulders, the strange feel of his body as he pressed closer to her. She tried to pull away.

"Bonnie Cathleen, why do you have to make this so difficult?"

She did not say anything, and soon she felt the pressure of his hands as he turned her around so that she was facing him. She melted against the welcome feel of him, aware of the sensation it caused when his body aligned with hers. He lowered his face, then just at the moment she thought he would kiss her, he said, "When you decide you can trust me, come into the parlor and I'll tell you what I've found."

She watched him go, stopping to pick up the yellow kitten, then carefully closing the door behind him. He had left her with weak knees and a hammering pulse, the image of his body permanently engraved upon her mind. He wasn't going to force her. He had given her the choice. Only it wasn't the choice she wanted. Trust him? How could she, when the very thing he was here for would provoke the duke? What would happen to her and her grandfather then?

She turned around, bringing the back of her hand up to her mouth and squeezing her eyes shut, hoping she would not cry. She liked Fletcher. She desired him. But could she trust him? It seemed that the pull, the attraction of him, was greater than her fear, for without really realizing it she had crossed the room.

It was only when she had her hand on the door that she heard herself say, "Well, perhaps I can trust him . . . just a little."

A moment later she stood at the table in the parlor, waiting until he moved a kitten from a chair so she could sit down. She took her seat. "What did you find?"

"I found a paper with Douglas Ramsay's name on it, but the rest was water damaged and I was unable to make it out. A little while ago I found another paper with Bride Ramsay's name on it. It appears to be some sort of a record of a ladies' church meeting, but there was no mention of any members of her family, nor that she was even married. It is, at least, proof that Bride Ramsay existed, but precious little more than that."

Hearing the disappointment in his voice, she searched her mind for a way to give him encouragement and consolation, finding it odd that she knew all about caring for kittens, rabbits, and owls but nothing about caring for a man, other than her grandfather. "I know you are disappointed. I wish I knew what to say."

He gave her a smile that she knew he did not feel. "How about, 'Keep looking'?"

"How many trunks are left?"

He sighed. "Only three."

She gave him a comforting look. "I know how much time you've spent going through those trunks. I'm sorry this is proving to be so fruitless for you."

"So am I." He tilted his head to one side, and gave her the once over. His entire countenance changed. Gone was the sad, melancholy look. In its place was one of amusement. He smiled.

The intensity of his gaze left her feeling flustered. "What are you smiling at?"

"You."

"Why?"

"Do you know, I think this is the first time I've seen you with your face dirty."

Her hand came up to brush her cheek.

"Other side," he said. Then, coming to his feet, he moved to stand in front of her. "Here, let me." He took her hand and drew her to her feet, then brought his thumb to his mouth and touched it with his tongue before he wiped the smudge from her face.

His thumb was warm and smooth as satin as it touched her cheek. A flutter of feeling washed over her, the blood pounding so hard in her brain that it drove away all the reasons why she should not be standing here with him like this; why she should not allow him to look at her as he was; why she should not return the look, seductive as it was.

She could not help herself.

She found that one act so endearing and so much more overpowering than anything more blatant, like a kiss. He had, after all, only touched her cheek with his thumb, so why was her heart bouncing so painfully against her ribs? And her clothes . . . why did they seem suddenly so horribly thin?— as if she could feel the warmth of his body against hers, which she knew was crazy, since he wasn't even touching her. How odd that her body burned in many more places than the one he had touched. She realized she was learning things about herself for the first time.

Looking into his gentle eyes, she wondered what he would say if she told him this was the first time she had allowed herself to think the kind of thoughts she was thinking or to feel the kinds of things she was feeling. The implications of it left her uncertain and unsure. To ease her discomfort, she laughed, but feared it had come out more as a nervous sort of twitter.

If it was a twitter, he was civilized enough to act as if he had not noticed. He was so close, close enough that she could feel the warm current of his breath, like a caress against her cheek. "Do I look funny?" he asked.

"Aye," she said, feeling suddenly shy, "you do. I've never seen a man do that before."

"What?" he whispered, one long, slender finger coming up to lift the wisps of hair and push them back, away from her face. "Wet his finger to clean a smudge?"

"Aye," she said, thinking it sounded dreadfully like a croak.

He shrugged. "I was on the receiving end of such an act more times than I can count. I suppose it comes natural to me."

"You are so different," she said, feeling herself drawn into the warm space that separated their bodies.

"Different? How do you mean?"

"You are very manly, with all the typical attributes—you're tall and strong, your voice is deep, you're brave, determined, and hardworking. But there is also a soft side to you, a gentleness I've never seen in a man, not even my grandfather."

"And you find that odd?" he asked in a slow voice.

She began to feel weak from the powerful feelings he stirred in her. It took great effort to respond, even greater effort to hide the way she felt. Unable to look at him, she answered, "Aye, most men would go to great lengths to hide such gentleness."

He looked at her for a moment before putting his hand under her chin, lifting her face to his. "I was taught that a man loses nothing by being gentle. I can be hard and forceful when I need to be."

She opened her mouth to respond to that, feeling her body straining weakly toward him. What would it be like to give in, to sway against him and close her eyes, to feel the soft press of his clothing against hers, his hands beginning a courtship of her body? What would he think if she wrapped her arms around him and began to stroke the firm, supple muscles of his back and shoulders? Carried beyond herself, she pressed forward, feeling the need, the desire to learn more about this wonderful man.

Suddenly, someone pounded frantically on the front door, and the spell was broken.

"Damn!" he said.

Dazed, she looked up at him and saw the same confused expression there that she was feeling.

"Cathleen . . ."

It was nothing more than a hoarse whisper, the sound of her name, but it carried a wealth of implication. Her hand weakly found his chest and lay there for a moment, as if she needed that connection to him.

The knocking came again, louder and harder this time, and his face came hazily into focus. As if drugged in a state of what-might-have-been, she could only murmur, "I . . . I wonder who . . ." as she turned toward the door. "It isna my grandfather's knock."

"Do you want me to answer it?"

"No, I'll get it," she said, wondering if her legs were up to the task of carrying her to the door.

She opened the door to see Alex Monzie, who appeared terribly upset. He was panting and unable to speak for a moment. She stepped outside. "What's wrong?"

" 'Tis me ma, Miss Lindsay. She's birthin' the babe, but the babe won't come. Me pa went for the doctor, but he isna home, so he sent me to fetch you. She needs help. Me pa's afraid she might die. You must come. You canna let her die."

Cathleen's heart began to pound. Her palms grew damp. For the longest time she stood there, not really seeing Alex but her mother. She closed her eyes, but still it was there: the ashen face; the smell of perspiration; the agonized screams; the sticky warmth of blood seeping into her clothes. Even now she could feel the bite of the metal buckle of her stepfather's belt cutting into her skin. *No. I canna. I canna . . .*

"Miss Lindsay?" Alex looked at her, panic gripping his features. "You'll come? You willna let me ma die?"

"I canna," she said, holding her hands up in front of her and backing away. "Please. I canna. Dinna ask me."

She turned to run, but Fletcher was there, taking her by the arms. "Cathleen—"

"Dinna ask this of me!" she screamed. "I can't do this! You know I can't!" She began to cry.

He drew her against him. "I won't force you to," he said, stroking the back of her head. "Do you know where the doctor is?"

"Aye." Her words were muffled against his blue shirt. "He went to the Finlaysons'."

Fletcher looked at Alex. "Do you know where the Finlaysons live?"

"Aye."

Releasing her, Fletcher said, "I'll go with Alex. You go on back inside."

Cathleen stepped back into the doorway, hating herself for her weakness, yet unable to do anything about it. It wasn't fair. She did so much for the people of Glengarry. She went whenever and wherever she was needed. There was nothing she wouldn't do for these people. Nothing.

Except this.

Trembling, she stood in the doorway and watched Fletcher and Alex ride away. When she turned back inside and closed the door behind her, the world around her seemed terribly small and very, very lonely.

Chapter Eleven

The next day was surprisingly warm and sunny after the early morning chill and mist had burned away, and Fletcher took advantage of it.

Standing beneath the branches of a grand old rowan tree, he groomed his horse. Before long, his thoughts began to wander and he placed his left arm on the gelding's broad back, his chin resting against the back of his arm, while the hand holding the brush lay idle a few inches away. He stared over the gelding's back, his gaze going beyond the paddock to rest on the line of trees that rode the hills in the distance. After spending considerable time thinking about Cathleen, his mind had wandered some five Scottish miles away to Glengarry Castle.

"Apparently horses aren't the only animals that sleep standing up."

The gelding snorted and sidestepped. Fletcher jumped, whipping his head around, a startled expression on his face as he saw Cathleen, who looked mighty bonny in a fetching color of blue violet.

"Are you going to brush your horse, or are you going to think about it all day?" she asked, giving him a smile whose bittersweetness tore through him.

Putting the brush down on the fence, he turned from the gelding, giving him a slap on the rump to move him out of the way, then crossed the paddock to where Cathleen stood on the other side of the fence. "I guess my mind wasn't on what I was doing."

She looked away. "It didn't look like it was on much of anything."

He was suddenly struck by how very alone she seemed, how isolated in her solitary dignity. At the sight of her wrapped in her wounded pride, he felt the stirring of his blood that always drew him to her. He stepped closer, standing just on the other side of the fence from her, close enough that he could touch her. "I was cogitating," he said at last, realizing the lunacy of his thoughts.

Her eyes told him that she too had been reflecting upon the things that had happened yesterday, but her voice remained detached—yet with an element of something else, which he could not identify. "Do you always think standing on one foot with your eyes closed?" she asked. "What were you thinking about?"

"I was thinking about last night."

"Don't," she said, and he was aware that what he had been hearing in her voice was shame. "There are no answers, and to search for them would only leave you more confused."

"And if I insisted?" he asked.

There was a silence, made more profound by the knowledge of what had happened, the unexplained reasons why.

He broke the silence. "And if I insisted we talk about it, Cathleen? What then?"

She closed her eyes, as if she could shut away what she was thinking. It must have worked, for when she opened them, Fletcher saw that her eyes were clear, showing no hint of what she was feeling inside, but even so, her eyes brimmed with tears, although he knew she would not allow herself to cry. "I would leave."

He did not push it, but in the look that passed between them, he realized that she was aware that something had changed between them. *She will tell me. It may not be today, or even tomorrow, but it will happen. There will come a time when she will tell me what I want to know.*

Confident in this newfound knowledge, he changed the subject. "I've been thinking of a way to get into Glengarry Castle."

If Cathleen was surprised by his shift in topic, she did not let on, but the look she gave him was one of displeasure. "Forget those kinds of thoughts," she said. "If there is anything Adair Ramsay is known for, it is having plenty of his men about. The place is heavily guarded. It wouldna be a good idea to try to get inside."

"I agree . . . at least for the time being," Fletcher said; then, seeing the expression on her face, he asked, "Does that surprise you?"

"Aye. We rarely agree on anything."

He chuckled. "Maybe this is a sign that I'm mellowing."

She studied his face for a moment before she spoke. "I ken there is another reason."

He gave her a smile that said she was right. "All right. I'm not ready to let Adair know what I'm up to."

"You think he doesn't know you are here?"

"Oh, he knows all right, but I'm hoping he does not know why."

"Humph! Suspicion is a dog that bites without a cause. It is the companion of mean souls, and Adair has a verra mean soul."

"Well, I'm *hoping* he doesn't know. He may have his suspicions, but until I act, he has no proof."

"Between suspicion and proof falls the shadow, calmly licking its chops."

He raised his brows. " 'Licking its chops'? Now you surprise me. I would have thought the granddaughter of a good and faithful minister would have said, *'God stands in the shadow, watching over his sheep'.*"

"Aye, He is there, but it has been my experience that man is like a bee that finds itself trapped inside the house. It dashes itself against the windowpane again and again, but God is less merciful than man. He never opens the window."

Fletcher felt a great sadness coming over him. Was there no optimism, no hope in her? Had her past reached out with long groping fingers to control her future? Never had he met anyone so accepting of such a bleak outlook, but then why should she not? She was a woman who had never known the comforting guidance of a loving mother, the feel of Brussels lace at her throat, the soft whispers of an ardent lover.

Her life had been as harsh and bleak as the windswept moors. In spite of that, he could not leave things the way they were. "Perhaps that is because He knows there is an open window nearby," he said.

"All my windows are closed," she said. "They always have been."

Without another word she turned away from the paddock and began walking back toward the house.

Climbing through the fence, Fletcher followed her.

Somehow he felt responsible for the loss of harmony between them, and that made him feel a certain accountability, as if it were up to him to lighten her spirits.

"Cathleen, wait up!"

"I don't need your good-humored efforts," she said, not breaking stride. "Leave me be."

He came loping up beside her. "I'm afraid my motives are more selfish than that. Will you give me a moment of your time?"

She stopped and breathed a deep sigh, as if his request were a tremendous burden to her. "What is it?"

Fletcher paused for a moment. He knew he had to make this good, for he would get this one chance and one chance only. "Have you ever seen the cemetery at Glengarry Castle?"

She gave him a suspicious eye, but answered his question readily enough. "Aye, but only to pass by."

"Is it in a place I could get to easily—without being spotted?"

"It's behind the chapel, set off from the castle by a grove of birch trees."

"Well hidden?"

"Relatively so. Are you going there?"

"I am considering it."

"I'll come with you!" she said, excitement in her voice.

Now he had done it. Now things were not going as he had planned. True, he had her mind off the painful past and bleak future, and onto the curious present, but he could not allow her to come with him. But that, he knew, would spoil her mood again.

Frustrated, he ran his fingers through his hair, considering the options. Then he realized that no matter what, he could not risk taking her along. "No," he said, seeing the expected disappointment in her eyes. "You have enough to keep you busy here."

"But I could show you where it is. Otherwise you could be searching for hours."

"I will find it. I cannot involve you in this, Cathleen."

She gave him a look he had never seen before, and her voice was undeniably soft as she said, "I ken I am already involved. More than you know."

Before he could reply, she quickened her pace and turned down the footpath to the garden, where the fawn—the one she had found in the gorse bushes on the moor, lying beside its dead mother—was sticking its head through the fence, its soft muzzle working frantically as it tried to get a bite of something more tasty than grass.

She had her bright hair tied up with a ribbon that he had not noticed before, due to the deep purple color that was difficult to see against the glossy darkness of her hair. The sight of that ribbon reminded him of how few treasures there really were in her life.

He watched her go to the fawn, which, seeing her, turned and trotted to her. Hugging it, she dropped down in the grass and the fawn lay down beside her in a limp heap of warmth, laying its head in her lap like a baby.

He was fascinated as he always was when he saw her with her creatures. He felt his heat soften as the fawn began to nuzzle at the folds of her skirts, butting its head with soft impatience. Cathleen reached down to pet its head, as if knowing the fawn was asking for it, and presently the animal lifted its head and looked around.

She had a way of communicating with wild things, like no one he had ever seen. As he stood watching her with her fawn named Bathsheba, he could not help wondering if this wasn't what God really had in mind when He created the animals and gave man dominion over them.

He saw Cathleen lean down and speak softly, in a language only the two of them understood. The fawn turned its head, then lay it in her lap again, and she, placing her cheek against the silky softness of its head.

What would it be like to have her turn to him for comfort like that?

Cathleen stood at the kitchen window, watching Fletcher ride off, knowing just where he was headed. She dried the last cup and put it away before removing her apron and hanging it on the hook by the door.

She went into the parlor, where she thought her grandfather was working on the Psalms, intending to tell him she was going visiting. She found him in his favorite chair by the fire, fast asleep. Leaving him a note, which she placed in his lap so he would not miss it, she went to her room to change into her brown dress.

Next, she made her way to the paddock where her fat little pony, Flora, stood munching a measure of oats. It was not much later that she was trotting down the lane in the direction Fletcher had taken.

When she came to a fork in the road, she took the less traveled one, cutting across an old stone bridge and riding by the mirrored waters of the loch. It was a shortcut that she hoped would put her at Glengarry Castle at about the same time as Fletcher.

Soon Glengarry Castle rose up out of the mists before her, a grim reminder of a bitter past of wars and betrayal. The heavy dark roof seemed to frown at her. The scraping of stout oak branches against the stone stronghold sent chills up and down her back. A breeze stirred the trees and sent the iron gate creaking. Cathleen shuddered and urged her pony forward, taking note as she passed of the lamps burning dim in the library windows.

And all about her, the darkness gathered, seeming eager to press in. Keeping to the trees, she took a long, raw, uneasy breath, circling the great gray stone fortress, riding around to the back where the cemetery lay near the chapel.

Riding over gravel paths and dew-sparkled grassy slopes, she passed the place where Fletcher had left his horse and kept on going, leaving her pony some distance from Fletcher's gelding, since she did not want the two to start nickering at each other and attract attention.

Several minutes later she was slipping through the birch trees behind the chapel. When she reached the clearing where she could see the ancient grave markers rising out of the ground, she paused, looking around her to make certain none of Adair Ramsay's men were about.

In the dimness, she searched the area for some sign of Fletcher. Seeing nothing, she could not help wondering if she had somehow gotten ahead of him. Feeling a little uneasy about being here, she made her way forward, going through the iron gate, thankful it did not creak, and spotted the guelder roses that grew along the fence.

Moving among the lichen-covered tombstones, her gaze took in the inscriptions, the late afternoon sun casting long, eerie shadows ahead of her.

She could not understand her apprehension. There was nothing to fear here. The dead were quite safe—safer, really, to be around than the living, but still there was an anxiety within her that she could not ignore.

Once, she thought she heard something and ducked down in the shadowy darkness behind a large stone where an angel peacefully spread its wings. As she waited, her fingers trembled as they traced over the inscription:

*Elizabeth Ramsay, beloved daughter, who departed
this world June 20, 1757, age three*

In a flood of fluttering pulse and flushed heat, she sensed another presence, but she saw nothing. Her fear surrounded her, paralyzing her. She seemed unable to move from this spot. Her hand came up to brush her forehead. She heard another noise, this time making it out to be footfalls, and wondered what she would say to the Duke of Glengarry's men if she was caught.

She heard another noise, this time closer. Her heart pounded and her throat grew too dry to swallow. She sensed movement behind her, and then someone stumbled against her, knocked her over, and fell on top of her. Then he cursed.

She blinked and looked up into angry blue eyes. She was not certain if she was more surprised by hearing such language or by seeing a man lying on top of her.

"What in the hell are you doing here?" a voice whispered.

Fletcher! She went limp with relief.

He shook her. "Don't you dare faint!" he said in a louder whisper.

She opened her eyes, barely making out his furious features scowling down at her. "I never faint," she whispered, "but this may be the first time—if you don't get off. You are crushing the breath from me."

Fletcher rolled off of her. "I'd like to crush some sense into that head of yours. That's what I'd like to do. Don't you have any sense, Cathleen? What if we are caught? How will you explain your involvement? Why did you follow me here?"

"I didn't follow you."

"What the hell is that supposed to mean?"

"Since I was here first, I'd say it was you who followed me."

"Don't be clever. You don't have a reason on God's green earth for being here."

"And you don't have a reason for swearing."

"All right. I won't swear and you won't lie. What are you doing here?"

"Shhhh! Don't talk so loud. I came to help you," she whispered softly.

"I don't want your help," he almost shouted.

"Well, you don't have to get spiteful about it," she said,

feeling a bit persecuted. After all, she was only trying to help. Was he too beef-witted to comprehend that?

He sighed. "I'm sorry. It's just that I would never forgive myself if anything happened to you. This isn't your fight. I don't want you suffering the consequences of what I'm about."

"I don't know how you can say it isn't *my* fight," she whispered hotly. "Not after all the help my grandfather and I have given you. We are involved in this up to our ears. We have helped you and given you a place to stay. If that isn't help, I don't know what is. Now, are we going to sit here like two fallen acorns, or are we going to look for what we came for?"

Fletcher looked around, then rose to his feet, taking Cathleen's hands and pulling her up to stand beside him. "You're right. We'll have to hurry. It will be dark soon ... too dark to read the inscriptions."

She took a step, tripped, and fell.

He dropped down in a crouch beside her. "Are you all right, Cathleen?"

"Aye."

"Well, that makes two falls. Perhaps you should just stay down and wait for me here. I'll search the graves and then come back for you."

"'*A just man falleth seven times and riseth up again,*'" she said, taking his hand and rising to her feet. "Proverbs."

He grunted, then turned away and began walking in front of the scattered gravestones. "Try to stay down," he said, "but not *all* the way down."

"Aye," she replied, looking at two more gravestones. Then it suddenly occurred to her to ask, "What are we looking for?"

"Hell's bells! You mean you came all the way over here, endangering your life, and you don't even know why you're here?"

She stopped, clamping her hands on her hips, looking remarkably like a sugar bowl. "Well, I couldn't very well ask you *before* I came, now could I?"

He looked heavenward and mumbled something about the

children of Israel getting manna, and look what he got. He looked around him, then said, "Bride."

She hit the ground, lying flat behind a gravestone. She could hear someone approaching. She closed her eyes and prayed.

"What are you doing?"

At the sound of Fletcher's voice, she opened her eyes. Looking up at the vicinity of the voice, she said simply, "I am hiding."

He peered over the top of the gravestone. "Would it be too much to ask why?"

She noticed he was standing up, in full view, so she scrambled to her feet. "Because you told me to," she said, dusting dirt and bits of twigs from her skirts.

"I did not tell you to hide."

"Yes, you did. I heard you. You said, "Hide.""

He sighed. "I said *Bride*. It's the name we are looking for. Bride," he repeated, "as in Bride Ramsay."

"Oh."

He didn't say anything more, but he mumbled under his breath again as he turned around and began reading gravestones.

Without speaking to him, Cathleen turned in the opposite direction and began reading the inscriptions on her side, having mentally divided the cemetery in half. When she had finished all the gravestones on her side, she turned to him. "Find anything?"

"No. Nothing."

Just at that moment, she heard voices.

Fletcher must have heard them too, for he said, "Damn!"

She gave him a chastening look, then whispered, "Do you think they've seen us?"

"I don't know, but I don't intend to wait around and find out. Come on!" He grabbed her by the arm and they ran toward the small stone chapel.

Finding the side door unlocked, he pushed it open and shoved her inside. He followed her in and pulled the door shut behind them.

The interior was quite dark, with only a few weak beams

of diffused light penetrating the darkness through two tall, narrow windows.

The voices were closer now.

He took her arm and hauled her along to the front of the chapel, their feet scuffling over the stone floor until they ducked down behind an ancient stone font.

The large door at the back of the chapel creaked open, and a beam of light shot into the room, striking the medieval effigy of St. Helen. Yellow shafts of light appeared on each side of them. Fletcher leaned over Cathleen, pushing her down farther and making it almost impossible for her to breathe.

"See anything?" asked a deep baritone voice.

"There is no one in here," replied another voice, much lighter in tone. "Are you certain you saw someone?"

"I ken I saw two people walking through the cemetery."

"Maybe it was just shadows you saw."

"No, I am certain it was two people."

"Maybe it was poachers, or some of the village children taking a shortcut home."

"Maybe."

The door creaked again. The light grew dim, then disappeared.

Cathleen pushed at him. "Get up," she whispered. "This is getting to be a habit."

"Not yet," he said.

"Why? Do you see something?"

"No, but I feel something . . . and it feels mighty good."

"Get up, you lecher! We've work to do."

"Maybe I've decided I like being here, on top of you," he whispered, nuzzling her throat.

"If this is your idea of being romantic, I . . ."

"Shhhhh," Fletcher said, clamping his hand over her mouth.

Suddenly the door creaked open and the light reappeared.

"See anything this time?" asked the baritone voice.

"No. Nothing."

"Weel, let's get out of here, then. This place gives me the shudders after dark."

The door closed, and again the chapel was left in darkness.

Fletcher made a move to get up, but now Cathleen clutched at him. "You aren't going to get up now, are you?" she whispered.

She knew he was grinning at her, although she could not see it, when he said, "Are you trying to tell me that you like me here?"

"No, but they might come back."

"They won't be back."

She dug her fingers into his arm. "Are you certain?"

He chuckled. "I'm certain, but if it's a reason to keep me on top of you that you're looking for, you've only to say so. I'm an accommodating man, Cathleen."

She gave him a shove. He rolled off her and lay there for a moment, chuckling softly in the darkness.

She shot to her feet, then nudged him with her foot. "Stop gloating and get up. I want to get out of here."

"For a lass who was raised in the church, you seem mighty uncomfortable in one."

"I attended church," she said. "I didna live in one. Are you coming or not?"

His voice was soft, lazy. "Maybe. Maybe not. Why is it that you are so anxious to leave *with* me? You didn't mind coming here all by yourself."

"That's different."

"What's different about it?" He rolled to his feet.

"It wasn't dark then," she whispered, scooting closer to him.

"Why, Mary Cathleen, are you afraid of the dark?"

"Only a wee bit." But she took his hand and did not let go of it until they were outside.

They ran until they were almost at the gates, then they waited in the bushes until they were certain no one watched. Making a dash for it, they ran through the gates, keeping low to avoid the pale oval of light cast by the lamps. Once they were away from there, the night seemed to fall into absolute darkness, only the ghostly outline of the trees visible, black against black.

"Where is your horse?"

"Just a little way past yours."

He drew up short. "Just a little way past mine? I thought you said you got here before me. Cathleen, I call that lying."

"It is not lying," she said matter-of-factly. "I said I was here before you. I didna say I was here before your horse."

He grunted, as if he was trying to figure out the logic of that. She smiled to herself. That would keep him busy for a while.

A sudden flutter of wings overhead made her jump. She reached for him, touching his sleeve, then inching downward, until she touched his hand. An unexpected, penetrating throb of pleasure flowed through her.

Slipping her hand firmly into his, she scooted closer, listening to the rising wind as it whistled through the lofty spires of pine trees. They walked on in silence until they reached the place where she had left her pony.

But Flora wasn't there.

Cathleen turned in a circle, her eyes scanning the line of trees and searching the darkness, certain that this was the place she had left Flora. "I left her right here."

"Are you certain this is the place?"

"Aye. This is the branch I tied her to," she said, pointing at a thick, jutting branch.

"You probably didn't tie her well enough."

She glanced around, taking his hand again and holding it tightly. "I think they have taken her."

"I don't want to hurt your feelings, Cathleen, but you couldn't pay someone enough to take that horse."

She went rigid. "Flora is a perfectly serviceable beast."

Fletcher leaned close to her ear. "Flora is an overweight nag."

"She got me here."

"Yes, but she won't get you back. Now the question is, how will you get home?"

"I can walk, thank you."

"Not while I'm around," he said, and before she could protest, he gently lifted her into his arms.

"What are you doing?"

"I'm taking you home."

"You're going to carry me?"

"Only to my horse."

She felt a twinge of disappointment. "I can walk."

"I know," he whispered in her ear, "but I like it this way and I'm bigger than you."

"Is that the only reason?"

"No . . . but the truth might send you into a swoon, or at least scampering back to your cottage—afoot."

They reached his horse and he lowered her to her feet, but he did not release her. Even in the darkness she could see that he stared down at her, and there was something in his look that caused her heart to race with breathless intensity.

It was as if he allowed his gaze to do the things to her that he dared not. Her lips felt strangely swollen, as if they would no longer stay closed. Parting them slightly, she felt a subtle pressure, cool and dry, against them, but all she had time to do was gasp before it was gone.

"Cathleen," he said softly, "my quaint little virgin. Don't you know I did not come here to hurt you?" Slowly, slowly, he pressed light, lazy kisses around her face before his lips came to rest upon hers.

Feeling as if she were floating out of her body, she dug her fingers into his arms to anchor herself to the ground. He pressed closer, and she was trapped between him and the warm shoulder of his gelding.

"Don't."

"What's the matter? Don't you like being with me?"

"I like being with you," she said in a shaky voice, "but I don't want to like it. I would never let you take such liberties, you know, if I were not afraid of the dark."

As far as answers went, that one must have surprised him, for she heard what she could only call a delighted laugh.

Cathleen's reaction was a strong one of guilt and self-disgust. She had sworn to be strong enough to resist his lure, but she had failed. It was a weakness within her, a powerlessness she tried to overcome but couldn't whenever they were together.

Something twisted in her chest and she found herself regretting her past—a past that had changed the course of her life, that made her future barren. She felt torn between the way history had formed her and the natural urges of a woman her age, a woman with all the normal feelings for a man to love and be loved by, to marry, to mate.

But her old fear of having a child remained. She had prayed many times to be barren, because only then could she have what she wanted—the love of a man, without the fear of having children. But even as she thought it, she knew that was not the answer. A man like Fletcher deserved more than a barren wife. He deserved a woman with gentility, the daughter of an earl or a duke. A lady. One who would gladly bear his children. She was none of these.

Overcome with emotion, she put her arms around his neck and buried her face in the warm cove of his shoulder, as if by hiding she could hold back the pain and the tears that threatened.

Misunderstanding her actions, Fletcher hugged her to him and kissed the top of her head. "That's better," he said.

Aye, that was better. She was in his arms, something that should have made her happy, and it did. But it also brought an element of pain, for she knew that the happiness now would be part of the sadness later. Fearing she could not hold back her tears any longer, she ground her nose against his neck and closed her eyes tightly.

"Keep that up and we might not make it home."

Fletcher, Fletcher, you are such a charmer, such a dear. How I wish things could have been different. . . .

He gave her a boost onto his horse, then he mounted in front of her.

"Hold on tight," he said, and she put her arms around him, laying her cheek against the powerful muscles of his back. He was formal once more, acting as if nothing had happened between them. She squeezed her eyes shut, a devastating loneliness growing inside of her. She had what she wanted. He had released her. He was leaving her alone. She had come out the victor.

Why was her success so bitter?

For a time, his cause had become her cause, but only for

a time. Soon he would finish his work here, and he would leave, and then it would be as before, with her and her grandfather working on their translations and forgetting all about the time when a man named Fletcher Ramsay was part of their lives.

Chapter Twelve

The afternoon was almost gone by the time Fletcher returned to the crofter's hut after spending the day in Glengarry. He had arrived in town feeling guardedly optimistic, hoping to find something—Bible records, old deeds—anything that might give him a clue as to where to look next. He returned home feeling frustrated and angry, as if his inability to find the proof he needed were an insult to the memory of his father.

After all, he had taken a vow the day that he had stood beside his father's grave, listening to the words of comfort David MacDonald offered those present at the duke's funeral. Fletcher hadn't listened, however, for even then, at the age of eight, he somehow knew that there would never be any peace for him until he restored his father's honorable name.

The frustration he felt now did not lie so much in his inability to find the proof he needed—for he knew that he would find it—but more in the fact that for twenty long years he had erroneously thought that the proving of it would be relatively easy.

Now he realized what a task he had set for himself.

As he rode toward the paddock, he was thankful not to see Cathleen or David. In his present state of mind, he wouldn't be the best of company.

As he unsaddled his horse, he thought about Cathleen and how odd it was that he had spent half of his life torn between two decisions: to return to Scotland to prove Adair a fraud, or to give his mother what she wanted most, by staying in California, and now he was once again faced with two decisions. While his obsession for proving Adair to be a murderer and a liar had not waned, his goal was now tempered somewhat by his desire for a certain fire-haired lass named Cathleen. The two goals were infinitely different, infinitely desirable, infinitely in conflict with each other.

It wasn't Cathleen that was causing his frustration, nor was it his obsession with taking back his title. It was his inability to give of himself completely to one or the other. He felt like a man trying to ride two horses at the same time.

Still thinking about his dilemma, he gave the gelding a measure of oats, then closed the paddock gate. A few minutes later, he walked into the crofter's hut, only to find a surprise waiting for him. Someone had been there.

As soon as he opened the door, he saw the chaos. Canisters of coffee and sugar had been dumped across the floor, making a gritty sound beneath his feet as he walked in. A jar of honey left a glossy trail across the top of Cathleen's tablecloth, then dripped into a puddle on the floor. The kitchen chairs had been overturned, while the chairs next to the fireplace had the stuffings ripped out. Pictures had been knocked off the wall, his trunk overturned, its contents scattered about.

In the bedroom, the down that had filled his mattress was spread across the room, leaving a dull grayish cast over everything. At the foot of the bed, his chest had been thrown over, its contents littering the floor.

Seeing his letter box, he opened the lid. The letters from his mother as well as the two papers he had found in the trunk with Douglas and Bride Ramsay's names on them were gone.

"Son of a bitch!" he shouted, kicking a chair across the room. Anger, white-hot and raging, seemed to explode inside his head. He kicked a boot out of the way, then picked up an armful of clothes and, unable to find a place to put them, threw them back on the floor.

Never could he remember being so angry or feeling so helpless. He felt violated, wronged, and angry enough to kill. His first reaction was to go to Glengarry and scc this thing out between himself and Adair. He wanted to finish what had started twenty years before. Cursing, he left the crofter's hut, not bothering to close the door, and headed for the paddock.

By the time he bridled his horse, his anger had cooled down a little—enough to make him realize the consequences of what he was about to do.

That was exactly the kind of thing Adair wanted him to do. Whatever happened, whatever approach he decided to take, Fletcher realized he must learn control. Rash, hot-headed anger would never accomplish his goal. Only clear, concise, rational thinking would do that.

He returned to the crofter's hut, now knowing that Adair was not only aware of his presence in Glengarry but knew the reason why he had come.

He stayed up until four in the morning, putting the crofter's hut in order, knowing that if he did not, Cathleen would add it to her endless list of benevolent responsibilities.

When he finished, he crawled wearily into bed, glad he had finished the task. There were many things Cathleen needed, but more work was not among them.

A few days later, David and Fletcher sat at the dining table long after Cathleen had cleared away the dinner dishes. They were discussing the ransacking of their two cottages.

"You know, in a way I'm almost glad it's out in the open," Fletcher said. "If Adair is sending his men to search our houses, it's proof that he is getting nervous."

"You say that like it pleases you."

"In a way it does," Fletcher said. "Nervous people make mistakes."

"How far do you intend to go with this? Will you be content to simply get your title back, or is revenge written upon your heart?"

"My mother tried to talk me out of killing Adair a long time ago."

"And did she?"

"Perhaps." Fletcher paused. "At times I feel she did, but then something like this happens and I find myself wondering. I cannot lie and say I have not thought about putting my hands around Adair Ramsay's scrawny neck and choking the life from him."

"There are other ways to seek revenge besides murder . . . none of them wise."

"I know, and I am probably guilty of them all. For as long as I can remember I've lived with the idea of returning to Scotland to set things to right between Adair and myself. If that means his death, so be it."

"And that doesna bother you?"

Fletcher shrugged. "It bothers me, although I sometimes think it does so only because it bothered my mother so much. She was fond of reminding me, *'The prayers of the righteous availeth much.'*"

"She was right, you know."

A smile flickered across Fletcher's face, then faded, the memory of Maggie strong within him. "My mother is a woman of strong faith and many quotes. I have had them hammered into me since I was in nappies. I grew to manhood with her quoting, *'Vengeance is mine sayeth the Lord.'*"

"But it didna change your mind?"

"No, I cannot say that it has—but who knows? Perhaps her sermons have greatly watered down my thirst for revenge, without my really knowing it. *She* was confident that it would."

David laughed at that, his face alight with recollection. "Aye, Maggie would be. *'Raise a child up in the way that he should go, and when he is old, he will not depart from it.'* That would be her guide and her assurance."

Fletcher frowned. "Yes, but it is not necessarily mine," he said, speaking with much passion. "Adair's death may not be foremost in my mind, but I have not wavered in my desire to regain what rightfully belongs to me. Like Esau, I have been cheated out of my birthright."

David's dry smile made Fletcher think he had not missed the impassioned tone in his voice. "Weel, perhaps like Job, whatever has been taken from you will be returned threefold."

Fletcher grinned, seeing why David was such a good minister. "I could live with that," he said. "I surely could."

They lapsed into silence.

Since the rifling of his crofter's hut, Fletcher had realized he needed to move on, to look for his proof in other places. He knew that he could not, in all conscience, involve David and Cathleen in his search any longer, for to do so would be to endanger their lives. Secondly, Glengarry seemed to be a dead end for him.

David offered him more tea, but he shook his head and said, "No, thanks. I'm not in a tea-drinking mood tonight. Now, if you had some good double-malt Scots whisky ..."

"Something is bothering you," David said. "Would it help to talk about it?"

Fletcher had never been one to hedge, so he blurted out, "I'll be leaving here in a few days."

David put down his teacup, his face registering surprise. "You are going back to Caithness?"

"I was, but I've had a slight change of plans."

David said nothing.

Fletcher went on talking. "I've been thinking it might be worth my while to go the Lowlands—to where Adair Ramsay lived before coming to Glengarry."

"There is a reason for that, I am certain, although it escapes me."

"If I cannot prove my lineage, then perhaps I can find some way to disprove his."

"And where will you be going?"

"To St. Abb's."

David's face registered surprise. "St. Abb's ... that's a stone's throw from Abbey St. Bathan's."

Fletcher knew that David was getting at something. "Abbey St. Bathan's? I have not heard the name before. Is there some reason you think I should go there?"

"No ... at least no reason that I know of. I just found it coincidental."

"You found what to be coincidental?"

"That St. Abb's is so close to Abbey St. Bathan's." As if seeing that this made no sense to Fletcher, David said, "I could save you a trip."

"How? By talking me out of going?"

"No, by going for you."

"I would not allow that."

"Not even if I was going anyway?"

Fletcher could not hide his surprise. "You are going to St. Abb's?"

"Well, not St. Abb's exactly, but I am going to Abbey St. Bathan's two days hence. It would be easy enough for me to make the short jaunt over to St. Abb's. It is a small enough place. Whatever records that exist there would not take long to check out."

Fletcher gave him a skeptical look, but a hint of humor laced his voice as he asked, "And when did you plan this trip to Abbey St. Bathan's? Five minutes ago?"

David laughed. "No, I have been corresponding with James Buchanan, a minister who lives near Abbey St. Bathan's. It seems he has some old papers, copies of songs . . . hymns in French, many of them adaptations of the Psalms. From what he says in his letters, he believes them to have been brought over by some of William the Conqueror's men. I just received a letter from him yesterday, inviting me to visit him so that I might view the papers firsthand."

Fletcher knew he could not even consider David's offer. Adair's decision to violate the crofter's hut on David MacDonald's property had put things in a new light. He would not allow anything to pose a further threat.

"Well, what have you decided? Will you trust this mission to me or no?"

"No."

David's face registered surprise. "But why?"

"When I made up my mind to leave here, I decided not to involve you further."

"Because of what happened to your place?"

Fletcher nodded. "And for good reason, I might add."

"I understand your concern and I thank you for putting

our safety first, but I don't think my going to St. Abb's has much bearing on the matter. I am going to Abbey St. Bathan's on business, regardless of what you decide to do. Who is to know if I stop by St. Abb's on my way back?"

"What about Cathleen?"

"Cathleen has stayed alone before."

"But not when your property has been ransacked. In view of the situation as it now stands, I don't think that would be wise."

"Perhaps you have a point." David was silent for a moment. "Considering what you just said, I think the best plan would be for you to stay here. Would you consider it a fair exchange—if I went to St. Abb's for you, while you remain here until I return? That way, you can keep an eye on Cathleen."

Fletcher grinned at him. "You mean to sit there and tell me that you trust *me*, here alone with Cathleen?"

"No, but I trust Cathleen. Besides, I didna offer you the use of our house. You will remain in the crofter's hut . . . a safe, respectable distance away."

"You are certain you want to do this? I mean, if you go to St. Abb's, you will be involving yourself."

"Laddie, I am up to my hipbones in this affair already, and by my own choosing, I might add. Now that I have confirmation that you don't intend to do Adair bodily harm, I have no ill conscience about helping you set things right. What say you?"

"I don't know. A few days ago I would have jumped at the chance, but now, in view of what has happened . . . You will have to agree that I have cause for worry. I came here to bring a situation to rightstanding. I don't want to bring about more problems."

"You have not caused any difficulties for us, Fletcher. In fact, your presence here has been a nice diversion in our staid existence. There is not much excitement in the lives of a retired minister and a spinster, you know."

Hearing David refer to Cathleen as a spinster took Fletcher by surprise. Although he knew that she did not intend to marry, he had never believed it as absolute fact. He was so shaken by what David had said that he could not reply.

"Then it is agreed. You will stay here with Cathleen, and I will go to Abbey St. Bathan's and then to St. Abb's—and somewhere in between I plan to do a little salmon fishing."

"Keep talking like that and I'll be tempted to go to Abbey St. Bathan's for you."

"I would turn you down in a minute. I have been looking forward to taking a fishing trip for some time."

"And you don't think Cathleen will mind your leaving her here alone with me?"

"Cathleen has stayed by herself before. I learned a long time ago that I couldna drag her away from her generosity to Glengarry's humanity. The lass has too many causes. You could sooner wrest a rabbit from the jaws of a wolf than you could pluck her from the midst of her commitments. As for you, I would say the lass likes you well enough to tolerate you for a week or so."

"When did you say you were leaving?"

"In two days' time. Are we agreed, then? You will stay here while I go to St. Abb's?"

Fletcher stood. "Yes, although I still have some reservations," he said, walking toward the door.

"Dinna fret about it," David said, opening the door for him. "I am glad that is settled." He clapped Fletcher on the back. "Now I'll see what bonny Cathleen has to say when I tell her that I am leaving."

"And that I am staying on a bit longer."

"Aye, that too."

Fletcher smiled. "She might not be too receptive to my staying on here as her guard dog, so for that reason I'm glad it is you that will be telling her."

"Aye," David said, looking as grim as a severed head. "I ken she willna be all too happy about it, but there is nothing I can do to change that. A man can do little more than stand reproved, can he?"

The next morning dawned cool and sunny, as perfect a Sunday morning as Fletcher had ever seen, but it wasn't perfect enough to make him accept David's offer to ride into Glengarry to attend St. Andrew's Church with him and Cathleen.

Reminding David that he had told him at their first meeting that he was a sinner, Fletcher saddled his horse and rode out to inspect a few old graves that he had heard lay near the ruins of an ancient castle—graves that proved to be of no value, since none of them bore the name Ramsay.

It was late afternoon when he arrived back at the crofter's hut, feeling his usual reaction of disappointment and frustration, only this time he also felt bewildered. He didn't know what to do next.

Fletcher wasn't ready to give up by any means, for he was as strongly dedicated to the task as ever, but he was feeling mighty irritable over the fact that he had not found even one shred of proof.

He dismounted, and had just put his horse in the paddock behind the house, when he met David coming down the path.

"How was church this morning? Did Robert stick to traditional Presbyterian theology, or did he hit you with a few surprises?"

"No surprises at church," David replied, "but we had one when we got home."

"Oh?"

"Seems we had a visitor while we were gone."

Fletcher's expression was grim. "Your house was searched?"

"Aye, searched, and wrecked this time. Cathleen is trying to put things in order now."

"The trunks?"

"Still there, but all the papers are gone. They burned the lot of them in the fireplace."

Fletcher tried to suppress his anger in front of David, but it was damn hard. He wanted to throw back his head and curse Adair Ramsay for the bastard he was. Well he knew that Adair was doing everything he could to draw him out into the open, to force his hand. He was like a fly that won't give up, and sooner or later Fletcher would have to take a swat.

However, this understanding did not make it any easier to

accept. "I'm sorry," he said with sincerity. "Was anything of yours destroyed?"

"No, nothing destroyed. Things were just tumbled."

Fletcher frowned. "This changes things, you know. I cannot in all consciousness allow you to go to St. Abb's for me now—not after what has happened."

"I suspected you would feel that way, and I have been thinking about it," David said. "I think I've come up with the perfect solution."

Fletcher crossed his arms. "Which is . . .?"

"We cannot alter our very lives out of fright. The Bible teaches us to 'fear not.' I ken it would be a good plan for me to go to Abbey St. Bathan's as planned, only instead of staying here in the crofter's hut to keep an eye on Cathleen, I think it best if you would return to Caithness."

Fletcher was astounded. "*What*? Leave her here, alone and unprotected?"

"Hear me out. If Adair is doing these things to use your concern for us as a way to force you to stop, then what better way to make him think that you have given up? If you have returned to Caithness, he will think you have given up your search—at least as far as Glengarry goes. Our lives will then return to normal and things will be as before. With you gone, Adair will have no reason to suspect us. I will go on my trip as planned, and Cathleen will remain here as she always does, going about her charitable work. None will be the wiser."

"I don't know."

"It is the perfect solution," David said. "I know it is."

Fletcher thought about that for a moment. Perhaps David was right. "As much as I would like to say you are wrong, I know you and Cathleen would be safer if I returned to Caithness."

"Yes, because it is the only solution. You cannot stay here and to go to the Lowlands about the same time that I go would raise suspicion. The wisest choice, then, is for you to return to Caithness Castle."

"I will agree to one thing. My remaining here would only increase Adair's interest in what I am doing."

"Aye, Adair will be watching you, I am certain. You must

take care when you leave here. They know you are here now, Fletcher, and they know why."

"I'll be careful."

Because of the condition of their cottage, Cathleen had to ignore the biblical admonishment against working on the Sabbath. The moment she and her grandfather had returned from church, she removed her bonnet and her Sunday best. Wearing her oldest dark blue dress, she tied a white apron about her waist, put her hair into a knot on top of her head, then gathered her cleaning supplies.

She was down on all fours cleaning out the ashes in the hearth—the ones left from all the burned documents—when she heard a noise behind her.

She turned and saw Fletcher coming into the room. He was alone. Her eyes dilated, and she felt herself shrinking back at the sight of his beloved presence, fearful that she might smile a bit too brightly, or that her eyes might follow him a bit too much . . . and then he would know.

"Where is my grandfather?" she asked, more to distract him than from any real curiosity.

He gave her a look that said her ploy had not worked and she found it exceedingly frustrating that he seemed to know what she was thinking.

"He said to remind you that he had been invited to dinner at the MacPhearsons'."

Distracted by her earlier thoughts, she could only stammer, "Oh . . . I—I think he told me about that . . . but I forgot."

"He thought you might, seeing as how you were quite busy when he told you."

She was sitting on her knees now, still in front of the fireplace, her gaze upon him as he walked around the room, taking in the disorder that lay about. Love-smitten and dizzy with the intensity of her feelings for him, she could only stare at him as dazed as a goose. Then a pain so intense that she almost doubled over stabbed into the heart of her, and Cathleen wondered if she would ever be able to get over her feelings for him.

True, he was a handsome devil, but it really wasn't his

looks that attracted her, nor was it his long legs, his engaging smile, the generally good nature of him, or any of a hundred other things she could readily list to describe him. In fact, she had trouble deciding just what it was about him that fascinated her so.

She sighed, in such a daze thinking about all the reasons why she felt as she did about Fletcher that she did not, at first, notice that he had picked up the broom. It wasn't until she heard the bristles sweeping against the floor that she realized it was a broom she heard, and that it had to be connected to someone.

She could not contain her gasp of surprise when she looked up and saw who it was. The sight of Fletcher sweeping absolutely astounded her. Her eyes grew large and round. Her mouth dropped open. Never had she seen a man sweep the floor. Stunned with disbelief, she could only ask, "What the devil are you doing?"

He did not miss a stroke as he went on sweeping around her grandfather's chair, making what she considered a fairly adept attempt at it. "I'm giving you a hand."

"You don't need to do that."

"I am doing it because I want to, Cathleen. I also feel responsible for what happened here."

"It wasn't your fault, and sweeping the floor is woman's work," she said, coming to her feet and dusting the ashes from her hands. "Here, let me do that." She reached for the broom, but he drew it back.

"Give me that broom!"

He grinned, moving the broom behind him. "Come and get it."

Cathleen did not miss the invitation in his voice. She tilted her head and looked at him. She could withstand anything but this humorous, boyish quality he had. She would have bet that if anyone stacked end to end the women he had felled with that charm, they would reach all the way to London and back.

"I don't intend to play games with the likes of you," she said. "Put the broom back where you found it. I refuse to allow a man to sweep my house."

He laughed heartily at that and kept on sweeping. "Don't go looking a gift horse in the mouth. You go on with cleaning your ashes, Cinderella, and I'll see to the sweeping."

"But . . ."

He stopped sweeping and leaned on the broom, and for a moment she thought she had never seen him looking as handsome as he did standing there in that blue shirt that brought out the color of his eyes. He was dressed casually in a pair of buckskins and riding boots, with his shirt open at the collar. His hair had been ruffled a bit by the wind, and she wondered what he would do if she ran her fingers through it to smooth it back in place.

"Cathleen," he said, "I don't want to hear any more. I am angry enough over what happened here to chew up nails, and if you don't let me take out my anger on this broom, then there is no other way for me to vent it, save riding over to Adair Ramsay's and calling him to task."

Cathleen understood that. "Well, why didn't you say that in the first place?" she said. Then, giving him her back, she leaned down and scooped up the last of the ashes and dumped them into the hopper, her mind not on what she was doing but on Fletcher.

Here he was, showing her yet another side of himself. *Just how many sides are there?*

Never in her wildest imaginings would she have thought he even knew which end of a broom to pick up, and here he was sweeping. Everything about him was so different, so dear. She could grow old with a man like that. Aye, she surely could.

She picked up the hopper full of ashes and was about to carry it outside when Fletcher said, "Here, let me take that out for you."

Cathleen was stunned. Her mouth parted with surprise as she watched him prop the broom against the wall and cross the room to where she stood. He moved with the quiet grace that she had come to associate with him.

Stopping in front of her, he looked for a moment like he was about to bend over and pick up the hopper, but something stopped him. He reached out and traced the shape of her mouth with one finger before dropping it beneath her chin and lifting it as he gave her a look that was warm enough to suck the air from her lungs.

"Close your mouth if you don't want to be kissed, sweet Cathleen."

She snapped her mouth shut but was able to do little more than that. He did not say anything, nor did he move. He simply stood there looking down at her for a time before reaching out and catching a loose tendril of hair. His hand brushed her neck, which set her heart to racing.

"Don't be afraid of me," he said. "You should know by now that I would never hurt you."

"I'm not afraid of you," she said, "but more of myself, of the way I am when I am with you."

His gaze searched her face so intently that she found herself wondering what he saw there. Did those deep blue eyes of his see into her? Did they see the feeling she had for him, the fabrications her mind created of how it would be to be loved by him?

Her gaze fixed upon his mouth, she began to feel light-headed, as if her blood had suddenly grown thin and warm. How long had the memory of those lips upon hers filled her with longing and despair? And once he was gone from her life, would the memory be enough to last throughout all the years that he would not be with her?

"What are you thinking?"

Her gaze flew quickly to his and she saw a look that she could only call desire. Stirred by her feelings of love for him, she felt her heart beat as constant as a flame burning steadily in the hearth. The love that she felt for him was so consuming, so intense, that it was something physical, something like pain. Sensing that he might see that written in her eyes, she turned her face aside.

"Cathleen, look at me," he said, his words coming like a breath touching the side of her cheek.

"I can't."

"Then let's see if I can help you." He took her hands in his, brought them up to his mouth, opening her fingers one by one, then kissing each palm and folding the fingers back, as if by doing so she could hold the kisses there.

Running his thumbs over the sensitive skin of her inner wrists, he felt her tremble, and drew her hands up to his neck. Then he brushed his lips across the skin of her forehead, and she swayed, leaning into him. He kissed her mouth lightly before whispering, "I would love to see where this leads, but something tells me you wouldn't like that."

Releasing her, he stepped back, giving her a soft look and one full of regret. "Maybe this wasn't such a good idea. I came here to help you, but judging from the expression on your face, I see I have succeeded only in adding to your confusion."

She gave him a blank stare.

Hugging her to him, he said, "Ahhhh, Cathleen ... my bonny Cathleen ... my desire knows no rest." He released her and turned away, crossing the room quickly.

Before she could call him back, he was gone, and she was left alone, standing in the middle of the room where the air was heavy with the smell of ashes.

Chapter Thirteen

When Cathleen's grandfather told her that Fletcher would be returning to Caithness, a sadness gripped her heart. She stared at David, dull and transfixed, like a person about to be bitten by a dog, unable to do anything about it.

The feeling of loss was new to her, for never before had she given her affections to a man. Her hands curled into fists. She resented his coming. She wanted her freedom back; her freedom to go about her day in a carefree manner, not lifting her eyes to stare across the room at the line of a nose or the curve of a jaw; her freedom to do her chores without pulling back a curtain to catch a glimpse of him coming up the road; her freedom to sleep at night without dreaming about what might have been.

Damn you, Fletcher Ramsay, for coming into my life, for making me care. . . .

Later that evening, after she had cleaned the house and put away the dishes from the evening meal, she went for a walk across the moors. She had not gone very far when she heard footfalls.

Someone was following her.

Cathleen paused. Her heart pounding, she wondered if it could be Adair's men behind her. She turned to confront whoever it was.

"Fletcher!" she said, releasing a nervous breath.

He was so very tall and regally slim. The bones of his face were masterfully put together, and his lightly tanned skin set off the blue of his eyes. As always when she looked at him, her blood began to flow in a heated rush. Bold as a harpie he looked, walking toward her with such confidence.

But he was leaving.

She closed her eyes, feeling a tightness in her throat. Since his coming, she had begun to see what it meant, how it felt to be really, truly alive. How could she bear the thought of his going?

He stopped. He was standing very close to her now. "Where are you going?" he asked in a mellow voice. "Were you running away from me?"

It's you who will be running away.

"No, I was just walking," she said in a hoarse whisper, forcing herself to look down at her feet, for it seemed to extract the energy and life from her to look into his face, a face that had become dearer to her than she had known before tonight.

"Then I shall walk with you."

He fell in step beside her. "Grandfather told me you are returning to Caithness."

"Yes," he said. "I can't think of any stones around here I have left unturned. If any proof ever existed here, it is gone now. Adair has covered his tracks well."

"When will you be leaving?"

"In two days' time."

"The same as Grandfather, then."

"Yes, did he not tell you that . . ."

"Aye, he told me he persuaded you to let him go to St. Abb's." She said the words in pain. It was one of the few times that she actually wanted his sympathy. She expected it.

She did not care. To have both of them leave at the same time—it was too much.

"I tried to convince him."

"I know," she said. "He can be a stubborn man when he wants to be."

"Do you mind his doing this . . . going to St. Abb's, I mean?"

"He is old, and I mind anything that takes him from me. But I cannot say his involvement in this displeases me. How could I? He is like a young puppy. This search of yours has energized him far more than my playing the Psalms ever did. I had not noticed it before, but there is a bit of the sleuth in him. I almost find myself wondering if he would have made a good barrister."

"I think he chose the right path. Spending your life as a man of God cannot be faulted."

"No, I suppose it canna."

"Will you be all right while he . . . we are gone?"

She smiled. "He has left me before, you know, and I am a grown woman, but I will miss him. It grows quite lonely here without him, and now that I have become accustomed to having the two of you around . . ."

She could not go on, for her throat felt as if it had narrowed, choking back the words she wanted to say. Feeling the burn of tears, she turned her head away, fearful that he would see how very much she had come to enjoy his company, how much she cared for him. Terror rose in her, an absolute irrational fear that he would somehow know that she had come to love him.

"Cathleen . . ." He leaned forward to kiss her, tentatively, like the fawn coming up to take food from her hand, with uncertainty as to how she would react. His lips covered hers, his long fingers slipping around her neck, his thumbs touching her jaw, caressing gently, then moving to her cheeks. A warm and delicious sensation seemed to drug her, spreading down to her loins.

She wanted to tell him that he must not kiss her, that he must let her go, but she realized that if he did as she asked, she would sink to the ground, for it was his strength that supported her, his arms that held her upright. Panic beat at her throat like the frantic wings of a trapped bird.

"Easy darling. You know I wouldn't do anything to hurt you, Cathleen. You know that. What pleasure, what joy would there be in that for me?"

His words seemed to wash over her like the melody of a song. He kissed her again and, when she thought he was finished, again. She felt as if her body were floating, weightless, anchored only by the heat that seemed to fuse their bodies together. He touched her breast then, rubbing the nipple, sending a new sensation fluttering through her. She pushed weakly against him.

He broke away. "I'm sorry. I always seem to forget myself when I am with you. You are like a drug that penetrates my skin, making me think things I should not be thinking, making me do things I know you do not want. You see? I have upset you now, when that was never my intention. Forgive me."

She wiped at her eyes with the back of her hand. "It's all right. I'm not upset about that. Truly. It's just the thought of both of you leaving at the same time."

He paused, taking her by the arms and turning her toward him. "Are you sure that's all it is?"

"Don't make this out to be more than it is," she said. "I have grown fond of you, that's all."

"Like you've grown fond of your horse?"

She gave him a watery smile. "Aye . . . like Flora."

"Well, knowing I rank right up there with an overweight nag—that is a humbling thought."

His attempt at humor left her feeling sad and shaky. His nearness. His dearness. His soon-to-be absence from her life.

It was too much. She could not think straight.

All Cathleen wanted to do was cry, which was odd, because she wasn't a woman prone to crying. She had always thought herself stronger than tears, yet she seemed prone to do nothing but shed them in Fletcher's presence.

His arms came around her and he pulled her against him, fitting their bodies together perfectly. Her only thoughts were of how good and warm and solid he felt, of how much she would miss him. He kissed her cheeks, her eyes, her forehead, her mouth, leaving a path of kisses across her skin. Her breathing became quick and shallow.

She pulled her head back to look at his face, wondering how she could ever ignore the temptation of that beautiful mouth, with its teasing words and soft kisses.

His eyes gazed at her with gentleness; eyes as blue as the sky overhead; eyes that were coaxing, promising all the things she had no right to think about.

"Dinna look at me like that," she whispered.

His sigh said it was a little late for that.

Dropping her head, she buried her face in her hands. She didn't know what to do. She was torn between her past and her desire. Her mind and her body seemed no longer capable of coexistence.

"You think too much," he said, lifting her face to his.

Before she could respond, he kissed her. At first, the touch of his mouth was no more than a whisper, stroking her mouth gently, as if learning its shape and contour, and the exact timing of her breath. He shifted his weight, drawing her more closely against him, his body pressing intimately. As she felt his body trembling against hers, fear shivered down her spine. His chest pressed against her breasts. His hips were flat against hers. His tongue stroked the inside of her mouth.

She tried to look at him but saw nothing but star-points, as if she had looked directly at the sun. He tried to kiss her again, but she put her fingers over his mouth. He sighed, then drew her against him, lowering his chin to rest upon the top of her head.

"Of all the women and all the times, I had to fall for you ... now. You complicate things, Cathleen. You surely do."

She turned her head so that it rested against his chest. For a long time she stood there savoring the sound of his words, listening to the beat of his heart.

"I'm a contradiction, aren't I? I tell you about my past and all the reasons why I will never marry, yet I melt whenever you touch me. I don't understand myself anymore. I feel like I'm floating on a block of ice that is slowly melting. I can't stay on it ... and I can't swim."

"No matter what your mind is telling you, your body wants me, Cathleen."

She looked at him, and she knew he had noticed the way her bonnet strings seemed to catch at her throat, for he traced them with his finger. She ignored that, responding to his statement instead. . . . *your body wants me, Cathleen.* "Aye, my body wants you, Fletcher Ramsay. I know it, and I can't seem to help that. My body seems to have a mind of its own. Unfortunately, my body is not capable of taking care of the rest of me."

She broke away from him. "Perhaps your returning to Caithness is best," she said. "Once you are gone, things will seem clearer to me than they do now. It will be like a burn that has been muddied by the steps of many horses, but once they are across, the sand will settle to the bottom and the water will run clear again. Right now, everything seems muddy to me, but once you are gone, things will settle down and soon I will have my old life back."

"Don't count on it," he said. "I may be harder to forget than you think." He gave her one of his charming lopsided grins, and as always, her heart melted at the sight. "Besides, I may come back."

She shook her head sadly. "No, you willna. There will be no reason for you to return." Then she turned away and started back toward the house, leaving him standing there alone in a field of heather.

The next day Fletcher was in Glengarry, having gone there a few hours earlier to leave his horse with the blacksmith. While the horse was being shod, he wandered around town. He crossed the street in front of the shoemaker's shop and encountered Annora Fraser coming into town in a smart, shiny carriage pulled by a smartly trotting horse.

"Fletcher Ramsay!" she called out. "What luck to come to Glengarry and find you."

"Hello, Annora," Fletcher said, looking at her and squinting against the sun at her back. "What brings you here on such a fine day?"

"A visit to the dressmaker's. I want to be certain I look

exceptionally lovely, just in case you decide to pay me a visit sometime."

"You always look lovely, Annora," he said, thinking that was true. She was like a doll, with perfect features—a rosy mouth and dusky cheeks, skin of the palest ivory, and hair that was so black it looked almost blue. Her dress was of a red and green plaid, trimmed in black velvet, tight-fitting to highlight an ample bosom and the kind of waist a man wanted to put his hands around. Oh, she was a beauty all right.

But she wasn't Cathleen.

She smiled, showing deep dimples and showing too how pleased she was to hear him say she looked lovely. "Really? And here I thought you had hardly noticed me."

He grinned at her, at the obvious way she had of fishing for a compliment. "Any man would notice you on his deathbed. He would have to be blind not to."

She smiled, apparently liking that comment as well. "So tell me, what are you doing here in Glengarry?"

"My mother was an old friend of David MacDonald's. She asked me to pay him a visit."

"Oh? How long have you been here?"

"Not long."

"When are you coming to Dunston to see me?"

"Whenever I can manage it. I've been quite busy of late."

"Doing what?"

"Working on some old family business. I like your rigging, by the way. Is it new?"

She drew her brows together in a way that made even that looked lovely. "Rigging?"

"Your carriage," he corrected himself, realizing she did not understand his American term.

"Oh aye, my carriage. Why, thank you, and yes, it is new, but don't think you can change the subject. When are you going to pay me a visit?"

"Whenever I can arrange the time, I guess."

"I know better than to accept something as vague as that. How about this weekend?"

"I'm afraid I can't. I'm returning to Caithness tomorrow."

Her face fell. "Oh. Well, perhaps I can pay you a visit at Caithness."

Not wanting to start that, Fletcher said, "I'll be returning to Glengarry before the month is out. Maybe I can stop by to see you when I return."

She gave him a curious look. "My, my, if you are coming back that soon, your mother must have been a *very* close friend of David MacDonald's." She paused, as if suddenly catching light of something. "Of course! How lapse of me. I had forgotten about David's little granddaughter . . . although I would not have pegged her for your type."

"That's not the reason I'll be coming back."

"Oh? What is the reason then?"

"David is tending to a little business for me in St. Abb's."

"In St. Abb's? Whatever for?"

"He is going to Abbey St. Bathan's, which isn't far from St. Abb's."

"Oh, I see. I didn't know you had business interests there."

"There are a lot of things you don't know about me, Annora," he said, feeling that he had already said far too much.

"You could always come to visit me at Dunston while David is away," she said, "and save yourself the trip back home."

"Thank you for the offer, but my aunt is getting anxious for my return. There are things I need to attend to at Caithness."

She picked up the whip. "All right," she said with a forlorn sigh and a sideways glance in his direction. "I'll concede defeat this time. I know when I'm bested."

He laughed. "Never defeated, just postponed."

"I do like the sound of that," she said. "Say you will pay me a visit when you return," she said.

"I will."

She smiled. "Now, why don't I believe that?" she asked. Then with a flick of her wrist she brought the whip down lightly on the chestnut's back and the carriage rolled on down the street.

He stood there in the street, watching her drive off, thinking that Annora Fraser was quite adept at gleaning information. He shook his head.

She was one inquisitive woman.

He crossed the street, then paused, remembering something his mother always said when chiding her children about being overly curious: "Remember what happened to Lot's wife."

Chapter Fourteen

Fletcher had been back at Caithness for two weeks when he got word that David MacDonald was dead. As soon as the messenger departed, Fletcher broke the news to Aunt Doroty.

Gripping the arms of her chair, she listened to the grim words. A moment later, Doroty came to stand before him, her hands coming out to cup his face as she looked him in the eye. "I know you will be wanting to go back and I canna prevent that. The good Lord knows that puir child will need some comforting. David was all the family she had in the world. But still, you are my family, Fletcher, and the only relative I have living in Scotland. I have grown verra fond of you, lad. It pains me overmuch to think what could happen if you go back to Glengarry."

"I will be careful, Aunt."

She gripped his cheeks, giving them a squeeze to emphasize her words. "Go with God, Fletcher Ramsay. If anything should happen to you, I don't know how I could break the news to your mama."

Fletcher left for Glengarry immediately.

The rain slowed his pace, for the roads were so deep in mud that even the horse had difficulty. After a while Fletcher left the main road and rode over high corries, before coming down again, past a stand of pines, and into an open glen where an old stone bridge spanned a narrow beck. The rain gave way to mist now, and by the time he reached Glengarry the mist was gone and the sun was shining.

Because of the slow traveling, he arrived at the village too late to go to Cathleen's, for there was scarcely enough time to make it to St. Andrew's Church to attend David's funeral.

Once he arrived, he dismounted in the churchyard and tied his horse. His gut was twisted in a dozen knots both from guilt and anticipation.

What would be Cathleen's reaction when she saw him?

Would she despise him and blame him—as he blamed himself—for David's death? Or would she be the loving, forgiving Cathleen he knew her to be?

The small church was filled with people when he entered. He stood at the back, his hat in his hands, as he listened to Robert speak words of comfort, his rich baritone giving David MacDonald the thanks and the praise he had never received in life.

Fletcher stared at the simple pine coffin, unable to see David from this distance and not really wanting to. He preferred to remember David the way he was when he saw him last. As he listened to Robert's words, Fletcher gazed around the church, searching for Cathleen, for a glimpse of her vivid wine-dark hair. Unable to spot her, his frustration and fear mounted, until he realized that the woman in the black veil sitting in the front pew would be Cathleen.

How small she looked. How broken. Without seeing her face, he knew her skin would be white, her beautiful violet eyes dull and filled with pain. He had never wished more than at that moment that it had been his body the Lowlanders' had found lying on the rocks with a broken neck. How could he tell her how he grieved, how his heart felt as if it had been ripped out, knowing that he had caused her such pain? *Cathleen ... Cathleen ... forgive me ... love me ...* his mind cried out, his chest constricted and aching, his heart heavy with grief.

He prayed for David's forgiveness then, promising to take care of Cathleen for the rest of his days. David, he thought, who had offered so much comfort in life. David, whose going left so much grief behind. David, whose death had been no accident.

They said it was an accident, of course, that something must have frightened David's horse along the wild coastline pounded by the sea where the highest cliffs on the east side of Scotland rise up more than three hundred feet. According to the young man sent by Robert Cameron to give Fletcher the news at Caithness, the reason why the carriage went over the side and crashed to the rocks below was unknown.

The only thing the man had said was, "His body was found lying peacefully in a bed of sea campion and rose root with the neck broken—a great and tragic accident."

A tragic accident ...

Fletcher almost snorted at that, for there were too many similarities between David's death and that of his father for it ever to be considered accidental. Like David, Bruce had plunged to his death, only Bruce Ramsay's broken body was not found lying peacefully in a bed of sea campion and rose root.

After the service, as the mourners began to leave the church to make their way to the cemetery for burial, Fletcher stood to one side, trying to catch Cathleen's attention, hoping for a few moments with her. He watched her accept the condolences of those around her, opening her arms to many who expressed their grief.

Unable to stay away from her any longer, he started to make his way toward her, but she was taken out a side door before he could get to her. Running as if the devil himself were after him, he tore back down the aisle to the front door, dodging people and leaping over hedges to get her before she was gone.

"Cathleen!" he shouted, catching sight of her standing beneath the bare branches of a tree that made her look even more desolate, the black of her mourning dress stark against the gray bark of the tree and the ghostly paleness of her face. She looked up, and even through the black veil he could see the ravages of grief upon her face. How pale she was, how lovely in her sorrow. How very, very beautiful she was in the elegance of woe.

He knew the moment she spotted him. His heart stilled in his chest. What if she turned away from him? His heart in his hands, he watched as she seemed to freeze, unable to say anything for a moment. She turned away and said something to a woman next to her. Then she turned around and hurried toward him. His heart pounded with relief.

"Oh, Fletcher!" she cried, as she came to him. She lifted her veil, using the back of her hand to wipe the tears away. His heart twisted.

Come to me, Cathleen, bonny Cathleen with the broken heart and sad, sad face. Come to me and let me take your grief. Lay your sweet head on my shoulder. Let me give you my strength. Let me hold you until the pain goes away. Give me this, for I need to hold you. I need to know that you understand the pain that I feel. Give me this so I know you don't blame me. Don't shut me out. I love you. . . . Dear God, don't let it be too late.

"I'm so glad you are here," she said, looking up at him, and he saw the path of her recent tears.

He could not speak, for all the words he wanted to say seemed to get tangled up with the pain he felt, knotting together to form a huge lump in his throat. Without a word, he opened his arms and she stepped into them. It was only when he closed his arms around her and heard her cry softly that he was able to say, "I'm so sorry. So very sorry."

"Oh, Fletcher, I was afraid you were not coming."

He looked down at her lovely violet eyes, which now were shadowed with grief. "Don't you know that I would ride through hell itself just to get to you? Surely you knew I wouldn't stay away," he said, aching to kiss her. "Not from you. Never from you."

"In my heart I knew, but still I was afraid. Oh, Fletcher, I miss him so much. How will I ever get on without him?"

He opened his mouth to reply, but Robert came up at that moment and, after shaking Fletcher's hand, told Cathleen that it was time to go to the cemetery. She gave him one longing look, then turned toward Robert, who took her arm. They started off, walking slowly toward the black carriage that would take her with her grandfather on his final journey.

A moment later, Cathleen paused and turned back to look at Fletcher. "You will be there at the cemetery, won't you?"

"I will always be there, Cathleen," he said softly.

After she had gone, he stood in the churchyard, watching the procession wind its way down the narrow, rutted road to the cemetery, then he headed toward his horse, to take his place among the mourners.

"Fletcher! Fletcher Ramsay!"

At the sound of the female voice, he turned to see Annora Fraser hurriedly making her way toward him in a rustle of black silk. His heart was heavy with the burden of David's death. The woman he loved needed him. He did not want to make small talk with Annora.

As she drew closer, he saw that her black dress was piped in green, and her black hat with its iridescent green feathers curving around her face was of the latest fashion. But she would never stop his heart as Cathleen had done in her simple muslin gown and straw bonnet with frayed satin ribbons.

"Faith! Am I glad to see you."

He sighed. *I don't want to be with you, I need Cathleen* . . . "Hello, Annora." His voice was flat and held no emotion.

She was a bit breathless from hurrying to catch up to him. "I had hoped I would see you here. It's terrible about David."

"Yes, it is. I didn't know you knew him well."

She smiled, slipping her arm through his. "*Everyone* in the Highlands knew David well. He was that kind of person. But let's talk about something more pleasant. I'm so very glad to see you. I've missed you."

He pulled his arm away from her, but she seemed not to notice. "I saw you a couple of weeks ago."

She smiled, keeping in step beside him. "To me, that is a

long time, especially when I was expecting you to come to Dunston. Fie on you for not coming to see me."

"I've been busy."

"Not at Caithness," she said. "I paid a call on your aunt ... hoping to see you, of course. She told me you would be gone for an extended period of time, but she would not tell me why or where you had gone."

He could not help smiling faintly at that, amused that Aunt Doroty had sent Annora packing and had not told him of her visit. It would take more than the likes of Annora Fraser to breach that stern and staunch Scots fortress he had come to know and love as Aunt Doroty.

"My aunt doesn't believe in discussing her personal life or her business," he said. "She is a very private person."

"A bulldog would be a more apt description of her, but I dinna want to discuss your guard dog old aunt. Tell me, what brings you back to Glengarry?"

"David's funeral."

She gave him a knowing smile. "I know, but I thought you had come back to stay."

Fletcher stopped walking and turned to look at her. "Why would you think that?"

For the briefest split of a second, Annora looked uncertain, then she smiled and said, "I—I talked to Robert before the funeral. He said you had been renting the crofter's hut from David—something you neglected to tell me that day I saw you in town, I might add. So naturally I thought you had finished your business at Caithness and were returning to your cozy little crofter's hut."

"I came back for the funeral," he said. "I have not decided how long I'll stay."

"It must have been something terribly important to bring you away from a lovely place like Caithness Castle to live in a crofter's hut in the first place."

"I told you why I came that day I saw you in town, remember?"

She smiled and drew a finger down the side of his cheek, then brought it to rest on his lips. "So secretive. You know that only serves to make a woman more curious."

"Does it?" he asked, looking toward his horse.

"Yes, and being both curious and shameless, I am not above asking what could possibly interest you in a dull little village like Glengarry?"

Fletcher had no intention of telling Annora anything. Fortunately, at that moment they reached the spot where he had tied his horse, and as he prepared to mount he said, "I would offer you a ride, but as you can see, I'm on horseback."

"I have my carriage," she said, "but I must tell you that if this were anything but a funeral, I would hitch up my skirts and ride behind you."

Fletcher mounted his horse, saying nothing, but he had an inkling that Annora would have done exactly what she said. A moment later, he tipped his hat, said, "Goodbye," and turned his horse up the road. His thoughts were of Cathleen and what he would say to her when they were alone.

Cathleen rode next to Robert Cameron, her mind on her grief. *Oh, Grandpa, why did you have to die? Why did you have to leave me? What shall I do now? Where shall I go? What will become of your beloved Psalms? I dinna want you to be dead. . . .*

But he was dead, and no amount of grieving or denial would change that. Her sorrow welled up inside of her to the point of overpowering her. How does one go on? she wondered. Where do you find the strength to get up each morning and face the day?

"Are you all right, lass?" Robert asked, placing his hand over hers and giving it a squeeze.

"Aye," she said softly, "I ken I am as right as one can be with their heart ripped out."

Robert nodded. "Nothing will ease the pain," he said, "nothing but time. Grief, in a way, is its own medicine."

"My heart is dead."

"It is only numb. It beats still. God would not have you suffer overlong."

"I canna believe that right now."

"You will, in time."

"Aye, when sugar turns to salt."

"God grant you peace," he said, but Cathleen was not listening.

Her mind was on her grief.

At the cemetery, Fletcher stood at the back of the crowd as he had done at the church service, preferring to keep his distance. It was not that he did not want to be with Cathleen, but that he wanted to keep an eye on Adair. He did not want Adair to see him with Cathleen any more than was necessary. And of course, there was Cathleen. She was always a consideration, for he was afraid that if she saw him right now she might lose her composure. From a distance he watched her, seeing even through her black veil the lost look, the abject grief that gripped her lovely features.

He had to force himself not to go to her, for he wanted nothing more than to take her in his arms, to hold her and keep on holding her until hell froze over and Adair Ramsay be damned.

Gazing around the crowd, Fletcher felt his blood run suddenly cold, for there, just a few feet from Cathleen, stood the bastard himself. Adair. That he could be the cause of David's death and then attend his funeral, cold as charity, infuriated Fletcher. With a thin thread of control on his anger, Fletcher managed to keep from confronting Adair then and there.

Standing on one side of Adair were two men Fletcher did not know. On the other side, he recognized Gavin MacPhail. Just then, Adair glanced up and looked straight at Fletcher, a triumphant gleam in his eyes.

Something inside Fletcher exploded, shattering his emotions beyond control. He felt his face turn red and his hands curl into fists. Adair was guilty as sin and Fletcher knew it. It was high time everyone else here knew it—after he got through smashing his murdering face. Consumed with a rage that had an intensity he had never known, he took a step toward Adair, when suddenly Cathleen moved, the back of her head coming into his line of vision.

Fletcher swore silently and stopped.

Seeing Cathleen was a reminder—a reminder as effective as a cold bucket of water thrown in his face. He could not confront Adair here, at her grandfather's funeral and in front of her, for to do so would only bring her added grief, and God knew she had more right now than she could bear.

He clenched his jaw and told himself there would be another time.

Fletcher looked at Adair again. The bastard was guilty as hell. Never before in his life had he had to control such a feeling of menacing fury. He could kill the man with his bare hands, and by God, he wanted to. He wanted to choke him until his eyes bulged out of his head. He wanted to watch him die as he had watched Fletcher's father die, and David, too.

With mastery he did not know he possessed, Fletcher turned toward Cathleen. As he did, he tore his thoughts from confronting that deceiving, murdering, thieving little bastard who had ruined so many lives. With an iron will, he forced those thoughts to the back of his mind, calming himself, knowing that Cathleen would sense his anger the moment she saw him.

Cathleen, he thought, looking at her. *You are my refuge and my strength. Give me your love, your generosity, your kind understanding. Temper the anger, the resentment, the obsession for revenge that eats away at me. Love me. Forgive me. Help me to be whole.*

Reaching her side, he took her hand and gave it a squeeze. He said nothing, but stood silently beside her, hoping she could feel his love for her, as if the very hand that held hers was capable of conveying all he felt, when words seemed so inadequate.

When it came time for Cathleen to toss a handful of dirt over her grandfather's coffin, Fletcher saw her shoulders shake. He heard the soft, muffled sounds of her sobs against the handkerchief she held pressed to her mouth. He wanted to take her into his arms, to hold her close, to give her all the comfort he was capable of, but he dared not. To do so in front of Adair would endanger Cathleen. So, doing what he could to play the part of the concerned friend, he released her hand but remained silently next to her, hoping that she understood . . . praying that Adair did not.

Looking around, Fletcher noticed that every face was filled

with sorrow. Even the toughest Scots, the most hardened men, seemed unable to hide their emotions.

Only one man appeared unmoved. With a blank expression, Adair Ramsay kept his gaze on the gaping hole into which they had lowered David MacDonald's coffin, as if he wanted to make certain David stayed there.

Fletcher moved to stand behind Cathleen and gave her the support of his body, warm against hers. He offered her the comfort of whispered words of solace, the assurance that he was there, behind her—all the while forcing himself to look concerned and at the same time detached and impersonal.

Once, he glanced over the top of her head, his eyes falling again on Adair, who stood beside his carriage watching them. As if he sensed Fletcher was looking at him, Adair turned around. Just before he stepped into the shiny black carriage that bore the Duke of Glengarry's crest, he paused to say something to Annora.

Fletcher did not get to observe them further, for at that moment Cathleen turned to him. With a heart full of vengeance, Fletcher Ramsay, possessor of a Scottish title and an old and noble name, stood looking down at the woman he had come to love, seeing her grief, her pain, and feeling utterly and completely helpless.

"I'm sorry," she said, wiping the tears from her face. "I wish I could stay here with you, but I must go. Robert is waiting for me." She rose on her tiptoes and pressed a cold kiss to his cheek. "Thank you for coming. You don't know what it means to know you are here. Please come to see me later."

Without another word, she turned and hurried to Robert, who paused just long enough to help her into his carriage.

The carriage started off, and Fletcher could have sworn he heard the sound of thundering hooves as a great black shadow seemed to pass over his mind. About him the wind picked up, and a thick and heavy mist rolled in from the sea. Thunder rumbled in the distance, a low, grumbling sound. He felt the first splattering drops of rain as the mist turned too heavy to be called mist. And still he stood there for a long time after Cathleen had gone, wondering what he should do now.

A jagged bolt of lightning ripped across the sky, and Fletcher looked at David's grave, bidding him a final goodbye. He turned away then and made his way to his horse, who was growing nervous with all the thunder and lightning. Mounting, he rode off, his thoughts turned toward what he should do.

Part of Fletcher wanted to stay in Glengarry and prove that Adair Ramsay had had something to do with David's death. Another part of him wanted to get as far away from Cathleen as he could, in order to protect her, for no matter how he looked at it, Fletcher knew in his heart that now that David was dead, Adair would not hesitate to harm Cathleen if he thought she was involved with him in any way, and that included friendship. For this reason, he ruled out going to St. Abb's himself. At least for now.

As he rode toward Glengarry, his mind was on going to Cathleen.

But his prayers asked for the strength to stay away.

Adair Ramsay was a deadly man. He played no games. His home was well guarded. He was a strong, cruel man without decency or compassion, a man who had murdered before. He was not above doing whatever he deemed necessary. He would go to any lengths to remove anyone he considered his foe.

Adair Ramsay knew he had a foe now. His name was Fletcher Ramsay. Adair had already decided what to do. To help carry out his plan, he summoned Annora Fraser.

Later that evening, Annora arrived at Glengarry Castle. Adair was waiting for her in his study.

Upon entering, she paused a few feet from his desk and began pulling the leather gloves from her hands. He knew she was doing her best to look calm and impassive, but he had seen the way her gaze darted around the room, the slight tremor in her hands. She would be easy to manipulate. He knew it as soon as she walked into the room, and he felt a thrill of triumph at seeing her cold shiver of fear. "You're late," he said.

"It was unavoidable." She sounded cool and detached, but she fidgeted anxiously with the gloves in her hands.

"I don't like tardiness."

When Annora didn't say anything, he nodded toward a chair on the other side of the desk. "Sit down."

"Thank you." She dropped gracefully into the leather chair.

He noticed the way she sat forward, her small frame looking lost and vulnerable. He liked that. "I suppose you are wondering why I sent for you."

"I was curious, yes."

"What did you talk to the Earl of Caithness about?"

"You mean today, at the funeral?"

"Aye," he said, wondering if there had been other times.

"I ask him what he was doing here in Glengarry."

"And what did he tell you?"

"That he came for David's funeral."

"And you believed him?"

"Should I not?"

Adair was silent, noticing the way her frightened eyes seemed hesitant to look at him.

"If you will remember, Your Grace, I told you the last time I saw you that I had seen him in town, that he said his mother had asked him to come to Glengarry, to call on David."

She spoke with a forcefulness he knew she did not feel. "Did he tell you why?"

She shook her head. "He just said his mother was fond of him."

"What do you know about Fletcher Ramsay and his past?"

"Only that his mother was the sister of the late Earl of Caithness and that she was married to an American."

"Did you know that Fletcher's father was the Duke of Glengarry before me?"

Annora's face registered shock. "No . . . I . . . that is, I had no idea. If Fletcher's father was the duke, then how did you—"

"How is not important. Suffice it to say, Fletcher's family had wrongfully taken the title from my family several generations ago. Only after years of intense searching was I able to find sufficient evidence of the deception. The case went to trial and I was awarded the title. This, of course, happened many years ago—before you married and arrived here. Everyone knows and accepts *me* as the rightful duke."

Her expression was drawn and scared as she asked, "What does this have to do with me?"

"What is your interest in Fletcher Ramsay?"

She smiled slightly. "Is it that obvious?"

He stared at her. Her smiled faded. She sat still and blank-faced, like a stone statue.

"It is obvious, yes, but you didn't answer my question, Annora. What is your interest in him?"

"Personal."

His eyes bored into her. "How personal?"

"As personal as I can get it," she said, in an attempt to be witty. But Adair was not amused. "He intrigues me. He is a very attractive man, and I find him quite appealing. I would be lying if I said I was not interested in things going a bit further. What I don't understand is your interest in all of this."

"Perhaps it pertains to the mortgage on Dunston."

She leaned forward, placing her hands on the desk in front of her. "You promised you would never demand my complete and total devotion. We made a deal when Simon died. My *occasional* favors in exchange for his gambling notes. One favor, one note. You cannot—"

"Calm yourself, Annora, and let me finish. I have an offer to make to you. I know you have not exactly enjoyed warming my bed these past few years since my wife died. What would you do if I told you I would give you *all* the remaining notes I hold on Dunston?"

She looked suspicious. "All of them, at once?"

"Aye, all at once."

She gave him a direct look. Annora was no fool. He knew she liked the idea of having all of her late husband's notes paid off, of course, but she was smart enough to be cautious. He realized too that she knew him well enough to know that he did not go around doing good deeds or favors unless there was something in it for him.

"And why would you do that for me?"

Adair raised one brow. "Why? Because I want something from you in return."

"Which is?"

"I want you to involve yourself with the Earl of Caithness. I want to know his every move, every plan he makes."

Her features were stiff. "In other words, you want me to be your spy?"

"If you want to call it that, yes." He gave her a cold smile. "I prefer to think of it as doing you a good turn. You want the earl in your bed . . . and so do I."

He could tell that Annora was liking this idea more and more. He had observed Fletcher with Cathleen Lindsay the day of the funeral. It hadn't taken him long to see there was more between them than grief. If Annora was as infatuated with the earl as she let on, then she too would have noticed this.

"Well, what do you say?" Adair asked.

"I say I like the sound of that." She gave him a thin smile.

"I always knew you were a smart woman." Adair rose to his feet. "I am sure you won't have any objections to inviting Fletcher to stay at Dunston with you."

She looked relieved. "I have already invited him."

"When he comes, just remember to keep your end of the bargain. I don't like to think about what might happen if you try to betray me."

Her face paled, and her hands began to tremble. Adair felt power coming to him from her fear and weakness. "I understand," she said, her voice unsteady.

"Good. I am glad we understand each other."

She stood. "You . . . you aren't going to kill him, are you?"

He came around the desk. "Of course not. That is why I'm going to all this trouble of having you keep me informed of his plans. I only want to discourage him, to keep stumbling blocks in his path."

"How can I be certain of that?"

Oh, he loved this. "My dear Annora, if I meant to do the lad harm, I could have done so before now." He knew by her expression that he had her now.

"Aye, I suppose you are right."

He smiled, feeling the power in him again. "I'm always right."

* * *

A few minutes later, Annora made her way to the stables, where she asked a young groom to bring her horse around.

"Hello, Annora."

Annora's heart constricted. There was something familiar about that voice.

She whirled around, stifling a gasp of surprise. The man was huge, well over six feet tall, and massively built, with a big ruddy face and kind blue eyes. Eyes that she had known before.

She blinked. *No . . . it can't be!*

"You dinna know me, Annora?"

"My God! Angus MacTavish!"

"Aye."

"I had no idea you were here. It's been such a long time."

"Aye, it has at that. Ten years, to be exact."

She looked around the stable, then back at him. "What are you doing here?"

"I am in the duke's employ. I have charge of his horses."

She smiled. "I should have guessed. You were always a lover of horses, as I remember."

"If you remember that, then you must remember there was also a time when I was in love with you."

She looked away. "That was a long time ago. We aren't the same people anymore."

"No, we aren't. At least you aren't, but still, one cannot forget."

"Some things are better forgotten," she said, taking her gloves out of her pocket. "I have put that life behind me. I want no reminders of it."

"Aye, I can see you are a fancy lady now, but it isn't the fancy lady I've come to give advice to. I don't give a tuppence for what you've become. It is only because I cannot forget the lass you were, the way things were between us once, that I interfere in this at all."

"Interfere in what? What are you talking about?"

"Don't involve yourself with the Duke of Glengarry. He is a treacherous man. This thing between him and Bruce

Ramsay's son doesn't concern you. Leave it be. It could be very dangerous for you."

Annora laughed and began to pull her gloves on. "I see you haven't changed so much after all. You were always overprotective of me, like a clucking old broody hen."

"I loved you."

Annora's voice grew soft, and her eyes held a gleam of fond recollection. "Aye, I know, and I loved you ... once. But that is over now. A lot of time has passed. Things have changed. I've changed. The past is dead to me. I don't want to be reminded."

Annora looked away again, her mind pulling up memories she had long thought forgotten. She remembered the bothy her father had owned, its heavy, peaty smell of whiskey and smoke, and the sweaty men and the sound of their boisterous laughter, the feel of their groping hands.

Only Angus MacTavish had been different. He was such a handsome man then, tall and strapping, and he had treated her like a lady.

Working for her father gave Angus plenty of opportunity to be around Annora. She was young and impressionable. He was young and full of optimism. He filled her head with fancy talk about how he was going to own a fine string of horses one day, and how there would be enough money for him to support her in the style she deserved.

Even before then, Annora had known that Angus was in love with her, and she found herself drawn to his handsome face, his fancy talk, his worshipful attitude toward her. She returned his affections and fell in love with him, for it was Angus who showed her the beauty of lovemaking, the way things could be between a man and a woman.

Young and in love, Annora gave herself to Angus frequently, and just as frequently they talked of marriage.

But then a wealthy landowner by the name of Simon Fraser began to frequent the bothy. Drawn by her youth and her extraordinary beauty, he began to pay attention to Annora. Attracted by his wealth and position and her father's encouragement, she found herself responding to him. Soon he began to court her openly. Angus was forgotten.

A few months later, she became another man's wife.

Although she had married Simon Fraser, Angus MacTavish had sworn to her on her wedding day that he would never forget her and would never marry anyone if he could not have her.

The past began to fade away then, and Annora looked at Angus.

"Have you a wife?"

"No. I told you I would never marry if I couldn't have you."

She had never thought he meant those words. It pained her now to know he had loved her so much and so deeply. "Did you ever get your herd of horses?"

"No," he said. "I lost the dream after you married."

She put her gloved hand on his arm, and the words she spoke were from her heart. "I'm sorry, Angus. I never meant to hurt you. I always thought you would find the love you deserved, that you would be a wealthy man with a lovely wife who suited you and many children to love."

"I meant what I said that day. Somehow I never felt you believed me."

"No, I don't think I did. But now it doesn't really make any difference," she said.

"No," he said. "It doesn't."

"I'm sorry," she said, looking at him and feeling something she rarely felt anymore: remorse.

He was a great-boned, ruddy-faced man, who reminded her of her past, yet she could never be unkind to him.

She had loved him once.

Chapter Fifteen

Cathleen grieved over the loss of her grandfather. She grieved also over the loss of Fletcher, for how else could she explain his continued absence?

She did not understand. How could he have been so loving and gentle the day of the funeral and then turn so cold? Why did he stay away?

Her heart breaking, she went about her life as cold and lifeless as a stone statue. All of the warmth, the joy, the reason for living was gone out of her. She could not believe that her grandfather was gone. He was all she'd had. She still did not understand why he had to die. *"'The Lord gave, and the Lord hath taken away; blessed be the name of the Lord,'"* she whispered. "Job."

As soon as she said those words, she had a flashing memory of the duke's face. She paused for a moment, deep in thought. Did Adair Ramsay have something to do with her grandfather's death? Was her grandfather killed because Ramsey found out that the old minister was helping Fletcher? Her heart began to pound. No, it couldn't be. Not even the duke would stoop that low. Grandpa was a man of the cloth, a man of God. Not even Adair would commit such a crime.

She picked up one of her rabbits and buried her face in its soft gray fur. Only the warmth of that furry body and the steady thumping of its heart told her she was still alive. Inside, she was as dead as her hopes, as cold as her dreams.

She put the rabbit down and forced herself to go into the kitchen. Fletcher had not come, nor would he. She began to wash the dishes that waited, finding herself taking a pause now and then to stare out the window.

The sun seemed to be waging a war with the dark clouds overhead. One minute it was sunny, the next minute the clouds turned everything dark.

Just like my life . . .

The sun came out from behind a cloud then, sending a burst of light and warmth through the kitchen window. Feeling the penetrating heat on her face, she found herself clinging to one small thread of hope. " *'If you have faith as a grain of mustard seed,'* " she whispered. "Matthew."

The sun did not go behind the clouds again that day.

Fletcher would have returned to Caithness immediately after the funeral except for two things. The first was that he wanted to do a little snooping around at Glengarry Castle; the second was Cathleen.

After David's funeral, Fletcher knew he could not go back to the crofter's hut because of the damage it would do to Cathleen's reputation and, more important, because it might make Adair suspicious.

He wanted to protect Cathleen, not draw Adair's attention to her.

At last he decided that if he could not be with her in person, the least he could do was to find someone to help her. The very next thing he did was to hire a neighbor of Cathleen's to help her with the farm chores and caring for the livestock.

Now that David was gone, she would need someone to help, and he knew that asking for help was something she would never do. As it worked out, the neighbor, Robert Skene, had a son Fionn, a strapping boy of sixteen who had a way with animals. Fletcher decided that Fionn would be good to help with the livestock as well as the orphan babies that kept turning up at Cathleen's. At the mere mention of Cathleen's fawn, Bathsheba, Fionn's eyes lit up.

Fletcher had another, ulterior motive for wanting someone to work for Cathleen. He would sleep much better knowing there was someone looking after her.

After paying Robert and Fionn for six months in advance, Fletcher took a room in the village from the Widow MacAlister, an absentminded old woman who introduced herself to him each time he came home.

On the second day after David was buried, Fletcher was surprised when the Widow MacAlister stopped him when he walked in the front door.

"Hello," she said. "I'm the Widow MacAlister. Who are you?"

He could not help smiling at her. "I'm Fletcher Ramsay, the Earl of Caithness. Remember me?"

"No," she said, looking him over critically. "Have I met you before?"

"Yes, several times. I'm the earl you rented a room to, so that makes me a guest here."

"Oh, you are the earl's guest!" she said her smile showing her front teeth, which protruded just enough to give her a rabbity look. "How lovely. Then you can tell the earl, when he comes, that he has a visitor . . . a *female* visitor waiting for him in the parlor."

Fletcher looked at Mrs. MacAlister, with her lopsided white top-knot hanging almost above her left ear, and thought about reminding her again that he was the earl, but thought better of it. An hour from now she would have forgotten it again. Instead, he thanked Mrs. MacAlister, promised to tell the earl, and offered to entertain the earl's guest until he arrived.

"Why, how verra kind of you," she said. "I am sure the earl will be pleased."

"I know he will be," Fletcher said. "Where is the young lady?"

"She is in the parlor."

Expecting Cathleen, Fletcher was surprised to find Annora

waiting for him. Disappointment lay heavy in his chest. There she sat—the wrong woman, waiting for him and looking beautiful as always, with her black, black hair and smooth-fitting blue dress with black braid and jet beads.

"Annora, this is a pleasant surprise," he said, forcing cheerfulness into his voice. "How did you know I was staying here?" He walked farther into the room and sat in the chair opposite the one she occupied.

She smiled brightly. "Glengarry is a small village. Everyone here knows everyone else's business. You were not hard to track down. Do you mind my coming?"

"Not at all. I've never been one to frown upon the visits of beautiful women. What drew you away from Dunston?"

"You."

"Me?"

"Oh, come now, Fletcher. You are a handsome, titled man . . . a prime catch for any lass about. And I know you are aware that I have been chasing you shamelessly. Now, you can't possibly tell me you are surprised to learn that a woman will do whatever is necessary to spend time with you."

He smiled, amused as he always was at her blatant honesty. "Is that what you're doing? You have come here to spend time with me?"

Her eyes gleamed with suppressed humor. "Ever on your guard, aren't you? All right. I'll be honest with you. I came here to invite you to stay at Dunston until you return to Caithness Castle. Dunston has *much* more to offer you than this humble cottage of Widow MacAlister's. She is so forgetful, you know—always putting on things to cook and then forgetting about them. . . . Why, I wouldn't be surprised to hear she had burned the place down one day." She paused. "I am known for being the perfect hostess. I promise you won't lack for . . . *entertainment* while you are there."

He was amused and had to admit it. In spite of her forward ways, Fletcher could not help liking her. Perhaps it was her straightforward manner. Perhaps it was her charming nature, or her beauty. Perhaps it was all three.

"So, what do you say, Your Lordship?"

"I'll think it over," he said, noticing the way her face seemed to fall.

"What is there to think over?"

"I'm not a man to make rushed decisions."

"It's her, isn't it?"

"Who?"

"I have been completely honest with you, Fletcher. I expect the same from you. You have feelings for David's granddaughter, don't you?"

"Of course. I'm concerned about her. David MacDonald was a longtime family friend and he was all she had. She is all alone now. Of course I worry about what will happen to her."

She rose to her feet in a rustle of taffeta. Her perfume seemed to swirl about his head. Annora could be had, and for the flash of a moment he found the thought tempting. A man would have to be dead not to find her desirable.

"You are wrong about her being all alone," Annora said with a knowing smile. "She has you."

Standing beside her now, he said, "Cathleen is a friend, nothing more."

"Perhaps," she said, "and perhaps not. But that is not the issue. I would still like to have you as my guest at Dunston. I will be in town again tomorrow. I will come by then for your answer, which I hope will be yes."

He walked her to the door. "Regardless of what I decide," he said, "I do appreciate the offer."

She turned to him, leaning close enough for him to see the invitation in her eyes. "You could be thanking me for much more than an offer. You know that."

"Yes, and you make it mighty tempting."

"You're a hard man, Fletcher Ramsay."

Before he could respond, she stepped through the door. She opened her parasol with a snap. "Until tomorrow, then." And with a flip of her skirts she was gone.

Half an hour later, Annora sat in the same chair in Adair Ramsay's study as she had occupied the day before.

Adair got right to the point. "You spoke with him?"

"Aye, I invited him to stay at Dunston."

"Did he accept?"

"He wants to think about it. He will give me his answer tomorrow."

"Oh, come now, you are canny enough to entice any man. What went wrong?"

"Thank you for the compliment, but in all fairness, I wonder if it is right for me to blame myself. It is possible that the problem lies not with me but with Fletcher."

"What do you mean?"

"Perhaps he finds David MacDonald's granddaughter more to his liking."

"He told you that?"

"Of course not. And he might not be interested in her in the least. After all, he did not hesitate to claim his only interest in her was nothing more than concern for her welfare. However, it is always a woman's place to be suspicious ... especially of another woman."

"You must convince him to visit you at Dunston so you can keep an eye on him. I want to know where he goes, who he sees, and just what he is trying to prove."

"I have done my best." She knew immediately that this was not the answer he wanted to hear. She braced herself.

He slammed his hand down on the desk, overturning an inkwell. Annora watched the ink spread in a slowly widening circle, the dark, shiny liquid reminding her somehow of blood.

"You will have to do better than your best, Annora," he said, his voice filled with sinister implication. "I warn you. Do not fail me in this."

She felt the blood run cold in her veins. She knew now what it felt like to dance with the devil. A shudder passed over her. "I have extended the invitation and made it quite clear that I would share his bed. What else would you have me do?"

Adair turned his chair toward the window and stared out, his mood suddenly pensive. "Perhaps we can use MacDonald's granddaughter to our advantage whether his heart is involved or not," he said. "Even if he is only concerned for her welfare, he would want to spare her any harm. His kind are ever merciful and compassionate to those less fortunate." He turned back to her. "There, you see? There is always another way."

"I won't be a part of murder."

"Annora, Annora," he said, his voice surprisingly smooth. "Was I speaking of murder? The chit is of no use to us dead. I only plan a little surprise, one that will stir to action all that protective blood of the Earl of Caithness."

Annora frowned, suspicious of his congenial air. He was like a demon who could take many forms. But his attempt to pose as an angel of light did not fool her. She swallowed, dryness sucking at her throat. "I don't know."

"What's the problem? You should be overjoyed. It is a way to send the earl scampering into your arms. That *is* what you want, is it not?"

"Aye," she said, feeling a sense of mounting dread, "it's what I want."

Annora's surprise visit and invitation to stay at Dunston caused Fletcher to think not about Annora's offer but about Cathleen.

By late afternoon, he knew he could not stay away from Cathleen any longer. He knew how she would be feeling, that she would think he had abandoned her. He could not hurt her like this without at least giving her some explanation other than the truth—that he stayed away because he feared for her safety. He had to see her, if only under the pretext of gathering his belongings from the crofter's hut.

As he rode toward her cottage, his thoughts conjured Cathleen, the way she would smile when she saw him, the way her eyes would look at him. He thought himself in complete control, for he had spent two days priming himself for the moment he would see her again. He intended to be diplomatic, courteous, understanding, and gentle.

He had not expected to feel so very deeply in love with her.

The thought caught him off guard. This put up a whole new set of circumstances to be dealt with. He had not meant to allow this to happen. The timing was all wrong.

She had her grieving to do.

He had the mission he had waited all his life to accomplish. It wasn't the right time to fall in love.

But he had fallen in love. And now there was nothing to be done about it. He would simply have to figure out a way to deal with it. Loving Cathleen did complicate things, enough that he wasn't certain how to handle it or what he should do.

He decided that, for starters, he would not let her know how he felt. To do so would only muddy up the waters more than they already were—and the good Lord knew they were muddy enough. He would see her, but it would be brief. No feelings exposed. No emotion. *I can do it. I can handle it. I'm a strong man. . . .*

She heard his horse approach, and even before she looked out the window, Cathleen knew it was Fletcher. Pulling back the curtain, her heart pounded with excitement, for as he rode into her yard, looking as bonny as a Her Majesty's Highland Regiment, a look of expectation upon his face.

She ran to the door and jerked it open before he had time to dismount. By the time he had both feet on the ground, she was in his arms.

"I thought you would never come," she whispered against the solid warmth of his chest. "I've never known such loneliness, such desolation. Oh, Fletcher, I've missed you terribly. I never knew what loneliness was until I lost the two most important things in my life . . . you and my grandfather."

"You could never lose me, Cathleen. Don't you know that?"

She squeezed her eyes closed and hugged him to her, her hands going around his chest. "I was afraid you had gone back to Caithness, that I might never see you again."

"Cathleen," he groaned, tilting her face up so he could look at her. "How could you think I could leave without seeing you? Do you not understand, I could go without air sooner than I could go without seeing you again."

He did not give her time to answer, but ground his mouth down upon hers, kissing her with a possessiveness, a fierceness that should have frightened her. But all she could think of was the agony she had endured these past few days, the way his absence had tormented her more than the emptiness she felt over the loss of her beloved grandfather. She knew now, with every fiber of her being, that she loved him, and that she had known he was the one since that day at the well.

To love and not to possess. That was the agony of it.

"Come on," he said hoarsely. "Let's go inside."

His arm around her, they walked into the cottage.

She lit one of the lamps, sending a dull, mellow light to penetrate the darkness left by the fading twilight. Then she turned to look at him, standing a short distance from her, framed in a shaft of dim yellow light.

"You know why I came?" he asked.

"Aye, to tell me you don't want to see me again."

She could not stop looking at him, at the way the lamplight turned his hair to fire and his skin to the color of antique gold, and she wondered how she would ever stand the loss. *Dearly beloved. Heart of my heart. How much better had I not come under your spell. To love. To want. To need like this and be undone. How can I face each morning, knowing it is another day that you will not come?*

Afraid she would cry now, she forced herself to turn away from him, and walked to her grandfather's chair and sat down.

"It isn't that I don't want to see you," he said. "It's a matter of what is best for you."

She could not hide her hurt look. "And of course you know what is best for me."

"Don't make this any harder for me than it is."

She crossed her arms in front of her now. "And is it hard for you to turn me away?"

"Dammit! I'm not turning away. It's just that the timing is all wrong. Can't you understand that? You need time to get over David's death, and I have to continue my search."

That isn't the real reason, she thought. *He's hiding something. How can I make him understand what I feel?* She smiled wistfully and looked into his beloved face. *Why do I suffer so, when I know there can never be anything for us?*

He came to where she sat, going down on one knee in front of her, his face breathtakingly close. "Cathleen . . ."

She shook her head. "Don't. Don't say anything. Please.

Just give me a moment. I don't seem to be very good at being strong lately." She felt again the urge to cry and again fought against it. She would not cry in front of him. She would save that for when he was gone, for all the times she would be without him. He would never know that inside she felt like an old rag doll, limp and forgotten.

"Damn you!" he said, closing his eyes as if in pain, and she knew he was trying to resist her. "It's too soon, don't you understand that? This wasn't supposed to happen. Not here. Not now." His eyes seemed to burn into her, and then he was pulling her out of the chair and into his arms. "God help me," he groaned, holding her tightly against him. "God help us both."

For the longest time they sat there, upon the floor, each of them holding the other, neither of them saying anything. She felt completely under his power, unable to resist him, although her mind urged her to use caution. She held her breath and closed her eyes, inhaling the scent of him, feeling his nearness, responding with both excitement and alarm. She should not care for him this much.

At last he broke the silence. "Cathleen, Cathleen, you make it so difficult. . . ."

Her fingertips stopped his mouth. "Don't talk," she whispered. "We do better when we don't say anything. Just hold me."

He groaned and buried his face in her hair.

"I make it harder for you, don't I?" she asked. "I'm like a child teasing a wild dog. I don't seem to understand that it can hurt me."

"It isn't your fault. I know that. We have so many things working against us. Sometimes I feel like we were plucked out of another time and dropped here, in the midst of turmoil, unable to find our way back. It isn't easy for me, but I know it's even harder on you. At least my wanting you is something I can deal with."

She was silent.

"Do you understand what I'm saying to you?"

She stiffened, her body tensing as his meaning became

clear. Her heart breaking, she could only whisper weakly, "Aye."

Drawing back slightly, he looked down into her eyes. "I'm not so certain you do. I understand how you feel. I know it's hard when your mind and body don't agree," he said. "Your body wants me, Cathleen. It's wanted me for some time now."

"Aye," she said, "it has." She looked deep into his eyes, and she knew that his body wanted hers, too. She did not know much about the things that went on between a man and a woman, but she had a feeling that he wasn't having an easy time controlling himself.

He desired her. She saw it in his eyes, heard it in his voice. Scalding tears ran down her cheeks and dropped onto her hands. "I wish there was some way," she whispered. "I want you, Fletcher, and that will be my undoing. I am like a child. I want to have it both ways. I want you so badly I can not think of anything else, but my fear of dying like my mother holds me back. My future is dark with 'ifs ands or buts.'" She laughed, a mocking, dry sound. "I stumble over them, do I not? If only I could think of a way, but I canna. I fear I could sooner turn chopped straw to gold."

He looked at her for some time, then at last, he spoke. "There is a way," he said, and he took her hands, pulling them around his neck as he drew her tighter against him. She watched his eyes darken with passion as he lowered his head to hers, and she felt herself lean into him, meeting him on equal terms.

Warm and soft his mouth moved over hers, his body pressing her back until she lay on the crocheted rug, his body spreading over hers, his weight welcome and oh, so right.

She kissed him with all the aching longing that she had kept inside of her, showing him in a way she could not speak of, feeling her body respond to his when he began to kiss her with a hunger that made her gasp. She could not get close enough to him.

"How?" she whispered, pulling her mouth away just long enough to say the words. "How can we?"

"Do you trust me, Cathleen?"

She would trust him with her life, her spirit, her soul. She would trust him until her dying day. She would trust him in all ways. "Aye, but . . ." She smiled. "There's that word again."

"You think too much. For once, trust someone. Trust me. I won't hurt you. I won't betray you. I won't do anything to leave you with child, but you will have to trust me. I want to make love to you, Cathleen. Can you trust me to do that? If I give you my word that you will not get with child, will it be enough for you?"

She made no attempt to hide the worry in her voice or the concerned look in her eyes. "I don't understand."

"You will," he said softly. "Trust me and I will show you a way . . . a way to give us what we both want."

For the first time since they had met, the restraints seemed to fall away and she felt as free as the wind at Martinmas. They both were free. Free to touch, to explore, to feel. There was no thought of going to the bedroom, of making things proper. No thought of taking their clothes off.

There were no thoughts. . . .

Only feelings guided them now, feelings too long denied, too long held in check.

Having him touch her like this, having him so near—it was nothing like she had imagined it would be. It was so much better. Awe seemed to whisper through her. Delight seemed to sing in her veins. Holding her face in his hands, he kissed her until her breathing was rapid and deep, and then he pulled the pins from her hair and tangled his hands in it, whispering how he had wanted to do that since the first time he had seen her.

Her hair tumbled down, covering his hands.

"Your hair," he whispered, crushing it, "it was always your hair that fascinated me and drew me to you, even from the beginning. God, you are so perfect for me."

She was not aware that he had unbuttoned her dress until she felt him tug at the ribbon of her chemise, and felt too the warmth of his hand upon her breast.

He turned, putting himself beneath her. She was trembling all over. She felt herself lean toward him, closing her eyes and feeling the weight and texture of his mouth upon hers. She steadied herself with one hand against his chest. Everywhere he touched her she burned.

She felt his hands trembling and knew it took some resolve on his part to maintain his control. He pulled her face gently to his, and his lips parted, luring her, inviting her to kiss him more deeply, and she did. A warm and vibrant current flowed through her, softening her limbs, until she trusted him with all her weight.

The shadows of her past and future seemed to scatter until nothing but the dream remained. She found herself nuzzling his throat, his temples, feeling pleasure at the sound of his indrawn breath. There was power in being with him like this, power in his being beneath her, and she on top of him.

"God," he groaned, "a thousand desires and so few choices."

"I trust you," she whispered, covering his face with a hundred kisses. "I trust you . . . I trust you . . . I trust you." And she knew by his response that it was enough, for he kissed her and kept on kissing her until she was mindless and as wild for his kisses as he was for hers.

Whenever he drew back, her mouth sought his of its own accord.

"You want me," he said, and she knew it was not a question, but she could not help answering.

"Aye," she said. "I didn't know how much until now."

His hands pushed her dress from her shoulders, then down until her arms were free and her breasts were just above him, her nipples brushing across his face lightly until they were hard with wanting. He drew one into his mouth, surrounding it with a warm wetness that made her moan low in her throat. Moving to the other breast, he drew its hard point into his mouth, his hands following the line of her legs downward and drawing her skirts upward until they lay bunched around her waist. He brought his knee between her legs and she gasped, feeling suddenly afraid.

"Do you want to stop?"

"No, but I'm afraid."

"Cathleen, you know what happens between a man and a woman, don't you?"

"Aye, I've seen animals . . ."

He almost choked. "A common mistake. And a frightening one. Believe me, it isn't exactly the same. A man doesn't make a woman stand on her hands and knees while he comes at her from behind."

"I am verra happy to hear that!"

"Do you understand what happens when a man is inside a woman? What happens that makes her have a child?"

"Aye. It's a man's seed."

"It is possible for a man to make love to a woman without leaving his seed inside her."

"How?" she asked, feeling his smile against her cheek.

"The question every man dreams of," he whispered. "Here . . . I'll show you."

He brought his knee up to ride against her, and she gasped. Then his hand replaced his knee, and she felt herself go limp with desire. A moment later, he eased her drawers down, his hands spreading across the flatness of her stomach, then sweeping up to cover her breasts, lifting, caressing, teasing, then kissing the firmness that responded to his touch.

"Everywhere I touch you're so delightful. I'm like a kid with his hand in a candy jar. I don't know what to try next."

"My mouth," she whispered.

"Wanton," he murmured. "Beguiling witch. You seduce me with your innocence, with your child's mouth."

His words were as seductive as his touch.

"Kiss me," he whispered, and her mouth was against his again. His mouth was hot, opening under hers, yielding, then taking control, slanting over hers with a hunger that threatened to devour them both. Her body was lost to her now, as if it were a thing separate from her, like a boat that loses its anchor and is swept down the rapids in a swirl of sensation. Each place he touched, each caress across yearning flesh sent her spinning off in another direction. She felt like a priceless jewel with many facets, each one catching the light, dazzling and leaving her blind.

How beautiful it was to love someone. Someone she could trust. Trust . . . a word she would always associate with him now. It did not matter that she was walking down a path she had never traveled, or that he was taking her to places unknown, for she had complete and utter faith in him. She knew him to be a man of his word.

How beautiful that she could be with him as a woman can be with a man, and yet not risk the gnawing horror, the wrenching reminder of where it could lead. She never knew she could make love with a man and not worry about having a child.

As she lost herself in the touch of his flesh against hers, she had a fleeting thought that the only thing better would have been not to have the fear in the first place.

His hands left her breasts, replaced by his mouth, and began touching her, making her arch upward against him, and she suddenly realized that they had somehow changed positions and she was beneath him now and they both were naked.

It both surprised and amazed her. He must have done this a lot, she thought, for only lots of practice could have allowed him to remove his clothes without her being aware of it. *What else have you practiced, Fletcher? No, don't tell me. Show me . . .*

Her hands began to explore him, learning the musculature of his back, his loins, discovering how he was naked, how lovely, how beautiful, how beloved. A wave of love blossomed within her, so strong she wondered if she would ever recover from it. And then he touched her in the most intimate place of all, and she knew he had much experience with this as well. For how else would he know just where to touch her and for how long, to drive her to the brink and no further?

Consumed with passion, she moved beneath him, murmuring incoherent words, trying to convey what she was feeling. Only her body seemed capable of communicating with him, and of its own volition it seemed to take charge, knowing instinctively just what to do to bring her pleasure and him too.

"I love you, Cathleen. Come with me, love. Come."

Slowly, he brought his hard flesh against her, and she whimpered, feeling his organ against her, surprised that there was no shock, only this wanting, this needing.

"Oh love," he whispered, and drove himself deep inside her.

She gasped, and his mouth covered hers. The pain lasted only a moment, and then she began to move with him, his slim hips above her, moving faster and faster until she thought she would shatter from the beauty of it.

He brought her knees up, and as she looked down between them, she thought she had never seen anything as beautiful, as arousing as the sight of him moving inside her.

She felt his body tense, and she heard him curse softly. Quickly he withdrew, and she felt the length of him, hard and hot, pressing against her belly. A moment later she heard him groan again, heard too his softly whispered apology, as his seed spilled and covered her, hot and wet.

He had kept his word.

The thought shattered her. He had kept his word. This beautiful, wonderful man cared more for her needs than he did for his own. He had kept his word . . . and never had she loved him more than she did at that moment. Nor had she ever detested her fear of childbirth as much as she did now.

"Are you all right?" he asked, his voice laced with concern.

"Aye," she said, never knowing that so much feeling could be expressed in one short word.

"Are you sorry about what happened?"

"No."

"Then what is it?"

"I love you," she whispered, holding him tightly against her. "It's as simple as that. I love you so much, but I don't know what I'm going to do about it."

"We will think of something," he said, and then he rolled to the side, taking her with him.

As she lay there beside him, her head cradled against his chest, he whispered, "Well, so much for strong men."

Chapter Sixteen

Fletcher stayed for dinner, then left. After he was gone, Cathleen fed the owls, cleaned the kitchen, and dressed for bed.

She had almost drifted off to sleep when she heard the horse and the pony in the paddock whinny. Since Robert and Fionn had come earlier to feed the animals, she knew it wasn't one of them. She was telling herself that it was probably just one of their equine disagreements and things would settle down soon, when the disturbance got louder.

Soon they were kicking up a ruckus, their whinnies turning to frightened screams. Even from the house she heard them running around the paddock, rearing and kicking, their hooves striking the side of the barn, the slats of the fence.

Throwing the covers back, she sprang to her feet, grabbed her wrapper from where it lay at the foot of the bed, and put it on as she crossed the room.

She was just about to light the lamp when she realized that she didn't need the light, for the room was filled with an eerie red glow that came through the window and threw grotesque shadows across the opposite wall. She rushed to the window and pulled back the curtains. Flames leaped high into the sky, like long bloody fingers that clawed at the blackness of the night.

The crofter's hut.

She ran from her cottage. Her heart pounded wildly in her chest, sending her blood racing faster than her feet. By the time she reached the crofter's hut, her heart felt as if it were about to burst. She saw immediately that there was no way to save the hut, for the straw roof was completely engulfed. Nothing but the chimney and the thick stone walls of the hut remained.

She brought her hand up to shield her face as she stepped back. The heat was too intense for her to go any closer. Thick clouds of dark gray smoke poured from the hut and swirled about her, making her choke. For a moment she was consumed with a fit of coughing as the smoke caused her eyes to water and her throat to burn.

When the coughing subsided, she stood there in her night-clothes and watched the flames devour the hut. She told herself that she could at least be thankful that it was not her cottage that had burned.

At about the time she remembered that fires often spread, a breeze stirred the smoldering rubble to new life, sending a tower of flame high into the sky. A shower of embers and burning debris swirled about her, and one flaming ember struck her cheek and stuck there. She smelled her scorched flesh and felt the searing pain. Quickly, she brushed the ember away and felt a burning sting on her hand.

She hurried to the barn and got the shovel, then began to throw dirt over the embers around the perimeter of the hut. She hoped this would keep the fire from reaching her cottage.

It was only when she paused to wipe the sweat from her face that she heard someone shouting. Looking up, she saw Robert and Fionn Skene riding toward her.

Robert dismounted and came to her straightaway. "I ken Fionn and I can finish this," he said, taking the shovel from her. "You dinna need to be here, lass. You look exhausted.

Go home and get some rest. There isna much to be done now. The fire will burn itself out."

"I couldn't sleep now," she said. "I might as well stay here."

Cathleen stayed until the fire had died down. A few more neighbors arrived, mostly to survey the damage and offer their opinions as to the cause.

Realizing that there was nothing more to be done, and that she was after all standing in front of a goodly portion of the population of Glengarry in her dressing gown, she thanked Robert and Fionn for their help and returned to her cottage.

By the time she arrived back home, she was too exhausted to do more than collapse across her bed. She fell asleep instantly.

When she awakened, bright shafts of morning light streamed through the open window, where the yellow dimity curtains fluttered, stirred by a gentle breeze that carried the scent of charred wood.

She glanced down and realized then that she was sleeping on top of the bed. It must have been a fretful sleep, for her gown and wrapper were twisted about her legs like iron bands. She made several weak attempts at extracting herself, then fell back on the bed, panting as a wave of nausea swept over her, which she attributed to having so much smoke.

As she lay there waiting for the nausea to pass, she suddenly remembered that she was now living alone, so if something happened to her, if she were to take sick, there would be no one to notice, no one to care.

She rested for a moment longer, then gathered what energy she could and came to a sitting position. She felt her head swim, but sitting up seemed to ease the nausea. Dragging herself out of bed, she noticed the black, charred holes in her gown.

She steadied herself on her feet, made her way to the mirror, and saw a clear blister that had formed on her cheek. Next, she held out her hand, and saw no blister there. Apparently it had been rubbed away by the shovel, for there was nothing there now save a bloody, raw spot.

She took a bath, having the devil's own time of heating

the water with only one hand, but she managed. She soaked for some time before she washed the smell of smoke from her hair. Then, she dressed, twisted her hair in a wet knot upon her head, and mixed a poultice for her cheek. She applied some to her hand, which she wrapped as best she could.

Tomorrow, if it was not better, she would pay a visit to Dr. Scott.

Robert and Fionn came later that morning to feed the livestock and do the chores. She reminded herself that she was ever so thankful that Fletcher had made arrangements for them to help her, when it occurred to her that Fletcher probably didn't know that the hut had burned.

He will come as soon as he hears.

The rest of the day passed. Night came, and then morning, when Robert and Fionn came early to break the sad news to her.

Bathsheba, the fawn, was nowhere to be found.

"You don't think the fire . . ."

"No, I dinna ken she is dead," Fionn said. "I ken she was frightened by the fire and ran away."

"She is so small."

"Someone will care for her, I ken. She's a friendly lass. I wouldna worrit overmuch." Fionn grinned at her. "You still have all the others."

"Aye," she said. "I still have them."

"How is your hand faring?"

Cathleen looked down at the bandaged hand. "It festers."

"You better see Dr. Scott."

"Aye, I am going to pay him a visit."

"I'll hitch the pony to the cart for you."

Without giving her a chance to say thank you, Fionn was off, loping down to the barn with his long-legged stride that reminded her so much of Fletcher.

A short while later, Cathleen was with Dr. Scott, who cleaned the burn with something that burned worse than the fire, then bandaged it. He told her not to use that hand for a few days and to keep it dry. She nodded.

"I'll take that in the form of a promise," said Dr. Scott.

"I promise," she replied.

On her trip home, she encountered danger once again.

As she guided the pony cart down a narrow trail alongside a rocky ledge that edged a burn, she heard the rumble of rocks overhead. She looked up and saw a large boulder rolling down the side of the cliff, heading straight toward her in a shower of smaller rocks. There was no time to think. Instinctively, she threw her arms up over her face.

A split second later, she was pelted with rocks, just as she heard a splintering crash and felt herself bounced into the air. She landed on the seat with a thump.

About that time her pony began to scream.

Opening her eyes, she saw the strangest thing. The boulder had hit the very back of the cart, splintering the end rail but leaving the floor in tact. The weight of the boulder had pressed the back of the cart down to the ground, while the wheels, acting as a balance in the middle, forced the front of the cart up in the air, seesaw fashion.

Poor Flora was still hitched to the traces and bars, her weight not enough to break the bars or counter the weight of the boulder, which left her suspended in midair, her short little legs thrashing as she tried to whinny and nicker her way out of this predicament.

Had Cathleen not still been fighting off the effects of being frightened out of her wits, she might have laughed, for it was a sight to see, poor Flora kicking and thrashing, her feet some two feet off the ground.

About the time she was trying to figure the best way to get herself out of the cart and safely on ground she heard the clipping gait of an approaching horse.

Looking up, she saw Fletcher riding toward her, a grin as big as a Highland loch on his face.

Seeing his beloved if somewhat amused face, she simply said, "Fletcher! Am I glad to see you."

Having heard about the fire, Fletcher had ridden directly from Glengarry to Cathleen's, only to find she was not there. Having learned from Fionn that she had gone to see Dr. Scott, he was headed there when he rounded a bend in the trail and came upon the oddest thing he had ever seen.

There was the object of his search, calm as June weather, sitting in her little cart, its back weighted down by a boulder, its front end a couple of feet off the ground, while her pony made it known to all and sundry that she was most unhappy.

The moment he pulled his horse to a stop, saw Cathleen's bright smile and realized that she was all right, he could not contain himself.

It was simply too damn funny.

"I've heard of women sticking their noses in the air, but this is going to the extreme a bit, don't you think?"

"I will thank you to offer us some assistance instead of laughing at our unfortunate circumstances. I might have been killed, you know."

As far as sobering him and driving away the urge to laugh, that did it.

In a flash he was off his horse and had her safely out of the cart and into his arms. Then he noticed the burn on her cheek and her bandaged hand.

"You're hurt," he said, tracing the blistered welt on her face. "Your poor, lovely face. Does it pain you overmuch?"

"No. Dr. Scott said I did the right thing by applying a poultice."

"Will it leave a scar?"

She lowered her face. "If it does, what does it matter. I was never the village beauty anyway."

"It matters to me," he said softly. "I should be horse-whipped for having left you out there by yourself."

"It wasn't your fault, Fletcher. Accidents happen. It could have been worse."

The pony whinnied again and resumed thrashing.

"Will you do something to help Flora? The poor thing has exhausted herself."

Fletcher helped Flora, but not before he made Cathleen comfortable in the shade. Then he set himself to the task of freeing the pony from her lofty perch.

Once the pony had all fours on solid ground, he turned her

loose. Seeing the look on Cathleen's face, he smiled. "Don't fret, little mother. She will go home."

"I know. I was just wondering how *I* was going to get home."

"I'll take you."

With Cathleen secured behind him, he turned his horse around and headed toward her cottage. The ride back was short, warm, and silent. Cathleen seemed content to sit behind him, her arms around his middle, her cheek resting against his back.

Fletcher knew he was the reason things were so quiet between them, for it was difficult for him to make conversation. His mind was on the series of accidents coming Cathleen's way.

And he knew why.

It was now obvious to him that no matter how much he cared for Cathleen, he would have to do more than to stay completely away from her. He would have to do something to make Adair think he had no interest in Cathleen whatsoever. As long as Adair suspected that there might be something between them, he would use Cathleen as a way to control him. The best way he could think of to make Adair believe there was nothing between them was to take Annora up on her offer.

With his heart wrenching from the thought of what he must do to her, Fletcher felt the moment drawing near as they rode into the yard of her cottage. Pulling his horse to a stop, he dismounted. After helping her down, he followed her into the house.

She turned to him. "You are as grim as the reaper. What's bothering you?"

"It's nothing that concerns you," he said. "Come here. I want to see the burn on your face."

She turned her face away. "The doctor has seen it. There is nothing more you can do. It does not pain me overmuch."

"In that case, I'll be on my way."

She turned to look at him, her eyes searching his face. He knew the exact moment when she realized what was happening, for he saw it in her eyes. She knew, now, that he would not be coming back.

The thought of doing this to her left a big hole inside of him, but the hardest part was not being able to tell her why. How could he tell her that he was turning to Annora in order to make Adair think he had no interest in Cathleen? How could he make her understand that he had made the decision to hurt her in order to protect her life? If she had any idea that he was doing this to protect her, she would not hear of it.

In order to protect her, he had to hurt her.

Her voice was soft, subdued, laced with pain. "Before you go, I have something to give you," she said. She turned away and crossed the room.

She went to her grandfather's desk, opened the drawer, and took out an envelope. She returned to his side and handed it to him. "Go on. Take it. It's for you."

He looked down and saw his name on the envelope. He recognized the handwriting immediately. It was David's.

He took the envelope, then he looked at her, waiting for some explanation.

"They found it in his possessions," she said, her lip trembling. "I suppose he meant to post it to you, but he never . . . g-got the chance."

He heard the break in her voice, saw the tears glistening in her eyes. He had never wanted anything more in his life than to take her in his arms. Yet, he could not. He knew what would happen if he touched her.

He vowed that someday, somehow, he would make it all up to her, that he would spend the rest of his life seeing to it that she never suffered or doubted his love again. He could not bring David back, but he would see that she never wanted for anything again.

But even as he thought it, he knew it wasn't enough. *She has suffered so much. Is there no mercy for her? This is my battle and yet she has paid the greater price. Give me the pain. Let me suffer. I can't bear to see her hurt.*

But when it was all over, and the anguished thoughts had

played themselves out in the agony of his mind, he knew he would hurt her again.

He pulled the letter from the envelope. David had written that he had searched church and land records in St. Abb's but found nothing out of the ordinary. He had noted, however, that there were several pages missing during the years in question, but there was no way ever to know what had happened to them.

I did check the church records and found the proof of Adair's ancestry, just as he claimed.

He ended the letter by expressing his sadness over not finding anything.

The answer is out there somewhere. I pray God will reveal it to you at the appointed hour.

Too many feelings seemed to jam in Fletcher's throat. There were so many things he felt, yet he had no words to express them. He looked out the window and saw the pony standing near the paddock. "Well, if there is nothing more I can do here, I'll see to your pony before I go."

"It is all right. Robert will see to her ... or Fionn. And thank you again for sending them here to help me."

"It is the least I can do. I will look for a woman to help you in the house as well."

"I don't need anyone, you needn't do this for me."

"I'm not doing it for you."

Suddenly she looked tired and waved her hand at him in dismissal. "Whatever. I don't want to argue with you," she said, sighing. "Thank you for all your help." She turned away, staring across the room.

Fletcher followed the direction of her gaze and saw her grandfather's chair. He knew she was thinking about their lovemaking, remembering how he had pulled her from that chair and into his arms, and he cursed the timing of it all.

If these accidents had occurred earlier, he would have never made love to her, knowing she was in so much danger, knowing he would have to turn away from her in the end. He knew the kind of woman she was, the thoughts she would be thinking, and he knew too what his betrayal would do to her.

She was so lovely that it hurt him to look at her. The thought that he would soon turn his back on her was killing him inside. He knew all too well what she would suffer, and he hated himself for what he knew he had to do.

With a sad, apologetic look, he prayed that she would know what was in his heart, that she would be able to see his love for her shining deep in his eyes. He had asked her once to trust him, and she had done so.

He could only hope that she would trust him in this as well. "Well, if you don't need anything else, I guess I'll be going," he said.

"Aye, I think that would be best. I know you have much to do, and I have fallen quite behind on my chores."

He picked up his hat. "I'll be seeing you, then."

"Aye, take care of yourself."

He nodded, and with a sudden turn he crossed the room and went out the door.

After he saw that Robert had put Flora into the paddock and fed her, Fletcher mounted his horse and headed toward Dunston and Annora. He rode out of Cathleen's life in much the same manner as he had entered it.

Trust me, Cathleen. Understand what this is all about.

This was just like a man, he thought—betraying the woman he loves and praying that somehow she will understand.

He knew that even for Cathleen, this was asking a bit much. Still, he could not help praying, *Light the candle of understanding in her heart. . . .*

Chapter Seventeen

Cathleen could not understand.

She had known the moment they reached her house that she would not see him again, but that did not mean she understood why.

Why had Fletcher made love to her and then turned his back on her?

She walked along the edge of the loch that was almost covered by a thick mist creeping in from the sea. She felt hot tears trickle down her face, mingling with the cool, damp air that lingered about her.

How would she live without him?

She had thought she would not be able to bear it, but time passed . . . three days, then four. Soon it was a week.

Still he did not return. In her heart, she knew he never would.

On Sunday morning, she went to church. After the service, as she was standing at the door talking to Robert Cameron, she heard a woman's gay laughter. She glanced around and saw a fancy carriage pass by.

It wasn't seeing Annora Fraser sitting in the back of that carriage that hurt her so deeply.

It was seeing Fletcher sitting beside her, his arm stretched lazily across the back of the seat as he looked down at Annora, smiling at something she had said.

The sight of him with another woman crushed Cathleen, leaving her breathless with heartache. After a week of grieving for him, she had thought her heart dead.

Her world shattered and lay like glittering fragments of glass about her feet. Blinking back her tears, she managed a calm demeanor, wishing she were anywhere right now but here.

"Cathleen?" Robert asked. "Are you all right?"

"Oh, aye."

Robert looked in the direction of the retreating carriage. "They make an attractive couple, don't they?"

"Aye, they are both handsome people."

Robert frowned. "Although I canna say I am pleased to hear the earl has taken up residence at Dunston."

"Dunston? But, I thought . . . I just assumed he had returned to Caithness."

"No, he has been Annora's houseguest for over a week now, I believe."

She turned away, feeling that there was no pain as intense as the pain of betrayal. She made her way to her carriage. She did not want believe that Fletcher had deliberately humiliated her by turning to another woman, but in the end that is exactly what she did believe. She was unable to find any other explanation for it.

As she drove herself home, she found her thoughts going to her grandfather. It was better that he was not here to witness this, for she knew that had he still been alive, she would have confessed everything to him. Would he have said that she was being punished for making love to him without the blessing of wedlock? Somehow, she knew he would not.

Oh, Grandpa, I never needed you more than I do now. . . .

Her heart heavy, her mind grieving, she arrived at her cottage. She did not go to her room, or to the kitchen to cook her lunch. She went to her grandfather's chair and sat there, crying, for the better part of the afternoon. When nothing was left but hiccuping sobs, she told herself that crying was good for her, that it would help ease her pain.

She remembered what her grandfather had always said: "It clears the lungs, washes the face, brightens the eyes, and blunts pain, so cry away."

She took a deep, trembling breath and wiped her eyes on the hem of her apron. There was nothing she could do now but wait, wait with winter patience for peace to come—like spring—back into her life.

Going to the kitchen to heat water for a cup of tea, she vowed she would not leave her cottage until the pain of betrayal had left her and she was whole again.

She wasn't able to keep her vow, for the following Wednesday, little Robbie MacHugh came down with the fever. Two days later he died. Mrs. Bowie died a day later. By the third death, Dr. Scott had diagnosed the strange fever.

Typhoid.

It hit the impoverished areas of the village first, where most of the people drank from the same well and sewage was a constant problem. From there it spread to other parts of the village, reaching the outlying farms by the end of the first week. Glengarry had not seen anything so devastating since the Clearances.

Working day and night beside Dr. Scott, Cathleen did not have time to think much about Annora and Fletcher, which she supposed was a blessing. There was enough suffering and dying around her; she needed no further sadness.

She found it odd that when she was devoting all of her efforts to helping the sick, when she had neither the energy nor the time to think about Fletcher, that was the time he thought about her, for during this time he came to see her three times.

"Fletcher Ramsay is here to see you," Dr. Scott's wife told her as she came into the room where Cathleen was assisting the doctor.

Feeling a jolt of surprise, she looked up. "What does he want?"

"He wanted to know how you were. He said he would like to speak to you."

"Tell him I am fine and that I am too busy to talk to him."

The second time he came, Cathleen again refused to see him.

"I ken he would like to speak to you, if only for a moment," Mrs. Scott said.

"Just tell him I'm doing fine, that there is no need to check on me. Dr. Scott will notify him if anything happens."

Two days after Fletcher's second visit, Dr. Scott became ill, but he kept on working. "I canna take time out to be sick," he said, and she supposed he was right. Over half the village was sick with the fever now.

When Cathleen went home that night, she was too tired to eat anything. As she had done the night of the fire, she fell across her bed and immediately drifted into a deep, deep sleep of utter exhaustion.

She had no idea how long someone had been pounding at her door before she was awakened. Opening her eyes and hearing the loud knocks, her heart began to thump painfully in her chest, as she realized it probably meant that Dr. Scott had taken a turn for the worse.

Dragging herself wearily from the bed, she made her way to the front door, hearing her own gasp of surprise when she opened it and saw it was none other than Fletcher Ramsay who stood there, an expression as dark as a mourning weed upon his face.

She returned his dark look with one of her own. "What do you want?"

"I came to see how you were."

"I thought Mrs. Scott told you. I am fine."

"I wanted to see for myself."

"Why?"

"I was worried about you."

"Don't be. I can take care of myself, and if I can't, there is always Dr. Scott."

"I've seen Dr. Scott. The man is too sick to care for himself, much less you."

"He has sent to Edinburgh for more doctors."

"Cathleen . . . please. May I come in?"

"I'm tired. I have to be up early. Thank you for coming, but please don't bother to come again. If anything should happen, if I find I need you, I'll send for you."

"Cathleen,—"

"Whatever you have to say, I don't want to hear it." She tried to shut the door but found she could not. She looked down and saw his foot wedged there.

"I'd like to explain . . ."

"You needn't bother. I'm not interested in anything you have to say. I'm sure you had your reasons for doing what you did. If you are happy, then I can only be happy for you. Please don't come here again. . . . And move your foot!"

He did not budge.

Without giving him a chance to say anything more, she slammed the door with all her might, which she feared was not much considering how weak she felt. She did feel a sense of satisfaction when she discovered it was enough to shove his foot back.

Once the door was closed, she leaned back against it, trying to stop the frantic pounding of her heart. Taking deep breaths, she stood there listening to the sounds of his horse riding away, as he had done before.

Two days after Dr. Scott announced that he thought the worst of the typhoid outbreak had passed, he took a turn for the worse.

Three days later, he was dead.

Doing what she could to help the sick and having no doctor to guide her, Cathleen managed to get by on even less sleep. Two days passed, then four.

Dr. Scott had been dead almost a week by the time the three doctors from Edinburgh arrived. She had expected them to ease her workload, but Cathleen found that she was still as busy as ever. By the second week of their stay, however, there was a drastic reduction in the number of new cases.

Now that the epidemic seemed to be subsiding, two of the doctors returned to Edinburgh. A few days later, Cathleen was again awakened in the dead of night, only this time it was not Fletcher Ramsay who pounded on her door.

Summoned to Glengarry Castle, where some of the help had taken ill, Cathleen went immediately. Upon her arrival there, she was taken directly to Angus MacTavish, since it was reported that he was the most seriously ill.

It did not take her long to see that this was the case, for out of the three people there who suffered from the fever, he was the most critical. He was now in the beginning of his third week of sickness, which was when typhoid reached its height and the danger of dying was greatest.

The moment she entered his room, Beitris, the scullery maid who had been caring for him, rose to her feet.

"I'm glad you are here. I dinna ken he will last the night. I'm so frightened. Please dinna make me stay here. I'm scared of the dead. I dinna want to catch the fever. Please tell me I can go."

Seeing the girl's agitated state, Cathleen knew that she would be of little help, so she nodded. "Go get some rest. I'll stay with him."

"Oh, thank you," the girl cried, kissing Cathleen's hand before she dashed from the room.

Cathleen went to Angus's bedside, wincing at the sight of the great strapping man who looked as if he had lost at least three stone.

There was not much she could do for him, aside from giving cold sponge baths to reduce the fever. As weak as a baby from much intestinal bleeding, he was able to eat only small sips of watery soup.

Day and night for five days she stayed with him, leaving the room only for short periods of time, when she went to a nearby room to clean herself up and rest.

On her way down to the kitchen to get a little dinner for herself one afternoon, Cathleen was startled to see Beitris rushing toward her.

"His Grace would like to see you," she said.

"Whatever for?"

"His Grace didna say, and saints above! I willna ask him. I willna ask anything of His Grace."

Cathleen nodded, well understanding that.

"If you will follow me, miss, I will take you to him."

Cathleen frowned. She wondered why the Duke of Glengarry wanted to see her.

It's probably about Angus and the fever.

She told herself that he was, more than likely, concerned about the typhoid spreading to other members of the household. Still, as she followed Beitris down the stairs and toward their meeting place, she could not keep from wondering if there was yet another reason why she had received such an urgent summons from the Duke of Glengarry.

Minutes later, she was escorted into a small, private study she had never seen before, where the duke awaited her.

"Come in," Adair said, turning away from the window and looking at her. He nodded toward a nearby chair. "Perhaps you should sit down."

"Oh, I don't mind standing."

"But I mind. Please sit down," he said firmly.

Cathleen sat down, adjusting her skirts about her, her gaze fastened on the duke's face. For a moment he simply returned her look, as if he were waiting for her to look away, with demurely downcast eyes, giving him the edge over her.

She remained steadfast, her gaze locked upon him, her stare unblinking, unwavering.

Adair sat behind a small desk, his hands resting on the top. "I wish to thank you for giving so unselfishly of your time. Angus has been quite ill, and it is my understanding he would have had no chance for survival had it not been for you."

"I am glad I was able to help. Angus is a decent man. It is my greatest hope that he has a speedy recovery."

"Aye. A speedy recovery," the duke said, his eyes boring into her.

Cathleen was uneasy. She shifted her position in the chair as she waited for the duke to say more, and when he did not, she wondered if this was all he intended to say to her. She was about to rise to her feet and excuse herself, when he spoke.

"While I have you here," he began, "perhaps you can answer a few questions for me."

"About what?"

"Various things ... most of them simply to satisfy my curiosity."

"I don't understand."

"I could not help but notice the Earl of Caithness lived with you for quite some time."

"The earl did not live with *me*. He rented the crofter's hut from my grandfather," she said. "It has since burned down, but that was after he left."

"Aye, I have heard he is visiting Dunston now."

She nodded. "That is my understanding."

"I do have a certain amount of curiosity about the earl's purpose in spending so much time in Glengarry."

"Then I suggest you ask the earl. He does not confide in me."

"Oh, come now," Adair said. "I find that hard to believe. I would think a woman as lovely as yourself would have no trouble drawing the earl's interest."

"Obviously, the woman who has drawn the earl's interest is Annora Fraser. Why don't you ask her these questions. The earl and his family were longtime friends of my grandfather. Since his death, I have seen little of Fletcher Ramsay."

"So, he was here on family business, then?"

"I don't know if you would call it business. It is my understanding that he did have a certain amount of interest in Glengarry. I believe he was born here and lived here until he was eight or so. It would only be natural to assume he would want to return to the place of his birth. He hardly knew his father, since he died when the earl was quite young, so he was most interested in hearing stories about him."

"What kind of stories?"

Cathleen was beginning to get a headache and wanted only to return home. She saw no point in all of this. What, for goodness sake, did the duke think she could tell him? In spite of his attempts to be somewhat friendly in his approach, the man made her nervous. She squirmed in her seat. "The usual kind of stories," she replied. "He wanted to know what his father was like, the kinds of things he enjoyed. Who his friends were. Places he had been. People who knew interesting stories about him. Is it so strange for a body to want to know something about their past?"

She saw immediately that her obvious irritation did not sit well with the duke. "I see it was a mistake to think I could talk to you. It is obvious that you are hiding something. The question is, why?" His look was cold, hard. "Just what is *your* relationship to the earl?"

Cathleen rose to her feet. "He is my friend. Nothing more. However, I really don't think it is any of your business, Your Grace. I think your interest in the earl has moved beyond the bounds of common courtesy."

He gave her a cold smile. "I would advise you to have nothing to do with the Earl of Caithness."

"I have not for some time now." She glanced toward the door and was about to start in that direction when the duke's voice stopped her abruptly.

"I have reason to believe the earl is not what he appears to be. It is rumored that he is involved in seditious activities. To involve yourself could implicate you in something that could turn quite nasty."

She gasped, staring at him. "I don't know what you are talking about, and in any case, I think your concern is rather like locking the barn door after the cattle are gone. The earl no longer lives in our crofter's hut, and, as I said before, since my grandfather's death I have seen him hardly at all."

"Perhaps I should make myself more clear—"

"And perhaps you are barking up the wrong tree. I have come here to Glengarry Castle out of concern for the health of your staff. I do not appreciate having my feet held over the fire and being interrogated. If you have questions about the Earl of Caithness, I can think of no one better endowed to answer them than the earl himself."

The duke's face turned a dark red. The dark, piercing eyes flicked over her with no more regard than they would have for a swarm of gnats. Cathleen felt goose bumps popping out under his intense scrutiny.

She did not like this man. He terrified her. To provoke him had been foolish. She vowed to keep her mouth shut.

"I had hoped that you would prove to be a sensible lass.

I know your grandfather did not leave a large fortune behind when he died. As overlord of this area, it is my responsibility to watch over those under my care. You might say that I believe that one good turn deserves another. Should you happen to remember anything that might be of interest to me, please feel free to call here at any time. Give me any information of interest and I will more than make it worth your while. I am sure you *understand*."

"Aye. I understand perfectly."

The Duke of Glengarry rose to his feet and came around the desk. Taking Cathleen's arm, he walked her to the door. "I will give you time to think about what I have said. Perhaps you will feel differently and we can speak of these things at another time, when your passions have cooled."

"There is nothing to speak of. Time will not change my mind. I was taught to tend to my own affairs and let others attend to theirs. I will tell the earl of your interest. Perhaps he will see fit to call upon you himself, so that he might answer all your questions."

That seemed to amuse him. She felt a coldness settle over her as she watched a slow, curving smile stretch across his face. "You are welcome to tell him anything you like, lass, but if you have any affections for him, you might wish to reconsider. I would hate to see the young earl lose his temper over such a trivial matter. Anger could cause him to do something both of you might regret."

For a moment she was so overcome with anger and fear that she thought she could not move. She realized then what kind of man she was up against. She had made a grave mistake in thinking that she could place Fletcher's stay here in an innocent light. To have tried to do so had only implicated her, for she knew that Adair knew she was hiding something.

Finding the strength from somewhere deep within her, she left the study, thinking she could not stay at Glengarry Castle any longer, at least for today. She needed to get away before the evil in the place contaminated her. She needed time to think.

As she made her way home, her mind was awash with

confusion. She wanted nothing more than to run to Fletcher and tell him, but she was afraid.

Afraid for Fletcher.

Afraid for herself.

In the end, she decided that it was best to remain silent. Adair had been right about one thing. If she told Fletcher, he would want to confront Adair, and if he did, it would only complicate things further. The best thing to do was to ignore it, to let Adair think she gave it no more importance than she would the skip of a flea.

Ignore it and it will go away. It is better to suffer a great evil than to cause a little one.

There were several times during the coming days when she felt certain that Angus MacTavish would not win his bout with typhoid, but when he survived the height of the fever, she knew from experience that by the fourth week he would be on the mend.

As Angus grew stronger, he grew more inquisitive. One of the first things he asked her was about the Earl of Caithness.

"Why does he spend so much time here in Glengarry?"

Cathleen felt her heart lurch, for his words sounded remarkably like Adair's, but she saw no reason not to be honest. Angus had already made his dislike of Adair known to her. When she told him about Fletcher's father, Angus said he had heard the rumor years ago.

"And did you believe it?" she asked.

"I would believe anything of the Duke of Glengarry. He is a cunning man and cruel. Tell me, just what it is that the earl is looking for?"

She explained it as best she could, but when she got to the part about there being no proof that Bride Ramsay was Douglas Ramsay's wife, Angus seemed to listen with even more interest.

"There are many Ramsays buried here at Glengarry. Perhaps the one you are looking for is here."

"We have searched the cemetery," she said, then went on to tell him how they had hidden in the chapel.

"Then you searched only the chapel cemetery?"

"Aye. Are there others?"

"There is one other graveyard, one that is older and smaller. The duke had it walled in many years ago, so it is overgrown and almost hidden in a grove of trees. There are only a handful of graves there, all of them much older than those in the cemetery behind the chapel."

"How can I find this place?"

Angus gave her directions, then grew too weary to talk any longer. She sat beside him until he slept soundly, then she quietly left the room.

The sound of dogs barking interrupted the Duke of Glengarry's train of thought. His pen lost a drop of ink and he watched with seething anger as it seeped over the letter he was writing. With a violent curse, he threw the pen down on his desk and came to his feet. Turning toward the window, he looked out.

He saw a woman run across the lawn, keeping to the edge where the shrubbery formed a hedge, then darting through the bushes. He knew instantly who the woman was. The question was, where was she going? The stables lay in the opposite direction. The only thing that lay in the direction she was going was the old cemetery.

So, the Earl of Caithness does not confide in you, hmmmmm? Weel, we will have to see what we can do about that. Perhaps we can arrange a little something for you, Miss Lindsay ... a nice little scare to make you tell me what you know. It would be a pity for one so pretty and young to end up like her grandfather.

Chapter Eighteen

The wind had come up, whipping the branches of the trees and blowing Cathleen's skirts about as she walked toward the grove Angus had mentioned. Arriving there, she saw nothing that resembled a walled-in graveyard, but Angus had been right about one thing—the place was terribly overgrown.

Another blast of wind blew some trailing branches of ivy, revealing what looked like a stone wall. Upon closer inspection, Cathleen decided this had to be the fence. Searching through the overgrown ivy, she followed the fence line until she found a gate. Her heart thumping wildly, she tore away the clinging vines to clear the gate, then pushed on it. The hinges were rusty, the gate difficult to open, but in the end her perseverance paid off and the gate slowly creaked open.

With a quick glance around her to make certain she had not been seen, she stepped inside the gate.

Just as Angus had said, the graves here were much, much older than the others. It was obvious that these graves had not been looked after, for everywhere she looked, the cemetery was terribly overgrown and showing obvious signs of neglect. She wondered at the high, stone fence that encircled the small graveyard, for it was not the type of enclosure usually found around graves. Then she remembered Angus saying that the duke had built the fence several years ago.

She felt a surge of excitement rush through her body, for she could not help speculating just why the wall had been built.

What was he trying to hide?

She hoped above all hopes that the proof Fletcher needed was secreted away behind these walls.

In spite of its overgrown state, the cemetery was as lovely as a garden. Behind the protection of the high walls and safe from the fierce winds that blew across the moors, the roses had found a sort of haven, and they bloomed in profusion, in every delicate color imaginable. Most of them were climbing roses, and with no one to prune and direct their growth, they had wound around everything they could cling to. Long tendrils hung down from the trees, a tangle of swaying color that seemed to leap from one tree to the other, spreading a fragrant mantle over this hidden family plot.

As she looked about, she began to make out the aged grave markers among the dense growth. She began to search the graves one by one, pushing away thick vines, occasionally rubbing moss and lichen from the inscriptions, in her search for one name: Bride Ramsay.

She was about to give up, for she had read half the stones in the plot, but a moment later she found her first bit of proof.

It was not the grave of Bride Ramsay she found but that of Fletcher's father, Bruce Ramsay. A short while later, she came upon a grave that she thought might prove to be a connection, for the stone read:

Madeline de Compiegne Ramsay
beloved wife of Alexander Ramsay

Cathleen stood there for a moment staring at the inscription, a memory stirring in her mind. She remembered that in the

church records they had searched there was proof that Alasdair
Ramsay had a son, Alexander.

Could this Alexander be the brother of Fletcher's Douglas?

She studied the stone again, wondering if there might be
proof somewhere that this Alexander and Fletcher's Douglas
were brothers, for it would prove that his Douglas was Alasdair's son as well.

She searched a few more stones and stopped dead still,
feeling a shiver pass over her as she looked at the stone in
front of her.

Douglas Ramsay
b. 1715   d. 1765

There was no mention of his wife, nothing to connect
Douglas with Bride, but it did prove that Douglas had lived.
Leaving Douglas Ramsay's grave, Cathleen continued her
search. Three stones later, she found what she was looking
for:

Bride Ramsay
b. 1720   d. 1780

It was both exciting and disappointing, for while the stone
bore the name of Bride Ramsay, it did not prove that she had
been the wife of Douglas Ramsay.

Cathleen left the family plot, careful to close the gate and
cover it over again with vines, and rode home. She was
saddened that she hadn't found all the proof Fletcher needed,
but she had part of it. At least it was a start. Somewhere, she
thought, there was proof that Alexander and Douglas were
brothers and the sons of Alasdair Ramsay.

I know it exists.

Back at the cottage, Cathleen bathed and ate a small bowl
of soup, finding she was too exhausted to finish even that.
Wearily dragging herself into bed, she closed her eyes,
expecting to fall asleep as quickly as she always did, but she
could not sleep.

Each time she closed her eyes, she saw the stone that marked Bride Ramsay's grave.

Won't Fletcher be elated to hear I've found it?

Fletcher. Fletcher. Fletcher. How that name haunted her. Would she never know peace?

She punched the pillow. Just the thought of his name sent a pain shooting through her. Why did she bother to search for graves? Why did she care anyway? It was his search, not hers. After all, he had abandoned her for another woman.

"Because it is ever your nature to be helpful, Cathleen," she heard her grandfather say, his voice as plain as if he were standing beside her bed.

The next day there were three new cases of typhoid, and Cathleen wondered if the sickness would ever end. She tried to keep her mind on her work, but all she could think about was having found the grave of Bride Ramsay.

In spite of her pain at the thought of seeing Fletcher with Annora Fraser, she decided she could not keep quiet about her discovery. She decided then that she would go to Dunston to see him as soon as she finished her work today. No matter what he had done to her, no matter how badly she hurt, she could not keep something so important from him.

Much later she made her way to Dunston. She stopped before an immense house that curved in a rambling way about a stone court. She climbed down from the carriage and made her way to the front of the house, where she rapped upon a huge door made up of oak panels reinforced with great iron bands and studded with nails.

The moment the butler opened the door, Cathleen saw the portraits on the wall that seemed to be staring down at her in a way that made her want to turn and run.

"I've come to see the Earl of Caithness," she said.

"This way, please." The butler showed her into a salon. "Wait in here," he said. "I will find Lady Fraser." He then departed.

Cathleen ran to the door. "But I want to see the Earl of Caithness!" she called after him, but if the butler heard her, he did not let on.

With an irritated sigh, she turned back into the salon but did not take a seat.

A few minutes later, Annora swept into the room, looking exceptionally beautiful in lavender silk. Cathleen looked down at her homespun dress, its rose color faded to the lifeless shade of a pale evening sky, and thought it no wonder that Fletcher preferred this exquisite bird in radiant plumage to her own coloring that more closely resembled a red grouse.

"Miss Lindsay, this is a pleasant surprise. Duncan tells me you have come to see Fletcher."

"Aye. I have discovered something he has been searching for. I thought he might like to know about it."

"Oh, I am certain he would. Why don't you tell me, and I'll relay the message for you. It will be dark soon. I'm sure you are anxious to be on your way."

"Aye, but I would like to speak with him personally before I go."

"That is not possible, I'm afraid."

"He is not here?"

Annora looked a little uneasy. "He is ... he is here, of course, but we aren't certain just where. He often disappears like this, only to pop up again when you've about given up on finding him. I am certain *you* know how he is."

"Aye," Cathleen said, "I know."

"I did send Duncan to look for him," Annora said cheerfully, "but it might be quite some time before he finds him."

"I will wait."

Annora's smile faded. "As you wish." Then with a swish of silk similar to the one she entered with, she was gone.

Cathleen waited for over an hour.

There was not much daylight left when she decided she could not wait any longer. She did not like to be out on the roads after dark. Leaving the sumptuous room, she hoped above hope that she could slip out without anyone seeing her.

Fletcher walked into the hallway just in time to catch a glimpse of Cathleen Lindsay tiptoeing down the hall. It took a moment for his mind to register the surprise.

She had almost reached the front door when he called out, "Cathleen! What are you doing here?"

She turned around. "I came to give you some information you've been searching for, but it grows late."

Fletcher frowned. "Surely Duncan did not leave you standing here in the entry?"

"No, *they* graciously left me sitting in the salon. I was just leaving."

"You can't leave now," he said, looking down into her face. "You just got here."

"I have been here for quite some time—over an hour now—but never mind. I must go. I don't want to be out on the roads after dark."

He took her by the arm. "Nor would I want you to be. I'm sorry you had to wait so long. Come with me."

"No . . . Please!" A look of panic froze her face. "I don't want to go back in there. I don't like it here. I shouldn't have come. Please. I must go."

His look softened. "We'll go outside, then. Come on." He took her arm, then opened the door and walked outside with her, ordering the coach to be brought around.

"That won't be necessary. I brought my grandfather's carriage."

"Then I'll have someone drive it over for you. You've been waiting overly long, and I apologize for that. The least I can do is take you home."

She opened her mouth, but he interrupted her.

"The least you can do is let me, Cathleen."

"It isn't necessary."

"I'll be the judge of that. You look exhausted, like you're about to drop on your feet. Besides, I *want* to take you home. Would you deny me the pleasure?"

She gave him a look that said she would sooner believe that chickens had teeth than she would believe he wanted to spend more than two minutes alone with her.

Ah, darling Cathleen, I can see that you don't understand . . . that you no longer trust me. "I know you probably don't believe this, but nothing has changed between us. I wish you could believe me, Cathleen."

A dark, wounded look passed over her face. "I don't believe you."

Her reaction left him stunned. He had actually had the gall to think she would be overjoyed to see him and grateful for his offer to take her home. He'd thought that his assurance that nothing had changed between them would make everything right, and that she would forgive him as had always been her nature. In his arrogance, he had simply assumed that because she had come to him in the first place, all he would have to do is say a few words—words that he figured she wanted to hear—and all would be as it had been before.

As he thought more about it, he realized that the love she had so freely given to him had seemed an ironclad part of his life, something dependable that would always be there whenever he reached for it. He had taken it for granted. In the secret part of his being that longed for love, warmth, and passion, he had kept Cathleen, and on a certain level he had imagined that she would readily understand, just as he had assumed she would love him unconditionally.

He contemplated taking her into his confidence, telling her about his suspicions that Adair was responsible for David's death, that he didn't give two flips for Annora Fraser.

Would she believe him if he told her that this had only been a ruse because he feared for her life?

One look at her stubborn chin and proud carriage, and he thought not. Her expression was as murderous as he knew her feelings toward him were. Soon, perhaps, he could tell her. He could only hope that when he did, it would not be too late.

In the twilight darkness of the stables, Annora put a detaining hand on the coachman's arm. He turned toward her.

"When you drive them to her cottage, do not take the coach. Take the smaller carriage. I don't want you sitting too far from them. I want to know everything they talk about. You must be my eyes and ears, you understand?"

"Aye. You want me to listen to their conversation."

She nodded. "Come to me as soon as you return. Do not forget."

The coachman nodded. "I willna forget."

Annora watched him hitch the team to the small carriage. She smiled as he climbed into the seat and drove the carriage around to the front of the house. She would not rest until she knew what the bit of news was that had brought Miss Lindsay clipping over to Dunston, humiliating herself in the process, knowing she was a spurned lover.

Annora stood in the dark shadows of the stable and watched as, a few minutes later, the carriage passed in front of the stables and rolled on down the driveway. She smiled at the sight. *Let them talk*, she thought.

Knowledge is power.

Once they were in the carriage, Cathleen glanced at Fletcher. He did not say anything, but sat there, his gaze moving over her, taking in every detail. She knew he was making a comparison, not between her and Annora, for, faith, there was little to compare, Annora being such a great beauty and all. Something Cathleen knew she was not.

No, his comparison was between the Cathleen he remembered and the Cathleen he now saw. Watching him study her, she felt her heart turn over with a sad little flutter. How long ago it seemed that she had drawn water from the well and seen him riding toward her.

She had changed a great deal since that day, more than he, she was certain. Whatever she had felt for him once, she had no illusions about herself, her appearance, or her station in life. What was he thinking as those blue, blue eyes swept over her? Was he wondering how he could have ever cared for someone like her, or was he simply feeling sorry for the woman for whom he had outgrown his attraction?

She turned her head and looked out the window, seeing the well-manicured lawns of Dunston as they passed by.

"It's good to see you again."

She glared at him. "You can dispense with any attempts at conversation. I have nothing to say to you."

The look on his face told her that her words had found their mark. Strange. Hurting him did not give her the pleasure she had thought it would. She turned her face away once more, leaning her head against the glass window. She felt numb.

"You look tired. Are you still helping with the fever?"

"Aye."

"I understand there are fewer cases of it now?"

"Aye. We are praying the worst is over."

"I hope so, as much for your sake as for anyone. You have lost weight."

She knew she had lost weight, but it hurt to hear him mention it. He would have noticed the other things as well, things that he was too gentlemanly or too kind to mention to her now: the deep purple circles under her eyes, which seemed to have lost their luster, the dull cast to her hair, which he had once called so vibrant.

"I've missed you."

She felt a faintness overcome her and had to grip the seat. Of all the things he could have said, this one hurt her the most. That he would say things that he did not mean because he was struck with an attack of guilty conscience ... it was almost more than she could bear. She had never felt such anger. "I find that hard to believe, touching sentiment though it is."

He smiled and reached for her hand. "No sentiment, I assure you."

She moved her hand out of his reach. "All of that is unimportant and has no bearing on the reason I came here." She held herself distant from him, willing herself to be separate, precise, and very businesslike.

The look he gave her said he had decided to let things ride for the moment. She found it both satisfying and disappointing that he would not try to get things on a friendlier ground.

"You said you found something?"

"Aye. Something important. I know where Bride Ramsay is buried, and Douglas, too."

"Go on."

He sat quietly as she went on to tell him in her businesslike manner about the grave of Bride and her suspicions about Douglas and Alexander being brothers. "Alexander's wife was named Madeline. She is buried there as well. Of course, you will want to see them for yourself."

"You bet your sweet life, I do," he said, then he took her hands in his before she could draw them away. "Cathleen, you don't know what this means."

She pulled her hands away. "I do, of course. It is the reason I came here, but I don't want to mislead you. There is no mention of Douglas being Alasdair's son, or Bride being his wife, nothing that would give you the proof you need."

"I understand," he said, "but it's the first break I've had. I know now, for certain, that Bride and Douglas both existed. It's something at least."

"Aye, it is a start," she said, "but nothing more." She glanced at him, and when he looked at her, she quickly looked away. "You must be careful going to Glengarry Castle," she said.

"I understand. I, of all people, know Adair is a treacherous bastard. I'll be careful."

"If you come at twilight, I will be finished then and I can show you where the graves are located."

His face hardened. "I don't want you involved in this, Cathleen."

She smiled sadly. "We have had this argument before, or have you forgotten?"

"No, I haven't forgotten. I will not allow you to involve yourself," he said, giving her a soft look that matched the softness in his voice. "I am not happy to know you have been snooping about Glengarry. It is too dangerous. I want you to promise me you won't risk it again."

"We will see," she said, then leaned her head back against the cushions and closed her eyes. "I don't want to talk anymore. I'm too tired."

"You won't stop, though, will you? You will keep on working and keep on giving to others until there is nothing left. I—"

As if he had suddenly noticed the dark circles beneath her eyes, the way she seemed to be sinking into the deep sleep of someone overly fatigued, he did not finish what he had intended to say. He gently pulled her into his arms.

Even in her extreme weariness her mind was telling her to fight, but her body was simply too exhausted to obey. With a sigh, she gave herself to the feeling of being held in his arms again.

Even if it was only for a little while.

Chapter Nineteen

Annora went to Glengarry Castle early the next morning, but Adair was not there. She inquired about Angus.

"He is ill, Your Ladyship," the housekeeper informed her. "He has been at death's door with typhoid these past weeks."

"Take me to him," Annora said, and when the housekeeper gave her a surprised look, she added, "He is an old friend. He worked for my father when I was a child."

The housekeeper nodded. "This way, please."

A few minutes later, Annora sat beside Angus's bed. "Are you certain there is nothing I can do for you?" she asked him.

Angus shook his head weakly. "I am much better," he said. "Miss Lindsay has been here every day. I don't think a doctor could have done more."

"I'm sorry I didn't come sooner. I had no idea you were ill."

"How did you find out?"

"The housekeeper told me."

"You came here for another reason?"

Annora shifted nervously in her chair. "I had business with Adair."

Angus's expression darkened. "Have no dealings with him, Annora. The man cannot be trusted. I did not tell you before, because I did not want to frighten you."

"Tell me what?"

"What I'm going to say will shock and horrify you. You may not believe me, although it is the truth. I swear it upon the love I have always held for you. I know Adair was responsible for the death of Bruce Ramsay."

"Fletcher's father?"

"Aye."

Annora's breathing quickened. Her hands began to shake. "How do you know?"

"How I know is not important, but I got it from someone who was in the duke's employ for a long time. He told me, just before he died."

"Why have you stayed here working for him when you know something like that?"

"Because it's too late for me. You know his power, his wrath. I fear what would happen to me if I ever left. Those who leave the duke's employ meet with fatal accidents. Leave here and you die."

"But if you stay . . ."

"You grow too old to work and the duke continues to take care of you—as long as you keep your mouth shut. But you never leave his employ. Never."

"I don't believe you."

He ignored her and went on talking. "Like you, most of us became involved—innocently, of course—and now it is too late to get out. We are part of his treachery. To talk would be to implicate ourselves."

Annora was more afraid than she had ever been in her life. She decided not to go to Adair with this information, because if Angus was right then Adair might do something to Fletcher and to Cathleen Lindsay.

She did not want Cathleen to have Fletcher Ramsay, but that did not mean she wanted to see her dead and Fletcher along with her.

Annora studied Angus's features. His face was a frozen mask as he spoke. She had known Angus for a long time. She realized now that he was telling her the truth, horrible as it was.

She did not want to tell Angus that she was already involved, and that she too would never leave the duke's employ.

"Promise me," he said. "Promise me you will get out while you still can."

"I will think about it," she said. A few seconds later, she stood. "I must go now. I'll come back to see you."

"No," Angus said. "Don't come back here for any reason, especially to see me. I would not want it on my conscience . . . if anything happened to you."

Annora gave him a stiff smile. "Nothing will happen to me," she said, wishing she could believe the words as easily as she said them. She felt sick inside. She could not stop thinking that Adair had caused the death of Fletcher's father. The thought disgusted her. She was not above doing a little snooping here and there, but she wanted no part in it if things went further.

She wanted no blood on her hands.

But how could she stop now? She was in this thing whether she liked it or not. Adair was not a man to reason with, nor was he prone to pity. She had struck a bargain with the devil, and, as Angus had said, once you were a part of Adair's treachery, you never escaped.

Her hands trembling, fear drawing the moisture from her throat, she decided she would have to continue with the charade, at least for a while. As long as she gave Adair the information, what harm could it cause if she waited one day? That way, she would still be giving him the information he wanted, but *after* Fletcher and Cathleen went to see the graves. After all, Cathleen had already seen the tombstones and said there was no proof there; nothing to give Fletcher the advantage he needed; nothing to cause Adair to lose ground.

What could be the harm in that?

Angus raised himself in the bed, resting on his elbows. His voice sounded weary and tired. "Promise me you won't get involved, Annora. Swear to me that you will stay away from this . . . this house of evil."

Annora swallowed and glanced toward the door. She had never wanted to run from a place so much in her life. She wanted to run and run and keep on running until she was out of Glengarry, out of Scotland as well. "I will stay away, if that is what you wish," she said, turning toward the door. When she opened it, Angus spoke one last time.

"Get out of this, Annora. While you still can . . . before it is too late."

She nodded, and with a sinking feeling, she left. As she walked down the long hallway, she felt gripped by terror.

For her, it was too late.

The day after Annora's visit with Angus, Fletcher met Cathleen near the grove behind Glengarry Castle. It was dusk. The sun was sinking low in the sky by the time she led him down the tree-lined path to the fence she had found hidden in the grove. He stood nearby, waiting as she searched the trailing vines of ivy looking for the door, and when she located it, he stepped forward and pushed it open for her.

It was as if a magical opening had suddenly appeared in the midst of the solid stone fence, and the two of them stepped inside. "It's like a secret cemetery," she said. "I was thinking that perhaps Adair had this particular plot walled off because he wanted to keep the graves hidden from view."

"I wouldn't put it past him," Fletcher said.

"This way," she said, starting off in another direction, stepping lightly over the grass, weaving through the overgrown shrubbery, ducking beneath creepers that dangled from branches. She stopped near an ancient oak tree whose bark was covered with lichen, parting a curtain of tangled vines. He watched her, seeing the way her simple green gown swirled about her legs as she moved, graceful as a deer.

Reminding himself that this was neither the time nor the place for softer things, he walked around her, almost passing a grave marker, then stopped and turned around slowly.

Cathleen went to stand beside him as he stood looking down at the simple stone.

Bruce Ramsay
Duke of Glengarry

His heart wrenched. It had been a long, long time since he had been this close to his father. He dropped down in a crouch, his hand coming out to trace the letters of his father's name. "Someone tried to scratch out the words *Duke of Glengarry*," he said.

"Aye, I saw it earlier."

"He will get a new marker," he said, "when this is finished."

"Aye. One with the dates on it. It would be fitting."

He clenched his fists at his sides, the muscle working in his jaw. It was back: the anger, the rage, the desire to confront Adair. Willing himself to keep his head, Fletcher pulled a few weeds from the grassy mound that covered his father's bones.

"I haven't forgotten," he whispered. "All the things you taught me. All the things you stood for. I have remembered. All the time I was away, you were always before me, like a beacon from a lighthouse, guiding my way. I will never forget. I loved you then. I love you now."

He felt Cathleen's hand, light upon his shoulder; felt too the warm splash of her tears upon his hand. "I wish he could have lived . . . that I could have known him," she whispered.

"Yes," he said softly, "so do I."

Fletcher rose to his feet and turned toward her, having pushed the feelings aside. His face was an iron mask as he said, "Lead on."

She brought the back of her hand to her face. "The other graves are over here."

He gave her a smile. "It's all right," he said. "There is no need for sadness. My father has been gone from my life for a long time, and yet he was always present."

"I love you, Fletcher Ramsay."

"And I, you."

She turned away from him then, and went ahead, going from grave to grave, searching the names, until they came to the graves of Bride and Douglas Ramsay.

Fletcher stood still, looking down at the names he had

searched for for so long. As Cathleen had said, there was nothing more there than their names and the dates of birth and death. Nothing to prove that Bride was the wife of his Douglas, or that Douglas was Alasdair's son. So much, and yet so very little.

"I'm sorry there isn't more written here," she whispered as she stood beside him, looking at the gravestones of Bride and Douglas.

"I am too. There isn't much to go on, save the fact that there was a Bride Ramsay and someone named Douglas Ramsay."

"But that doesn't prove it was your Douglas."

"Or my Bride," he said, unable to keep the disappointment from his voice. "It isn't proof of anything. They could have been cousins, or even brother and sister." He turned away, taking her arm. "Come on, there is no reason to tarry here. I'll feel better when I see you safely home."

They started to leave, then Fletcher stopped suddenly, his gaze locking on another grave.

Cathleen stared at the stone, the one she had seen earlier with the name Madeline de Compiegne Ramsay written on it. "What is it?" she asked.

"I'm not sure," Fletcher said, not taking his eyes from the marker. "It's strange, but I have the feeling I've seen this stone before."

"You couldn't have seen it before. It is obvious that no one has been in here for ages."

"I know, but there is something oddly familiar about it."

"Familiar?" Cathleen studied the headstone again, then shrugged. "You couldn't have seen this stone before," she said. "Perhaps it's just the name that seems familiar. You've been searching records for a quite some time now. I'm certain you've come across the name Madeline Ramsay more than once."

"Perhaps I have," Fletcher said, shrugging, yet still feeling a mysterious premonition about that name.

He turned then to see Cathleen standing quietly in the shadows beside him. He gave her a tentative smile, then picked up her hand and held it between both of his, his thumb rubbing lightly on the inside of her wrist. "It looks like we are back where we started."

"No, it only seems that way because you are disappointed. Now you have proof that there was a Bride Ramsay, and you know she was buried beside someone named Douglas Ramsay. Now all you have to do is find out why."

"Oh, is that all I have to do?" He gave her a sad smile. "Ever the optimist," he said. "Do you know that just being around you seems to lighten my spirits?"

"Hah!" she said. "It may be nigh close to dark, Fletcher Ramsay, but I can see well enough to know that a more woeful face I have never seen. If your spirits were any heavier they would be sinking into the soil."

He looked at her, seeing her elfin face in the twilight and the way she smiled up at him, knowing her words had been nothing more than an attempt to cheer him. She had a smile that didn't seem to know its own power, and he found himself thinking he had never before met a comely woman who made no attempt to charm. Everything about her was as natural and pure as the evening air they breathed. He became aware, then of an odd tightening in his chest, a fluttering in the vicinity of his heart.

Why her?

Why was it that this woman, out of all the women he had met, caused such a response in him? Why did he delight in everything about her?

"Come on," she said, taking charge and tugging his hand. "We have been fortunate so far that no one has seen us. I am not in the habit of pressing my luck."

Her determination almost erased his disappointment. He did not release her hand, nor did he allow her to pull him along. "What if I said I like standing here in the darkness with you, that I would rather take my chances on being discovered if it meant I could hold your hand a bit longer?"

"I would say you were daft! If it is my hand you want to be holding, Fletcher Ramsay, then come along with you. There will be time enough for that when we are away from here."

"Is that a promise then?" he asked, drawing her closer. He could tell by the panicked look in her eyes that he was being a bit too forward, that she was uneasy about being here, because of her fear of the dark and, more important, because she was still feeling the bite of his rejection.

Still, all he could think about was being with her again. "What if I told you I wanted to make love?"

"Then I would tell you to hie yourself to Dunston and tell that to Annora. You have made your choice."

"Have I? Are you so certain?"

She gave him a frustrated look. "Aye, I am certain, but it sounds like you are having a wee bit o' trouble. If you can't make up your mind, then perhaps what you need is to get your mind on something else."

That intrigued him. "Something else, hmmmm? Like what, for instance?"

She yanked back her hand and gave him a shove. "Like mounting your horse and getting out of here."

She walked around him, and he followed her through the gate. When they reached the place where their horses were hidden, it was hard for Fletcher not to laugh as he watched her mount her fat, shaggy Highland pony, Flora. She glanced at him, seeing his amusement. "I will thank you not to laugh. My cart, as you well know, was smashed."

"Laugh at you? I would never be so despicable," he said, "even though your legs are scraping the ground."

"Aye," she replied, "you would laugh, and my legs are not scraping the ground."

"I've seen bigger goats."

"In America, more than likely. Everything is bigger there, I am told. Even braggarts."

He was laughing so hard he had difficulty mounting his horse, but he managed. He followed her then, wondering if she felt the chill of the evening now that the warmth of the sun was gone.

They kept off the main road, following narrow trails or blazing their own, riding beneath the crags that sheltered the valley, following for a while the meandering path of a gurgling beck that seemed in a hurry to reach the river Garry. They passed a few farm houses and abandoned crofter's huts, keeping to the hollows of the fells, startling a flock of sheep, and finding themselves chased by a barking dog.

He did not realize they had reached her cottage until he saw the burned-out shell of the crofter's hut where he had once stayed. They rode into the front yard.

She did not dismount straightaway, but waited a moment, staring at her house. Her pause of inspection seemed to satisfy her, for before he could dismount and come to help her down, she had both feet firmly planted upon the ground.

"Here," he said, taking the pony's reins from her, "I'll put fat Flora away for you before I go, and don't tell me Robert will do it. I know he doesn't come here after dark."

"Go easy," she said, handing Flora over to him. "She has been quite skittish since our accident with the cart."

"I can be gentle," he said, wondering if she heard the implication in his voice.

Apparently she did, for even in the darkness he saw signs of her sudden shyness, the way she dipped her head and turned toward her house, stepping across the lawn and opening the front door, slamming it with just enough force to let him know that she had.

He chuckled, then led the pony to the paddock, whistling a little ditty as they went. A short while later, he made his way back to the house.

He found her in the kitchen. She had a fire going and was putting on the kettle for tea. She did not hear him come in, and that gave him a moment to study her.

Although she was still a young and vigorous woman, obviously in the prime of health, she had lost weight since her grandfather's death, for the lines of her form were rather thin and spare, softened somewhat by the long full skirt and the looseness of her bodice, which was almost hidden beneath the folds of a large white muslin fichu that she had crossed over her breasts and tied behind her.

She turned around then. "Oh!" she said, startled, her hand coming up to her chest. "I did not hear you come in." She frowned, and he knew she was thinking that she should send him packing, and yet that good and kind part of her wanted to invite him to stay for tea. He stood there watching her, waiting to see if it would be her wounded pride or her infinite goodness that won out.

"Would you like some tea?"

He grinned. Her goodness was too ingrained for even her to overcome. "I'd love some," he said, coming farther into the room, stopping a few feet from her and leaning against the hutch, where he could watch her.

He studied her face, wondering why it was that he found her beautiful, for in truth her beauty was spoilt somewhat by the prominence of her cheekbones, the fullness of her mouth, and the pointedness of her chin. Perhaps it was her eyes, that lovely shade of blue-violet that seemed particular to her, sparkling and full of life. Or was it the delicate nose, the perfectly smooth brow? And then again, it might be her skin, which seemed to catch and hold the freshness of Glengarry's air and running becks.

"I'll only be a moment," she said, and he sensed that her words were inspired more from self-consciousness than from any idea that he was impatient.

Watching her, he decided that there was something about her face and figure, something that seemed in harmony with the bare stretches of moor and the lonely crags of the fells, something that seemed to mark her a true daughter of the Highlands, a partaker of their sadness.

A silence fell upon the room.

At last, when she spoke, she seemed too nervous. "If you would like to go into the parlor, I'll bring the tea in there."

"I'm off to the parlor, then," he said, with as much good-natured charm as he could muster.

Cathleen watched him go, then went to her room. Taking her Bible from her small desk, she picked up her pen, dipped it in ink, and wrote the names she had seen on the gravestones today. After spelling out Madeline de Compiegne Ramsay and Alexander Ramsay, she wrote the names Bride Ramsay and Douglas Ramsay, then sat back with a satisfied sigh. The names were recorded. There would be no chance of her forgetting them now.

After putting the Bible away, she returned to the kitchen to get the tea.

* * *

A short while later, Cathleen carried in two cups of tea to the parlor, where Fletcher waited. "I remembered you didn't take anything in your tea, so I decided not to bring the tray." She placed the cup and saucer on the table beside the chair he had taken.

She took a chair across from him, the one he had come to think of as her chair.

"How have you been? Are you able to keep up with the chores around here?"

"Aye. Robert and Fionn have been a big help, thanks to you."

"It was the least I could do."

She ignored that. "Everyone has been so kind. My grandfather was a much loved and respected man."

"Yes, he was. I'm glad to hear you've had plenty of help. Are you sure there is nothing else I can do to help you?"

"No," she said, obviously eager to change the subject. "I will be going back to Glengarry Castle tomorrow, to check on Angus. Perhaps while I am there I could ask him about the name Madeline Ramsay."

"I don't want you asking any questions, nor do I want you to do any snooping around," he said, feeling the worst kind of cad when he saw the way his words seemed to puncture her and leave her flat. "Stay away from the castle and from Adair Ramsay. It isn't that I don't appreciate your help."

"What is it, then? Is it me? Are you afraid you will have to spend time with me if I involve myself in this?"

He understood then the depths of the pain his rejection had caused her. He sighed, uncertain as to what he should do. He did not want to involve her further, yet to continue his farce with Annora would only cause Cathleen more pain, and the more she suffered, the further away from him she became. Now he worried that there would be a point of no return, a point where, no matter how much of the truth he confessed to her, it would make no difference.

He would not risk that.

He put his tea down on the table beside him, then rose to his feet and moved his chair in front of hers, so that when he sat down, their knees would almost be touching. Then, taking the cup of tea from her trembling hands, he placed it on the table beside her.

"What are you doing?"

"You know what I'm doing."

"I think you better go."

He sat down. "I think it's time we had a talk."

"Put your chair back. You can talk from over there."

"No, I can't."

"Why not?"

"Because I want to be close to you, Cathleen."

" *'Lying lips are an abomination to the Lord,' "* she said. "Proverbs."

"It is no lie. I do want to be close to you, Cathleen. I want to be as close to you physically as I feel in my heart."

"As if I believe that."

"What I've done ... this thing with Annora—it means nothing. Don't you understand that?"

"You don't have to explain anything to me. What you do is your own affair."

"No, it's not. I know what you are thinking, how you feel."

She gave him a look that said he could not possibly understand what she was feeling.

"You think I callously made love to you, to satisfy my own lust, without any feeling for you at all. After all, I did go to Dunston to stay. But it isn't the way you think. I have never made love to Annora Fraser, nor do I intend to."

"Then why did you go there?"

He pushed his chair back and rose to his feet. He paced the room two or three times, then went to stand at the window, his hands rammed in his back pockets. A moment later, he threw his head back and closed his eyes.

What should he do?

He stayed that way for some time, weighing the consequences, trying to decide what to do. At last, he decided he had to be honest with her. He could not risk losing her, would not risk her continued involvement in his search. If she understood the danger she was in, then she would stay away from him and out of his quest for proof.

He turned around at last, and never took his gaze from her as he spoke. "I was trying to protect you, Cathleen. All of this—my pretending to care for Annora, my going to stay at Dunston . . . it was all to protect you."

"Protect me from what?"

He shook his head, staring down at his feet for a moment. "This is not going the way I had planned. I wanted to keep you safe, Cathleen. I don't want to frighten you or cause you more pain."

"Keep me safe? Frighten me? What are you talking about?"

He went to her then, and taking her hands, he drew her to her feet and gently enfolded her in his arms, holding her close. "I didn't want to tell you this, but you leave me no choice. In order to protect you, I have to tell you the truth now."

"I don't understand."

He saw the confusion in her eyes, the look of despair. Her lovely violet eyes were stormy with panic. He was so acutely conscious of her nearness, of the fragrance of her hair and her skin, of the natural tint of her lips, which were too full for fashion but perfect for kissing. He clenched his jaw, forcing back those thoughts. Now wasn't the time to think of softer things. Now he needed to be strong, for in a moment she would need his strength as well as her own.

She seemed suddenly fragile to him and that made him want to say the right thing to her, but that was no longer a choice for him. In order to keep her near him, in order to protect her, he had to hurt her.

With a deep breath and a prayer, he said, "David's death was no accident."

He had never realized you could actually witness the blood drain from a person's face, but he saw it now.

"No!" she whispered. "It can't be true." Pulling back, she searched his eyes, as if looking for something that would assure her what he said was not the truth. But she saw only honesty and sincerity there. Then she buried her face in her hands, shaking her head from side to side. "Who would want to kill my grandfather? Everyone loved him. He had no enemies."

"No, he didn't . . . at least not until I came to town."

She shuddered and her hands fell away. He saw the glisten of tears brimming in her eyes and he knew that in a moment they would spill down her cheeks. "Adair," she whispered, as if her chest were crushing the breath from her lungs. "You think he killed Grandpa because he was helping you?"

"I am certain of it. Even the way he died ... it was too much like the way my father died. You never suspected he might be involved?"

"Only once. It was right after the funeral ... but I could not believe anyone could be so demented, so callous in regard to their immortal soul that they would stoop to killing a man of God. No, I could not believe that even Adair was capable of such."

Suddenly she turned and dropped back into her chair. Her face had a blank expression as she stared across the room, shaking her head slowly, the anguish she felt so obvious in her voice. She buried her face in her hands and sobbed. "Oh, Grandpa, not this way. Why did you have to die like this? You always gave so much. It isn't fair. You should have had an honorable death, at least."

Fletcher dropped to his knees in front of her, taking her hands in his. "Now you see why I went to Annora's. If Adair even so much as suspected I harbored any feeling for you, he would use you to get back at me."

"Aye." Her lovely eyes held fast to his, but the tears would not hold back. "I understand now," she said. "I'm glad you told me. While I understand why you left, it makes my grandfather's death harder to accept. But I ken even that will heal in time."

He felt a quiver of desire and sympathy, a warmth that wanted to reach out and touch her, a cold chill that swept down his spine.

He took her face in his hands, wiping the path of tears from her cheeks with his thumb. "Once this is over, if I have it in my power, Cathleen, I will spend the rest of my life seeing that you never have to suffer again."

Her eyes studied him, unconsciously wooing, responding to the soft allure of his words. His hands slipped around to her neck, drawing her closer. She turned her head to kiss his wrist, then pressed her cheek against it.

He kissed her neck, feeling her breath coming quickly. His hands were in her hair now, his mind paying no attention to the sound of her hairpins hitting the floor. The silky, fragrant mass tumbled down around them, like a waterfall they could secret themselves behind.

Whispering her name became a litany, a sonnet he committed to memory. But that was not enough, he thought. No matter how close he got to her, it was never enough. There was never a point that was sufficient, and he thought that he would feel this same acute frustration even if he were able to absorb her into his very bones.

Where did she begin and he leave off?

He quivered with excitement, his body hard and ready as he covered her face with scattered kisses, dragging his tongue along the delicate curves of her ear, his hands massaging her back. His skin was hot, as was hers. She was the creation of his desire, a fantasy of his imagination, the invention of a thousand dreams.

She was his.

His breath was rapid now, mingled with hers, and his mouth sought the warmth of her with a kiss. He stroked her mouth gently, his chest pressing hard against her breasts. His thoughts no longer rational, he wanted her to the point of desperation, but even then, deep inside, he knew it would be a mistake to take her here, now. He could not use her grief as a way of drawing her into his bed.

It was this knowledge that gave him the strength he needed to break the kiss and pull away.

His body responded with fury, and not even his mind seemed to understand. For a moment he could not say anything, so he simply sat there, with her head pressed against his chest. Then, after a long while, he found the strength to speak. "Forgive me," he whispered.

Her head came up and she stared at him oddly, then dipped her head, turning it away. "What made you stop?" she asked.

She wanted him and she was hurting. He could see that, and it made it all the more difficult for him. "Because you deserve so much more than what I was offering you. I have done nothing but bring death, grief, and amorality into your life. I have taken and taken and given nothing back. You are too innocent, too trusting. You have never been taught to watch out for people like me. As Ben Franklin said, 'A man in a passion rides a mad horse.'"

"Ben who?"

He could not help smiling at the way her nose seemed to turn up in unison with her question. "Benjamin Franklin is . . . was . . . Oh, never mind. What you really want to know is why I stopped." He shrugged. "I don't know. It couldn't be honor." He gave a sort of laugh. "I haven't had an honorable thought since I met you. Maybe it's just because I see something beautiful in you, something I don't want to take away or destroy."

"I'm not that fragile."

"No, but you're vulnerable." He came to his feet, drawing her up with him, then he picked up her hand, kissed it, and turned to walk to the door. He understood now how a condemned man feels walking the last few steps to the gallows.

She followed him, stopping just a short distance away. "Would you like to stay to dinner?"

"If I stayed, sweet Cathleen, it wouldn't be for dinner. I would want far more than you are offering."

She said nothing, but he could see in her eyes that his words warmed her. "And if I offered it?"

He smiled. "Sleep on it," he said, "and if you still feel that way, then we'll see what we can do."

She gave him a shy smile. "I'll sleep on it," she said softly.

"Sleep," he said, then nodded, reaching out to caress her cheek. "I'm glad one of us can."

When he was outside and she had closed the door, he made his way to his horse. It wasn't until he turned up the road to Glengarry that he said, "It must be love, because I would love to sleep . . . just sleep, beside you."

Chapter Twenty

Annora glanced nervously at Adair, wishing she had not involved herself in this affair. She did not feel well. Her head ached abominably. Her body felt warm. And for good reason. She was worried now, worried just how far this thing would go before someone was hurt. She was not foolish enough to think there was a point at which Adair would stop. He would not quietly submit to Fletcher's inquisitiveness, his nosy prying. He would keep Glengarry at all costs. A shudder passed over her at the thought.

"Come, come, I haven't all day. What do you have to report?" Adair asked, his eyes boring into her with an intensity that made her remember all the things Angus had said.

Annora moistened her lips, finding her mouth almost too dry to speak, yet her palms were damp. "Cathleen Lindsay came to Dunston to see Fletcher. It seems she discovered some graves. . . . "

"Graves? Here? At Glengarry?"

"Aye. She said they were the graves of Bride and Douglas, and a woman named Madeline."

He brought his palms together, his long fingers extended, the index fingers resting against his mouth as he listened, but when Annora finished speaking, he nodded. "In the old cemetery," he said. "Did he say anything about coming here to see them?"

"Yes, but Cathleen told him there was no information on the stones . . . nothing that would give him proof."

"That much is true. There isn't any useful information there, or Bruce Ramsay would have used it years ago, but that does not matter. The Earl of Caithness will want to see for himself." Adair came to his feet. "I'll put extra guards around there."

She shifted uneasily in her chair, lowering her gaze to study her hands, which were clasped tightly together in her lap.

He stood there for some time, looking down at her as if considering something. "When did Miss Lindsay come to Dunston?" he asked. "What day?"

Annora swallowed and looked straight at him, knowing that she could not let him see her fear. "Day—" her voice croaked, then broke off. "It was day before yesterday."

"Day before yesterday," he repeated, his face growing dark with anger. He had never looked more like a predator than he did now. "Day before *yesterday*, and you are just now coming here to tell me this?"

"I came here before, but you were not here," she said, her voice sounding weak and uncertain.

He slammed his hands down on the desk. "I will give you one warning, Annora, and one warning only. Don't lie to me—ever!"

"I didn't . . . "

He held up his hand to cut her off, then smiled coldly. "Do not cross me, Annora. This is the last warning I will give you. Do you understand?"

"Aye, I understand," she whispered.

"What? Speak up! I want to be certain there is no confusion about this, because your life depends upon it."

"I understand," she said. "Completely."

"Good," he said, "because there are no second chances."

By the time Fletcher arrived at Dunston, he had already decided to move back into the village. He would take the room he had rented previously from the Widow MacAlister.

After packing his belongings, he came down the stairs and met Annora, who had just returned home.

She stopped, looked at him, then glanced down at his packed bags. "You are leaving?"

"I think it best."

"Why?"

"I've work to do, Annora, and you are a distraction."

She gave him a hesitant smile. "Thank you for the compliment," she said, "but I don't want you to go."

"I have to. You knew this was not a permanent thing."

"Is it because of her?"

"Who?"

Annora licked her lips. Her face was clammy and pale. She seemed nervous. "You know who. Cathleen Lindsay."

"No, it isn't because of her," he lied.

"Where will you go when you leave here? To her house?"

"You know better than that. I will take a room at Widow MacAlister's . . . after I pay a short visit to my aunt at Caithness."

"I need you to stay here, Fletcher. Please don't go." He could not help noticing the strange way she spoke. She *needed* him to stay here? It did not make sense. Besides her strange way of talking, she was acting a bit peculiar, as if she was agitated about something.

"I have to go, Annora."

She began to wring her hands. Her color was gone, leaving her face even more pale and ghostly than before. "You . . . you don't know what you are doing, Fletcher."

He studied her face. "Something is wrong," he said. "Tell me what it is, Annora. Maybe I can help. Are you worried? Afraid of something?"

She shook her head, laughing lightly, but it was not Annora's laugh that he heard, but a forced, artificial one. "I'm not afraid of anything. Why should I be? I simply don't want you to go. Is that so strange? You know I had plans . . . plans for us to do more than converse with each other politely over dinner."

"I know," he said softly, "and I'm sorry for that. You are a beautiful woman. . . . "

"But not, I take it, the right woman?"

"No," he said, taking a deep sigh. "You are not the right woman."

Her face seemed to fall, and her shoulders stooped in a defeated way. He could see something akin to despair in the depths of her eyes. She stepped aside. "Go then," she said. "Go, and the rest of the world be damned."

He hesitated. "Are you certain there is nothing wrong?"

She nodded, then opened the door. "Go with God, Fletcher Ramsay."

Fletcher gave her a light kiss, then stepped through the door. A moment later, he mounted his horse and rode out of Annora Fraser's life.

As luck would have it, his decision to move from Dunston was a wise one, for the day after, Annora came down with typhoid fever.

Two weeks after Annora had taken ill, Cathleen was summoned to Dunston. By the time she arrived there, the housekeeper, Mrs. Farquar, was waiting for her, her face splotchy from crying.

"Thank God ye've come, Miss Lindsay. I fear my mistress willna make it through the night. I ken the fever has taken a mighty hold on her. Out of her head, she is, with her puir body burnin' like it was on fire."

"I'll do what I can." Cathleen hurried along the hallway, following Mrs. Farquar to Annora's room, finding Annora in a very bad state.

For two days and nights she stayed with Annora, not sleeping save for a few small naps she managed while Annora slept. Her weariness went beyond mere exhaustion now, for the past few weeks were taking a heavy toll upon her. Cathleen's body no longer seemed capable of distinguishing night from day, and when she had the opportunity to sleep, she often found she could not.

"Can a body be too tired to sleep?" she asked Mrs. Farquar.

"Aye, a person can push their puir body until it canna function properly. It is called mistreatment, and I ken you have been guilty of a lot of that, lass. Why, just look at you— and pardon me for saying so—but you look as if you are about to drop. You are pale as a ghost, and your eyes look as if they are sinking into your head. You are thin as a pikestaff, and your hands are shaking and raw as a piece of meat."

Cathleen looked down at her trembling hands. They were raw and swollen from repeatedly wringing out wet towels to cover Annora's body. It was something that had to be done in order to keep the fever down.

"If I have ever seen the walking dead, you are it. Keep going the way you are, lass, and you willna be any good to anybody, not even yourself. You need rest, Miss Lindsay, and a great deal of it. Now, why dinna you let me sit here with my mistress, and you go get yourself a bit of sleep?"

Cathleen left Mrs. Farquar with Annora, going to the room across the hall, but when she lay down in the bed she could not sleep. Tears began to roll down her cheeks until her body was shaking with great, heaving sobs. She cried until she thought her body could take no more, finding that the more she cried, the more she had to cry for.

How strange it all was, really, for she had no idea just *why* she had started crying in the first place. But once she'd begun, she realized that she was dragging up all the old ghosts in her life, the things she had closeted away and never allowed to come forth.

The tears she shed were for a multitude of things: the loss of her mother; the fear she had of childbirth; the lost years of her youth, when she could have been a normal young woman who loved and allowed herself to be loved in return; the children she would never bear; the man she would never marry; the grandfather she had adored . . . and she cried for Fletcher, the one man she had come to love, and the hopelessness of that love. She cried too for herself, for the deep feelings of being all alone, for the monster that seemed to have hold of her, that drove her toward the need to be everything to everyone, yet nothing to herself.

Why was it so difficult for her to say no?

She cried until, at last, complete and utter exhaustion took over and she drifted off to sleep.

During the next few days at Dunston, Fletcher came to see Cathleen twice. The first time was to tell her that he was returning to Caithness Castle but would be back as soon as he could.

The second time was to leave her a message. "What was it?" Cathleen asked Mrs. Farquar.

"His Lordship said to tell you that since you would not take care of yourself, he hired Mrs. MacGillvry to cook for you."

"Mrs. MacGillvry?"

"Aye, the best cook in all the Highlands."

"Did he say anything else?"

"Aye. He said he was providing nourishing food. He hoped he did not have to hire someone to make certain that you ate it."

Thanking Mrs. Farquar, Cathleen turned away, feeling less weary than she had before. He had said he would always be there. She found it uplifting to know that Fletcher was a man of his word.

The dogs were howling when Annora woke up and saw Cathleen Lindsay's face. She did not know, at first, where she was. She was bewildered, like a bird in a wind storm, blown far from its home.

"How are you feeling?" Cathleen asked, placing her hand on Annora's forehead. She smiled. "It's cool for the first time in weeks."

"How . . . how long have you been here?"

"Over two weeks, now."

"I can't have been sick for two weeks."

"You were quite ill, Annora."

"Aye," she said, trying to raise herself on her elbows, but falling weakly back against the pillows.

"Don't try to get up now," Cathleen said. "I'll send for Mrs. Farquar. I think you will feel better after you have a nice bath and some clean clothes. Then I'll have the kitchen send you some of Mrs. MacGillvry's soup. I know you will feel stronger after that. Then we'll talk."

"Is Mrs. MacGillvry here?"

"No, but Fletcher hired her to cook for those in your household who are ill."

Annora looked at Cathleen for a moment. This woman had given two weeks of her life to care for someone who had not been very nice to her. This kind of sacrifice was difficult for Annora to understand. *Perhaps this is why Fletcher cares so much for her, for she is so giving to everyone, no matter who they are or what their needs.* "I ken Fletcher hired Mrs. MacGillvry for you, not for me or anyone else," Annora said.

"Nonsense. He cares for you very, very much."

"Aye, but it is you that he loves."

"That is the fever talking," Cathleen said, giving her hand a pat. "I'll call Mrs. Farquar now."

"Will you be back?"

"Aye, after you have eaten."

Cathleen visited Annora a few hours later. Stepping into the room, she heard the dogs barking again. Looking at Mrs. Farquar, who was just leaving Annora's bedside, she said, "Would you please have someone put the dogs out? They are making a dreadful ruckus."

"Aye, I will see to it straightaway."

Cathleen approached Annora's bed. "How are you feeling?"

"Tired."

"It will take time to get your strength back, but it will return. In the meantime, you must be patient."

"I'm sorry to have been such a bother," Annora said. "Thank you for what you've done. Mrs. Farquar said I wouldn't be here if it weren't for you."

"You were always in God's hands." She smiled. "And I cannot think of a better place to be."

Annora sighed, then turned her head to look out the open window. "I wish I had your faith, your wisdom."

"Och! My grandfather would disagree that faith and wisdom could walk hand in hand. He was fond of saying, 'The less you understand, the greater your faith.'"

"Your grandfather was a wonderful man," Annora said, seeing the look of sadness that passed over Cathleen's face.

"Aye, he was. He was everything to me. I never really understood loss until he was gone."

"I didn't have a chance before to tell you how sorry I was about what happened."

"Thank you for caring," Cathleen said, smoothing out the blanket on Annora's bed. "Don't you think you should rest now?"

Annora gave her a weak smile. "I have rested for weeks. Talking is the best way to prove to myself that I am still alive."

Cathleen brushed the hair back from the woman's face. "Very much alive and still very beautiful."

Annora saw the warmth and honesty in her eyes. She clutched Cathleen's hand and, bringing it to her lips, kissed it, then turned her cheek to lie against it. "I understand now why the villagers call you an angel."

Annora saw the way Cathleen looked down at her hands, her embarrassment obvious. "You mustn't call me that," she said. "I'm no angel. Far from it."

"You will always be an angel of mercy to me." She saw the faraway expression in Cathleen's eyes. "What are you thinking about?"

"I was just remembering something."

"What?"

"When you said angel of mercy, it made me remember. That is what my grandfather always called me."

"Did they ever find out what happened to him?"

"No. Some speculated his horse was frightened. Others said he must have guided the horse too close to the edge of the road. Fletcher seems to think . . . " Cathleen's voice drifted off to nothing.

Annora stared at her. "Fletcher seems to think what?"

"He . . . he feels a little responsible, that's all."

"Why? Surely he had nothing to do with it?"

"No, of course he didn't. It's just that my grandfather was on his way back from St. Abb's, where he had gone on an errand to check some family matters for Fletcher. Naturally, Fletcher felt that my grandfather might still be alive if he had not gone there. So you see . . . "

Cathleen went on, but Annora was no longer listening. Her heart began to hammer. A loud, buzzing noise filled her ears. Suddenly she remembered talking to Fletcher in the village that day. She also remembered telling Adair Ramsay everything that Fletcher had told her.

Oh, dear God, it was my information that doomed David!

Panic beat at her throat like a frightened bird. Her heart was racing so fast that she felt it might explode. Fighting to hold back her tears, she blinked her eyes. "I am tired now. I would like to sleep."

The dogs were howling again.

Annora watched as Cathleen turned to look out the window, frowning.

"The dogs," Annora said. "They are howling for me."

"Nonsense. They are howling because I had them put outside."

"No," Annora said, "they are howling for me. Dogs howl, you ken, when a member of the household is about to die."

"You have just survived typhoid, Annora. If you were going to die, it would have already happened."

"Perhaps." Annora turned her face away, knowing the truth. She knew . . . in her heart she knew just why the dogs howled. How strange it was that the moment she understood that, the fear seemed to flow out of her. She lay there feeling relaxed, the hammering in her heart gone now. The fear had gone, and in its place was a calmness she had never known before—a complete and total peace.

"Are you all right?"

"Aye. Thank you for coming, Cathleen . . . for all you have done."

"Sleep then," Cathleen said, patting her hand. "The rest will do you good."

Annora listened as Cathleen slipped from the room, closing the door behind her. When she was gone, Annora opened her eyes and stared at the ceiling, not mindful of the tears that slid from her eyes to soak the pillow beneath her head. She tried once to get up but found she was too weak. So she lay there listening to the dogs howl and knowing it was for her. How odd, she thought, for even knowing that the their howling was the herald of her death, that was not the cause of her sorrow.

The thing that grieved her most was knowing that she was responsible for David MacDonald's death.

The next morning, Annora awoke shivering and covered with perspiration. She had slept hardly at all, for thinking about David MacDonald's death and listening to the wailing of the dogs outside. Feeling very weak, she forced herself to get up, calling upon a strength she did not know she had. Once she was out of bed, she dressed herself and made her way to Glengarry Castle.

She was trembling by the time she arrived, but nothing would have stopped her. Nothing save her own death, which she knew was imminent.

As she rode to Glengarry, she had a premonition that the Angel of Death had come for her during her bout with typhoid. Now it was clear to her that her life had been spared for a purpose, which was to confront Adair Ramsay. Once that was done, she would be dead . . . as dead as the mallows in the garden.

As she was led to Adair's library, she could not help thinking that she could not bring David MacDonald back to life, but perhaps in some way she could atone for causing his death.

Chapter Twenty-one

"**Y**ou look ghastly," the duke said.

Annora said nothing.

"It must be very important news indeed to draw you away from your sickbed."

"I came to tell you that I will no longer be a part of what you are doing. I want out."

"What are you talking about, Annora?"

"I'm through with all of this . . . the deceit, the spying. It is over."

"And the markers I hold on Dunston?"

"Call them in. Sell them. Eat them for breakfast. I don't care anymore."

He was amused at her show of defiance. "Then perhaps I can help you . . . give you a reason to care."

"Whatever reason you chose, it would not matter. I am beyond that now. I know you killed David MacDonald, and I want you to know that if anything—I mean *anything*—happens to Cathleen Lindsay or Fletcher Ramsay, I will confess everything I know about you."

"That would be a big mistake." He saw the fear on her face. It was so strong that he could almost smell it. It was like an aphrodisiac, and he was filled with a feeling of power.

"You killed him," she said. "A man of God! How could you?"

He rose and came around the desk, stopping beside her. He gave her that cold, confident smile, the one he knew worked so well. "I did not kill him. I had him killed."

Annora sprang to her feet, going wild. Nails as sharp as eagle claws lashed at his face, cutting a deep groove across his forehead. Already he felt the blood in his right eye, blurring his vision. He drew back his hand and slapped her hard, knocking her against a table.

She looked up at him through her long, dark hair, which had fallen down about her face like a black veil. "Murderer! Bloody murderer! I would kill you myself if I could. You killed him and you tried to kill Cathleen! I hope you rot in hell for what you've done!"

He drew back his hand to hit her again, but stopped, seeing she was no longer a threat to him. Her energy was gone.

Weak, trembling, and looking like she might faint, Annora buried her face in her hands and sobbed uncontrollably.

He turned away and walked to the cupboard where he kept his spirits. He made her a drink and brought it to her.

"Annora," he said.

She looked up at him, her hair wild about her face. He saw the red print of his hand on her cheek and the tears in her eyes. How strange. Nowhere on her face did he see fear. "Here," he said, "drink this."

She looked at the glass, then at him. With a trembling hand Annora took the glass, and for a brief moment he thought he saw her smile. Then she raised the glass as if giving a toast, as if she knew. For a moment Adair thought she would hurl it into his face. And then she seemed to grow calm and relaxed before his very eyes. "I never knew you were the Angel of Death, Adair."

Without another word, Annora lifted the glass to her lips and drank the wine.

When she finished, she looked at him. "I want to go home now."

"I'll call for your carriage," he said, taking her elbow to help her out.

"I rode my horse. I can show myself out. Get your murdering hand off me." She snatched her arm from his grip.

He stood aside and watched her weave her way toward the door.

A moment later she was gone.

Annora reached the stables, intending to get her horse and ride home, but she did not have the strength to climb into the saddle.

Suddenly, Angus appeared out of the shadows. How appropriate it was that the last man she would see was the one she had loved first. "Angus," she said weakly. "Help me up."

Angus came to her, taking her in his arms. "You shouldn't be out," he said. "You are as weak and trembling as a newborn lamb."

"I must get home, quickly."

"There is no rush. Rest a moment. I'll get the carriage and drive you home."

"No," she said, seeing the love for her on his great ruddy face. She lifted her hand and stroked his cheek. "You were always there, whenever I needed you. I should have married you, you know. We would have a dozen beautiful horses by now, and just as many children. I did love you, Angus."

"Aye. I know. Don't try to talk."

She groaned, doubling over with pain.

"Annora, what is wrong?"

She shook her head. "No time," she whispered. "Angus, I've been poisoned."

"Poisoned? What are you saying?"

"Adair . . . I know he poisoned me."

"No!" he said, his voice laced with anguish. "Not this! Not you, Annora! I won't let you die!"

"It's all right," she said. "I have made my peace with God." She groaned again, the pain cutting into her, twisting, burning. "Promise me you will help them."

"Who?"

"Fletcher," she whispered, "and the girl. He killed her grandfather, you know. . . . Adair had him murdered, just as he murdered Fletcher's father . . . and now he has murdered me." Darkness began to close in upon her and she called his name again. "Angus . . ."

"I am here." Still holding her, he put his face next to hers and whispered, "I am here, Annora. I will always be here. Don't leave me."

Annora jerked suddenly, pulling away from him, trying to sit up. He helped her into a sitting position. "Light," she said. "So much beautiful light. Angel light. Take me. Take me away from this pain. I am ready."

"Annora, don't go . . . don't leave me."

She looked upward. "Forgive me, Father, for I have sinned. Into thy hands I commit my spirit."

"Annora!" Angus cried, staring down at her.

She slumped over. Her spirit was gone.

Adair walked into the stables and found Angus holding Annora. "Is she dead?" he asked.

Angus did not speak.

"I asked you a question. Is she dead?"

Angus raised his head slowly. He looked at Adair for a long time. "Aye."

Cool, aloof, detached, Adair looked down at her body. "She was a beautiful woman. It is a pity she never learned to use her beauty in the right way. Beauty and compassion do not mix."

A muscle in Angus's jaw flexed. "She is dead now," he said, looking away. "Let her rest in peace."

"Peace? Nothing would please me more. She has caused me nothing but trouble. She didn't even die the way I had planned. The poison I gave her was slow-acting. I had hoped she would reach home before she died. It must have been her weakness from the typhoid. Take her close to home, then leave her on the road with her horse. When they find her, they will think she simply went out riding before she was well. Typhoid has killed many of late. They will suspect nothing. She will simply be one more victim."

Angus did not move.

"Did you hear what I said?"

"Aye."

"Then get a move on. Get her out of here, and when you do, find Gavin MacPhail and send him to me."

It was ten o'clock that night when Gavin MacPhail slipped into Adair's library.

Annora's body had been found hours ago.

"What took you so long?" Adair asked. "I sent for you a long time ago."

"I didn't get the message until two hours ago," he said. "I came as soon as I could. Did you hear about Annora Fraser? They found her body on the road, not far from Dunston."

"I know that, you fool! I had to kill her."

"She got in the way?"

"Aye. She wanted out."

"And the Earl of Caithness?" Gavin asked. "Is he suspicious?"

"Not of Annora's death, if that's what you mean. At least not yet. He and David MacDonald's granddaughter have been snooping around Glengarry. They found the old graves behind the fence in the grove."

"It won't do them any good. There isn't anything there to help him."

"Still, too much has happened," Adair said. "He is too determined. I don't want to wait until it's too late. Find them."

"Who?"

"Fletcher Ramsay and Cathleen Lindsay, you idiot!"

"And when I find them?"

"Kill them. Kill them both."

Fletcher looked down at Cathleen. "You are taking Annora's death too hard."

" '*Weep ye not for the dead,*' " she said, wiping her eyes. "Jeremiah." And still the tears came.

"It hurts me to see you cry, Cathleen."

"I can't help it. I worked so hard . . . for weeks I worked

to save her life, only to lose her, just when I thought she had recovered."

"Sometimes death is like that," he said. "It comes unexpectedly."

"It wasn't unexpected," Cathleen said. "Annora knew she was going to die."

"What do you mean she knew?"

"She was acting strange the last few days, all during that time the dogs were howling. She heard them, Fletcher. She heard them and she knew."

Fletcher gave her a puzzled look. "She heard the dogs howl and that made her know she was dying?"

"I don't expect you to understand," she said. "If you had been raised here, you would believe in such omens."

"That howling dogs mean death?"

"Aye. It is an old superstition that the household dogs will howl whenever someone in the family is about to die."

"Cathleen, it was a coincidence, nothing more," he said with a dismissive air.

"No," Cathleen said flatly. "You were not there. You did not see Annora before she died. You did not see the resigned look on her face when she spoke of death."

Fletcher looked down at Cathleen. She was standing next to him at Annora's funeral, her Bible clutched tightly against her breast. Tears rolled down her face as she stared at Annora's coffin, listening to Robert Cameron's words of comfort as he buried yet another victim of typhoid.

In spite of his efforts to convince Cathleen that there was nothing suspicious about Annora's death, Fletcher was not so certain. Outwardly, he accepted the official cause of death, because he did not want to raise Cathleen's concerns. But inwardly, he was not so sure.

What is the connection between Annora and Adair?

He could not ignore the feeling that there was a connection between his search for his past, Adair Ramsay and Annora, and David's death. He wouldn't upset Cathleen by mentioning his suspicions to her, but they had prompted him to reach a decision—a decision based upon one simple fact.

Too many people were dead. People who, in one way or

another, were connected with his search. No matter how important it was to him, he could not in all conscience continue, for there was little doubt in his mind that if Adair killed again, it would be Cathleen.

"I have decided to call things off," he said as they left the funeral. Giving the reins a slap, he urged the gelding into a faster pace.

Cathleen, sitting on the seat beside him, clamped her hand on top of her bonnet. "Call what off?"

"My search."

She stared at him, aghast. "You are giving up? Quitting? You are going to let Adair win?"

"Yes."

"Why?" she asked, grabbing hold of the seat to keep from falling off. "Will you slow this thing down and tell me one good reason why?"

He pulled back on the reins. "It isn't worth it," he said.

"Not worth it? My grandfather's death is not worth it? How dare you say that!"

"That isn't what I meant."

She grabbed his arm. "Don't you dare let that wonderful old man's death be for nothing. Don't let him have died in vain."

Fletcher stopped the carriage, turned to her, and took her hands in his. "Cathleen . . ."

"Don't try to explain. I don't want to hear anything except that you are *not* giving up."

He took her in his arms. "I'm doing this because of you."

"Don't use *me* for an excuse. You aren't doing it for me, Fletcher, because I don't want you to. Never would I ask this. Never, do you hear?"

"Cathleen . . . If you would only listen to reason, you would see that I am doing it for you."

"Well, *undo* it for me, then."

He sighed, frustrated because he could not express his thoughts in a manner that she would understand. "I don't want anything to happen to you. I'm not afraid for myself, Cathleen, but for you. I love you. Can't you understand that?"

Cathleen pulled away and scooted across the seat. She gave

him a direct look. "No, I canna. A month ago you were living with Annora. Now she is dead, so you suddenly love me. A finer duck never wet a feather. I don't think you know what you want."

"You don't believe that any more than I do," he said.

"Understand this, Fletcher Ramsay. I want no part of you if you are going to let Adair keep what he has stolen from you." Her eyes flashed with anger. "If you don't prove he's a liar, a fraud, and a murderer, I will." She started to climb from the carriage.

He grabbed her arm. "Where in the hell are you going?"

"I'm going to walk home."

"Why?"

"I'm going to find the proof that you're too afraid to look for."

He snorted. "You couldn't find your head with both hands."

"Perhaps not, but I'm beginning to doubt that you even have a head."

He seemed amused. "All right. Just answer me one thing. How do you plan to prove anything, since I haven't been able to?"

"I don't know, as yet," she said, "but I will find a way, even if I have to dig up . . . Oh, fie! What was her name?" Cathleen picked up her Bible from where it lay on the seat next to her, and opening it up, she read the first name she had written inside. "If I have to dig up the remains of Madeline de Compiegne Ramsay to do it."

The moment the words left her lips, Fletcher must have felt his head snap, so fast did he turn toward her. "What did you say?"

Her face wore an odd expression. "What?"

"Say that again."

She closed the Bible and gave him a suspicious look. "Say what again?"

"The name," he said. "The name of the woman you want to unearth."

"Madeline de Compiegne Ramsay," she said. "Don't try to tell me that it's wrong, because I know it's not. I wrote it down, just so I wouldn't forget." She opened the Bible again and, turning to the proper page, pointed her finger at the name. "You see? It's right here in my Bible. Madeline de Compiegne Ramsay."

Bible. De Compiegne.

Judging from the way he looked, the name must have exploded like cannon fire inside his head. "That's it!" he said. "That's where I've heard that name before."

"What?"

"The Bible," he repeated. "The one in my mother's old trunk."

"What Bible? What trunk? Fletcher, you are as pale as a fish belly. Are you all right?"

He grabbed her and kissed her hard. "You wonderful, adorable woman. You may have given me just the break I need."

She gave him a bewildered look, albeit a curious one. "I have?"

"Yes, I think you have."

First she looked pleased, then she looked puzzled. "What have I given you?"

At that, Fletcher threw back his head and laughed. "If you promise not to throw any more fits between here and your house, I'll tell you."

"If you stop making foolish statements about giving up your search, I'll stop throwing fits."

"Agreed," he said. "Now, about that name—Madeline de Compiegne. I knew I'd heard it before, but I could not remember when or where. Not until you picked up your Bible. Then it all came back to me. It's in the Bible."

"Fletcher, I hate to disappoint you, but I was raised on scripture. The name Madeline is not in the Bible anywhere. Mary, yes. Magdalene, yes. Madeline, no."

He laughed. "I didn't mean it was written in the scriptures and I did not mean the name Madeline. It's the last name, de Compiegne, that is so familiar."

She cringed at his botched pronunciation of the French name. "De Compiegne isn't in the Bible either," she said.

"It is in the Bible I'm speaking of," he replied.

She crossed her arms in front of her. "And which Bible would that be?"

"There is an old trunk at Caithness. One that has been in my mother's room for years. Inside it is an old French Bible. I would swear the name written on the inside of that Bible is Madeline de Compiegne."

"Well, fancy that," she said, a pleased look on her face. "I may have given you the break you needed after all. *Me*," she said, poking herself in the chest and giving him a superior look, "who could not find her head with both hands."

"Okay, so I was wrong . . . for the first time in my life."

He received a jab in the ribs for that. "Fletcher Ramsay, *'Thou shalt not bear false witness.'* Exodus."

"I wasn't bearing false witness," he said. "I was telling a lie."

The laughter that followed was good for them, she decided.

They rode along in silence for a while. Then Cathleen said, "Now that you've got a new clue, what are you going to do about it?"

"We are going to Caithness to see that Bible, of course."

"We?"

"We. As in you and I. Surely you know you can't stay here. It isn't safe."

She frowned, shaking her head. "I can't go to Caithness with you."

"Why not?"

"I've things to attend to at home."

"Such as?"

"The animals and the farm chores."

"Which Robert and Fionn can handle while you are gone."

"The owls have to be fed frequently."

"Give the owls to Fionn. You told me yourself he loves them."

"Aye, he does."

"Well, let him take your orphans home with him to care for them there."

"And there's the typhoid."

"Which is on the wane." He stopped the carriage again. "Cathleen, mankind managed to survive for centuries without you. I think it is capable of doing so again."

Chapter Twenty-two

They left for Caithness Castle early the next morning, going on horseback to make better time.

Two hours out of Glengarry, the sky grew dark, the rumble of thunder booming like cannon fire in the distance. A jagged bolt of lightning split the sky, lighting up the moors like a sunny summer day. The rain began to fall, first coming with great splatters, then coming down faster, until everything in front of them looked like a dull gray curtain.

The beck nearby, which had been gurgling merrily, was now running swiftly with a great rushing sound. The wind came up, pelting the cold rain against them, whipping it beneath her bonnet. Soon she was soaked and her bonnet dropped dejectedly.

Fletcher knew he wasn't faring any better, for he was soaked as well—the rain running off the brim of his hat in little rivulets, running down inside his collar and soaking his shirt.

He looked at Cathleen, who was shivering from the cold. All around them there was nothing but grayness broken by the swaying branches of the trees that lined the beck, the muddy tracks of the road ahead.

"We have to find shelter," he said, his words almost drowned out by the thunder. "We'll leave the main road here. We'll be safer out on the heath, away from the trees."

She nodded, urging her horse closer to his as she followed him to a trail that wound across the moors. A nearby tree branch cracked under the burden of wind, sending a shower of leaves over them and causing the horses to become skittish. Urging them forward, they picked up the pace.

It was growing darker now, and Fletcher wondered if they would be able to find shelter in the blackness that surrounded them. They rode for what seemed at least another hour when a bolt of lightning lit up the sky and he saw what appeared to be a house in the distance.

As they rode closer, another lightning bolt illuminated the darkness, and he saw that they had come upon a large farmhouse, its roof covered with thatch. A sheepdog barked as they rode up to the front door.

There was no other sign of life.

"You go on inside," he said, dismounting and coming around to help her down. "I'll see to the horses."

He knew that ordinarily Cathleen would have been a bit shy about dashing into someone's house uninvited, but she was shivering, and her clothes were soaked through to her skin. He figured that was enough incentive, and he was right.

With mud-logged feet, she made her way to the front door. Finding it unlocked, she knocked. No one answered. She knocked again and then a third time. When she opened the door, a blast of wind whipped it out of her hand, driving it back against the wall with a loud crash.

Hearing the sound, Fletcher turned. He called to her, telling her it was only the wind, but she said that she thought she had heard someone scream.

"Go on inside," he said.

Cathleen nodded, then bent down to remove her muddy shoes before going inside, wrestling the door shut.

Fletcher put the horses and the sheepdog in the barn, then came inside to find her standing just inside the door, shivering.

"What are you doing?"

"Waiting for my eyes to adjust to the darkness," she said.

He grunted and stood beside her, unable to see anything either, for the interior was dark and chilled from the downpour.

He waited for a few minutes, until his eyes adjusted and he saw a fire laid in the fireplace, ready to be lit.

"Is anyone here?" he asked, looking around.

"No, I don't think so, but it doesn't look deserted. It is well kept and furnished."

"Perhaps they are just away."

"Aye. Should we stay?"

"We don't have a choice. It's raining a blooming river out there."

Fletcher found a lamp on a table and lit it, sending a golden glow into the room to chase away the dark gloom. "There," he said, "that's better."

"Aye," she said, still shivering, staring wistfully at the fireplace.

He gave her an understanding smile. "I'll start a fire in a minute. I want to look around first."

She nodded and, rubbing the chill from her arms, moved closer to the fireplace, as if to make certain that he wouldn't forget.

He lifted the lamp and made his way farther into the house, going into a small bedroom, finding a little bed neatly made. Just then he heard a moan coming from the room next door. Hurrying there, he paused a moment at the door, listening.

When he heard nothing, he knocked. No one answered, so he slowly opened the door and looked inside.

A young woman lay in the bed, very pregnant and, judging from the look of things, in very advanced labor. *Damn! Not here . . . Not now!*

In spite of the chill in the room, the woman's gown and the bed were drenched with sweat. Her face was pale, her forehead ashen and shiny. Fletcher did not know "come here" from "sic 'em" when it came to childbirth, but he knew one thing: Something about *this* particular birth was not right.

Feeling inept but knowing that the woman needed help, he

stepped closer to the bed. "Are you all right?" he asked softly, not wanting to frighten her.

She opened her eyes, and the moment she saw him she reached for him. Her hands twisted in the folds of his jacket, clutching him as if she never intended to let him go. "Help me," she whispered. "I am dying. The babe willna come."

"You are going to be fine," he said, patting her hand. "Is there anyone here with you?"

Too weak to hold on to him, she fell back against the bed, shaking her head from side to side. "No, no one."

"You husband?"

"Went for the doctor," she whispered weakly. "Gone too long. Help me. I know I'm dying."

Fletcher's heart hammered in his chest. He believed every word the woman had said. She did look like she was dying, and he did not know what to do about it. He could not ride off and leave her in this state.

Cathleen . . .

He turned toward the door, intending to go after her, when he saw her standing in the doorway. He looked at her stricken face, her hands tightly clenching the fabric of her rain-soaked skirts, and he knew he would get no help from that quarter, for it was the same look of terror he had seen on her face that day in the meadow when she saw the ewe giving birth.

"Cathleen . . ."

"No," she whispered.

"Love, this woman needs our help. She's all alone. There's some problem. The baby won't come. We've got to help her."

Cathleen stared at him as if in a trance. "No," she whispered, and began backing through the door. "I can't!" she cried. "You know I can't!" She whirled around then and dashed from the room.

He caught her in the kitchen and spun her around to face him. "All right, dammit! I'll do what I can. At least you can help by getting that fire started," he said, nodding in the direction of the fireplace.

He gave her a gentle shake to make sure she understood. "Can you get the fire started?"

"Aye," she whispered.

He thought back to the times when his mother had given birth and her friend Molly Polly had come to help. "Put some water on to boil," he said. "Then see if you can find some clean cloths, a knife, and some twine."

He looked at her standing there in the middle of the kitchen, her face frozen, her eyes huge with fright. "Do it, dammit! At least help me with this! You can't let that woman die in there, just because you're afraid."

She stood as still as a block of ice.

His heart went out to her and he reached out and took her in his arms. "It will be all right, Cathleen," he whispered. "Don't worry, love. It won't be like before. This time, I'm here. I won't let anything happen. It won't be like your mother. I promise you, she'll make it. But you've got to help me. Do you understand?"

She nodded.

"Can you help me?"

"Aye," she said weakly. "I'll see to the fire."

"Good girl," he said. "That's my lass."

He went to the basin and poured water over his hands, then picked up the soap. When he had finished scrubbing, he dried his hands and turned to see that Cathleen had the fire going.

"Do you need any help?"

She shook her head. "I can manage."

He started for the woman's room, saying as he passed, "Say a prayer for me."

"I already have."

He took a deep breath. "I cannot ever remember feeling so alone."

She gave him a soft look. " 'As I was with Moses, so I will be with thee: I will not fail thee, nor forsake thee. The Lord is with thee withersoever thou goest,' " she said. "Joshua."

Fletcher gave her one last look, then turned and went to the woman again. This time, she did not open her eyes. "I'm going to try and help," he said, "but I'll be honest with you— I don't know the first thing about delivering a baby. If you can help me in any way, please speak up."

She shook her head weakly. "Too late," she whispered. "The babe willna come."

He heard a noise and turned to see Cathleen standing in the doorway, her face pale, her eyes huge and filled with fright. She held a pan of hot water.

"Bring the water over here, where I can get to it," he said. Cathleen did not move.

"Damn," he said, crossing to where she stood, taking the water from her. "Go get the other things. Hurry!"

By the time he had put down the water, she was standing in the doorway just as she had done before, her face a mask of fear, her color gone, her breathing rapid. He went to her again, took the things from her, and put them on a clean cloth on the table beside the bed.

He looked back at her, saw that she had not moved, then looked again at the woman, swallowing back the taste of his own fear. He could not do this alone. "Cathleen, something is wrong. I don't know what to do. The baby won't come. You've got to help me."

She said nothing.

"Cathleen! Did you hear me?"

"Aye," she whispered.

"Please. Help me. Help her."

"I canna." Tears formed in her eyes.

"I know you aren't the kind to stand and watch a woman die without lifting a finger to help. Is your fear more important than this woman's life?"

She was silent for a long time, and then, when he thought he had lost the battle, she walked toward him, stopping a few feet away. Her eyes were glassy and her breathing was rapid as she glanced down at the woman.

"You've worked with the doctor before," he said. "You must know what could be wrong. Cathleen, this poor soul looks as if she's been at this for hours. What can it be? Help me."

He swore inwardly, seeing her frozen countenance, thinking that he would get no help from her, when suddenly she said, "Perhaps the babe is turned wrong."

"Turned wrong?"

"Feet first, it willna come," she said, glancing down at the woman again.

He saw her sway on her feet. "Take a deep breath, Cathleen. Don't pass out on me now. I need you! Don't look if it makes you faint. Just tell me what to do. How can I tell if the baby is feet first?"

She took a deep breath and turned her face away. "You will feel the foot," she said. "It will be first."

Feel the foot? How?

He remembered a similar problem, with a horse that was in foal. The foal had one foot out, and the only way his stepfather could help the mare was to put his hands inside and turn the foal around, so that it came out head first.

Fletcher looked at the woman's distended stomach and felt a flush of heat sweep over him. There was a world of difference between putting one's hand inside a woman's body and that of a horse. Besides, how would he be able to tell if that was the problem here? For a moment he felt dizzy, but he told himself this was no time to get queasy and afraid. One terrified person was enough.

He looked at Cathleen. She looked as if she could pass out any minute. If putting his hand inside the woman was necessary, what other choice did he have? He couldn't let her die.

He reached out, intending to smooth the woman's wet hair back from her forehead, when he remembered that he had just washed his hands. He settled for a few words of comfort and assurance.

"All right," he said. "Let's see what we've got here." He pulled back the sheet and saw that her gown had ridden up, leaving her huge belly exposed. Her legs were naturally spread wide. He didn't know why he did it, but he pushed both legs up until they were bent at the knees, and saw that it gave him better access.

He put his hand on the woman's stomach. It was rock hard and cramping. There was no sign of a baby's head, but the area beneath her hips was wet and streaked with blood. He put his hand just inside the birth canal, groping, feeling, until he touched something. He felt around it. "Jesus, a foot," he whispered. "The baby's foot." He glanced at Cathleen. "I can feel it."

She stared at him, then down at the bed. He knew the

moment she saw the blood, for her face grew deathly white. "What do I do now?" he urged, afraid she might faint before she could tell him. "Tell me what to do!"

"Turn it," she said, turning her face away and grabbing the bedpost for support. "You will have to turn it."

All right, Fletcher. You've got a foot here. What are you going to do with it? You've got to push it back, Fletch. Push it back as far as you can, then see if you can turn the baby.

He closed his eyes and whispered a prayer: "You must have had a reason for this. I'm certain of it. I don't think it would be very sporting of You just to leave me here now . . . not like this. We're in this thing together, right?"

He did not expect an answer, of course, but an earnest prayer was always in good order, and the good Lord knew that if this prayer was anything, it was earnest.

The woman moaned, and Fletcher knew he must act now. He located the baby's foot again. "I can feel the foot, Cathleen. I'm holding it. How do I turn it?"

"Push it back."

Using his right hand to push, he splayed his left hand across the woman's belly as he began to push.

The woman moaned and began writhing.

He looked back at Cathleen. She was staring at him, her face frozen. He pushed for what seemed an eternity, and just when he thought this would not work, that he would have to try something else, he felt the baby's foot move. "It's moving! By God, it's moving!"

Using his left hand as a guide, he felt the baby's rump down toward where it shouldn't be. Once he had the foot back far enough—or what he hoped was far enough—he began pushing on her stomach with both hands, trying to manipulate the baby around so its rump moved up and its head turned down toward the woman's pelvis. He pushed firmly, but not too hard, feeling the baby move slightly, then a little more.

There had never been a feeling like the one he felt when the baby's head began rotating downward. Fletcher knew he would never forget the elation he felt at that moment. He did not have long to wallow in his success though, for the moment the baby was in the right position, the woman began to moan and pant. Beneath his hands he felt powerful contractions, and this scared him.

Keeping his left hand on the woman's abdomen, he shifted his position, experiencing tremendous awe as he watched the birth passage widen and a small head covered with dark hair appear. A tiny, wrinkled face turned toward him. Then came a shoulder, then another shoulder. A second later, the wet, slippery baby slid into his hands, followed by a slush of liquid and blood.

He heard Cathleen gasp, and yet he could not help grinning. It was a boy . . . with all the necessary equipment.

His heart hammering, his head light with a combination of thrill, pride, and panic, Fletcher looked down at the baby and gave him a shake. The infant sputtered, waved his tiny arms, then grew stiff. Terror gripped Fletcher. He shook the baby again, trying to think of what else he could do, then suddenly the boy let loose with a royal wail.

It was the most beautiful sound Fletcher had ever heard.

Shaking, like the idiot he felt he was, he didn't know what to do now. He looked at the water, the cloths, the knife. He hadn't used any of them. What were they for? He glanced at Cathleen, but she was still staring at him as if in a trance.

He looked down at the baby and the cord that still connected him to his mother. *Maybe that's what the knife is for*.

Placing the baby on the bed beside the mother, he took the knife in his hand, turning to look at Cathleen. Her gaze was fixed upon the baby, who was bawling his head off. He gave her a helpless look, but Cathleen did not respond.

He turned back to the woman, knowing that he had to cut the cord but not certain where. Then suddenly Cathleen was beside him. He watched her tie the string around the cord near the baby's body. "Cut it there," she said, "next to the string."

He cut the cord.

The baby, bawling his head off, was a whole, complete human being, now separated for life from his mother. Fletcher felt a great satisfaction in that. He picked up the infant, not even noticing that both of them were covered with blood.

Grinning like a baboon, he turned to Cathleen, who was looking at him with an expression not of fear or terror but of complete and utter awe.

He held the baby up proudly for her to see. "A boy," he said. "As perfect a baby boy as I've ever seen."

He hadn't actually seen one this new, of course, but he was the closest thing the wee one had to a papa right now, and somebody had to crow. He knew he was grinning like a fool, but he could not help it as he stood there grinning at Cathleen, the baby in his hands. As he watched her face, he found himself wishing that, just once, he would see this expression on her face again.

She didn't take the baby at first, but simply stood there looking at him. "A boy," she said.

"In every sense of the word," he replied, offering the baby to her.

Her gaze came quickly to his, then she held out her arms and let him place the baby there. The moment he did, she started to cry.

He thought he had done the wrong thing by handing the baby to her, so he reached to take him back, noticing the blood and thinking that this was the reason she cried. "I'm sorry," he said. "I guess that wasn't the right thing to do. I know how this must seem to you . . . how ghastly it was for you to watch."

She hugged the baby to her. "No. It's not that," she said, "it's just that this was the most wondrous, the most glorious and holy thing I've ever seen."

"Yes," he said softly, "it was, wasn't it?"

"And you are the most beautiful man I could ever hope to meet."

At that moment, after what he had just been through, Fletcher could not help but agree with her.

Chapter Twenty-three

Cathleen cleaned up the baby and the mother, whom they had learned was named Mary MacMillan. Mary then fed her son, telling them she had decided to name the lad Fletcher Lindsay MacMillan in honor of the two of them. When Mary and the baby were resting, Cathleen and Fletcher slipped out of the room, closing the door behind them.

"Now it's time to attend to us," he said. "What's for dinner?"

She smiled. " '*A man hath no better thing under the sun, than to eat, and to drink, and to be merry.*' Ecclesiastes," she said, going into the kitchen.

While Cathleen found enough ingredients to make soup, Fletcher lowered himself into a sagging chair and watched her.

Outside, the storm raged on, but they were as snug and comfortable as a body could be, and Fletcher nodded off. A while later, Cathleen roused him by waving a steaming bowl of soup beneath his nose.

Cathleen went to Mary's room once more, opening the door slowly and peeking in, then closing it. Turning to Fletcher, she said, "They are both sleeping soundly."

"That's good."

"Aye." Suddenly feeling shy, she looked around the room, wondering if he was thinking about the same thing as she. "I suppose we should get a little sleep as well."

He moved the chair closer to the fire. "I know you're tired. Why don't you sleep in the bedroom and I'll sleep here."

"No. You take the bed. I'll stay in here, in front of the fire."

He gave her a curious stare. "I couldn't do that. Nary a one of these chivalrous bones in my body would rest a bit if I was in that feather bed and you were all squashed up in this little chair."

"Well, you did deliver the baby, and not one of my Christian bones would rest if I allowed *you* to sleep in the chair."

"Hmm," he said, giving her a wicked grin. "Then I guess there are only two choices left."

"Only two?"

"Yes. Either we both sleep in the chair or we both sleep in the bed."

"Hmm," she said, doing her best to mimic his sound. "I guess if you put it that way, I'd have to choose the bed."

"I always had you pegged for a wise lass," he said, springing out of the chair and sweeping her up into his arms. She buried her face in the warm cove of his neck. *Fletcher, Fletcher ... How much I love you!*

A moment later, he was pushing the bedroom door open with his foot.

He walked to the bed and stood her on her feet beside it as he began to remove her clothes. "You had best get out of these wet clothes," he said. "I don't want my lass getting sick."

"Aye," she said, unbuttoning his shirt. "So had you."

When they were both as naked as young Fletcher Lindsay, Fletcher put his arms around her and, kissing her, lowered her down to the bed with him. Her arms came around his neck as she began stroking his hair. "I was verra proud of you tonight. You were wonderful, Fletcher. I've never in all my born days seen anything like that."

He snorted deprecatingly, but she knew her words pleased him immensely. "It was I who was proud of you," he said. "I could not have done it if you had not helped."

"You would have done fine without me."

"Never," he said. "Of course, it was only the birth of a baby, which is a perfectly normal process, and women have been giving birth for centuries without any aid at all. I had never had any experience with this sort of thing, you see, but—"

She put her hand over his mouth, laughing as she said, "Shut up, you wonderful, dear man, and kiss me."

He obliged, kissing her with all the love that she knew was in his heart and stroking her with his hands, which began to inch lower.

There was little doubt that the thrill of birthing the babe was now becoming a thrill of another kind.

"Do you think Mary will hear us?" she asked.

"I doubt it, but what if she does? She has given birth, so she is bound to know what happens when a man and woman get in bed together." He paused. "You aren't trying to make excuses, are you?"

"Would I stoop so low? I want you, Fletcher. So bad, I canna think of anything else," she said, kissing him soundly upon the mouth, her own mouth opening beneath his.

"Cathleen . . . love," he said, his hand slipping inside her. "Lord, you're as slippery as a trout and as wet as . . ."

"Please," she said, laughing, "no more comparisons. It will take me a month of Sundays to live that first one down. Some women get flowery verses of poetry or whispered words of love, and what do I get?" She kissed him again. "'As slippery as a trout.' Fletcher Ramsay, where did you learn to speak like that?"

He seemed to swell up with pride. "I don't know. It's just a natural talent, I guess."

"No, it isn't."

"Did I ever tell you that you talk too much?" he asked, not giving her time to answer, for he rolled over on top of her, pinning her to the bed, spreading her thighs with his knee, sheathing himself within her as far as he could go, a single, hard thrust that made her gasp.

"This is ever so much better than talking," he said, moving inside of her with slow, sure strokes, but soon he could not hold that pace and she felt him moving harder, faster, until she moaned and began to writhe beneath him.

"You belong to me," he whispered. "When this night is over you will think of no one but me. I will have you, now and forever, whether you agree or not. I will not let you go, Cathleen. You are a part of me that cannot be severed. You will never be free of me. Never."

She moved in a mindless way beneath him. Sweat bathed their bodies, a slippery feel that made his hard thrusting moves so much faster and easier. He drove himself deep, deep into her, wanting to make her remember what it was like to be loved and loved well. There was no end, only the need to drive himself deeper, to move faster, each thrust going beyond the limits of the last, until the moment was near.

He groaned, and she knew he had to withdraw now or spill his seed within her. With one swift move, he began to withdraw.

She clutched at him.

"Cathleen . . ."

"No," she whispered.

"Cathleen . . . love . . . please. I promised you . . ."

"No," she said, her legs going around his hips, her arms holding him to her. "I want you. All of you. Don't leave me now."

He only had time to cover her mouth with his, before she felt his release, a continuous shudder that gripped him harder with each thrust. Soon she could think of nothing else, for she felt herself coming with him, beyond pain, beyond pleasure, to a point of pure and complete sensation.

"God!" she cried. "I never knew. I never knew."

"You know now," he whispered, keeping pace with her. "And I'll see that you never forget it."

She arched up against him, panting, digging her nails into

his back, clawing, writhing beneath him as if she were trying to become one with him, and then he seemed to understand.

"Come with me," he whispered. "Come."

Her cry mingled with his, and for a moment they were both lost, out of touch with reality, with the world, as they seemed to dissolve into a timeless, formless being before taking their shape again, the world about them suddenly righting itself as sanity slowly returned.

But even then, as he held her against him, she knew that from this moment on, nothing for them would ever be the same.

It was some time later before she returned to herself, lying in his arms, her head resting on his chest, their bodies still wet with sweat and the rewards of their lovemaking. His breathing was deep, heavy, and she tapped her fingers on his chest, establishing the rhythm of his heart that she knew pounded out a message of love for her, just beneath her ear.

"Why did you stop me?" he asked. "Didn't you realize it could get you with child?"

"Aye," she said, kissing his chest, his throat, his mouth, "I knew."

"But why?"

How could she tell him? How could she explain to him that after she had seen the birth of Mary's babe, she could think of little else save having a babe of her own? Where were the words that would make him understand that she loved him enough to want his child; too much ever to expect anything more?

"Because I want that part of you," she whispered. *A part that can never be taken away.*

That seemed to satisfy him, for he said nothing more as he lay there, stroking her back with his hand, stirring occasionally to kiss the top of her head.

"When did you know it was a boy?" she asked, wondering if he had had a premonition that Mary's child would be a boy.

"When I saw his . . . that is . . ."

Cathleen doubled over with laughter. "That's one way to

do it," she said in a fit of laughter, not having the heart to tell him that that wasn't exactly what she'd meant.

"Go to sleep, sweet love," he whispered, pulling the blanket over them. "Little Fletcher MacMillan will be making demands early in the morning, and I fully intend to let you take care of him."

She smiled, thinking there was nothing she would like better. Then with a satisfied sigh she closed her eyes and drifted off to sleep.

She awoke early the next morning, when Mary MacMillan's husband, Ian, arrived with the doctor.

Hearing the approach of horses, Cathleen woke Fletcher, then dressed quickly. She had barely reached the main room when the door burst open and two men stepped inside.

After getting over the initial surprise of seeing her standing there, the larger of the two men said, "Who are you?"

Cathleen explained who she was and what she was doing there in his house, introducing Fletcher when he walked into the room.

"You must be Mary's husband," Fletcher said.

"Aye," he said, "I'm Ian MacMillan. This is Dr. Ross." He frowned. "My wife . . ."

"She is doing fine," Fletcher said. "And you have a fine, healthy son. I know, because I delivered him myself."

Dr. Ross went with Ian into Mary's room.

A few minutes later, Ian came out, a look of awe upon his face. "Mary told me what happened. How can I ever thank you?"

"We were glad to help," Fletcher said. "All in all, I'd say it was a pretty fair exchange for a hot bowl of soup and a good night's sleep. We were worried about you, however."

"Aye. I had the devil's own time of it," Ian said. "I was plagued with bad luck from the time I left here. By the time I reached the bridge, the rains had washed it away. I had to go miles out of my way to get to the village, and once I found Dr. Ross, we had to come back by the same way. I was worried sick about my Mary."

Dr. Ross came out of Mary's room. Looking at Ian, he

said, "You can go in. Everything with her and the babe is as well as could be."

With a wide grin, Ian hurried into Mary's room.

"'Tis a fine job you've done, lad," the doctor said, looking at Fletcher. "I couldna done a better job myself."

"I'm glad I was here to help, but it isn't something I would want to do again," Fletcher said, smiling at Cathleen, his arm going around her. "Although I would have doubted it at the time, I know now that God in his infinite wisdom knew exactly what He was doing. He gave me the strength to do the job, but it was Cathleen who had the wisdom."

Cathleen looked at Fletcher and smiled. "Aye. *'Wisdom always prevails over strength.'* Proverbs," she said, basking in the sunshine of Fletcher's warm laugh.

Chapter Twenty-four

They left for Caithness Castle shortly after lunch, Cathleen lifting her skirts to accept Fletcher's boost into the sidesaddle.

They were off again, riding toward their destiny and Fletcher's home. Cathleen settled in with the rhythmic motion of her horse, feeling her excitement mount. Soon they would be near the western coast of Scotland, with its wild granite crags, bleak moorlands, and wooded glens.

Although the world about her seemed grim and melancholy, and a heavy mist clung to the ground, making it seem as if the sky had come down to earth, Cathleen's spirits were at their sunniest. And why not?

She sighed, her gaze going, as it had a habit of doing, to Fletcher's back as he rode just ahead of her. Was any woman ever more blessed than she, to be loved and protected by such a man?

They rode until twilight, stopping for a while to rest beside a small loch. "We can seek lodgings nearby, or we can keep riding until we reach Caithness, but it will be late," Fletcher said, bringing her a drink of water.

She took a drink and mulled over what he had said. It was her excitement to reach Caithness, as well as caution, that prompted her to say, "I'm not that tired. Let's keep riding." She glanced around. "I ken I will feel better when we're there, where we can be certain Adair or his men won't be sneaking up on us."

"That's my lass," he said, helping her to mount. A moment later, he was in the saddle again, urging his horse ahead, Cathleen falling in behind him.

My lass . . . She gave his back a smile, liking the sound of those words when he spoke them, not with the usual Scots burr, but with his American accent, which she found quite seductive.

It was well after midnight when they rode through a stand of firs that bordered a churning river. The mist had turned to rain now, and the weather was much colder. She considered taking her cloak out, but looking down at her sodden skirts, she knew the cloak would be in a similar state before long.

"It won't be much longer," Fletcher said, turning around to look at her. "Can you make it?"

"Aye," she said. "If you can make it, I can make it." She heard him chuckle and it warmed her to know she could amuse him.

They rode along the bank of the river, then turned where the trees began to grow thinner and a steep, granite mountain seemed to rise up out of nowhere before them, its peak hidden in the clouds. The trail grew steeper now, made even more narrow by many boulders that had fallen from the heights above.

She leaned back in the saddle, her hand pressing the small of her back. It was a miserable night and she wondered at her sanity for saying that she was ready to go on this journey, which was looking more and more like a lesson in misery. Every part of her body either ached or felt wet and frozen.

Presently the trail grew less steep and wider, until they reached the summit and began their descent. Before long, they were over the mountain and riding into a sparsely wooded glen, the moon peeking out of the clouds from time to time, quite stingy with its light.

Another mile and she saw a road ahead. The moment they turned up the road, she could see it. Caithness, huge, black, and hulking in the distance.

The next morning, Fletcher watched with amusement as Lady Doroty Lamont, looked down her long, aristocratic nose and gazed at Cathleen with stony dignity, as if she were trying to decide what she was: mistress, a bit of charitable baggage Fletcher had picked up somewhere along the way, traveling companion, or a woman toward whom he had honorable intentions. As Fletcher made the introductions, she showed no hint that she had chosen any one of them as being more likely.

"Cathleen Lindsay, I would like you to meet my aunt, Lady Doroty Lamont."

Doroty nodded and said, "Miss Lindsay," in much the same manner as he would have expected Queen Victoria to say, "Off with her head."

Fletcher then began to tell his aunt about his and Cathleen's namesake and the bit of adventure they'd had with Mary MacMillan.

"And you delivered the child all by yourself?" she asked, giving Cathleen a questioning look.

"Cathleen had an unfortunate situation with childbirth and it left her quite terrified of it."

"Indeed? And how many children do you have, *Miss* Lindsay?"

"Oh ... well ... I don't have a husband ... I mean, I've never been married," she added, with the sudden feeling that she had not explained anything but had somehow made things worse.

"You have *children*," Doroty said, "but no husband?"

Fletcher laughed. "This seems to have gone off in the wrong direction, and I have a feeling I'm the one who started it all. Let me see if I can straighten it all out."

"Please do, if you can," Doroty said, "or send for the hartshorn."

Cathleen kept her gaze fixed on the heavy, green damask

draperies that covered the sitting-room window directly behind Lady Lamont as Fletcher went on to explain briefly about Cathleen's experience with her mother, telling Doroty how it had left her terrified of childbirth. He ended by telling her how watching young Fletcher MacMillan being born had changed all that."

"You are David MacDonald's granddaughter?"

"Aye."

Lady Lamont's entire expression re-formed itself into one of kind regard. She turned to Fletcher. "It would have made things easier, you scoundrel, if you had told me *that* in the first place." Then, without giving him a chance to respond, she smiled at Cathleen. "I thought very highly of your grandfather. I was sorry to hear of his death."

"A death which was partly my fault," Fletcher added, then explained the circumstances that had led to David's death.

"Of course you did the right thing by bringing her here," Lady Lamont said, sounding positively motherly. "But you should be horsewhipped for bringing her without an escort, Fletcher. Did you give no thought to her reputation?"

"There wasn't time for that, I'm afraid," Fletcher said. "Besides, what difference does that make?"

Lady Lamont's stony demeanor resurfaced. "It may not make much difference in America, but in Scotland a woman does not travel with a man without another female as her companion. To disregard that tradition can bring about the most unfortunate set of circumstances."

"What kind of circumstances?" Fletcher asked, giving Cathleen a quick glance.

"Marriage," Doroty said. "I cannot . . ."

But Fletcher was not listening. He was watching Cathleen, who had begun to wring her hands and had turned pale as a ghost. Her eyes, which had been droopy with sleep only a short time before, were open wide, her mouth parted in stupefaction.

Fletcher turned back to his aunt and, in prime form, said, "Then rest easy, for I don't find that unfortunate at all. In fact, I find it a rather workable solution, since I have intended for some time to marry Cathleen."

Cathleen's teacup crashed to the floor. She would have laughed, had she not been in such a state of shock. *Marriage*?

She watched Aunt Doroty leave the room and soon the silence seemed to close in around her. For some strange reason, she could not bring herself to look at Fletcher as if to do so would be to bring an end to the spell she was certain she was under.

At last he broke the silence. "Are you angry, Cathleen?"

"No, I haven't gotten that far, yet. Numb is about as far as I've made it."

"Surely this came as no surprise to you. You know how I feel."

"I know you care for me, but that isn't the same as marriage. Truly, Fletcher, I had no idea."

"You think I would do the things I did with you and then go on my merry way, leaving you with nothing but dishonor?"

"The thought crossed my mind," she said. "I daresay you have not proposed marriage to every woman you have made love to . . . or have you?"

"Hardly."

"Then what was different this time?"

"You are different. My feelings for you are different. Everything about it is different. What the hell kind of question is that to ask, anyway?"

She shrugged. "Your aunt thinks you have been a bit hasty."

"I don't care what my aunt thinks," he said, coming to stand just inches from her. "She isn't the one asking to marry you."

"Perhaps you should care. She seems to be a very level-headed woman, and it is obvious she cares a great deal about you."

"She may care about me, but she isn't the woman I plan to marry, nor is she the one in love with you. I am," he said, poking himself in the chest for emphasis. "Marry me, Cathleen."

"Fletcher, I have no heritage. I am an orphan, the daughter of a soldier . . . the granddaughter of a poor village minister. I am a spinster, a woman of five and twenty years, and past the age of marriage. I have no bloodlines, no titles, no money, and no hopes of such."

"I don't care about any of that." He drew her close against him and kissed her.

Cathleen followed Fletcher upstairs to the door of his mother's room, where she paused for a moment, seeing the possessions of a woman from her childhood through to her adult years. Upon first glance, it was a room that spoke to her, a room that seemed to call out, asking her to come inside and to linger for a while.

She stepped over the threshold and into the room of the woman who had had such a profound impact upon the life of a man she had come to respect and to love. The room seemed to enfold her, to offer its wisdom of years and its infinite understanding. She felt welcome here, accepted, and somehow she had a feeling that that was exactly how she would have felt had she met Maggie Mackinnon herself.

Fletcher crossed his mother's bedroom and lifted the lid of an ancient, yet sturdy, humpbacked trunk.

She watched, an amused look on her face as he began rummaging through the contents, looking much like a young boy digging through his toy chest.

When he had emptied almost everything from the trunk and dumped it on the floor, he shouted, "Here it is!"

Cathleen watched with mounting excitement as he removed a false bottom, then withdrew a large, leather-bound Bible, the gilt lettering on the cover long faded. She took a seat beside him on the bed as he opened it.

"Here," he said at last. "You see?" He turned the Bible so that she could read the inscription more easily. Even then it was difficult, for the writing was quite elaborate, with many embellishments and flourishes.

It was also written in French.

"Brigitte de Compiegne," she read. "Honfleur, France, 1740." She looked up at him. "But this name is Brigitte, not Madeline."

"No, it isn't Madeline, but that isn't important. It's the last name that is significant—de Compiegne."

She shuddered at the way he pronounced the name. "That is French," she said, "and it is pronounced *de-com-pyen*, not *de-com-pi-eg-ne*."

He smiled. "I had no idea you spoke French."

"My grandfather did, so I learned a little from him. I have never actually studied it formally, but Grandpa spent enough evenings with me that I can make myself understood." She looked down at the name again.

"They must be sisters," she said. "Brigitte and Madeline."

At that moment they heard a sound behind them and turned in unison to see Doroty come into the room. "I thought I might find the two of you here." She looked at Fletcher. "What are you trying to do? Talk her to death?"

Fletcher laughed. "I'd have to get an early start to do that."

Aunt Doroty looked down at the scattered contents of the trunk, then at the Bible in his hands. "Have you found anything?"

"Nothing much," Fletcher said, "just a suspicion that the Brigitte de Compiegne in this Bible is a sister of the Madeline de Compiegne Ramsay that is buried at Glengarry."

"Well, that is something, at least," she said.

"But not what I need," Fletcher said, frowning. "All I have proven so far is that Madeline and Brigitte are probably sisters, and that Madeline was married to Alexander Ramsay, who is probably my Douglas's brother. But I still don't know anything more about Douglas and Bride Ramsay than the fact that they are both buried at Glengarry Castle."

Suddenly, Cathleen sprang to her feet. "Of course! That's it!" she said. "Douglas and Alexander were brothers ... brothers who married sisters!"

"You might be on to something," Fletcher said, then he paused, thinking. "No, that can't be right. Douglas was married to Bride, not Brigitte."

Cathleen's euphoria sank, and she sat back down on the bed with a dejected sigh. "Aye, you're right."

"'Bride' is Gaelic for 'Brigitte,'" Aunt Doroty said. "I think your lass has made the right connection. They probably *were* sisters. Besides having the same last name, it was quite common in those days for such to happen—sisters marrying brothers. And if that were the case, then that meant they were both from Honfleur, France," she said, pointing to where *Honfleur, France, 1740*, was written.

"It is possible," Fletcher said. "The grave of Bride Ramsay said she was born in 1720. The date on this Bible is 1740. She would have been twenty."

"And the right age to marry," Aunt Doroty said.

"If they were sisters and they were both from Honfleur, then it is quite possible that they were married in France, so the records of their marriages would be there," Cathleen said, feeling the tension mounting as her excitement grew.

Fletcher's face grew pale. His hands shook. "And that is why no one has ever been able to find the records here," Fletcher said, looking down at the old trunk. "All this time . . . and the answer was right here, under our very noses."

Tucking the Bible safely back in the trunk, Fletcher replaced the contents, then closed the lid and locked it, before he started for the door.

"Where are you going?" asked Cathleen, springing up to follow him. "You aren't going to Honfleur now, are you?"

"No, I'm just going to the library to find out where Honfleur is, and if you say France, I'll throttle you."

"I would never be so bold," Cathleen said, hearing Aunt Doroty's chuckle.

As Fletcher left the room, Cathleen said, "Wait!" and rushed after him down the hallway.

Left behind, Doroty came slowly to her feet. "I had forgotten," she said, "just how exhausting it is to be young."

With that, she headed to the library, not with the friskiness of a puppy but with the wisdom and understanding of a wise old dog.

Fletcher had already rolled out a map of France across the desk, holding it down with a magnifying glass, an ink blotter, a brass figurine of a hunting dog, and a crystal paperweight, by the time Cathleen reached the library.

"Have you found it yet?" she asked breathlessly, coming into the room.

"Yes. It's a small town on the Seine River, not far from Le Harve."

She began to study the map, her gaze going to the tiny dot that indicated Honfleur. "Such a small dot to signify so much."

"Let's hope I find it even more significant when I get there," Fletcher said.

"Thankfully, it should be easy to get to. Le Havre is on the coast," she said. "From there it should be easy to go up the Seine. When are we leaving?"

"'We'?"

"Aye." She crossed her arms and began to tap her foot. "Fletcher Ramsay! You weren't thinking of leaving me *here*, were you?"

His expression was as mild as milk. "Of course. I want you safe, Cathleen, and the safest place is here at Caithness with my aunt."

"This is as much my investigation as it is yours, Fletcher Ramsay, and in case you have forgotten, I have plenty invested in it. If you think I'm going to stay here knitting while you're off having the adventure of your life, you are mistaken. You can either take me with you, or I'll follow you on my own."

"Not if I have you kept here as a prisoner."

"You wouldn't dare."

"I would."

"And it wouldn't do you a bit of good," Aunt Doroty said, huffing into the room like a winter wind. "I'd let her loose the minute you left."

Fletcher stared at his aunt.

He didn't say anything for a moment. He did not dare. He was waiting until the urge to strangle Aunt Doroty had passed.

Cathleen, he noticed, brightened like a newly lit lamp, her eyes twinkling merrily, her mouth stretched into a wide smile.

"Why, thank you, Aunt," he said. "It's nice to know my family will always rally behind me in a time of need."

"Your lass is trying to rally behind you, oak wit ... if you'd only let her."

"Cathleen isn't family," he said; then, apparently seeing the dark scowl on Cathleen's face, he added, "yet."

"I beg to disagree with you, lad, but you expressed your intent right here in the library, and I bore witness to it. Now, to my way of thinking that makes *you* betrothed, and being betrothed to you makes *her* family."

"Are we getting technical?"

"If that is what it takes, then I guess I am. Think upon it, Fletcher. From what you've said, it has been Cathleen who has found the clues you needed and Cathleen who began putting the pieces together . . . with a little help from me, I might add."

"That's right," Cathleen said. "I'm the one who found Madeline's grave, and I'm the one who guessed the brother-sister thing."

"And I'm the one who told you about 'Bride' being Gaelic for 'Brigitte'," Doroty added. Then, giving him a scowl, she said, "What have *you* found?"

"A reason to keep my mouth shut."

"And don't be forgetting that I speak French," Cathleen said, "something you will have need of."

"All right, you can come. I only hope I don't live to regret this."

"You won't," Cathleen said, giving both him and Aunt Doroty a kiss on the cheek.

It was about that time that the housekeeper, Mrs. Mac-Cauley, came into the library and announced, "There is a gentleman at the door to see you, Your Lordship."

Fletcher turned around. "Did you get his name?"

"Aye. He said his name was Ian MacMillan, and then he said something about you delivering his baby."

Fletcher felt three pairs of eyes upon him. Feeling a little embarrassed, he said, "Tell Mr. MacMillan I'll see him in my study."

As Mrs. MacCauley left, Cathleen asked, "What could he want? You don't suppose anything has happened to little Fletcher, do you?"

"If you'll stop asking questions, I'll go find out." He started to leave, then turned back to her. "Don't worry. I am certain nothing has happened to little Fletcher, and even if it has, I don't think Ian MacMillan would track us down with the news. You wait here with Aunt Doroty," he said, giving her a kiss on the nose.

Fletcher walked into his study. Ian was sitting in a side chair but sprang to his feet immediately, yanking his cap from his head. "Your Lordship! It's good to see you again. You are looking much more rested than you did the last time I saw you."

"And you are looking like you've been losing a little sleep. The newest little MacMillan isn't keeping you up at night, is he?"

Ian chuckled. "Aye, that he is, Your Lordship. That he is."

"Have a seat. Would you like some brandy or a glass of port?"

"No, thank you," Ian said, sitting down. "I need to be getting myself back home, soon as I'm finished here. One glass of brandy and I might be tempted to stay."

Fletcher laughed. "Well then, what brings you to Caithness?"

Ian began twisting his cap in his hands. "We had a peculiar incident that occurred yesterday. A man came to the door asking for you."

"Really? Did he give his name?"

"No, and when I asked it, he said he would only give his name to you."

"That is odd. What did you tell him?"

"At first I told him I didn't know you, but then he gets all angry and grabs me by me collar and starts to talking real low in his throat, like he intends to do me body harm. He said he knew that I was lying and that if I wanted to keep that pretty wife of mine and that new baby, I'd better tell him what I knew."

Fletcher felt his mouth go dry.

Ian gave him an apologetic look. "I had to tell him then, you ken."

Fletcher nodded.

"When I said you had just happened by, he grabbed me again and said he knew you had stayed at my place for a couple of days. He wanted to know why you stayed there so long, what kind of business we had together.''

''What did you tell him?''

''The truth. I told him about your delivering the baby and all.''

''Did he believe you?''

''Aye, I ken he believed me then, but I could tell it wasna what he wanted to hear.''

''What happened then?''

''Nothing. He left, but I ken he was verra angry.''

''Was he a small, weasel-looking man with gray, thinning hair?''

''No, this man was younger—at least his hair was red, not gray. He was short, but stocky. He looked more like a bulldog than a weasel.''

The description did not fit Adair Ramsay, but it likely fit someone sent by him. Gavin MacPhail had red hair. . . . Fletcher stood and came around the desk, and Ian rose to his feet.

''I felt you should know, Your Lordship.''

Fletcher put his hand on Ian's shoulder. ''I'm glad you came, Ian. Thank you for going to so much trouble.''

''It was the least I could do after all you did for Mary and me.''

''Speaking of Mary . . . Wait a moment. I have something— something I want to send for my namesake.''

''Oh, you needn't do anything like that, Your Lordship.''

''It's my pleasure.'' Fletcher opened a chest on his desk, from which he took out a small pouch of coins. ''Put this away for young Master Fletcher,'' he said. ''I think Cathleen wants him to go to Edinburgh University.''

Ian laughed, then looked down at the pouch. The laughter drained away. ''This is too much money, Your Lordship. I canna accept this much.''

''But you can accept it for your son.''

''Thank you.''

Fletcher walked with him to the front door. ''Give my best to Mary, and tell her that Cathleen sends her love.''

''I'll do that, Your Lordship. And thank you again.''

* * *

"What was that all about?" Cathleen asked, coming out into the hallway as Fletcher closed the door.

He gave her a suspicious look. "Have you been snooping again?"

"Aye, because it's the only way I can find out anything. Who do you think it was that went to his house?"

"Someone under Adair's thumb, of course."

"We are being watched, then?"

"More than likely."

"We will have to be careful when we leave for Le Havre."

"We'll leave during the dead of night," he said.

Cathleen shivered, rubbing her arms. "Could you please phrase it another way?"

"*Late* at night, then," he said, smiling at her. "If we are lucky, they won't be expecting us to go anywhere, certainly not to leave the country."

Cathleen, swept up in the intrigue of it all, could not hide the excitement in her voice. "We should wear dark clothing and ride horses with no white markings."

He smiled again, stroking her cheek. "We'll be careful, but there is no need to disguise yourself as Dick Dauntless."

"Perhaps I've always wanted to dress as Dick Dauntless," she said saucily, "or at least as Mrs. Dauntless."

"Mrs. Dauntless, is it? How about dressing as the Countess of Caithness instead?"

"How about keeping your mind on getting us out of this box we are in, and then I'll think about being your countess."

He pulled her against him, gazing deep into her eyes. "Is that a promise?"

"Aye," she said. "You didn't forget to thank Ian for coming here?"

"I thanked him," he said, "and I gave him a little something for young Fletcher."

"That was thoughtful of you."

"It was the least I could do for the man who probably just saved our lives." Fletcher shook his head. "I would never have suspected that Adair would have us followed to Caithness. He must be getting quite worried."

"We will have to be even more cautious now."

"Yes—and, thanks to Ian, we will."

"Perhaps I should reconsider your offer to become a countess. The name Mrs. Dick Dauntless, and the idea of being married to a highwayman, is sounding better all the time."

"You may get your wish. I have a feeling there is a big price on our heads."

Cathleen felt a shiver go over her, as if someone were walking over her grave. "*Our* heads? You mean mine too?"

"Every wine-colored strand of it. Now come here, wench, and kiss me. They say the threat of danger brings out the beast in a man and makes him amorous."

She laughed, kissing him soundly. "Anything makes you amorous," she said. "Even breathing."

"That too . . ." he said, taking her in his arms.

Chapter Twenty-five

They left for France in the middle of night.

The sun was up by the time the small ship that carried Cathleen and Fletcher across the Channel docked at Le Havre, an important port on coast of France. But it wasn't Le Havre's importance as a port, or the fact that it was on the French coast, that had drawn them there.

Le Havre lay at the mouth of the Seine River, just a short distance from Honfleur.

As she stood in the warm sunshine on the deck of the boat that carried them upriver from Le Havre to Honfleur, Cathleen was lost in thought, her mind spinning backward, as if she were reliving the time since Fletcher had come.

How much her quiet, orderly life had changed in the past few months because of him.

In spite of her circumstances, she could not help smiling at that. Never in her wildest imaginings had she pictured herself gallivanting about the country, living in sin with a man to whom she was not married. Indeed, she wouldn't have believed herself capable even of considering marriage, much less of actually looking forward to it. No, she would have not believed it, not even if the angel Gabriel had appeared before her in the flesh and told her so.

In Honfleur, they made their way to a small inn, Le Petit Chat, where they registered as man and wife.

Cathleen looked down at the register, reading what Fletcher had written in his flowing script; *Sir Gaylord Hawthorne and Lady Hawthorne*.

She frowned, giving him a look that voiced her displeasure. "Our staying together is absolutely necessary," he explained. "I don't intend to let you out of my sight."

She understood then that he was merely being cautious, that he did not know whether they were being followed.

Shortly after they closed themselves into the small room on the second floor, Cathleen stood at the window, looking down at the courtyard where a young girl herded a flock of unruly geese.

Had the girl been sent to spy on them? Cathleen began to rub her temples, wondering if this is how one went insane. What was wrong with her? She was suspicious of everyone, and she couldn't get the thought of Adair's men out of her mind.

"Are you all right?" Fletcher asked, coming up behind her, putting his hands on her arms.

She did not want him to know, for worrying about her would only distract him. She forced a lightness she did not feel. "Aside from the fact that my rib bones are clacking together, I'm fine. Are you going to feed me or starve me to death?"

He turned her to face him and kissed her lightly on the mouth. "Here I'm thinking about making love, and your mind is on food."

She smiled, coming up on tiptoe to give him a light kiss of her own. *Be wise, Fletcher. Be wary.* "Where is it written," she said with a hint of seduction in her voice, "that we can't have both?"

"I don't know, but I have little doubt that you'll find it somewhere . . . probably in the 'Book of Abstinence,' chapter twelve."

She laughed, curling her arms around his middle. "I don't feel much like reading right now. However, if you don't feed me soon, it won't matter. I won't have the energy to do either."

"I'll be right back," Fletcher said, and with Cathleen's laughter following him, he shot from the room, pausing only long enough to tell her, "Lock the door behind me and don't open it for anyone except me."

My idea exactly. "Not even the landlord?"

"Not anyone, landlords included." With a teasing look, he added, "I'll be back in a minute with something for you to eat. Then we'll see if you're a woman of your word."

" *'Faithful in little, faithful in much,'* " she said. "Luke."

He nodded. "See that you remember that when your belly is full." And with that he was off, closing the door softly behind him, his voice reaching her from the other side of the door: "Lock it."

Her hand was already on the lock. Only after she had shoved the bolt home did she hear his satisfied grunt and retreating footsteps.

She was sitting on the bed when she heard a knock at the door. Her heart hammered. She looked around the room for something to use as a weapon in case they broke down the door.

Stop it! You're becoming too fearful. God would have you vigilant, not terrified of your own shadow.

Getting up, she crossed the room and pressed her ear to the door. "Who is it?"

"It's me," he said, "Fletcher the faithful. Revelations, eight hundred. Open up."

She smiled, shoving back the bolt and opening the door. He strolled into the room, pulled something from the inside of his coat, and handed it to her.

She looked down at the unappetizing mass of something white, veined with green mold. "Was it alive once, or has it always been dead?"

He looked at it again. "I'm not certain. What do you think?"

She shrugged. "Always dead, I think. What is it?"

"Cheese." He produced a loaf of bread and a bottle of wine, which he set on the table by the window. "Don't complain, just eat it. I had the devil of a time finding even that."

She eyed the hideous lump. "I never eat green cheese."

"All of it isn't green," he said, looking at it, "only parts of it."

"I'll have the bread," she said, handing the lump of cheese back to him.

He took it, breaking off a healthy lump and poking it into his mouth. "Mmmmmm. . . . delicious."

She picked up the loaf of bread, returned to the bed, and sat down. She tore at the long, dry loaf, succeeding at last in tearing a hunk of it loose. Poking it into her mouth, she chewed gingerly, trying to swallow without much luck.

"*Aaak!*" The dry crumbs sucked at what little moisture there was in her mouth and lodged in her throat.

"Here," he said, handing her a cup of wine, "wash it down with this."

She drank thirstily, then tore off another hunk of bread, chewing it in much the same manner as she had the first, following it with the wine.

At last she sighed and fell back. "I think I could sleep for a week."

"What happened to poor ol' *'faithful in little, faithful in much,'* Luke?' Did you forget him *and* his faithful ways?"

"No," she said, stretching like an overfed cat, rolling onto her side. "I'm just resting up a bit, waiting for you to pounce." She closed her eyes.

He pounced.

She expected him to make love to her, so she was surprised when he gathered her into his arms and said, "Sleep," kissing her lightly. "I think you need it more than you need me right now."

She raised her head, looking at him. "Are you trying to get out of it, then?"

He grunted. "Hardly. I only have enough self-restraint for a short delay." He pushed her head down. "Go to sleep. I feel my saint's veneer wearing thin."

She closed her eyes, feeling relaxed and sleepy. Fletcher

watched over her, and she felt as if nothing could harm her now.

When she awoke, the room was dark, save for a faint light coming through the window. Looking in that direction, she saw him standing there, both hands braced against the window frame as he stared out, lost in thought.

He was naked, a magnificent godlike being, and she studied him. How beautiful he was. How perfect. She thought that this must be how Adam looked in the beginning, for she could see tremendous power held in check—power seen through the tense contours of his body, the flexing knee, the bent arms, the head inclined forward as if awaiting the moment of life.

And the Lord God formed man of the dust of the ground, and breathed into his nostrils the breath of life; and man became a living soul . . .

Even in the faint light, she could see the dusting of dark hair on his arms and legs, the firm muscles of his buttocks, the long, straight legs.

A ripple of desire coiled low in her belly. She found herself wishing he would turn around.

"Make love to me," she whispered softly.

He turned quickly, and she saw the hesitation in his stance.

"I thought I'd let you rest," he said. "You were exhausted."

"As were you."

"I couldn't sleep."

"I could."

"Yes, the sleep of the innocent."

"Not so innocent since I met you," she said, wishing she could take the words back when she saw the effect they had upon him.

He came to sit beside her on the bed. He stroked her face. "I regret the way this has gone," he said, "but not the fact that we've made love. If things had been different . . . normal, I would have made an honest woman of you long before now."

"I know," she said, taking his hand, turning her face into his palm to place a kiss there.

"I love you," he whispered, leaning over her and kissing her cheek, her neck, her throat.

"Show me."

Her hand came down between them, and she stroked his hard flesh.

He did a little stroking of his own. "You have the softest skin. It feels—"

She gasped as his hand found the juncture of her thighs.

"Lord," he groaned, "you're sleek and warm as wet velvet."

He rolled over on top of her, his knee going between her legs as he began to move, rubbing her. Her legs parted, and she thought how quickly she seemed to have forgotten all that she had been taught. She was a minister's granddaughter, but a thousand sermons would not have been enough to still the instinctive action of her body moving in response.

His mouth found hers and he kissed her, long, deep, and hard, his tongue restless, seeking, and welcome in her mouth.

"Come inside me," she panted, her hand searching and guiding him.

"God in Heaven," he said, "I can resist anything save the sound of your voice when you want me." He pressed against her, moaning softly as he entered her, his body tensing when he could go no farther.

She raised her knees, drawing him in deeper. He began to move with slow, sure strokes. Her hands spread across his back, stroking the taut, hard muscles. "Too soon," he whispered. "I want you too much to hold back."

She felt his entire body quiver, then the muscles of his legs grew tense, his buttocks clenching tight. She felt the warmth of his release flow into her, the close intimacy of it shattering her, as her body convulsed, the low, moaning sounds she knew he loved coming from deep inside her.

He rolled to his side, taking her with him and settling her body against his. "Sleep," he whispered, "while you can."

But sleep was the last thing on her mind.

Something troubled her, robbed her of her peace. She was afraid for him, afraid that something might happen to him, something horrible and he would be taken away.

Just like Grand father ...

Closing her eyes, she lay with her head against his chest, listening to the sound of his heart beating. So much had happened since that day at the well when she had looked up and seen a little bit of heaven riding toward her, a part of heaven come down to earth to change her life forever. And he had changed it, giving her far, far more than he had taken. *Don't let anything happen to him. Please don't take him away. Please, God, protect this man and give him to me....*

She lay there until the rapid pounding of his heart slowed and his breathing became deeper. "I love you," she whispered, knowing that he could not hear her.

Somehow that did not seem to matter.

The loud clang of a nearby church bell woke Fletcher. He opened his eyes, feeling a numbness in his left shoulder. He glanced at his shoulder.

The numbness had a name: Cathleen.

Smiling down at the profusion of long, flowing hair, he could not help thinking how perfectly she suited him. He had expected many things when he came to Scotland, but to find the love of his life had not been among them. He slipped his hand under her head, lifting it, needing to get up but not wanting to disturb her.

"What time is it?" she asked, raising a sleepy head to look at him. She smiled. "Good morning."

He kissed her. "Good morning to you, love. If those blasted church bells are right, it is seven o'clock." He kissed her again. "I've got to get dressed. Why don't you go back to sleep?"

"Dressed? Where are you going?"

He rolled from the bed and walked across the room to the washbasin. Filling the bowl with water, he began to wash his face. She could not take her eyes off him. A naked man was a beautiful thing, she thought. How sad God must have been when man sinned, his newfound awareness forcing him to cover all that newly created beauty.

Drying his face, he turned toward her. "I've got to find a carriage or some sort of transportation for us. Lord knows how many records we'll have to search, how many churches and graves."

"Wait and I'll come with you."

"Stay here. I shouldn't be long. Rest awhile. I'll be back before you know it. I'll bring you something to eat."

She sat up, leaning against the headboard, crossing her arms in front of her, giving him a scowl.

He stopped and looked at her. "I've said something wrong again, haven't I?"

"No. I just wonder why you said we had to have a room together so you could keep me with you, and here you are leaving me here alone."

"Maybe that wasn't the only reason I wanted us to share a room," he said, ducking when she sailed a pillow at him.

He finished dressing, then kissed her before he left, reminding her to lock the door.

When he had not returned by the time she was dressed, she decided to go downstairs. She was starving and could not wait for him to come back. Perhaps the innkeeper would have something to tide her over. She thought briefly about Adair, but surmised that she would be safe as long as she did not leave the inn.

She left the room and walked along the dimly lit hallway to the stairs. Her hand on the rail, she started down, hearing the sound of voices coming from the taproom below.

The men were speaking in French, so she paid them little heed, but when they said the name Ramsay, in English, it caught her attention.

She froze.

"Ramsay?" the innkeeper repeated. *"Mais non, monsieur,"* he said, saying that he had no guests registered by that name.

"He is an American. He is traveling with a young English woman with dark hair."

Not even the inn was safe from Adair's men. Her heart pounding, Cathleen turned around quietly and tiptoed back up the stairs. When she reached the second floor, she ran back to the room and closed the door behind her, ramming the bolt in place. She threw the few possessions they had into the small bag they carried, then hurried to the window.

Opening it, she leaned out and looked down to the courtyard to see if there was a way to escape. It had rained during the night, washing the red tiles on the roof and leaving a few puddles in the inn yard.

At that moment she saw a small carriage come into the courtyard, its wheels splashing through a large puddle as it stopped. A moment later, the door opened and Fletcher climbed out.

"Fletcher!" she called, keeping her voice as low as she could.

He looked up.

She held up a hand, then pointed behind her. "They're here," she said. "Stay there. I'm coming out." She tossed their bag down to him.

"Wait there," he said, "I'm coming up."

"No, there isn't time!" She crawled to the edge of the roof. On all fours, she peered over the ledge and saw him standing below her. She inched her body around until she was in a sitting position, her feet dangling off the ledge.

"Catch me," she said, then shoved herself off the roof.

"Cathleen!"

She dropped down into Fletcher's arms.

"I'm glad to know you can trust me at least about some things," he said.

"Hurry," she said as he lowered her to her feet. "We haven't much time."

He took her hand, and they ran across the courtyard to the carriage. Opening the door, he stuffed her inside.

"Hold on," he said, climbing in beside her. Then, sticking his head out, he told the driver to hurry.

They did not move.

She poked her head out and told the driver to hurry, in French.

The driver cracked the whip and the carriage took off with a lurch. Digging her hands into the seat beneath her, Cathleen held on for dear life.

"Don't say it," he said.

"What?"

"That you warned me I would need someone to speak French."

"I won't."

"What was that all about back there? Did someone come up to the room?"

"No. I heard two men talking to the innkeeper," she said, then told him what had happened.

It seemed that Fletcher was more upset over the fact that she had not stayed in the room, as he had told her, than he was about the men looking for them.

"If you can't behave yourself and do as I ask, I'll send you back to Caithness."

She gave him her most contrite look. "I'll behave."

"Did you recognize either of the men?"

"No. I stopped on the stairs and didn't go down far enough to see them."

"It's just as well. We know who sent them and why."

"Fletcher," she said, putting her hand on his arm. "Do you think they are here simply to spy on us, or to do us bodily harm?"

"Something tells me they are here for more than just spying."

"You mean . . ."

"I won't let anything happen to you, Cathleen. I'll protect you. I promise."

She snuggled close to him, tucking her arm through his, burying her face against his shoulder. She did not want him to see the look of sadness on her face. How could she tell him it wasn't herself she worried for? She knew he would protect her. Even if it cost him his life . . .

Chapter Twenty-six

They searched records at two churches before the driver took them to a small country church called St. Benedictine's.

The priest, Father Sebastian, was more than helpful, and Fletcher was grateful that he also spoke English.

Father Sebastian informed them that the de Compiegne family had attended his church for centuries. "In fact, monsieur, St. Benedictine was built on de Compiegne land and paid for by them. There are many members of the family buried in the churchyard. The earliest dates back to the year 1163."

"The years I'm interested in are much later than that," Fletcher said.

Father Sebastian nodded, then glanced toward the window. "It looks as if the Lord has blessed us with another fine day. Would you like to visit the churchyard?"

"Perhaps, if we don't find what we are looking for elsewhere. May we see your marriage and birth records?" Fletcher asked. "I'm mostly interested in the 1700s."

"Of course. I would be delighted to show them to you," Father Sebastian said.

He led them into a small room that contained floor-to-ceiling shelves filled with books. A long table and four chairs stood in the middle of the floor.

"The years you are interested in would be in one of these," he said, pulling two large books from the shelves and placing them on the table. "I will come back later to see how you are doing." Father Sebastian left them alone in the room.

Cathleen's heart throbbed with anticipation as she waited, seeing Fletcher's hands tremble as he opened the first book. His eyes scanned the first page and then the next. Page after page, she watched him, his jaw clenched tightly as he skimmed the names recorded there.

Suddenly she realized that her heart was no longer pounding, that a remarkable calm had settled over her. It was at that point that she felt herself surrounded by an incredible warmth.

A moment later, Fletcher took a deep breath, closed his eyes, threw his head back, obviously overcome with emotion.

"What is it?" she asked, looking down at the book.

"It's ... here," he said, his voice choked with feeling. "After all these years, it's right here. The proof. My family. I am the true duke," he said, "just as my father said."

She looked down at the page, seeing the faded brown ink, but the writing was quite legible. There before them was recorded the marriage of Alexander Ramsay, son of Alasdair Ramsay, Duke of Glengarry, to Madeline de Compiegne, daughter of the Comte de Compiegne. Six months later, on June 23, 1740, was recorded the marriage of Douglas Ramsay, son of Alasdair Ramsay, Duke of Glengarry, to Brigitte de Compiegne, daughter of the Comte de Compiegne.

The proof was there. All of it. Douglas and Alexander *were* brothers. They were the sons of Alasdair Ramsay, and Alasdair was the Duke of Glengarry. And, as they had suspected, Brigitte and Madeline were sisters.

They searched further, finding it recorded that one year after their marriage, Brigitte and Douglas Ramsay baptized their infant son, Ian.

"There are no other births recorded," Cathleen said.

"That is because Douglas and Brigitte must have taken their son and returned to Scotland. The dates coincide with the time of Alasdair's death."

"Aye. Alasdair's death would have made Douglas the Duke of Glengarry," Cathleen said. "That is the reason they returned to Scotland."

"If my father had only known . . ."

She touched his arm. "I have a feeling that he does," she whispered.

"You and your unshakable faith," he said, looking at her. "Sometimes . . ." He stopped, not finishing the thought.

"Sometimes what?" she asked.

"Sometimes I find myself wishing I had that kind of faith."

"You can."

He shook his head. "It's a bit late for me, I'm afraid."

"It's never too late, Fletcher. One of these days something will happen, something that will bring you closer to God."

"Perhaps," he said, drawing her against him. "Until then, I guess you'll just have to have enough faith for both of us."

"I do."

He pulled back, giving her a quick kiss. "If I tell you to wait here for me, will you do as I say?"

"Where are you going?"

"To speak to Father Sebastian. I need to find a scribe. This information must be copied in a legal document and certified, if it is to stand up in the courts at Edinburgh."

"I hadn't thought about that," she said, realizing he was right. "I don't suppose Father Sebastian would take too kindly to our taking these old books with us."

"Nor would I want to. They are safer here," Fletcher said, then he started to leave.

"Wait!"

He turned toward her. "What?"

"Where are you going?"

"To find Father Sebastian and then to visit the scribe."

"You can visit Father Sebastian, but you can't go to the scribe."

"Why not?"

"Because you don't speak French."

Fletcher stared at her, and Cathleen knew the exact moment when the truth of her words sank in. He did not look happy, but he agreed with her. "I guess that means we'll both have to go."

"No, I think it would be better if—"

"Absolutely not." His expression grew dark, and he did not bother to hide his irritation. "You are not going alone and that is final."

"Just hear me out," she said. "It would be better if I went. Adair's men are looking for a man and a woman, not a woman alone . . . and certainly not a French-speaking woman."

Just as she knew he would, Fletcher saw the truth of her words and consented to let her go, but not before lecturing her thoroughly on being extremely cautious.

It was quite warm by the time she reached town. Cathleen wanted to remove her bonnet but dared not, fearing that the color of her hair would be a dead giveaway. She looked out the window as the carriage drove down the streets of Honfleur, passing the vendors' carts, the shops where the proprietors were carrying on their normal day's business. But for her, something about this day was not normal. Uneasiness pricked at her spine.

Suddenly the carriage stopped, and she heard the driver shouting. She poked her head out the window. "What is the matter?"

"There is an overturned cart blocking the street, mademoiselle," the driver replied.

"How long will it take to clear it?"

He shrugged. "Who knows? Perhaps a few minutes, perhaps hours."

Cathleen glanced out the window again. "I'll get out here. If the cart is cleared from the street before I get back, drive to the address I gave you and wait for me there."

The driver nodded. *"Oui, mademoiselle."*

Cathleen climbed out of the coach, closing the door behind her, then she turned to make her way down the street, which was narrow and twisting, the cobbles difficult to walk upon.

The air here seemed warmer and more humid, stifling. She opened the top button of her dress.

She came to a corner and turned up another street. A few minutes later, she noticed that there were no shops here, no people. Thinking that she had taken a wrong turn, she stopped. It was then that she heard the sound of running feet coming up behind her.

Turning around, she saw two men swiftly approaching her, their footsteps echoing with a hollow clap. She darted down an alley, finding it difficult to navigate its narrow lane, which was littered with garbage and refuse. Too late, she realized her mistake—the alley had no way out. She gave a quick glance back. The two men rushed into the alley behind her.

She ducked behind a large barrel, holding her breath at the rancid smell of rotting garbage and God knew what else. The slime beneath her began to soak into her clothes. She could feel it on her hands. Something small and scuffling ran over her hand and she jerked it back, flinging the slime across the front of her dress as she did so. Her stomach turned at the smell. For a moment she was afraid she would be sick.

It was all she could do to keep from jumping up, trying her luck at outrunning them, but she found herself calling upon a reserve of strength she did not know she had, a strength that enabled her to remain levelheaded. She reasoned with herself: No amount of garbage, no matter how foul-smelling, was worth losing her life over.

The sound of running feet slowed. She could tell that they were closer, walking now, searching. She heard their voices as they spoke, but she could not make out what they said. She knew it would be only a matter of time before they found her.

Looking about her, she searched for something, anything, that she could use to defend herself. She saw nothing, but an old fishing net and an oak bucket.

"She isna here. Where could she have gone?"

"I dinna ken, but she has to be in here somewhere. I ken we both saw her turn into this alley."

"Aye, but she doesna seem to be here now."

Fear had a metallic taste in her mouth. *The Lord is my shepherd* . . .

Her heart hammered as she began reciting the Twenty-third Psalm in her mind. *Yea though I walk through the valley of the shadow of death* . . .

It wasn't much, but it was all she had available, so she reached forward, her fingers feeling around in the slime until she had both the net and the bucket in her hands.

I will fear no evil . . .

She listened to the sound of the voices until she was certain the men had just passed by her.

For thou art with me . . .

Springing to her feet, she tossed the net over one of them.

The man cursed, taking God's name in vain, as he turned around and stared at her. He had a frightening face with a hideous scar that slashed horizontally from his left temple to the right side of his chin, disfiguring his nose and leaving him blind in one eye.

She heard herself make a small moaning sound, and for a moment she was frozen, as she stared in horror. He seemed to hold her transfixed with that one eye of his as he fought against the net. A second later, he freed one hand and grabbed for her.

She screamed and jumped backward. He lunged, losing his balance. He fell to the ground with a thud, his body still trapped, and fighting against the netting.

The other man whirled around and looked at her with a hate-filled grin. He took a step forward, and she countered it with a backward step of her own. He lunged, his hand whipping out snakelike to grab her. She sidestepped and turned at the same time. His grimy hand grabbed a fistful of her hair. She felt his nails scrape against her scalp, felt the burning pull as she was yanked backward by her hair.

Biting back the pain, she twisted her body until she was certain her hair would come out by the roots. But her endurance paid off, and she broke away from him. A second later, she spun around and brought the bucket down over his head, holding it in both hands and swinging it with all her might.

The bucket shattered, pieces flying in every direction, then clattering to the cobbles below. The man staggered, then stopped still, his eyes wild, more white than color showing. Winded, her scalp burning, she stared at him, watching, waiting, wondering if the blow had been enough.

Without a single oath, he dropped, silently and blessedly, to the ground.

"*'His enemies shall lick the dust,'*" she whispered. "Psalms."

Not waiting to take another look, she whirled around and dashed back the way she had come, running until she had a stitch in her side and her lungs felt as if they were on fire, and still she ran, following the twisting streets, stumbling twice on the uneven cobbles and scraping her hands.

Just as she left the narrow sidestreets and rushed out onto a larger street she saw the carriage coming toward her. "Help!" she screamed. "Help me!"

The driver stopped and climbed down, running toward her. "Mademoiselle, are you all right?"

So winded that she could not talk, she nodded.

He helped her to the carriage and held the door open for her. Not worrying about her dignity now, Cathleen almost threw herself inside. "Take me to the scribe," she said, gasping for breath. "I've decided not to walk after all."

"*Oui, mademoiselle*, a most sensible choice," the driver said, urging the horse into a faster pace. "*Je n'ai jamais d'espirit qu'au bas de l'escalier.* 'I never have any wit until I am below stairs.'"

"Aye," she said. "After wit is ever best."

An hour later, she stood next to Fletcher, watching as the scribe copied the information they needed. Her scalp still burned, her scraped palms were stinging, and she was feeling just a little sorry for herself. After all, she had suffered a very close encounter with two ruffians, and Fletcher seemed unconcerned.

Of course, she had not told him about the incident, but in her woman's mind that did not matter. In all fairness, she had to admit that he had noticed her disarray when she stepped out of the carriage. However, it was her opinion that he was far too accepting of her lame excuse that she had tripped and fallen.

Perhaps it was just her nerves, she decided at last.

What she really needed was for Fletcher to hold her while she had a good cry. She scooted closer to him, hoping he could see her need written in her eyes.

Fletcher sniffed the air, turning toward her. His nose wrinkled and he made a face.

"What is it?" she asked.

He sniffed again. "Do you smell something?"

"No. Do you?"

"Most definitely."

"What does it smell like?"

"Garbage," he said. "Very old, reeking garbage."

"Oh. I can't imagine where it could be coming from," Cathleen said, looking down and seeing the grimy, wet stains along the hem of her gown. She held out her hands, where grime seemed to ooze from beneath her fingernails.

Quietly, she slipped her hands behind her and stepped a few feet away.

After the scribe finished his work and left, Fletcher turned to Father Sebastian. "If I could rely upon your kindness for one more request . . ."

"I would be happy to help in any way I can."

"The contents of those books are very important to me. There are those who would give anything to destroy the evidence we found here. I would like to say it is my concern for this old relic that prompts my actions, but my motives are selfish ones, I'm afraid."

Father Sebastian smiled. "I will hide them in a safe place, monsieur. Have no worry."

"Thank you," Fletcher said, handing the priest an envelope. "I would like to make this contribution as a way of expressing my gratitude."

Father Sebastian nodded. "Contributions for the needy are always appreciated. Bless you."

Fletcher nodded, then took Cathleen by the arm. "We have

what we came for," he said, "and I find I am anxious to take the news back to Scotland, post haste."

She looked up at him. "Will we go to Edinburgh first?"

"No. I want to take you to Dunston, where you'll be safe. Then *I'll* go to Edinburgh. Alone."

He did not miss the knowing smile she gave him. "Thank you for your concern, but I have a suspicion that the real reason is that you first want to share the good news with your aunt."

Fletcher grinned. "I am never so transparent as when I think I am hiding something."

"Aye, I think that sometimes I have a grasp of what you are thinking before you do."

"Talk like that makes a man feel downright transparent."

"Dinna fret. I am certain you will think of some way to muddy the waters."

He puffed up. "Good at that, am I?"

"No, but you're getting better," she said, laughing.

"You're a long way from home, lass. Keep talking like that and I might be tempted to leave you here."

She gave him a confident smile. "You might be tempted, but you canna leave me here."

"And why is that?"

"Because once a woman has given you her heart, it is impossible to get rid of the rest of her."

Father Sebastian looked at Fletcher and laughed. "Thunderbolts and fires come as fate requires," he said.

Fletcher looked from him to Cathleen and back again, then he said, "Pray for me, Father."

Father Sebastian laughed again. "I have been, my child. I have been."

Returning to their hired carriage, Fletcher tried to explain to the driver that they wanted to go to Le Havre, using sign language to emphasize his words. He must have suspected he wasn't doing a very good job of it when he saw the bewildered look on the driver's face, for he said,

"Okay, you tell him."

She spoke to the driver in his native tongue.

He helped her into the carriage, then climbed in beside her and closed the door. The driver shouted and cracked the whip, and the carriage lurched forward.

Cathleen looked down at his hand resting on his knee. For a moment she was distracted by the sight of the crested signet ring, the expensive fabric of his coat, the fine cotton of his shirt.

A beam of sunlight slanted through the window, catching the gold of the ring and sending a flash of light into her eyes, blinding her for a moment. She closed her eyes against its glare.

When she opened them a moment later, she saw Fletcher make a face. "I can't believe it," he said.

She stared at him curiously. "You can't believe what?"

"That same wretched smell," he said. "It's here, in the carriage. I can't imagine where it is coming from."

"Oh. Neither can I," she said, slipping her hands beneath her skirts.

The carriage clattered on down the road, and Fletcher leaned back and closed his eyes, hoping to fall asleep, but the smell was so strong it made sleep impossible. He kept thinking about that smell. Then suddenly he remembered the way Cathleen had looked when she met him at the scribe's.

He opened one eye and glanced at her. There she sat beside him, the picture of innocence. Yet, the more he thought about it, the more he remembered the way she had rounded her mouth as she said the word *Oh*.

It seemed more than a bit suspicious to him, and on top of that, there were her eyes. Big as pumpkins they were, and the expression in them was guilty. "Want to tell me about it?" he asked, crossing his arms and doing his best to look sagacious, but feeling that he looked more like Father Christmas with a merry twinkle in his eye.

She sighed. "How did you know?" She laughed then. "Aside from the smell, I mean."

"Cathleen, you had better stick to telling the truth, because you can't lie worth a damn. The truth is written all over your face. Now, tell me what happened."

She settled herself back into the carriage and told him about her bit of adventure. When she got to the part about the net and the bucket, he said, "My God! I should be horsewhipped for letting you go alone. I would never forgive myself if something happened to you. Never."

"I wanted to go . . ."

"I won't allow you to do something like that again."

She laughed. "Go, saith the King. Hold, saith the wind."

He couldn't help smiling at her, despite the fact that his guts were churning at the thought of those two slimy bastards chasing her. Then look turned serious. "I'm sorry for what happened. I know you must have been terrified."

"Aye, I was frightened," she said, "but, *'he that fleeth from fear shall fall into the pit.'* Jeremiah."

For a stunned moment, Fletcher simply stared at her, then he laughed heartily. For the life of him, he could not get out of his mind the picture of her jumping up to toss a net over one man and bashing a bucket down over the other one's head. "That's my lass," he said, drawing her into his arms and giving her a quick kiss.

A second later, and gasping for breath, he released her. "Bad idea," he said, and moved to sit on the seat across from her, opening the window.

"Is it that bad?"

"Love, you are as rank as a pole cat."

She looked down at her soiled dress and sniffed. "I don't smell a thing."

"Count that a blessing," he said, turning his head for a blast of fresh air coming through the window.

The harbor of Le Havre lay before them, glittering in the sunlight, half a dozen boats and ships riding the gentle waves that splashed against the wharves.

Once they docked, they went straight to an inn, Fletcher ordering "the best-smelling bath money can buy" the moment they were shown to their room.

The landlord looked Cathleen over good and proper, then agreed to have it sent up immediately, and left as if he could not get out of the room fast enough.

"You stay here and don't open this door for anyone except the landlord bringing your bath. Is that understood?"

"Aye. Where are you going?"

"To arrange passage back to Scotland for us. I won't be gone long."

"Just long enough for me to smell better?"

"Definitely that long," he said, laughing and dodging her shoe as she tossed it at him.

Not long after he left, Cathleen went to the window and stood watching the street below, waiting for a glimpse of him. The sun they had enjoyed earlier was gone, replaced by a slow, steady drizzle that drenched the city and kept the smoky smell of fires and cooked food huddling close to the houses that lined the cobbled streets.

Catching sight of him as he crossed the street, she watched until he turned the corner and disappeared from sight, then she closed the window.

The chambermaid brought buckets of steaming water to fill the copper tub. Once she was alone, Cathleen scrubbed herself and washed her hair twice before leaning back and closing her eyes.

The joy she had felt earlier was leaving her. She felt it as if it were a physical thing, as if someone had turned a spigot inside her and let all the happiness flow away. She glanced at the window, where a bleak half-light crept timidly into the room.

How foreign this place was. Everywhere she looked, the world seemed forlorn and forbidding, lonely and withdrawn.

She rose and stepped from the bath, finding no pleasure now in its warm, fragrant depths. Drying quickly, she dressed in fresh clothes, then towel-dried her hair before twisting it into a quick braid and coiling it at her nape.

Suddenly feeling tired, she lay down on the bed. A dark gray mist seemed to settle over her, and she felt its liquid heaviness upon her face. She wiped away her tears, feeling their saltiness burn the scrapes on her hands, as she thought back over the months since Fletcher had come into her life.

She loved him, and she knew he loved her, too. But she also knew it was not to be. They were too different, their worlds too different, their futures too far apart. She remembered the way his hand had looked with the signet ring, remembered too the way the sunlight had flashed off it, blinding her. It occurred to her that that was exactly what she had been: blind. Blind to the reasons why things would never work out between them. Blind to the things that ring stood for. Blind to who he was and to her own station in life.

She was the heather, dancing in the wind on the hillside, rooted there until she died, living and enjoying each day to the fullest, but never losing sight of the fact that she was heather.

Fletcher knew no such bounds.

He was the sunlight that passed over her, bringing warmth and light into her world, but only temporarily. Soon, darkness would come to cover her, and he would go on, spreading warmth and light to others he met along the way.

She was earth.

He was wind.

She was bound by what she was, always to be solid, immobile.

He knew no bounds, nor was it in his nature to stay.

He had taught her love. It would have to be enough. She would have to end it soon.

It would be better that way, but it would also bring her pain.

When Fletcher returned two hours later, she was asleep on the bed. For a while he stood over her, looking at her, seeing her beauty, feeling her sadness.

He sat down beside her, leaning over to kiss her cheek. She stirred but did not awaken. He did not let that deter him, but went on to kiss each soft hollow, every sleepy and warm place. He smoothed his palm over the petal softness of her skin, feeling the loyalty and devotion of the muscles below. He spanned the narrowness of her waist and cupped the fullness of her soft breasts.

Every place he touched she was lovely.

And she was his.

He rolled her over to her back and began to unbutton her

dress, pulling the bodice apart until her loveliness was bared to him. Kissing her throat, her neck, her breasts, he tasted the residue of herbal soap, then easing her skirts up, he moved her legs apart, touching the warm dampness there, between her thighs. Hearing her moan, he looked up and saw her eyes open.

"I love you," she said.

"And I you. You are so beautiful," he said, "inside and out. I will never tire of seeing you like this, of being with you this way. If I live to be a hundred, each day with you will be like the first."

He saw a flash of pain in her eyes and thought to ask her about it, but at that moment she unfastened his trousers and took him in her hand. He was hard and stiff with wanting her, needing her, desiring her. . . .

When he could stand it no longer, he removed the rest of his clothes and hers, taking her as a ship comes to its mooring, moving hard against her, feeling her response, pressing, wanting, each needing the other so desperately that they seemed to fear that moment of complete intimacy, that utmost connection that would take them beyond what they could comprehend, as if somehow they both sensed that their time together was fleeting.

Again and again he brought her to the edge of the summit, then held himself back, feeling the twisting need, the shuddering gasp that threatened to overwhelm him.

On and on it came, until she writhed beneath him and cried out his name, and dug her hands into his hair and held him to her, refusing to let him go. She arched against him. "Now," she whispered. "Come with me. Love me. Now. Give me this memory."

He groaned, yielding to her, and the power of it drew her with him, his whispered words of encouragement and her panting cries of pleasure blending for a moment into one, as two raindrops come together on a windowpane.

They lay together until the heat of their passion cooled and the perspiration of their bodies dried in the twilight chill of the room, yet they stayed as they were, until he felt himself grow smaller and slip from the mingled wetness of her desire and his seed. And even then they remained as they had been, solid and together, filled with love and life, as if by staying this way they could hold at bay what was to come.

Knowing that she was worried about what lay ahead, and understanding that her frightening encounter had caused this fear, he gathered her close and rolled over, cradling her in his arms, holding her against him, wanting her to feel the security and protection he offered. "It is almost over," he said, trying to assure her.

"Aye. It won't be long now."

Her melancholy touched him.

"Don't worry, angel mine. I've waited too long and gotten too close to let anything happen to either of us. We will see this thing done and we will see it through together. We have been through much, each of us suffering our losses."

"Aye. *'A man of sorrows, and acquainted with grief.'*"

His heart felt weighted down. She failed to mention where that quote was found, and he knew it had been intentional.

"Job?" he asked, as if by doing so he could put things back the way they had been before.

"Isaiah," she said so woefully that he had to laugh.

"Ah, Isaiah . . . the foreteller of doom and wearer of sackcloth."

"Aye." She snuggled against him, and soon they were asleep.

He awoke sometime during the night and made love to her again before both of them drifted off to sleep once more. The early morning light had barely started to penetrate the room when he awoke to her touch, feeling a throbbing hardness where she stroked him, an aching to take her again. "Cathleen?"

"Aye."

"I love you."

She sighed and closed her eyes for a moment. "I love you too. More than you could possibly know."

"Show me."

"Again?"

He grinned. "Are we keeping a tally?"

"Perhaps I would . . . if I didn't always find myself so distracted."

"But you like to be distracted, don't you?"

"Aye. I like the way you are made," she said, rolling over to kiss him as her hand tightened and she began to stroke him faster.

"And I have never liked it better than at this moment," he said, turning and putting her beneath him.

Later that morning they made their way toward the wharf, while the mist was still heavy and close to the ground. The streets were quiet, deserted. Not even the sound of a church bell broke the silence.

They passed a shop and she turned her head, looking at her reflection in the shop window, thinking she looked scrawny and pale.

Wanting her to walk faster, Fletcher took her arm and they hurried along. She glanced at him and saw that his face was hard, his eyes darting here and there, lingering for a moment at each doorway, each shadowy entrance to a narrow alley. Their footsteps echoed against the buildings, making her remember the sound of the men running behind her.

She shivered and drew her shawl more closely about her.

"Are you cold?"

"No. I am uneasy."

"So am I. I will feel better when we are on board the *Angelique*."

"*Angelique*? Couldn't you at least find a ship named after me?"

He gave her a look that said he knew what she was trying to do. The squeeze he gave her arm said he appreciated her attempt to lighten their mood.

"I tried," he said, "but the *Steadfast* sailed this morning."

Cathleen did not have time to say anything, for they rounded a corner and saw the ships docked in the harbor a short distance away. She felt immensely relieved at the sight, although she knew that danger could just as easily await them there.

It was at that moment that two men suddenly appeared out of nowhere.

With a gasp, she stared at them. They were the same men from whom she had escaped before.

"It's them!" she said.

Fletcher grabbed her hand and they started running toward the men. Fletcher hit one of the men with his shoulder, a glancing blow that knocked him against the other one.

It gave them a little time, but not much.

Soon they heard the footsteps running behind them. A pain twisted Cathleen's side. Their feet pounded the cobbles, the jarring force causing her hair to fall down in a long braid that began to come unraveled.

And still they ran.

The pain in her side was greater now. She knew she was slowing him down. From out of nowhere, a hand grabbed her, pulling her backward until she lost her balance and fell.

Her assailant tripped over her and went down as well. She heard Fletcher curse and knew it was because he was busy with the other man and could not come to her rescue.

She rolled to her knees, preparing for the man's attack, when she realized that he was lying still. Blood trickled over the cobbles. Apparently, his head had struck the curbstone when he fell.

She wondered if he was dead. She hoped so.

The pain in her side had lessened as she came to her feet. Fletcher was still fighting. She crouched in the doorway of a shop, watching the fury of two men beating each other with their fists. But when the attacker pulled out a knife, she screamed, "He's got a knife, Fletcher! Look out!"

What happened next came so fast that she was not altogether certain what she had seen. She saw the knife glide in a sweeping arc toward Fletcher. She screamed again. Fletcher grabbed for the man's hand, and the two of them came together in a twisting mass.

Fletcher's back was to her now, blocking her view. Still locked together, each struggled to gain the advantage. Even she could see that they were well matched. She dared not scream, for fear that it might distract Fletcher, so she covered her mouth with both hands, then turned and buried her face in the corner of the alcove where she stood, unable to bear what might happen.

She had no way of knowing how long she stood there like that, with her mouth covered, her eyes closed, her face pressed against the cold stone walls that met in the corner. She had no recollection of hearing any sound, so she jumped when she felt a hand on her shoulder.

Whirling around, her only thought was that Fletcher was dead and now the man had come for her.

"It is over."

Weakness swept over her. Her knees buckled, and she would have fallen save for the strong arms that came out to support her. She felt a wave of nausea. "I think I'm going to be sick."

She was sick, and he held her head as she leaned over into the gutter. When she felt better, she glanced at the man lying in the street. The bloody knife lay nearby. "Is he dead?"

"Yes."

"And the other one?"

"He's alive, but he won't be doing much but nursing his aching head for a while." He held her close. "You are unharmed?"

"Aye. A tad shaken up, is all. I'll probably be a bit jumpy for a while, afraid of my own shadow."

"And for good reason. I'm sorry I've gotten you into this. You don't deserve it."

"No," she said, "and neither do you."

Warm, safe, and protected in the comfort of his arms, she could think only of him. "Are you hurt?"

"Only my pride. If Adrian Mackinnon ever hears how long it took me to wrestle a knife away from a man, he will never let me live it down."

"Adrian? Your stepfather?"

"Yes, the man who made certain that all his sons learned how to fight and how to protect themselves—and what better place to learn it than in a lumber camp. The men there were as big and strong as tree trunks."

He took her hand. "Come on," he said. "I've had enough of France."

"Aye," she said. "Let's go home."

As they walked to the wharf, Cathleen breathed deeply, but somehow the fresh air about her seemed stagnant, stifling, and stale . . . reminiscent of her life.

Chapter Twenty-seven

It was early afternoon when they arrived in Scotland. Cathleen wanted to go straight to Edinburgh, and thought she had Fletcher convinced, but by the time they hired a carriage, he had decided against it.

After that last incident with Adair's men in Le Havre, he told her, he could not endanger her life any further.

"Once you are safely at Caithness, I will go to Edinburgh alone."

"I don't want to go to Caithness," Cathleen said. "I won't rest until you get those documents into the right hands. I think we should go to Edinburgh. It is the logical thing to do."

"Yes, it is, and that is precisely what Adair will think. He will expect us to go to Edinburgh first, and unless I miss my guess, he will have men waiting for us there."

He handed Cathleen into the carriage, then climbed in next to her and kissed her on the nose. "And *that* is the logical thing for him to do."

Frowning, she sighed dejectedly. "I suppose you are right, but that doesn't mean I have to like it."

He laughed. "My bonny love, you are a lass who never learned to hide her disappointment. It is written all over your face."

She opened her mouth to reply, but he silenced her with his fingers and said, "Don't argue."

"When have I ever dared?" she asked, basking in the sound of his laughter.

This I will miss, too. . . .

They rode along in silence. Cathleen had closed her eyes, but she was not asleep, despite the gentle rocking motion of the coach and the deep, comfortable squabs.

"What are you thinking?" he asked at last.

"I was just wondering . . ." she said, opening her eyes.

"About what?"

"You."

"In what regard?"

"When you go to Edinburgh, then what?"

"Why, I will see my documents safely into the right hands."

"And then what?"

Now it was his turn to frown. It was obvious that he did not like the direction the conversation was taking. He turned his head and stared out the window, as if by doing so he could stop the flow of her thoughts.

Cathleen would not be deterred. Not now.

"You are going to Glengarry, aren't you?"

His jaw clenched. "I don't know. What difference does it make?"

"It makes a great deal of difference, because if you go to Glengarry, we both know why. You won't be happy with simply getting your title back, will you?"

"Adair cannot be trusted. I realize now that my life would never be safe. . . . not as long as he lives."

"I don't agree. Once the truth is known and the title is returned to you, his hands will be tied, for if something happened to you, he would be implicated. The courts will decide his fate."

"And a lot of good that would do me once I'm dead," he said. "He has managed to evade the noose for many deaths.

What makes you so certain he could not evade punishment for mine? Are you willing to take the gamble?''

Cathleen did not answer. She was shaken, for she knew the kind of man Fletcher was. She also knew Adair Ramsay. If Fletcher went to see Adair, one of them would die.

She knew how long Fletcher had lived with the desire to set things right, only now, that seemed not to be enough. Now that the title was safely within his grasp, he wanted more, and she had a feeling that it was due partly to the danger Adair had placed her in.

While it warmed her to know that Fletcher wanted to protect her, to make her life secure, she could not bear the thought that his thirst for revenge was because of her. Guilt gnawed at her insides. With her heart aching, she knew she would have to try to stop him.

At last he sighed and looked at her. ''Cathleen, why are you making this much bigger than it is? Don't become an albatross around my neck. Let me handle things. It isn't your place to worry about it.''

''But it is! I know what a visit to Adair means. I know you have murder in your heart. If you go there, one of you will die. There is always the chance that it could be you. Is that your idea of love?''

As if dismissing her, he leaned his head back against the seat and closed his eyes.

She sat there watching him, but he did not speak for a long time. When he finally did, he did not look at her, but kept his eyes closed, mumbling, ''Even the Bible teaches the doctrine of an eye for an eye, a tooth for a tooth.''

''Blood will not wash away blood, Fletcher.''

He should have known better than to try to argue scripture with a minister's granddaughter. For he had barely thought the thing put to rest when she replied that his words were from the Old Testament.

He opened one eye and looked at her. ''Now, why do I have a feeling I am about to be force-fed a liberal dose of the New Testament?''

She smiled. '' *'Recompense to no man evil for evil. Avenge not yourselves, but rather give place unto wrath: for it is written, Vengeance is mine; I will repay, saith the Lord.'"*

He looked at her, waiting for her to finish.

"Romans," she said.

But even then she saw that her words had no effect upon him. Leaning forward, she dropped down to the floor of the carriage, sitting in front of him as she put her hand on his arm. "Please," she said. "On my knees I humble myself and beg you not to seek Adair's death by your own hand. Let the authorities in Edinburgh handle it. With the proof you have, it should be easy enough to reopen the case of your father's death. Don't do this thing, Fletcher. Do not let it turn you into a bitter man."

He reached down wrapped his hands around her waist, and lifted her up into his lap. He pushed her head down to nestle her against his chest said, "Go to sleep, Cathleen."

She closed her eyes, for she did not want him to see the tears that had collected there.

Do not let it turn you into a bitter man . . .

Over and over these words echoed through his head. Cathleen's words. But also the words of his mother, for it had been Maggie's concern as well, that he would let this thing with Adair turn him into a bitter man.

Fletcher had been raised with a deep regard and respect for women. He loved their comfort and their beauty, of course, but he also respected their wisdom, their intuition, their advice. That the two most important women in his life had given him the same admonition left him shaken.

He cursed softly, then looked at Cathleen, afraid of what he might see.

As if she knew the moment his gaze rested upon her, she opened her eyes, and he saw what he feared most, the message that was written in her eyes.

He could have his vengeance. . . .

Or he could have her.

He could not have both.

"Cathleen. . . ."

"There is nothing to say." She pulled away from him and

returned to her seat across from him. "You have made your choice. I can only pray you do not come to regret it."

But I do regret it, I regret anything that comes between us. Anything that takes you away from me.

He wanted her. There had never been any doubt about that. But how could he forget what he had lived with for so long? How could he forget the dream he had had, the dream when his father came to him?

He had waited such a long, long time.

He looked at her again, seeing her face turned from him but knowing even then what those frozen features meant.

God! Why does it have to come to this?

He closed his eyes, trying to harden himself against her, against what she was asking, but it was no use. Instead of being able to recall the hatred he had harbored for so long, he remembered his mother's loving face and the loving kindness in Cathleen's eyes. Instead of vengeance, he saw the faces of his brothers and sisters. Instead of revenge, he remembered the ways of a man taught to him by Adrian.

And he knew . . .

He knew within the very marrow of his bones that what he sought was against them all, against everything they stood for, against everything he had been taught.

But how could that have happened? How could he have been so wrong? Could he have misunderstood his dream?

He thought back over the years. He was eighteen years old when he saw his father in that dream. Cathleen would have been what? Fourteen?

Fourteen, and much too young for me to have fallen in love with.

Was that it? Was that why he was supposed to wait? So that the love of a woman would turn him away from wrath, away from the very thing that would destroy him?

He opened his eyes and looked at her. There she sat in her gray silk dress with her beautiful wine-colored hair tied back with a black riband. Her face was like a sweet flower, and his heart began to ache. How beautiful she looked. How sad. How lost to him she was now. How much the thought of it hurt.

"I suppose this way is best," she said, "for I have always known that it was not meant to be."

"What isn't meant to be?"

"Our being together," she said quite simply. "It was my eternal hope and your desire, but it was never part of God's plan."

"What are you saying, Cathleen?"

"I am saying that all of this really doesn't matter. You will do what you have to do, but not because of your desire for me. It is impossible, you see. You can love me, but you cannot have me. I will love you to the end of my days, but I will not share them with you. We cannot marry. Not ever. Even my grandfather knew that. We love, but we are worlds apart. We love but are kept apart by our worlds."

"Cathleen . . . love . . ."

"Don't," she said, her gaze leaving his face and dropping to his hand that lay palm down against his thigh. He looked down, wondering what she was staring at. He saw only his signet ring bearing the crest of the Earl of Caithness.

He had lost her.

He had never prayed as earnestly as he did at that moment when he asked God to show him the way to heal what had come between them, to give him some sign, some way to rid her of her fears and doubts.

He did not open his eyes but he could feel hers upon him. Watching. Waiting.

I love her more each time I look at her. Her love is like an arrow that pierces my heart. Her very presence perfumes my soul. What a plague love can be! Thoughts of her torment my mind. My strength fails me and I am like a newborn, unable to stand and weak at the knees. When I look at her I am undone. Heaven is reflected in that face. God help me . . .

As the coach rounded a curve and came out of a wooded glen, a beam of sunlight came through the window and struck the signet ring on his finger, sending a brilliant shaft of light bouncing into his eyes.

The ring of the Earl of Caithness.

Suddenly he understood. At last, he knew.

He looked down at the ring, seeing it for what it symbolized. "I would give it all up, you know. Everything."

Her gaze flew to his face. Her skin was as white as alabaster. "What are you saying?"

"I am saying that all of this, the titles, the estates, they mean nothing without you." He pulled the ring from his finger. "If that is the only way I can have you, sweet Cathleen, then so be it." He put his hand out the window.

"No!" she shouted, grabbing his wrist. "Don't throw it out. You cannot mean that. It is your family crest, the ring that has been handed down to the earls in your family. You have a responsibility—"

"To myself. I am American enough to flaunt tradition and do as I please. I am Scot enough to see that I get it."

"I cannot let you do it," she said.

"Then say you will marry me, my sweet Cathleen."

Tears ran down her face. "I . . ."

He took her hand in his, placed the ring in her open palm, then closed her fingers one by one, kissing each of them in turn.

"You keep it," he said. "I will not force you. The decision is yours. I am asking you to be my wife. If your answer is yes, return the ring to me by the time this is all over, and we will marry. If you keep the ring, I will understand your answer is no and I will return to America."

"And Adair?"

He looked at her, seeing nothing but love, hope, and promise shining in her eyes. Something physical happened within him at that moment and he felt the love that she bore him reaching out, a tangible thing that surrounded him, offering him solace, comfort. It was as if a spring within him, which had been blocked suddenly came to life and flowed over him.

On and on it came, until it filled his body, cleansing, healing.

"To hell with Adair," he said. "It's you I want."

For a long time she stared at him as if she were stunned, and then she did the damnedest thing.

She burst into tears.

"I will never understand you," he said, "even if I live to be a hundred years old. Here I offer to give up everything for you, but that isn't enough. Then I give up something I have planned for half my life. And what happens? You cry.''

She was really weeping now, and, soft heart that he had for her, he could not bear it. Gathering her into his arms, he dragged her from her seat and onto his lap. ''If we don't pick a spot and light there, we're going to wear out these seats.''

That only made her cry harder.

''Cathleen, love, what is it? Is it something I did? Something I should have done? Something I didn't do?''

She hiccuped, then her shoulders began to shake. He was truly at a loss, when suddenly he realized that she wasn't crying now.

She was laughing.

He drew her closer, cuddling her against him. Hearing her deep, satisfied sigh, Fletcher had never known such contentment.

He decided then and there to tell his sons one day that there wasn't a feeling in the world as good as the one that comes when a man knows his lass is happy.

So this is what happens when love comes along. . . .

Love. Not revenge.

For it was love that had taken him by the hand and guided his steps from America to Scotland. It was love that had willed that they should meet, love that had drawn him to ride that day by the hay field where she was drawing water.

And it was love that had made a place for her in his heart.

He felt her hand come up to stroke his cheek. He looked down and saw her smile. He shook his head. ''Somehow, I feel you have plucked my destiny out of my pocket.''

Her smile deepened, and, tucking her arm through his, she rested her head against his shoulder. ''Aye, and saved your soul in the doing of it. You won't regret it, Fletcher.''

He took her in his arms and kissed her. ''It will be your lifelong task to see that I don't.''

''I ken I am up to the task,'' she said. ''It is good to learn life's lessons and to benefit from them.''

He gave her a skeptical look. ''And what lessons have you learned?''

She took his hand in hers and placed the signet ring on his finger.

He looked down at the ring. "You didn't answer me," he said. "What lesson have you learned?"

"That love is the strongest bond of all."

Chapter Twenty-eight

Adair Ramsay was furious.

He walked into his study, where Gavin MacPhail waited. The room was dark, with only one low-burning candle on his desk, casting its stingy light in a small semicircle. The shutters were closed, keeping the evil within.

Darkness lay all about.

Adair liked the dark. He felt at home in it. It was like an aphrodisiac to him. It gave him a feeling of power to know he enjoyed what others feared. He felt safe in it, as if no one could see what he was doing, could know what he was about.

He did not look at Gavin, but he did not need to. He could smell the man's fear. It gave him an exhilarating feeling, like the moment of ejaculation.

Seeing the duke come in, Gavin rose to his feet, seeming to shrink before him, his eyes cast down, looking like a whipped dog.

Fear was power.

Adair crossed the worn oriental carpet. He could smell the

candle wax, and he smiled. His senses were more acute now. Power did that to him.

Without a word, Adair walked behind his massive oak desk and took a seat, his gaze locked on Gavin. "So," he said, "the faithful chronicler coming to report." His voice was as mild as mead. "What have you to say?"

Gavin licked his lips. His forehead was glossy with sweat, and he shifted nervously in his chair. "I . . . we didn't get him. He killed one of the men I sent. The other was badly wounded."

Normally, Adair would have jumped to his feet, ranting and raving, making threats. But today he did none of those things.

Today he was as serious as a barrister, his face a hard mask. He sensed that it was this cool detachment, this iron control, that worried Gavin the most. Ranting and raving he was accustomed to, but this new, icy control would leave him shaken. Adair smiled. Now, for the first time, Gavin would realize what he had gotten himself into, and what could happen to him if he did not get the results Adair wanted.

Adair balled his hands into fists, feeling the power there. It coursed through his veins like warm brandy. He looked at Gavin, then steepled his fingers as he asked, "What else is there? What haven't you told me?"

Gavin swallowed. "He found the proof he needed."

" 'He'?"

"The Earl of Caithness. He found the proof of his ancestors."

"In France?"

"Aye, in Honfleur."

"Are you certain?"

"Aye."

"And how do you know?"

"There was a priest that helped them. A priest by the name of Father Sebastian."

"You talked to him?"

"Aye."

"And he told you?"

Gavin's eyes traveled around the room before coming back to Adair. "No, he wouldn't talk."

"Torture?"

He shook his head. "No. Not even then."

"Bloody fool! If he didn't talk, then how did you find out?"

"I went into town and learned that the earl had hired a solicitor to go out to the church and copy the records."

"You talked to this solicitor?"

"Aye."

"And silenced him, I hope?"

"Aye."

"And the priest?"

"Him too."

"And the books this scribe copied from—you destroyed them?"

Gavin licked his lips and swallowed again. "No."

"Fool! Have you found them?"

"No."

"Well then, you leave me little choice," Adair said.

"It isn't too late," Gavin said as if pleading. "We can still get him . . . and the girl."

"Where are they now?"

"I think they are in Scotland."

"You *think*? Idiot! You do not know?"

Gavin looked down at his feet. "We lost them after they set sail for Scotland."

"Edinburgh," Adair said. "That is where he would go. He would not want to waste a moment of precious time. If he has copies of those documents with him, he will want to see them into safe hands as soon as possible."

"Aye, you are right. He would go to Edinburgh."

"And that is where you will go. Take as many men as you need. I want him stopped this time. Before they can talk to anyone. Is that clear?"

"Aye."

"The bastard means to do away with me. I will see him in hell—and you along with him—before I let that happen. If you fail this time, it will be the last time you fail anything."

"Yes, Your Grace. You can count on me."

"For your sake, I hope that is so. If you don't stop him this time, my days are numbered . . . and so are yours. Now get out of my sight!"

After Gavin MacPhail had left, Adair began to think about the girl.

"Of course!" he said, slamming his hands down on the desk and rising to his feet. He began to pace the floor. "The girl changes things."

There was no doubt that Fletcher Ramsay was in love with her, for he had gone to too much trouble to keep her with him. Only a man in love would be so obvious or so foolish.

Perhaps that could be used to his advantage. Adair smiled. The girl changed things, and he could use that bit of information to predict what Fletcher would do.

Of course he wouldn't go to Edinburgh first, because he would want to protect the woman he loved.

Adair felt foolish. How could he have forgotten about her? Poor, stupid Gavin. He had sent him on a wild goose chase. But perhaps that, too, was a blessing. Of late, Gavin seemed capable of nothing but failure.

And failure was something Adair could not tolerate.

If he knew anything at all, it was that Fletcher would see to Cathleen Lindsay's safety before he took his proof to Edinburgh.

And what better place to ensure her safety than his home at Caithness Castle?

Immediately, he dispatched a man to watch Caithness and to report back to him the moment Fletcher Ramsay arrived.

Then Adair poured himself a glass of Scots whisky and sat back, waiting to see which of his traps would catch the young Earl of Caithness.

Adair blew out the candle, letting the darkness settle about him. His title was safe. Fletcher Ramsay would never be the Duke of Glengarry for one simple reason: He was a fool, a fool just like his father.

* * *

Riding across the moor in the coach with Fletcher, Cathleen stared out the window. It was a dark night. The coach lamps cast rays but a little distance, but enough that she caught a few glimpses of things as they passed.

On and on through the night they went, past villages of whitewashed cottages, past full public houses and inns posting signs that they were full for the night. They passed a church and a parsonage and she thought of her grandfather, feeling his loss so much more now that she was back on Scottish soil.

After a few hours, the coach slowed as the horses began climbing. Looking out, she now saw nothing but darkness and a rough-looking road that sliced through heather and gorse, while all about them the wind seemed to be rising, making a wild rushing sound, like a low, wailing moan.

She closed her eyes and slept.

It was much later when Fletcher woke her, for they had arrived at Caithness.

She looked out the window and saw nothing more than the dark turrets rising before them, the windows all dark, but it was enough to tell her they were home.

Having helped Cathleen out of the coach, Fletcher banged on the front door, rousing the entire household, for immediately after he knocked, lights went on all over the house.

They heard Mrs. MacCauley grumbling as she furiously yanked the door open. Holding a lamp aloft, she barked out into the darkness, "Who in the name of heaven is it out here on a night like this?"

"It is I, Fletcher," he said, stepping into the foyer, Cathleen in tow.

"Weel, you made enough noise to wake the devil," she said.

"Apparently," Fletcher said, giving her an appraising glance.

Cathleen heard a chuckle and looked up to see Aunt Doroty coming down the broad, curved staircase, tying her wrapper.

"I see success written all over your face," Doroty said. "The title is yours, I take it?"

"Aye, if we live long enough to get to Edinburgh with the proof."

She looked from Fletcher to Cathleen and back again. "You didn't go to Edinburgh first?"

"No."

"Why not?"

"Because of me," Cathleen said.

Aunt Doroty nodded. "Of course," she said. Then, smiling and giving Cathleen a pat on the arm, she added, "It was the right choice, my dear."

Cathleen stared at the floor to keep from looking at Fletcher, wanting to avoid the expression of I-told-you-so that she would see there.

Fletcher turned then, asking Mrs. MacCauley to bring them something to eat in the library. "We've got work to do," he said.

Immediately after Mrs. MacCauley left, they sequestered themselves in the library with Aunt Doroty, with Fletcher hurrying them along, telling them that there was no time to waste.

After much debate, they agreed upon one thing: Adair Ramsay had to be stopped.

"It would take a silver bullet to do it," Aunt Doroty said.

Fletcher and Cathleen laughed, Cathleen finding that a bit of humor was just what she needed to relieve the tension that had been tightly wound within her all day. She relaxed, feeling glad to be home.

In the end, they decided unanimously that what they really needed was a foolproof way to get the information Fletcher had acquired in France to the authorities in Edinburgh, without further loss of life.

"Do you think he's gotten word so quickly?" Aunt Doroty asked.

"Yes."

"But you said you killed one of the men and the other was badly wounded," she replied.

"Yes, but I know Adair wouldn't send just two men. I am certain there were others there, and they would have gotten word back to him by now. He knows we escaped."

"Do you think he knows about the records we found?" Cathleen asked.

"I can't see know how he could. I am certain Father Sebastian would not have said anything."

"And the scribe?" asked Cathleen.

Fletcher thought for a moment, then shook his head. "If Father Sebastian didn't tell them anything, how would they know about the scribe?"

"Didn't you say they attacked Cathleen when she went to find the scribe?" Aunt Doroty asked.

"Of course!" Fletcher said. "I had forgot about that. They could have followed her. . . ."

"And gotten word back to Adair as soon as they knew," Cathleen added.

"So, what will you do now?" asked Aunt Doroty.

"I don't know. If Adair knows, and I am certain that he does, then he will be watching Caithness."

"What if you left for Edinburgh at night?" Aunt Doroty asked.

Fletcher shook his head. "Adair is too shrewd. He would be expecting that."

"What if you acted as a decoy?" Cathleen asked.

"A decoy for what?"

"You could leave for Edinburgh in the afternoon. Anyone watching Caithness would follow you, thinking you would be taking the documents to Edinburgh. Only you wouldn't be carrying the documents."

"What would I be carrying?"

"Nothing."

Fletcher crossed his arms and gave her a displeased look. "And if I wouldn't be carrying the documents, who would?"

"I would," Cathleen and Aunt Doroty said at the same time.

Fletcher looked from one to the other. It amazed him how quickly women could band together.

"That would be even better," Cathleen said. "If your aunt and I left together, no one would suspect anything. Even if they were still watching Caithness, it would simply look as if we were going to rendezvous with you in Edinburgh. They would never suspect we had the documents, simply because they would never think you would trust something so important to the two of us."

"That is certainly true," he said, "but I don't want to put you at risk."

Cathleen sighed with exasperation. "Fletcher, you have no choice. What will you do if you take the documents and they overpower you? We are your only hope."

"Then I am doomed," he said, putting his hands over his head and doing his best to look distraught.

"Do not make light of this. We are serious," Aunt Doroty said.

"All right," Fletcher said. "I am serious now."

"I think the documents can be hidden in the coach," Aunt Doroty said. "Even if we were stopped, they wouldn't find them on us. They have no reason to harm us if we aren't with you."

"She's right," Cathleen said. "We are your only hope of getting those documents to Edinburgh."

In the end, Fletcher agreed, not because he wanted to but because he was outtalked and outwitted—and because they were right.

Much later that night, a rider came thundering into the stables at Glengarry Castle, his horse lathered and heavily winded from a long run.

Angus MacTavish took the man's horse, but instead of grooming him himself, he woke the young stableboy and assigned the task to him. He then went to the gardens at the back of the castle. A few minutes later, a light illuminated the windows of the library.

Making his way through the darkness, Angus went to the library's only open window, and crouching beneath it, keeping well out of the light, he listened.

Inside, Adair was getting a report from one of the men he had sent to watch Caithness Castle.

"They arrived there early this morning?"

"Aye, Your Grace."

"You are certain it was the earl?"

"Aye. I saw him and heard him speak with his American accent. It could have been no other."

"And the girl?"

"She was there too."

"You are certain?"

"Aye, Your Grace."

"Good. That means he has not gone to Edinburgh yet, which gives me the time I need."

"Do you want me to take care of the earl, Your Grace?"

"No. I don't trust the lot of you to do anything. So far, nothing has been carried out the way I planned." Adair paused, a gleam coming into his eyes. "I will take care of the young earl myself."

"Aye, Your Grace."

"You are dismissed," Adair said, "but stay close, in case I have need of you."

"Aye, Your Grace."

After he had gone, Adair sat at his desk, a smile upon his lips. Just as he had suspected, the young Earl of Caithness had made a mistake—a *big* mistake—and it would cost him the title he coveted. Adair hoped it would also cost him his life.

Too bad for the earl that he had let his feelings for a woman stand in the way. He had not gone to Edinburgh first. Putting the one he loved above all else, he had taken the woman to Caithness, ruled by his heart and not by his head.

Foolish. Very foolish.

Because of that one mistake, Fletcher Ramsay would pay dearly. He would never become the Duke of Glengarry now. He would even lose the title of the Earl of Caithness.

For how could a dead man hold a title?

Adair clenched his fists. He would have to plan the earl's death carefully. It would have to look like an accident.

How ironic, everyone will say, that the young Earl of Caithness lost his life so tragically, in much the same manner his father had lost his some twenty years before.

Adair settled back, deep in thought. He knew that Fletcher would lose no time in going to Edinburgh with his proof, now that he had the Lindsay woman safe at Caithness. Now was the time to end this thing once and for all. Only this time he would not trust so important a mission to one of those bumbling fools who worked for him.

No, this time he would take care of Fletcher Ramsay himself.

Just as I did his father.

Early the next morning, before the first rosy fingers of dawn spread over the moors, Adair hurried into the stables.

Angus, who always rose early, was spreading a pitchfork of hay in an empty stable. He looked up when the duke entered. "Good morning, Your Grace."

"Morning, Angus. Saddle Brigadoon for me."

"Brigadoon, Your Grace? Are you going on a long trip?"

"Aye, and I need speed and endurance."

Angus nodded and went to saddle the horse. While he was gone, Adair went outside and paced back and forth, slapping a riding crop impatiently against his leg. He cursed, then paused, looking back toward the stables, wondering what was taking Angus so long.

Just at that moment, Angus appeared in the doorway and led the stallion out to where Adair waited.

Not wasting a moment, Adair mounted the great gray and spurred him hard. The mighty horse leaped forward with a shrill cry, and soon his great hooves pounded out a rhythm as he ate up the miles between Glengarry and Caithness Castle.

Adair rode as if under a spell as the powerful stallion raced across the sunlit purple moors, but it was not purple moors that he saw, but moors stained red with blood. The taste of blood was in his mouth now, salty and metallic, and the hoofbeats seemed to be tapping out the names of those he had murdered.

Adair felt a sense of exhilaration. At last, he was off to settle an old score. One that he should have settled long before now, for he realized that he had made a big mistake those many years ago. He should have never allowed Maggie Ramsay to leave Scotland alive.

And that included her three children as well.

He reached his destination—the point where the road from

Caithness intersected the road to Edinburgh—ahead of schedule.

He turned off the main road, riding the stallion along the track above the sea.

He waited a little more than an hour before he heard approaching hoofbeats. He saw him then, the Earl of Caithness, riding his gelding down the road from the castle.

Adair waited until Fletcher was almost even with him, then he put his whip to his stallion and dug in his spurs.

Brigadoon leaped forward, thundering out of the fringe of trees, galloping down the road, heading straight for the narrowest point—a place where only a few feet of solid earth separated any passerby from the edge of nowhere. It was a place where the rock gave way, and far, far below lay nothing but foam and the echo of the tides thrashing against sharp cliffs, where the howling wind raged and whistled and seabirds shrieked as if to give warning for what lay below.

On he came, spurring his horse until blood ran down Brigadoon's sides and the great stallion's mouth was white with foam.

The approaching hoofbeats caught Fletcher's attention. He turned around in the saddle and saw a man on horseback thundering straight at him on a huge gray horse. He had only a moment to think, for he realized immediately that the rider intended to run him off the road.

Just like my father ...

From out of nowhere appeared a brilliant, blinding light, and then something seemed to suspend time. From out of the intense brightness he saw a man like unto an angel, dressed in white and standing in the middle of the road in front of him, his being shining as a flash of lightning, his countenance one of immeasurable beauty.

Suddenly, as if seeing the vision as well, Fletcher's gelding shied, stopping a split second before the moment of impact, as if Fletcher himself had jerked back on the reins.

Instead of hitting Fletcher's horse dead center and forcing him over the edge, the great gray beast Adair rode hit Fletcher's horse with only a glancing blow to the shoulder.

The blow wasn't enough of an impact to force Fletcher and his horse over the cliff, but it was enough to cause the gray's girth strap to break.

Adair's saddle came off.

At that moment, the gray stallion screamed and made a sharp turn to the right, sending Adair over the side to the death he had so carefully planned for someone else.

As soon as it was over, Fletcher looked around for some sight of the man he had seen standing in the middle of the road.

But there was no one there.

He dismounted, his body trembling and weak. He had no explanation for what had happened. It was something far beyond his comprehension. Some being, stronger than he, had been watching over him, and it had been that being of immeasurable beauty that had stopped his horse and saved his life.

An hour later, Cathleen and Aunt Doroty came down the road to Edinburgh in the Earl of Caithness's coach. They were deep in conversation when the driver pulled the coach to a stop.

Her heart feeling as if it had lodged in her throat, Cathleen looked at Aunt Doroty. "Well, it looks like this is it," she said. "We had better make this good."

"Aye. I always fancied myself an actress," Aunt Doroty said. "Only I never thought I would have the chance."

Cathleen opened the door and helped Aunt Doroty out.

"Well, bless me! What are you doing here?" Aunt Doroty asked.

Cathleen, right behind her, looked up to see Fletcher standing a few feet away, holding two horses. One she recognized as Fletcher's horse, but the other was one she had never seen before—a huge gray beast with no saddle.

She ran to him, her mind fertile with questions. "What are you doing here? Where did you get that horse? What happened? Were you attacked?"

Fletcher took her in his arms and said, "The strangest thing has happened."

"Strange? What do you mean?"

"I'm not sure I can explain it. You may think me insane, but I could swear I saw an angel."

"It's the sun," Aunt Doroty said. "You've been out in it too long with your head uncovered."

"No," Fletcher said. "You don't understand. It was a being, but it wasn't human, although it was in human form."

"Perhaps it was an angel," Cathleen said, sounding perfectly accepting. "What did it look like?"

"It is difficult to say, for there was so much light, like looking into the sun, a brilliance that seemed to stop everything." Fletcher went on to tell her about the experience and how the apparition had caused his horse to stop, thus saving his life.

"I know this sounds strange," he said, "but I cannot shake the feeling that this was connected with my father."

"And perfectly fitting it would have been, too," Aunt Doroty said, going over to the edge of the road and looking down to the thrashing sea below. "Perhaps it *was* the spirit of Bruce Ramsay you saw today. At any rate, it is more than appropriate that Adair Ramsay met the same fate he gave your father."

"And planned for you," Cathleen said, going to the edge of the cliff and standing next to Aunt Doroty. Fletcher joined her there, and she put her hand through his. " '*For he shall give his angels charge over thee, to keep thee in all thy ways. They shall bear thee up . . . lest thou dash thy foot against a stone.*' "

A short time later, as they were preparing to take the coach into Edinburgh, Fletcher watched Walter, the coachman, pick up Adair's saddle. He was about to heave it into the luggage boot at the back of the coach when he paused and looked down at the saddle, a strange, bewildered look upon his face.

"What is it?" Fletcher asked.

"I dinna ken, Your Grace, but there is little doubt that the cinch strap was cut."

Fletcher checked the saddle, seeing that the cinch had indeed been cut. The question was, by whom?

"Has it been cut?" Aunt Doroty asked.

"Yes," Fletcher said.

"But who would have done it?" Cathleen asked.

"Any number of people, I would think," Fletcher said. "Adair was not a well-liked man."

Aunt Doroty returned to the edge of the cliff and looked down. "A fitting end," she said. "At last the bastard gets his just rewards."

After tying his horse and Adair's gray to the back of the coach, Fletcher came around to help the ladies into the coach.

"If it's all the same to you," Aunt Doroty said, "I will ride up front with Walter for a while. I would imagine the two of you have plenty to talk about, and I much prefer fresh air to being cramped inside that stuffy coach."

"You cannot ride up there, Aunt."

"I would like to know why not. I spent many an hour riding up here when I was younger."

Before Fletcher could say more, she turned to Walter and said, "Weel, dinna stand there looking confused. Help me up!"

Fletcher handed Cathleen into the coach. Then, just as he was about to join her, he had the strangest feeling that someone was watching him. He turned and saw a man on horseback sitting in the shade of a towering crag, not very far away. At that moment, Cathleen looked out and, seeing Fletcher's gaze, glanced in that direction.

"Angus?" she whispered.

Fletcher turned to her. "What did you say?"

"That man. I am almost certain it was Angus."

"Angus? But what would he be doing here?" Fletcher asked, then turned to look again.

The man was gone.

As the coach started down the road to Edinburgh, Cathleen and Fletcher looked out the window taking one last look at the rocks where Adair's body lay. " 'They that take the sword shall perish with the sword,' " she said. "Matthew."

Fletcher put his arm around her and drew her against him. She buried her face against his chest, her arms going around his middle as she hugged him tightly to her.

Fletcher held her, feeling that his life was now complete.

Suddenly she pulled back, and looked at him in a way that made his breath catch.

"You have nothing standing between you and being the Duke of Glengarry now," she said.

"Nothing except you. I meant what I said, Cathleen. I would give it all up in a heartbeat if that was the only way I could have you." He looked down at the signet ring, shiny and golden, that circled his finger. "You gave the ring back to me."

"Aye." She turned in his arms and kissed him softly. *"'Whither thou goest, I will go; and where thou lodgest, I will lodge: thy people shall be my people, and thy God my God: Where thou diest, will I die'.* I love you, Fletcher Ramsay. What a story we will have to tell all our grandchildren one day."

Fletcher had a wicked gleam in his eye. "If we're going to have all those grandchildren, we will have to become parents first."

"We will," she said, laughing. "In about seven months."

When he got over his shock and finished scattering a dozen kisses about her face, asking her an equal number of times if she felt all right, he seemed to relax. "It's a good thing you agreed to marry me," he said. "When did you know?"

"The afternoon I threw up in France."

He laughed, remembering the afternoon in Le Havre when they had been attacked. At the time, he had merely thought her frightened.

Holding her in his arms, he felt a peace he had never known before, and he knew how it would be with them.

He had always known that there would come a time when he would regain all that had been taken from him, a time when he would avenge his father's death and set everything right.

It was now twenty-two years since the murder of Bruce Ramsay, Duke of Glengarry. The year was 1879, and Fletcher Ramsay, Duke of Glengarry, Earl of Caithness, was twenty-nine.

Outside, the road looked towards Edinburgh, winding its way across miles of empty Highlands. Beyond it, on the summit of a towering crag, half-veiled in cloud, hovered a brilliance, an intense brightness like a flash of lightning. It lingered there, calm, assured, and holy, impervious to wind, mist, snow, and time, the very essence of Scotland.

Fletcher closed his eyes, feeling that their story, his and Cathleen's, would one day take its place in history. It would be a story that wove its way across treeless moors, crossing narrow, winding roads and silent heaths where shaggy Highland cattle grazed the distant slopes, just beyond the ancient ruins of a roofless castle.

It would be a story woven into the history of Scotland itself, where the turbulent drama of kings, queens and sagas lingered like the haunting echoes of the Gaelic tongue, the skirl of the pipes, the roar of thrashing seas and wild birds, and the ever-present silence of bleak landscapes.

Perhaps their descendants would come here one day, many years after they were gone, and they would ride along this winding, twisting road to Edinburgh, passing the very spot where history was played out. And perhaps, if they were sensitive enough and Scot enough, they would feel an eeriness reaching out to them, and they would stop, and walk to the edge of the cliff and look down at the churning sea below. They might wonder what had happened here that day so long ago and why they felt as if they were standing upon hallowed ground.

They would not hear the thundering hooves of a mighty stallion or the cry of the seabirds overhead, nor would they catch the reflection of sun upon a signet ring or hear the softly whispered prayers of a woman in love. They would stand there wondering, with their faces to the sea and their backs to the moors, never seeing a towering crag half-veiled in mist or a flash of brilliance hovering there.

Dear Readers,

You're never too old to learn—I found this out the hard way. In *Heaven Knows*, I wrote my first letter to readers saying how sad it was to finish the Mackinnon books. I learned to never say never!

Over six hundred letters arrived telling me the Mackinnon saga was NOT over. It was this overwhelming interest in the Mackinnons that inspired Fletcher's story, *When Love Comes Along*. Now before you go and grab your pen and start another letter, let me say that I have just finished writing Margery's story. *If You Love Me* will be released by Warner Books in the fall of 1996.

Please know that I always love hearing from my readers, both the old faithfuls who have been with me from the start and the new arrivals. It is knowing how eagerly you await my next novel that keeps me going, your encouragement to "write just a little faster" that keeps me sitting up late at night, when anyone with half a brain would have gone to bed. You are my inspiration and my guiding light.

With much appreciation,

Elaine Coffman

Elaine Coffman